SWALLOWTAIL BOOKS

Swallowtail Books are republishing classic detective stories. Other titles are:

Death on the Oxford Road by E. C. R. Lorac
Murder at School by James Hilton

For further details about these books and for future publishing plans please contact:

Swallowtail Books
3 Danesbrook
Claverley
Shropshire
WV5 7BB
England

Telephone number : 01746 710837
E-mail : swallowtail.books@claverley88.freeserve.co.uk

THE EYE OF OSIRIS

R. AUSTIN FREEMAN

Swallowtail Books

SWALLOWTAIL BOOKS

Published by Swallowtail Books
3 Danesbrook, Claverley, Shropshire, WV5 7BB, England

First published by Hodder & Stoughton Ltd 1911

This edition published by Swallowtail Books 2000

A CIP catalogue record for this book is available from the British
Library

ISBN 1 903400 01 5

Printed by Antony Rowe Ltd, Bumper's Farm, Chippenham,
Wiltshire, SN14 6LH, England
Book cover and logo designs by Simon & Erica Minter Design
Services, 96 Cardigan Road, Reading, RG1 5QW, England

THE EYE OF OSIRIS

CHAPTER I   **The Vanishing Man**

The school of St. Margaret's Hospital was fortunate in its lecturer on Medical Jurisprudence, or Forensic Medicine, as it is sometimes described. At some schools the lecturer on this subject is appointed apparently for the reason that he lacks the qualifications to lecture on any other. But with us it was very different: John Thorndyke was not only an enthusiast, a man of profound learning and great reputation, but he was an exceptional teacher, lively and fascinating in style and of endless resources. Every remarkable case that had ever been reported he appeared to have at his fingers' ends; every fact—chemical, physical, biological, or even historical—that could in any way be twisted into a medico-legal significance, was pressed into his service; and his own varied and curious experiences seemed as inexhaustible as the widow's cruse. One of his favourite devices for giving life and interest to a rather dry subject was that of analysing and commenting upon contemporary cases as reported in the papers (always, of course, with a due regard to the legal and social proprieties); and it was in this way that I first became introduced to the astonishing series of events that was destined to exercise so great an influence on my own life.

The lecture which had just been concluded had dealt with the rather unsatisfactory subject of survivorship. Most of the students had left the theatre, and the remainder had gathered round the lecturer's table to listen to the informal comments that Dr. Thorndyke was wont to deliver on these occasions in an easy, conversational manner, leaning against the edge of the table and

5

apparently addressing his remarks to a stick of blackboard chalk that he held in his fingers.

"The problem of survivorship," he was saying, in reply to a question put by one of the students, "ordinarily occurs in cases where the bodies of the parties are producible, or where, at any rate, the occurrence of death and its approximate time are actually known. But an analogous difficulty may arise in a case where the body of one of the parties is not forthcoming, and the fact of death may have to be assumed on collateral evidence.

"Here, of course, the vital question to be settled is, what is the latest instant at which it is certain that this person was alive? And the settlement of that question may turn on some circumstance of the most trivial and insignificant kind. There is a case in this morning's paper which illustrates this. A gentleman has disappeared rather mysteriously. He was last seen by the servant of a relative at whose house he had called. Now, if this gentleman should never reappear, dead or alive, the question as to what was the latest moment at which he was certainly alive will turn upon the further question: 'Was he or was he not wearing a particular article of jewellery when he called at the relative's house?'"

He paused with a reflective eye bent upon the stump of chalk he still held; then, noting the expectant interest with which we were regarding him, he resumed:

"The circumstances in this case are very curious; in fact, they are highly mysterious; and if any legal issues should arise in respect of them, they are likely to yield some very remarkable complications. The gentleman who has disappeared, Mr. John Bellingham, is a man well known in archæological circles. He recently returned from Egypt, bringing with him a very fine collection of antiquities—some of which, by the way, he has presented

to the British Museum, where they are now on view—
and having made this presentation, he appears to have
gone to Paris on business. I may mention that the gift
consisted of a very fine mummy and a complete set of
tomb-furniture. The latter, however, had not arrived from
Egypt at the time when the missing man left for Paris, but
the mummy was inspected on the fourteenth of October
at Mr. Bellingham's house by Dr. Norbury of the British
Museum, in the presence of the donor and his solicitor,
and the latter was authorised to hand over the complete
collection to the British Museum authorities when the
tomb-furniture arrived, which he has since done.

"From Paris he seems to have returned on the twenty-
third of November, and to have gone direct from Charing
Cross to the house of a relative, a Mr. Hurst, who is a
bachelor and lives at Eltham. He appeared at the house at
twenty minutes past five, and as Mr. Hurst had not yet
come down from town and was not expected until a
quarter to six, he explained who he was and said he
would wait in the study and write some letters. The
housemaid accordingly showed him into the study,
furnished him with writing materials, and left him.

"At a quarter to six Mr. Hurst let himself in with his
latchkey, and before the housemaid had time to speak to
him he had passed through into the study and shut the
door.

"At six o'clock, when the dinner bell was rung, Mr.
Hurst entered the dining-room alone, and observing that
the table was laid for two, asked the reason.

"'I thought Mr. Bellingham was staying to dinner, sir,'
was the housemaid's reply.

"'Mr. Bellingham!' exclaimed the astonished host. 'I
didn't know he was here. Why was I not told?'

"'I thought he was in the study with you, sir,' said the

housemaid.

"On this a search was made for the visitor, with the result that he was nowhere to be found. He had disappeared without leaving a trace, and what made the incident more odd was that the housemaid was certain that he had not gone out by the front door. For since neither she nor the cook was acquainted with Mr. John Bellingham, she had remained the whole time either in the kitchen, which commanded a view of the front gate, or in the dining-room, which opened into the hall opposite the study door. The study itself has a French window opening on a narrow grass plot, across which is a side-gate that opens into an alley; and it appears that Mr. Bellingham must have made his exit by this rather eccentric route. At any rate—and this is the important fact—he was not in the house, and no one had seen him leave it.

"After a hasty meal Mr. Hurst returned to town and called at the office of Mr. Bellingham's solicitor and confidential agent, a Mr. Jellicoe, and mentioned the matter to him. Mr. Jellicoe knew nothing of his client's return from Paris, and the two men at once took the train down to Woodford, where the missing man's brother, Mr. Godfrey Bellingham, lives. The servant who admitted them said that Mr. Godfrey was not at home, but that his daughter was in the library, which is a detached building situated in a shrubbery beyond the garden at the back of the house. Here the two men found, not only Miss Bellingham but also her father, who had come in by the back gate.

"Mr. Godfrey and his daughter listened to Mr. Hurst's story with the greatest surprise, and assured him that they had neither seen nor heard anything of John Bellingham.

"Presently the party left the library to walk up to the

house; but only a few feet from the library door Mr. Jellicoe noticed an object lying in the grass and pointed it out to Mr. Godfrey.

"The latter picked it up, and they all recognised it as a scarab which Mr. John Bellingham had been accustomed to wear suspended from his watch-chain. There was no mistaking it. It was a very fine scarab of the eighteenth dynasty fashioned of lapis lazuli and engraved with the cartouche of Amenhotep III. It had been suspended by a gold ring fastened to a wire which passed through the suspension hole, and the ring, though broken, was still in position.

"This discovery of course only added to the mystery, which was still further increased when, on inquiry, a suit-case bearing the initials J. B. was found to be unclaimed in the cloak-room at Charing Cross. Reference to the counterfoil of the ticket-book showed that it had been deposited about the time of the arrival of the Continental express on the twenty-third of November, so that its owner must have gone straight on to Eltham.

"That is how the affair stands at present, and, should the missing man never reappear or should his body never be found, the question, as you see, which will be required to be settled is, ' What is the exact time and place, when and where, he was last known to be alive?' As to the place, the importance of the issues involved in that question are obvious and we need not consider them. But the question of time has another kind of significance. Cases have occurred, as I pointed out in the lecture, in which proof of survivorship by less than a minute has secured succession to property. Now, the missing man was last seen alive at Mr. Hurst's house at twenty minutes past five on the twenty-third of November. But he appears to have visited his brother's house at

Woodford; and, since nobody saw him at that house, it is at present uncertain whether he went there before calling on Mr. Hurst. If he went there first, then twenty minutes past five on the evening of the twenty-third is the latest moment at which he is known to have been alive; but if he went there after, there would have to be added to this time the shortest time possible in which he could travel from the one house to the other.

"But the question as to which house he visited first hinges on the scarab. If he was wearing the scarab when he arrived at Mr. Hurst's house, it would be certain that he went there first; but if it was not then on his watch-chain, a probability would be established that he went first to Woodford. Thus, you see, a question which may conceivably become of the most vital moment in determining the succession of property turns on the observation or non-observation by this housemaid of an apparently trivial and insignificant fact."

"Has the servant made any statement on this subject, sir?" I ventured to enquire.

"Apparently not," replied Dr. Thorndyke; "at any rate, there is no reference to any such statement in the newspaper report, though otherwise the case is reported in great detail; indeed, the wealth of detail, including plans of the two houses, is quite remarkable and well worth noting as being in itself a fact of considerable interest."

"In what respect, sir, is it of interest?" one of the students asked.

"Ah," replied Dr. Thorndyke, "I think I must leave you to consider that question yourself. This is an untried case, and we mustn't make free with the actions and motives of individuals."

"Does the paper give any description of the missing

man, sir?" I asked.

"Yes; quite an exhaustive description. Indeed, it is exhaustive to the verge of impropriety, considering that the man may turn up alive and well at any moment. It seems that he has an old Pott's fracture of the left ankle, a linear, longitudinal scar on each knee—origin not stated, but easily guessed at—and that he has tattooed on his chest in vermilion a very finely and distinctly executed representation of the symbolical Eye of Osiris—or Horus or Ra, as the different authorities have it. There certainly ought to be no difficulty in identifying the body. But we hope that it will not come to that.

"And now I must really be running away, and so must you; but I would advise you all to get copies of the paper and file them when you have read the remarkably full details. It is a most curious case, and it is highly probable that we shall hear of it again. Good-afternoon, gentlemen."

Dr. Thorndyke's advice appealed to all who heard it, for medical jurisprudence was a live subject at St. Margaret's, and all of us were keenly interested in it. As a result, we sallied forth in a body to the nearest newsvendor's, and, having each provided himself with a copy of the *Daily Telegraph*, adjourned together to the Common Room to devour the report and thereafter to discuss the bearings of the case, unhampered by those considerations of delicacy that afflicted our more squeamish and scrupulous teacher.

CHAPTER II   The Eavesdropper

It is one of the canons of correct conduct, scrupulously adhered to (when convenient) by all well-bred persons, that an acquaintance should be initiated by a proper introduction. To this salutary rule, which I have disregarded to the extent of an entire chapter, I now hasten to conform; and the more so inasmuch as nearly two years have passed since my first informal appearance.

Permit me, then, to introduce Paul Berkeley, M.B., etc., recently—very recently—qualified, faultlessly attired in the professional frock-coat and tall hat, and, at the moment of introduction, navigating with anxious care a perilous strait between a row of well-filled coal-sacks and a colossal tray piled high with kidney potatoes.

The passage of this strait landed me on the terra firma of Fleur-de-Lys Court, where I halted for a moment to consult my visiting list. There was only one more patient for me to see this morning, and he lived at 49 Nevill's Court, wherever that might be. I turned for information to the presiding deity of the coal shop.

"Can you direct me, Mrs. Jablett, to Nevill's Court?"

She could and she did, grasping me confidentially by the arm (the mark remained on my sleeve for weeks) and pointing a shaking forefinger at the dead wall ahead. "Nevill's Court," said Mrs. Jablett, "is a alley, and you goes into it through a archway. It turns out of Fetter Lane on the right 'and as you goes up, oppersight Bream's Buildings."

I thanked Mrs. Jablett and went on my way, glad that the morning round was nearly finished, and vaguely conscious of a growing appetite and of a desire to wash in hot water.

The practice which I was conducting was not my own. It belonged to poor Dick Barnard, an old St. Margaret's man of irrepressible spirits and indifferent physique, who had started only the day before for a trip down the

Mediterranean on board a tramp engaged in the currant trade; and this, my second morning's round, was in some sort a voyage of geographical discovery.

I walked on briskly up Fetter Lane until a narrow arched opening, bearing the superscription "Nevill's Court," arrested my steps, and here I turned to encounter one of those surprises that lie in wait for the traveller in London by-ways. Expecting to find the grey squalor of the ordinary London court, I looked out from under the shadow of the arch past a row of decent little shops through a vista full of light and colour—a vista of ancient, warm-toned roofs and walls relieved by sunlit foliage. In the heart of London a tree is always a delightful surprise; but here were not only trees, but bushes and even flowers. The narrow footway was bordered by little gardens, which, with their wooden palings and well-kept shrubs, gave to the place an air of quaint and sober rusticity; and even as I entered, a bevy of workgirls, with gaily-coloured blouses and hair aflame in the sunlight, brightened up the quiet background, like the wild flowers that spangle a summer hedgerow.

In one of the gardens I noticed that the little paths were paved with what looked like circular tiles, but which, on inspection, I found to be old-fashioned stone ink-bottles, buried bottom upwards; and I was meditating upon the quaint conceit of the forgotten scrivener who had thus adorned his habitation—a law-writer perhaps or an author, or perchance even a poet—when I perceived the number that I was seeking inscribed on a shabby door in a high wall. There was no bell or knocker, so, lifting the latch, I pushed the door open and entered.

But if the court itself had been a surprise, this was a positive wonder, a dream. Here, within earshot of the rumble of Fleet Street, I was in an old-fashioned garden enclosed by high walls and, now that the gate was shut, cut off from all sight and knowledge of the urban world that seethed without. I stood and gazed in delighted astonishment. Sun-gilded trees and flower-beds gay with blossom; lupins, snapdragons, nasturtiums, spiry foxgloves, and mighty hollyhocks formed the foreground, over which a pair of sulphur-tinted butterflies flitted, unmindful of a buxom and miraculously clean white cat which pursued them, dancing across the borders and clapping her snowy paws fruitlessly in mid-air. And the background was no less wonderful; a grand old house, dark-eaved and venerable, that must have looked down on this garden when ruffled dandies were borne in sedan chairs through the court, and gentle Izaak Walton, stealing forth from his shop in Fleet Street, strolled up Fetter Lane to "go a-angling" at Temple Mills.

So overpowered was I by this unexpected vision that my hand was on the bottom knob of a row of bell-pulls before I recollected myself; and it was not until a most infernal jangling from within recalled me to my business that I observed underneath it a small brass plate inscribed "Miss Oman."

The door opened with some suddenness and a short, middle-aged woman surveyed me hungrily.

"Have I rung the wrong bell?" I asked, foolishly enough, I must admit.

"How can I tell?" she demanded. "I expect you have. It's the sort of thing a man would do—ring the wrong bell and then say he's sorry."

"I didn't go as far as that," I retorted. "It seems to have had the desired effect, and I've made your acquaintance into the bargain."

"Whom do you want to see?" she asked.

"Mr. Bellingham."

"Are you the doctor?"

"I'm *a* doctor."

"Follow me upstairs," said Miss Oman, "and don't tread on the paint."

I crossed the spacious hall, and, preceded by my conductress, ascended a noble oak staircase, treading carefully on a ribbon of matting that ran up the middle. On the first-floor landing Miss Oman opened a door and, pointing to the room, said, "Go in there and wait; I'll tell her you're here."

"I said *Mr.* Bellingham——" I began; but the door slammed on me, and Miss Oman's footsteps retreated rapidly down the stairs.

It was at once obvious to me that I was in a very awkward position. The room into which I had been shown communicated with another, and though the door of communication was shut, I was unpleasantly aware of a conversation that was taking place in the adjoining room. At first, indeed, only a vague mutter, with a few disjointed phrases, came through the door, but suddenly an angry voice rang out clear and painfully distinct:

"Yes, I did! And I say it again. Bribery! Collusion! That's what it amounts to. You want to square me!"

"Nothing of the kind, Godfrey," was the reply in a lower tone; but at this point I coughed emphatically and moved a chair, and the voices subsided once more into an indistinct murmur.

To distract my attention from my unseen neighbours I glanced curiously about the room and speculated upon the personalities of its occupants. A very curious room it was, with its pathetic suggestion of decayed splendour and old-world dignity; a room full of interest and character and of contrasts and perplexing contradictions. For the most part it spoke of unmistakable though decent poverty. It was nearly bare of furniture, and what little there was of the cheapest—a small kitchen table and three Windsor chairs (two of them with arms); a threadbare string carpet on the floor, and a cheap cotton cloth on the table; these, with a set of bookshelves, frankly constructed of grocers' boxes, formed the entire suite. And yet, despite its poverty, the place exhaled an air of homely if rather ascetic comfort, and the taste was irreproachable. The quiet russet of the table-cloth struck a pleasant harmony with the subdued bluish green of the worn carpet; the Windsor chairs and the legs of the table had been carefully denuded of their glaring varnish and stained a sober brown; and the austerity of the whole was relieved by a ginger-jar filled with fresh-cut flowers and set in the middle of the table.

But the contrasts of which I have spoken were most singular and puzzling. There were the bookshelves, for instance, home-made and stained at the cost of a few pence, but filled with recent and costly new works on archæology and ancient art. There were the objects on the mantelpiece: a facsimile in bronze—not bronzed plaster—of the beautiful head of Hypnos and a pair of fine Ushabti figures. There were the decorations of the walls, a number of etchings—signed proofs, every one of them—of Oriental subjects, and a splendid facsimile reproduction of an Egyptian papyrus. It was incongruous in the extreme, this mingling of costly refinements with the barest and shabbiest necessaries of life, of fastidious culture with manifest poverty. I could make nothing of it. What manner of man, I wondered, was this new patient of mine? Was he a miser, hiding himself and his wealth in this obscure court? An eccentric savant? A philosopher? Or—more probably—a crank? But at this point my meditations were interrupted by the voice from the adjoining room, once more raised in anger.

"But I say that you *are* making an accusation! You are implying that I made away with him."

"Not at all," was the reply; "but I repeat that it is your business to ascertain what has become of him. The responsibility rests upon you."

"Upon me!" rejoined the first voice. "And what about you? Your position is a pretty fishy one if it comes to that."

"What!" roared the other. "Do you insinuate that I murdered my own brother?"

During this amazing colloquy I had stood gaping with sheer astonishment. Suddenly I recollected myself, and dropping into a chair, set my elbows on my knees and clapped my hands over my ears; and thus I must have remained for a full minute when I became aware of the closing of a door behind me.

I sprang to my feet and turned in some embarrassment (for I must have looked unspeakably ridiculous) to confront the sombre figure of a rather tall and strikingly handsome girl, who, as she stood with her hand on the knob of the door, saluted me with a formal bow. In an instantaneous glance I noted how perfectly she matched her strange surroundings. Black-robed, black-haired, with black-grey eyes and a grave sad face of ivory pallor, she stood, like one of old Terborch's portraits, a harmony in tones so low as to be but a step removed from monochrome. Obviously a lady in spite of the worn and rusty dress; and something in the poise of the head and the set of the straight brows hinted at a spirit that adversity had hardened rather than broken.

"I must ask you to forgive me for keeping you waiting," she said; and as she spoke a certain softening at the corners of the austere mouth reminded me of the absurd position in which she had found me.

I murmured that the trifling delay was of no consequence whatever; that I had, in fact, been rather glad of the rest; and I was beginning somewhat vaguely to approach the subject of the invalid when the voice from the adjoining room again broke forth with hideous distinctness.

"I tell you I'll do nothing of the kind! Why, confound you, it's nothing less than a conspiracy that you're proposing!"

Miss Bellingham—as I assumed her to be—stepped quickly across the floor, flushing angrily, as well she might; but, as she reached the door, it flew open and a small, spruce, middle-aged man burst into the room.

"Your father is mad, Ruth!" he exclaimed; "absolutely stark mad! And I refuse to hold any further communication with him."

"The present interview was not of his seeking," Miss Bellingham replied coldly.

"No, it was not," was the wrathful rejoinder; "it was my mistaken generosity. But there—what is the use of talking? I've done my best for you and I'll do no more. Don't trouble to let me out; I can find my way. Good-morning." With a stiff bow and a quick glance at me, the speaker strode out of the room, banging the door after him.

"I must apologise for this extraordinary reception," said Miss Bellingham; "but I believe medical men are not easily astonished. I will introduce you to your patient now." She opened the door and, as I followed her into the adjoining room, she said: "Here is another visitor for you, dear. Dr. ——"

"Berkeley," said I. "I am acting for my friend, Dr. Barnard."

The invalid, a fine-looking man of about fifty-five, who sat propped up in bed with a pile of pillows, held out an excessively shaky hand, which I grasped cordially, making a mental note of the tremor.

"How do you do, sir?" said Mr. Bellingham. "I hope Dr. Barnard is not ill."

"Oh, no," I answered, "he has gone for a trip down the Mediterranean on a currant ship. The chance occurred rather suddenly, and I bustled him off before he had time to change his mind. Hence my rather unceremonious appearance, which I hope you will forgive."

"Not at all," was the hearty response. "I'm delighted to hear that you sent him off; he wanted a holiday, poor man. And I am delighted to make your acquaintance, too."

"It is very good of you," I said; whereupon he bowed as gracefully as a man may who is propped up in bed with a heap of pillows; and having thus exchanged broadsides of civility, so to speak, we—or, at least, I—proceeded to business.

"How long have you been laid up?" I asked cautiously, not wishing to make too evident the fact that my principal had given me no information respecting his case.

"A week to-day," he replied. "The *fons et origo mali* was a hansom-cab which upset me opposite the Law Courts—sent me sprawling in the middle of the road. My own fault, of course—at least, the cabby said so, and I suppose he knew. But that was no consolation to me."

"Were you hurt much?"

"No, not really; but the fall bruised my knee rather badly and gave me a deuce of a shake-up. I'm too old for that sort of thing, you know."

"Most people are," said I.

"True; but you can take a cropper more gracefully at

twenty than at fifty-five. However, the knee is getting on quite well—you shall see it presently—and you observe that I am giving it complete rest. But that isn't the whole of the trouble or the worst of it. It's my confounded nerves. I'm as irritable as the devil and as nervous as a cat. And I can't get a decent night's rest."

I recalled the tremulous hand that he had offered me. He did not look like a drinker, but still——

"Do you smoke much?" I inquired diplomatically.

He looked at me slyly and chuckled. "That's a very delicate way to approach the subject, Doctor," he said. "No, I don't smoke much, and I don't crook my little finger. I saw you look at my shaky hand just now—oh, it's all right; I'm not offended. It's a doctor's business to keep his eyelids lifting. But my hand is steady enough as a rule, when I'm not upset, but the least excitement sets me shaking like a jelly. And the fact is that I have just had a deucedly unpleasant interview——"

"I think," Miss Bellingham interrupted, "Dr. Berkeley and, indeed, the neighbourhood at large, are aware of the fact."

Mr. Bellingham laughed rather shamefacedly. "I'm afraid I did lose my temper," he said; "but I am an impulsive old fellow, Doctor, and when I'm put out I'm apt to speak my mind—a little too bluntly perhaps."

"And audibly," his daughter added. "Do you know that Dr. Berkeley was reduced to the necessity of stopping his ears?" She glanced at me as she spoke, with something like a twinkle in her solemn grey eyes.

"Did I shout?" Mr. Bellingham asked, not very contritely, I thought, though he added: "I'm very sorry, my dear; but it won't happen again. I think we've seen the last of that good gentleman."

"I am sure I hope so," she rejoined, adding: "and now I

will leave you to your talk; I shall be in the next room if you should want me."

I opened the door for her, and when she had passed out with a stiff little bow I seated myself by the bedside and resumed the consultation. It was evidently a case of nervous breakdown, to which the cab accident had, no doubt, contributed. As to the other antecedents, they were of no concern of mine, though Mr. Bellingham seemed to think otherwise, for he resumed:

"That cab business was the last straw, you know, and it finished me off, but I have been going down the hill for a long time. I've had a lot of trouble during the last two years. But I suppose I oughtn't to pester you with the details of my personal affairs."

"Anything that bears on your present state of health is of interest to me, if you don't mind telling it," I said.

"Mind!" he exclaimed. "Did you ever meet an invalid who didn't enjoy talking about his own health? It's the listener who minds, as a rule."

"Well, the present listener doesn't," I said.

"Then," said Mr. Bellingham, "I'll treat myself to the luxury of telling you all my troubles; I don't often get the chance of a confidential grumble to a responsible man of my own class. And I really have some excuse for railing at Fortune, as you will agree when I tell you that, a couple of years ago, I went to bed one night a gentleman of independent means and excellent prospects and woke up in the morning to find myself practically a beggar. Not a cheerful experience that, you know, at my time of life, eh?"

"No," I agreed, "nor at any other."

"And that was not all," he continued; "for at the same moment I lost my brother, my dearest, kindest friend. He disappeared—vanished off the face of the earth; but perhaps you have heard of the affair. The confounded papers were full of it at the time."

He paused abruptly, noticing, no doubt, a sudden change in my face. Of course, I recollected the case now. Indeed, ever since I had entered the house some chord of memory had been faintly vibrating, and now his last words had struck out the full note.

"Yes," I said, " I remember the incident, though I don't suppose I should but for the fact that our lecturer on medical jurisprudence drew my attention to it."

"Indeed," said Mr. Bellingham, rather uneasily, as I fancied. "What did he say about it?"

"He referred to it as a case that was calculated to give rise to some very pretty legal complications."

"By Jove!" exclaimed Bellingham, "that man was a prophet! Legal complications, indeed! But I'll be bound he never guessed at the sort of infernal tangle that has actually gathered round the affair. By the way, what was his name?"

"Thorndyke," I replied. "Dr. John Thorndyke."

"Thorndyke," Mr. Bellingham repeated in a musing, retrospective tone. " I seem to remember the name. Yes, of course. I have heard a legal friend of mine, a Mr. Marchmont, speak of him in reference to the case of a man whom I knew slightly years ago—a certain Jeffrey Blackmore, who also disappeared very mysteriously. I remember now that Dr. Thorndyke unravelled that case with most remarkable ingenuity."

"I daresay he would be very much interested to hear about your case," I suggested.

"I daresay he would," was the reply; "but one can't take up a professional man's time for nothing, and I couldn't afford to pay him. And that reminds me that I'm taking up your time by gossiping about purely personal affairs."

"My morning round is finished," said I, "and, moreover, your personal affairs are highly interesting. I suppose I mustn't ask what is the nature of the legal entanglement."

"Not unless you are prepared to stay here for the rest of the day and go home a raving lunatic. But I'll tell you this much; the trouble is about my poor brother's will. In the first place it can't be administered because there is not sufficient evidence that my brother is dead; and in the second place, if it could, all the property would go to people who were never intended to benefit. The will itself is the most diabolically exasperating document that was ever produced by the perverted ingenuity of a wrong-headed man. That's all. Will you have a look at my knee?"

As Mr. Bellingham's explanation (delivered in a rapid *crescendo* and ending almost in a shout) had left him purple-faced and trembling, I thought it best to bring our talk to an end. Accordingly I proceeded to inspect the injured knee, which was now nearly well, and to overhaul my patient generally; and having given him detailed instructions as to his general conduct, I rose and took my leave.

"And remember," I said as I shook his hand, "no tobacco, no coffee, no excitement of any kind. Lead a quiet, bovine life."

"That's all very well," he grumbled, "but supposing people come here and excite me?"

"Disregard them," said I, "and read *Whitaker's Almanack*." And with this parting advice I passed out into the other room.

Miss Bellingham was seated at the table with a pile of blue-covered note-books before her, two of which were open, displaying pages closely written in a small neat handwriting. She rose as I entered and looked at me inquiringly.

"I heard you advising my father to read *Whitaker's Almanack*," she said. "Was that a curative measure?"

"Entirely," I replied. "I recommended it for its medicinal virtues, as an antidote to mental excitement."

She smiled faintly. "It certainly is not a highly emotional book," she said, and then asked: "Have you any other instructions to give?"

"Well, I might give the conventional advice—to maintain a cheerful outlook and avoid worry; but I don't suppose you would find it very helpful."

"No," she answered bitterly; "it is a counsel of perfection. People in our position are not a very cheerful class, I'm afraid; but still they don't seek out worries from sheer perverseness. The worries come unsought. But, of course, you can't enter into that."

"I can't give any practical help, I fear, though I do sincerely hope that your father's affairs will straighten themselves out soon."

She thanked me for my good wishes and accompanied me down to the street door, where, with a bow and a rather stiff hand-shake, she gave me my *congé*.

Very ungratefully the noise of Fetter Lane smote on my ears as I came out through the archway, and very squalid and unrestful the little street looked when contrasted with the dignity and monastic quiet of the old garden. As to the surgery, with its oilcloth floor and walls made hideous with gaudy insurance show-cards in sham gilt frames, its aspect was so revolting that I flew to the day-book for distraction, and was still busily entering the morning's visits when the bottle-boy, Adolphus, entered stealthily to announce lunch.

CHAPTER III   John Thorndyke

That the character of an individual tends to be reflected in his dress is a fact familiar to the least observant. That the observation is equally applicable to aggregates of men is less familiar, but equally true. Do not the members of the fighting professions, even to this day, deck themselves in feathers, in gaudy colours and gilded ornaments, after the manner of the African war-chief or the Redskin "brave," and thereby indicate the place of war in modern civilisation? Does not the Church of Rome send her priests to the altar in habiliments that were fashionable before the fall of the Roman Empire, in token of her immovable conservatism? And, lastly, does not the law, lumbering on in the wake of progress, symbolise its subjection to precedent by head-gear reminiscent of the days of good Queen Anne?

I should apologise for obtruding upon the reader these somewhat trite reflections, which were set going by the quaint stock-in-trade of the wig-maker's shop in the cloisters of the Inner Temple, whither I strayed on a sultry afternoon in quest of shade and quiet. I had halted opposite the little shop window, and, with my eyes bent dreamily on the row of wigs, was pursuing the above train of thought when I was startled by a deep voice saying softly in my ear: "I'd have the full-bottomed one if I were you."

I turned swiftly and rather fiercely, and looked into the face of my old friend and fellow-student Jervis, behind whom, regarding us with a sedate smile, stood my former teacher Dr. John Thorndyke. Both men greeted me with a warmth that I felt to be very flattering, for Thorndyke was quite a great personage, and even Jervis was several years my academic senior.

"You are coming in to have a cup of tea with us, I hope," said Thorndyke; and as I assented gladly, he took my arm and led me across the court in the direction of the Treasury.

"But why that hungry gaze at those forensic vanities, Berkeley?" he asked. "Are you thinking of following my example and Jervis's—deserting the bedside for the Bar?"

"What! Has Jervis gone in for the law?" I exclaimed.

"Bless you, yes!" replied Jervis. "I have become parasitical on Thorndyke! 'The big fleas have little fleas,' you know. I am the additional fraction trailing after the whole number in the rear of a decimal point."

"Don't you believe him, Berkeley," interposed Thorndyke. "He is the brains of the firm. I supply the respectability and moral worth. But you haven't answered my question. What are you doing here on a summer afternoon staring into a wig-maker's window?"

"I am Barnard's locum; he is in practice in Fetter Lane."

"I know," said Thorndyke; "we meet him occasionally, and very pale and peaky he has been looking of late. Is he taking a holiday?"

"Yes. He has gone for a trip to the Isles of Greece in a currant ship."

"Then," said Jervis, "you are actually a local G.P. I thought you were looking beastly respectable."

"And judging from your leisured manner when we encountered you," added Thorndyke, "the practice is not a strenuous one. I suppose it is entirely local?"

"Yes," I replied. "The patients mostly live in the small streets and courts within a half-mile radius of the surgery, and the abodes of some of them are pretty squalid. Oh! and that reminds me of a very strange coincidence. It will interest you, I think."

"Life is made up of strange coincidences," said Thorndyke. "Nobody but a reviewer of novels is ever really surprised at a coincidence. But what is yours?"

"It is connected with a case that you mentioned to us at the hospital about two years ago, the case of a man who disappeared under rather mysterious circumstances. Do you remember it? The man's name was Bellingham."

"The Egyptologist? Yes, I remember the case quite well. What about it?"

"The brother is a patient of mine. He is living in Nevill's Court with his daughter, and they seem to be as poor as church mice."

"Really," said Thorndyke, "this is quite interesting. They must have come down in the world rather suddenly. If I remember rightly, the brother was living in a house of some pretensions standing in its own grounds."

"Yes, that is so. I see you recollect all about the case."

"My dear fellow," said Jervis. "Thorndyke never forgets a likely case. He is a sort of medico-legal camel. He gulps down the raw facts from the newspapers or elsewhere, and then, in his leisure moments, he calmly regurgitates them and has a quiet chew at them. It is a quaint habit. A case crops up in the papers or in one of the courts, and Thorndyke swallows it whole. Then it lapses and everyone forgets it. A year or two later it crops up in a new form, and, to your astonishment, you find that Thorndyke has got it all cut and dried. He has been ruminating on it periodically in the interval."

"You notice," said Thorndyke, "that my learned friend is pleased to indulge in mixed metaphors. But his statement is substantially true, though obscurely worded.

You must tell us more about the Bellinghams when we have fortified you with a cup of tea."

Our talk had brought us to Thorndyke's chambers, which were on the first floor of No. 5A King's Bench Walk, and as we entered the fine, spacious, panelled room we found a small, elderly man, neatly dressed in black, setting out the tea-service on the table. I glanced at him with some curiosity. He hardly looked like a servant, in spite of his neat, black clothes; in fact, his appearance was rather puzzling, for while his quiet dignity and his serious, intelligent face suggested some kind of professional man, his neat, capable hands were those of a skilled mechanic.

Thorndyke surveyed the tea-tray thoughtfully and then looked at his retainer. "I see you have put three teacups, Polton," he said. "Now, how did you know I was bringing someone in to tea?"

The little man smiled a quaint, crinkly smile of gratification as he explained:

"I happened to look out of the laboratory window as you turned the corner, sir."

"How disappointingly simple," said Jervis. "We were hoping for something abstruse and telepathic."

"Simplicity is the soul of efficiency, sir," replied Polton as he checked the tea-service to make sure that nothing was forgotten, and with this remarkable aphorism he silently evaporated.

"To return to the Bellingham case," said Thorndyke, when he had poured out the tea. "Have you picked up any facts relating to the parties—any facts, I mean, of course, that it would be proper for you to mention?"

"I have learned one or two things that there is no harm in repeating. For instance, I gather that Godfrey Bellingham—my patient—lost all his property quite suddenly about the time of the disappearance."

"That is really odd," said Thorndyke. "The opposite condition would be quite understandable, but one doesn't see exactly how this can have happened, unless there was an allowance of some sort."

"No, that was what struck me. But there seem to be some queer features in the case, and the legal position is evidently getting complicated. There is a will, for example, which is giving trouble."

"They will hardly be able to administer the will without either proof or presumption of death," Thorndyke remarked.

"Exactly. That's one of the difficulties. Another is that there seems to be some fatal defect in the drafting of the will itself. I don't know what it is, but I expect I shall hear sooner or later. By the way, I mentioned the interest that you have taken in the case, and I think Bellingham would have liked to consult you, but, of course, the poor devil has no money."

"That is awkward for him if the other interested parties have. There will probably be legal proceedings of some kind, and as the law takes no account of poverty, he is likely to go to the wall. He ought to have advice of some sort."

"I don't see how he is to get it," said I.

"Neither do I," Thorndyke admitted. "There are no hospitals for impecunious litigants; it is assumed that only persons of means have a right to go to law. Of course, if we knew the man and the circumstances we might be able to help him; but for all we know to the contrary, he may be an arrant scoundrel."

I recalled the strange conversation that I had overheard, and wondered what Thorndyke would have thought of it if it had been allowable for me to repeat it.

Obviously it was not, however, and I could only give my own impressions.

"He doesn't strike me as that," I said; "but, of course, one never knows. Personally, he impressed me rather favourably, which is more than the other man did."

"What other man?" asked Thorndyke.

"There was another man in the case, wasn't there? I forget his name. I saw him at the house and didn't much like the look of him. I suspect he's putting some sort of pressure on Bellingham."

"Berkeley knows more about this than he's telling us," said Jervis. "Let us look up the report and see who this stranger is." He took down from a shelf a large volume of newspaper cuttings and laid it on the table.

"You see," said he, as he ran his finger down the index. "Thorndyke files all the cases that are likely to come to something, and I know he had expectations regarding this one. I fancy he had some ghoulish hope that the missing gentleman's head might turn up in somebody's dust-bin. Here we are; the other man's name is Hurst. He is apparently a cousin; and it was at his house the missing man was last seen alive."

"So you think Mr. Hurst is moving in the matter?" said Thorndyke, when he had glanced over the report.

"That is my impression," I replied, "though I really know nothing about it."

"Well," said Thorndyke, "if you should learn what is being done and should have permission to speak of it, I shall be very interested to hear how the case progresses; and if an unofficial opinion on any point would be of service, I think there would be no harm in giving it."

"It would certainly be of great value if the other parties are taking professional advice," I said; and then, after a pause, I asked: "Have you given this case much consideration?""

Thorndyke reflected. "No," he said, "I can't say that I have. I turned it over rather carefully when the report first appeared, and I have speculated on it occasionally since. It is my habit, as Jervis was telling you, to utilise odd moments of leisure (such as a railway journey, for instance) by constructing theories to account for the facts of such obscure cases as have come to my notice. It is a useful habit, I think, for, apart from the mental exercise and experience that one gains from it, an appreciable portion of these cases ultimately comes into my hands, and then the previous consideration of them is so much time gained."

"Have you formed any theory to account for the facts in this case?" I asked.

"Yes; I have several theories, one of which I especially favour, and I am awaiting with great interest such new facts as may indicate to me which of these theories is probably the correct one."

"It's no use your trying to pump him, Berkeley," said Jervis. "He is fitted with an information valve that opens inwards. You can pour in as much as you like, but you can't get any out."

Thorndyke chuckled. "My learned friend is, in the main, correct," he said. "You see, I may be called upon any day to advise on this case, in which event I should feel remarkably foolish if I had already expounded my views in detail. But I should like to hear what you and Jervis make of the case as reported in the newspapers."

"There now," exclaimed Jervis, "what did I tell you? He wants to suck our brains."

"As far as my brain is concerned," I said, "the process of suction isn't likely to yield much except a vacuum, so I will resign in favour of you. You are a full-blown lawyer, whereas I am only a simple G.P."

Jervis filled his pipe with deliberate care and lighted it. Then, blowing a slender stream of smoke into the air, he said:

"If you want to know what I make of the case from that report, I can tell you in one word—nothing. Every road seems to end in a cul-de-sac."

"Oh, come!" said Thorndyke, "this is mere laziness. Berkeley wants to witness a display of your forensic wisdom. A learned counsel may be in a fog—he very often is—but he doesn't state the fact baldly; he wraps it up in a decent verbal disguise. Tell us how you arrive at your conclusion. Show us that you have really weighed the facts."

"Very well," said Jervis, "I will give you a masterly analysis of the case—leading to nothing." He continued to puff at his pipe for a time with slight embarrassment, as I thought—and I fully sympathised with him. Finally he blew a little cloud and commenced:

"The position appears to be this: Here is a man seen to enter a certain house, who is shown into a certain room, and shut in. He is not seen to come out, and yet, when the room is next entered, it is found to be empty; and that man is never seen again, alive or dead. That is a pretty tough beginning.

"Now, it is evident that one of three things must have happened. Either he must have remained in that room, or at least in that house, alive; or he must have died, naturally or otherwise, and his body have been concealed; or he must have left the house unobserved. Let us take the first case. This affair happened nearly two years ago. Now, he couldn't have remained alive in the house for two years. He would have been noticed. The servants, for instance, when cleaning out the rooms, would have observed him."

Here Thorndyke interposed with an indulgent smile at his junior. "My learned friend is treating the inquiry with unbecoming levity. We accept the conclusion that the man did not remain in the house alive."

"Very well. Then did he remain in it dead? Apparently not. The report says that as soon as the man was missed, Hurst and the servants together searched the house thoroughly. But there had been no time or opportunity to dispose of the body, whence the only possible conclusion is that the body was not there. Moreover, if we admit the possibility of his having been murdered—for that is what concealment of the body would imply—there is the question: 'Who could have murdered him?' Not the servants, obviously, and as to Hurst—well, of course, we don't know what his relations with the missing man may have been—at least, I don't."

"Neither do I," said Thorndyke. "I know nothing beyond what is in the newspaper report and what Berkeley has told us."

"Then we know nothing. He may have had a motive for murdering the man or he may not. The point is that he doesn't seem to have had the opportunity. Even if we suppose that he managed to conceal the body temporarily, still there was the final disposal of it. He couldn't have buried it in the garden with the servants about; neither could he have burned it. The only conceivable method by which he could have got rid of it would have been that of cutting it up into fragments and burying the dismembered parts in some secluded spots or dropping them into ponds or rivers. But no remains of the kind have been found, as some of them probably would have been by now, so that there is nothing to support this suggestion; indeed, the idea of murder, in this house at least, seems to be excluded by the search that was made the instant the man was missed.

"Then to take the third alternative: Did he leave the house unobserved? Well, it is not impossible, but it would be a queer thing to do. He may have been an impulsive or eccentric man. We can't say. We know nothing about him. But two years have elapsed and he has never turned up, so that if he left the house secretly he must have gone into hiding and be hiding still. Of course, he may have been the sort of lunatic who would behave in that manner or he may not. We have no information as to his personal character.

"Then there is the complication of the scarab that was picked up in the grounds of his brother's house at Woodford. That seems to show that he visited that house at some time. But no one admits having seen him there; and it is uncertain, therefore, whether he went first to his brother's house or to Hurst's. If he was wearing the scarab when he arrived at the Eltham house, he must have left that house unobserved and gone to Woodford; but if he was not wearing it he probably went from Woodford to Eltham, and there finally disappeared. As to whether he was or was not wearing the scarab when he was last seen alive by Hurst's housemaid, there is at present no evidence.

"If he went to his brother's house after his visit to Hurst, the disappearance is more understandable if we don't mind flinging accusations of murder about rather casually; for the disposal of the body would be much less difficult in that case. Apparently no one saw him enter the house, and, if he did enter, it was by a back gate which communicated with the library—a separate building some distance from the house. In that case it would have been physically possible for the Bellinghams to have made away with him. There was plenty of time to dispose of the body unobserved—temporarily, at any rate. Nobody had seen him come to the house, and nobody knew that he was there—if he *was* there; and apparently no search was made either at the time or afterwards. In fact, if it could be shown that the missing man left Hurst's house alive, or that he was wearing the scarab when he arrived there, things would look rather fishy for the Bellinghams—for, of course, the girl must have been in it if the father was. But there's the crux: there is no proof that the man ever did leave Hurst's house alive. And if he didn't—but there! as I said at first, whichever turning you take, you find that it ends in a blind alley."

"A lame ending to a masterly exposition," was Thorndyke's comment.

"I know," said Jervis. "But what would you have? There are quite a number of possible solutions, and one of them must be the true one. But how are we to judge which it is? I maintain that until we know something of the parties and the financial and other interests involved we have no data."

"There," said Thorndyke, "I disagree with you entirely. I maintain that we have ample data. You say that we have no means of judging which of the various possible solutions is the true one; but I think that if you read the report carefully and thoughtfully you will find that the facts now known point clearly to one explanation, and one only. It may not be the true explanation, and I don't suppose it is. But we are now dealing with the matter speculatively, academically, and I contend that our data yield a definite conclusion. What do you say, Berkeley?"

"I say that it is time for me to be off; the evening consultations begin at half-past six."

"Well," said Thorndyke, "don't let us keep you from your duties, with poor Barnard currant-picking in the Grecian Isles. But come in and see us again. Drop in when you like after your work is done. You won't be in our way even if we are busy, which we very seldom are after eight o'clock."

I thanked Dr. Thorndyke most heartily for making me free of his chambers in this hospitable fashion and took my leave, setting forth homewards by way of Middle Temple Lane and the Embankment; not a very direct route for Fetter Lane, it must be confessed; but our talk had revived my interest in the Bellingham household and put me in a reflective vein.

From the remarkable conversation that I had overheard it was evident that the plot was thickening. Not that I supposed that these two respectable gentlemen really suspected one another of having made away with the missing man; but still, their unguarded words, spoken in anger, made it clear that each had allowed the thought of sinister possibilities to enter his mind—a dangerous condition that might easily grow into actual suspicion. And then the circumstances really were highly mysterious, as I realised with especial vividness now after listening to my friend's analysis of the evidence.

From the problem itself my mind travelled, not for the first time during the last few days, to the handsome girl, who had seemed in my eyes the high-priestess of this temple of mystery in the quaint little court. What a strange figure she had made against this strange background, with her quiet, chilly, self-contained manner, her pale face, so sad and worn, her black, straight brows and solemn grey eyes, so inscrutable, mysterious, Sibylline. A striking, even impressive, personality this, I reflected, with something in it sombre and enigmatic that attracted and yet repelled.

And here I recalled Jervis's words: "The girl must have been in it if the father was." It was a dreadful thought, even though only speculatively uttered, and my heart rejected it; rejected it with an indignation that rather surprised me. And this notwithstanding that the sombre black-robed figure that my memory conjured up was one that associated itself with the idea of mystery and tragedy.

CHAPTER IV Legal Complications and a Jackal

My meditations brought me by a circuitous route, and ten minutes late, to the end of Fetter Lane, where, exchanging my rather abstracted air for the alert manner of a busy practitioner, I strode briskly forward and darted into the surgery with knitted brows, as though just released from an anxious case. But there was only one patient waiting, and she saluted me as I entered with a snort of defiance.

"Here you are, then?" said she.

"You are perfectly correct, Miss Oman," I replied; "in fact, you have put the case in a nutshell. What can I have the pleasure of doing for you?

"Nothing," was the answer. "My medical adviser is a lady; but I've brought a note from Mr. Bellingham. Here it is," and she thrust the envelope into my hand.

I glanced through the note and learned that my patient had had a couple of bad nights and a very harassing day. "Could I have something to give me a night's rest?" it concluded.

I reflected for a few moments. One is not very ready to prescribe sleeping draughts for unknown patients, but still, insomnia is a very distressing condition. In the end I temporised with a moderate dose of bromide, deciding to call and see if more energetic measures were necessary.

"He had better take a dose of this at once, Miss Oman," said I, as I handed her the bottle, "and I will look in later and see how he is."

"I expect he will be glad to see you," she answered, "for he is all alone to-night and very dumpy. Miss Bellingham is out. But I must remind you that he's a poor man and pays his way. You must excuse my mentioning it."

"I am much obliged to you for the hint, Miss Oman," I rejoined. "It isn't necessary for me to see him, but I should like just to look in and have a chat."

"Yes, it will do him good. You have your points, though punctuality doesn't seem to be one of them," and with this parting shot Miss Oman bustled away.

Half-past eight found me ascending the great, dim staircase of the house in Nevill's Court preceded by Miss Oman, by whom I was ushered into the room. Mr. Bellingham, who had just finished some sort of meal, was sitting hunched up in his chair gazing gloomily into the empty grate. He brightened up as I entered, but was evidently in very low spirits.

"I didn't mean to drag you out after your day's work was finished," he said, "though I am very glad to see you."

"You haven't dragged me out. I heard you were alone, so I just dropped in for a few minutes' gossip."

"That is really kind of you," he said heartily. "But I'm afraid you'll find me rather poor company. A man who is full of his own highly disagreeable affairs is not a desirable companion."

"You mustn't let me disturb you if you'd rather be

alone," said I, with a sudden fear that I was intruding.

"Oh, you won't disturb me," he replied; adding, with a laugh: "It's more likely to be the other way about. In fact, if I were not afraid of boring you to death I would ask you to let me talk my difficulties over with you."

"You won't bore me," I said. "It is generally interesting to share another man's experiences without their inconveniences. 'The proper study of mankind is man,' you know, especially to a doctor."

Mr. Bellingham chuckled grimly. "You make me feel like a microbe," he said. " However, if you would care to take a peep at me through your microscope, I will crawl on to the stage for your inspection, though it is not *my* actions that furnish the materials for your psychological studies. It is my poor brother who is the *Deus ex machina,* who, from his unknown grave, as I fear, pulls the strings of this infernal puppet-show."

He paused and for a space gazed thoughtfully into the grate as if he had forgotten my presence. At length he looked up and resumed:

"It is a curious story, Doctor—a very curious story. Part of it you know—the middle part. I will tell it you from the beginning, and then you will know as much as I do; for, as to the end, that is known to no one. It is written, no doubt, in the book of destiny, but the page has yet to be turned.

"The mischief began with my father's death. He was a country clergyman of very moderate means, a widower with two children, my brother John and me. He managed to send us both to Oxford, after which John went into the Foreign Office and I was to have gone into the Church. But I suddenly discovered that my views on religion had undergone a change that made this impossible, and just about this time my father came into a quite considerable property. Now, as it was his expressed intention to leave the estate equally divided between my brother and me, there was no need for me to take up any profession for a livelihood. Archæology was already the passion of my life, and I determined to devote myself henceforth to my favourite study, in which, by the way, I was following a family tendency; for my father was an enthusiastic student of ancient Oriental history, and John was, as you know, an ardent Egyptologist.

"Then my father died quite suddenly, and left no will. He had intended to have one drawn up, but had put it off until it was too late. And since nearly all the property was in the form of real estate, my brother inherited practically the whole of it. However, in deference to the known wishes of my father, he made me an allowance of five hundred a year, which was about a quarter of the annual income. I urged him to assign me a lump sum, but he refused to do this. Instead, he instructed his solicitor to pay me an allowance in quarterly instalments during the rest of his life; and it was understood that, on his death, the entire estate should devolve on me, or, if I died first, on my daughter Ruth. Then, as you know, he disappeared suddenly, and as the circumstances suggested that he was dead, and there was no evidence that he was alive, his solicitor—a Mr. Jellicoe—found himself unable to continue the payment of the allowance. On the other hand, as there was no positive evidence that my brother was dead, it was impossible to administer the will."

"You say the circumstances suggested that your brother was dead. What circumstances were they?"

"Principally the suddenness and completeness of the disappearance. His luggage, as you may remember, was found lying unclaimed at the railway station; and there was another circumstance even more suggestive. My brother drew a pension from the Foreign Office, for which he had to apply in person, or, if abroad, produce proof that he was alive on the date when the payment became due. Now, he was exceedingly regular in this respect; in fact, he had never been known to fail, either to appear in person or to transmit the necessary documents to his agent, Mr. Jellicoe. But from the moment when he vanished so mysteriously to the present day, nothing whatever has been heard of him."

"It's a very awkward position for you," I said, "but I should think there will not be much difficulty in obtaining the permission of the Court to presume death and to proceed to prove the will."

Mr. Bellingham made a wry face. "I expect you are right," he said, "but that doesn't help me much. You see, Mr. Jellicoe, having waited a reasonable time for my brother to reappear, took a very unusual, but, I think, in the special circumstances, a very proper step; he summoned me and the other interested party to his office and communicated to us the provisions of the will. And very extraordinary provisions they turned out to be. I was thunderstruck when I heard them. And the exasperating thing is that I feel sure my poor brother imagined that he had made everything perfectly safe and simple."

"They generally do," I said, rather vaguely.

"I suppose they do," said Mr. Bellingham; "but poor John has made the most infernal hash of his will, and I am certain that he has utterly defeated his own intentions. You see, we are an old London family. The house in Queen Square where my brother nominally lived, but actually kept his collection, has been occupied by us for generations, and most of the Bellinghams are buried in St. George's burial-ground close by, though some members of the family are buried in other churchyards in the neighbourhood. Now, my brother—who, by the way, was a bachelor—had a strong feeling for the family traditions, and he stipulated, not unnaturally, in his will that he should be buried in St. George's burial-ground among his ancestors, or, at least, in one of the places of burial appertaining to his native parish. But instead of simply expressing the wish and directing his executors to carry it out, he made it a condition affecting the operation of the will."

"Affecting it in what respect?" I asked.

"In a very vital respect," answered Mr. Bellingham. "The bulk of the property he bequeathed to me, or if I predeceased him, to my daughter Ruth. But the bequest was subject to the condition I have mentioned—that he should be buried in a certain place—and if that condition was not fulfilled, the bulk of the property was to go to my cousin, George Hurst."

"But in that case," said I, "as you can't produce the body, neither of you can get the property."

"I am not so sure of that," he replied. "If my brother is dead, it is pretty certain that he is not buried in St. George's or any of the other places mentioned, and the fact can easily be proved by production of the registers. So that a permission to presume death would result in the handing over to Hurst of almost the entire estate."

"Who is the executor?" I asked.

"Ah!" he exclaimed, "there is another muddle. There are two executors; Jellicoe is one, and the other is the principal beneficiary—Hurst or myself, as the case may be. But, you see, neither of us can become an executor until the Court has decided which of us is the principal beneficiary."

"But who is to apply to the Court? I thought that was the business of the executors."

"Exactly, that is Hurst's difficulty. We were discussing it when you called the other day—and a very animated discussion it was," he added, with a grim smile. "You see, Jellicoe naturally refuses to move in the matter alone. He says he must have the support of the other executor. But Hurst is not at present the other executor; neither am I. But the two of us together are the co-executor since the duty devolves upon one or other of us, in any case."

"It's a complicated position," I said.

"It is; and the complication has elicited a very curious proposal from Hurst. He points out—quite correctly, I am afraid—that as the conditions as to burial have not been complied with, the property must come to him, and he proposes a very neat little arrangement, which is this: That I shall support him and Jellicoe in their application for permission to presume death and to administer the will, and that he shall pay me four hundred a year for life; the arrangement to hold good *in all eventualities.*"

"What does he mean by that?"

"He means," said Bellingham, fixing me with a ferocious scowl, "that if the body should turn up at any future time, so that the conditions as to burial should be able to be carried out, he should still retain the property and pay me the four hundred a year."

"The deuce!" said I. "He seems to know how to drive a bargain."

"His position is that he stands to lose four hundred a year for the term of my life if the body is never found, and he ought to stand to win if it is."

"And I gather that you have refused this offer?"

"Yes; very emphatically, and my daughter agrees with me; but I am not sure that I have done the right thing. A man should think twice, I suppose, before he burns his boats."

"Have you spoken to Mr. Jellicoe about the matter?"

"Yes, I have been to see him to-day. He is a cautious man, and he doesn't advise me one way or the other. But I think he disapproves of my refusal; in fact, he remarked that a bird in the hand is worth two in the bush, especially when the whereabouts of the bush is unknown."

"Do you think he will apply to the Court without your sanction?"

"He doesn't want to; but I suppose, if Hurst puts pressure on him, he will have to. Besides, Hurst, as an interested party, could apply on his own account, and after my refusal he probably will; at least, that is Jellicoe's opinion."

"The whole thing is a most astonishing muddle," I said, "especially when one remembers that your brother had a lawyer to advise him. Didn't Mr. Jellicoe point out to him how absurd the provisions were?"

"Yes, he did. He tells me that he implored my brother to let him draw up a will embodying the matter in a reasonable form. But John wouldn't listen to him. Poor old fellow! he could be very pig-headed when he chose."

"And is Hurst's proposal still open?"

"No, thanks to my peppery temper. I refused it very definitely, and sent him off with a flea in his ear. I hope I have not made a false step; I was quite taken by surprise when Hurst made the proposal and got rather angry. You remember, my brother was last seen alive at Hurst's house—but there, I oughtn't to talk like that, and I oughtn't to pester you with my confounded affairs when you come in for a friendly chat, though I gave you fair warning, you remember."

"Oh, but you have been highly entertaining. You don't realise what an interest I take in your case."

Mr. Bellingham laughed somewhat grimly. "My case!"

he repeated. "You speak as if I were some rare and curious sort of criminal lunatic. However, I'm glad you find me amusing. It's more than I find myself."

"I didn't say amusing; I said interesting. I view you with deep respect as the central figure of a stirring drama. And I am not the only person who regards you in that light. Do you remember my speaking to you of Dr. Thorndyke?"

"Yes, of course I do."

"Well, oddly enough, I met him this afternoon and we had a long talk at his chambers. I took the liberty of mentioning that I had made your acquaintance. Did I do wrong?"

"No. Certainly not. Why shouldn't you tell him? Did he remember my infernal case, as you call it?"

"Perfectly, in all its details. He is quite an enthusiast, you know, and uncommonly keen to hear how the case develops."

"So am I, for that matter," said Mr. Bellingham.

"I wonder," said I, "if you would mind my telling him what you have told me to-night? It would interest him enormously."

Mr. Bellingham reflected for a while with his eyes fixed on the empty grate. Presently he looked up, and said slowly:

"I don't know why I should. It's no secret; and if it were, I hold no monopoly in it. No; tell him, if you think he'd care to hear about it."

"You needn't be afraid of his talking," I said. "He's as close as an oyster; and the facts may mean more to him than they do to us. He may be able to give a useful hint or two."

"Oh, I'm not going to pick his brains," Mr. Bellingham said quickly and with some wrath. "I'm not the sort of man who goes round cadging for free professional advice. Understand that, Doctor."

"I do," I answered hastily. "That wasn't what I meant at all. Is that Miss Bellingham coming in? I heard the front door shut."

"Yes, that will be my girl, I expect; but don't run away. You're not afraid of her, are you?" he added as I hurriedly picked up my hat.

"I'm not sure that I'm not," I answered. "She is rather a majestic young lady."

Mr. Bellingham chuckled and smothered a yawn, and at that moment his daughter entered the room; and, in spite of her shabby black dress and a shabbier handbag that she carried, I thought her appearance and manner fully justified my description.

"You come in, Miss Bellingham," I said as she shook my hand with cool civility, "to find your father yawning and me taking my departure. So I have my uses, you see. My conversation is the infallible cure for insomnia."

Miss Bellingham smiled. " I believe I am driving you away," she said.

"Not at all," I replied hastily. "My mission was accomplished, that was all."

"Sit down for a few moments, Doctor," urged Mr. Bellingham, "and let Ruth sample the remedy. She will be affronted if you run away as soon as she comes in."

"Well, you mustn't let me keep you up," I said.

"Oh, I'll let you know when I fall asleep," he replied, with a chuckle; and with this understanding I sat down again—not at all unwillingly.

At this moment Miss Oman entered with a small tray and a smile of which I should not have supposed her capable.

"You'll take your toast and cocoa while they're hot,

dear, won't you?" she said coaxingly.

"Yes, I will, Phyllis, thank you," Miss Bellingham answered. "I am only just going to take off my hat," and she left the room, followed by the astonishingly transfigured spinster.

She returned almost immediately as Mr. Bellingham was in the midst of a profound yawn, and sat down to her frugal meal, when her father mystified me considerably by remarking:

"You're late to-night, chick. Have the Shepherd Kings been giving trouble?"

"No," she replied; "but I thought I might as well get them done. So I dropped in at the Ormond Street library on my way home and finished them."

"Then they are ready for stuffing now?"

"Yes." As she answered she caught my astonished eye (for a stuffed Shepherd King is undoubtedly a somewhat surprising phenomenon) and laughed softly.

"We mustn't talk in riddles like this," she said, "before Dr. Berkeley, or he will turn us both into pillars of salt. My father is referring to my work," she explained to me.

"Are you a taxidermist, then?" I asked.

She hastily set down the cup that she was raising to her lips and broke into a ripple of quiet laughter.

"I am afraid my father has misled you with his irreverent expressions. He will have to atone by explaining."

"You see, Doctor," said Mr. Bellingham, "Ruth is a literary searcher——"

"Oh, don't call me a searcher!" Miss Bellingham protested. "It suggests the female searcher at a police station. Say investigator."

"Very well, investigator or investigatrix, if you like. She hunts up references and bibliographies at the

Museum for people who are writing books. She looks up everything that has been written on a given subject, and then, when she has crammed herself to bursting-point with facts, she goes to her client and disgorges and crams him or her, and he or she finally disgorges into the Press."

"What a disgusting way to put it!" said his daughter. "However, that is what it amounts to. I am a literary jackal, a collector of provender for the literary lions. Is that quite clear?"

"Perfectly. But I don't think that, even now, I quite understand about the stuffed Shepherd Kings."

"Oh, it was not the Shepherd Kings who were to be stuffed. It was the author! That was mere obscurity of speech on the part of my father. The position is this: A venerable archdeacon wrote an article on the patriarch Joseph———"

"And didn't know anything about him," interrupted Mr. Bellingham, "and got tripped up by a specialist who did, and then got shirty———"

"Nothing of the kind," said Miss Bellingham. "He knew as much as venerable archdeacons ought to know; but the expert knew more. So the archdeacon commissioned me to collect the literature on the state of Egypt at the end of the seventeenth dynasty, which I have done: and to-morrow I shall go and stuff him, as my father expresses it, and then———"

"And then," Mr. Bellingham interrupted, "the archdeacon will rush forth and pelt that expert with Shepherd Kings and Sequenen-Ra and the whole tag-rag and bobtail of the seventeenth dynasty. Oh, there'll be wigs on the green, I can tell you."

"Yes, I expect there will be quite a skirmish," said Miss Bellingham. And thus dismissing the subject she made an energetic attack on the toast while her father refreshed himself with a colossal yawn.

I watched her with furtive admiration and deep and growing interest. In spite of her pallor, her weary eyes, and her drawn and almost haggard face, she was an exceedingly handsome girl; and there was in her aspect a suggestion of purpose, of strength and character that marked her off from the rank and file of womanhood. I noted this as I stole an occasional glance at her or turned to answer some remark addressed to me; and I noted, too, that her speech, despite a general undertone of depression, was yet not without a certain caustic, ironical humour. She was certainly a rather enigmatical young person, but very decidedly interesting.

When she had finished her repast she put aside the tray and, opening the shabby handbag, asked:

"Do you take any interest in Egyptian history? We are as mad as hatters on the subject. It seems to be a family complaint."

"I don't know much about it," I answered. "Medical studies are rather engrossing and don't leave much time for general reading."

"Naturally," she said. "You can't specialise in everything. But if you would care to see how the business of a literary jackal is conducted, I will show you my notes."

I accepted the offer eagerly (not, I fear, from pure enthusiasm for the subject), and she brought forth from the bag four blue-covered, quarto notebooks, each dealing with one of the four dynasties from the fourteenth to the seventeenth. As I glanced through the neat and orderly extracts with which they were filled we discussed the intricacies of the peculiarly difficult and confused period that they covered, gradually lowering our voices

as Mr. Bellingham's eyes closed and his head fell against
the back of his chair. We had just reached the critical
reign of Apepa II. when a resounding snore broke in upon
the studious quiet of the room and sent us both into a fit
of silent laughter.

"Your conversation has done its work," she whispered
as I stealthily picked up my hat; and together we stole on
tiptoe to the door, which she opened without a sound.
Once outside, she suddenly dropped her bantering
manner and said quite earnestly:

"How kind it was of you to come and see him tonight!
You have done him a world of good, and I am most
grateful. Good-night!"

She shook hands with me really cordially and I took
my way down the creaking stairs in a whirl of happiness
that I was quite at a loss to account for.

CHAPTER V   The Watercress-Bed

Barnard's practice, like most others, was subject to those
fluctuations that fill the struggling practitioner alternately
with hope and despair. The work came in paroxysms with
intervals of almost complete stagnation. One of these
intermissions occurred on the day after my visit to
Nevill's Court, with the result that by half-past eleven I
found myself wondering what I should do with the
remainder of the day. The better to consider this weighty
problem, I strolled down to the Embankment, and,
leaning on the parapet, contemplated the view across the
river; the grey stone bridge with its perspective of arches,
the picturesque pile of the shot-towers, and, beyond, the
shadowy shapes of the Abbey and St. Stephen's.

It was a pleasant scene, restful and quiet, with a touch

of life and a hint of sober romance, when a barge swept down through the middle arch of the bridge with a lugsail hoisted to a jury mast and a white-aproned woman at the tiller. Dreamily I watched the craft creep by upon the moving tide, noted the low freeboard, almost awash, the careful helmswoman, and the dog on the forecastle yapping at the distant shore—and thought of Ruth Bellingham.

What was there about this strange girl that had made so deep an impression on me? That was the question that I propounded to myself, and not for the first time. Of the fact itself there was no doubt. But what was the explanation? Was it her unusual surroundings? Her occupation and rather recondite learning? Her striking personality and exceptional good looks? Or her connection with the dramatic mystery of her lost uncle?

I concluded that it was all of these. Everything connected with her was unusual and arresting; but over and above these circumstances there was a certain sympathy and personal affinity of which I was strongly conscious and of which I dimly hoped that she, perhaps, was a little conscious too. At any rate, I was deeply interested in her; of that there was no doubt whatever. Short as our acquaintance had been, she held a place in my thoughts that had never been held by any other woman.

From Ruth Bellingham my reflections passed by a natural transition to the curious story that her father had told me. It was a queer affair, that ill-drawn will, with the baffled lawyer protesting in the background. It almost seemed as if there must be something behind it all, especially when I remembered Mr. Hurst's very singular proposal. But it was out of my depth; it was a case for a lawyer, and to a lawyer it should go. This very night, I resolved, I would go to Thorndyke and give him the whole story as it had been told to me.

And then there happened one of those coincidences at which we all wonder when they occur, but which are so frequent as to have become enshrined in a proverb. For even as I formed the resolution, I observed two men approaching from the direction of Blackfriars, and recognised in them my quondam teacher and his junior.

"I was just thinking about you," I said as they came up.

"Very flattering," replied Jervis; "but I thought you had to talk of the devil."

"Perhaps," suggested Thorndyke, "he was talking to himself. But why were you thinking of us, and what was the nature of your thoughts?"

"My thoughts had reference to the Bellingham case. I spent the whole of last evening at Nevill's Court."

"Ha! And are there any fresh developments?"

"Yes, by Jove! there are. Bellingham gave me a full detailed description of the will; and a pretty document it seems to be."

"Did he give you permission to repeat the details to me?"

"Yes. I asked specifically if I might, and he had no objection whatever."

"Good. We are lunching at Soho to-day as Polton has his hands full. Come with us and share our table and tell us your story as we go. Will that suit you?"

It suited me admirably in the present state of the practice, and I accepted the invitation with undissembled glee.

"Very well," said Thorndyke; "then let us walk slowly and finish with matters confidential before we plunge into the madding crowd."

We set forth at a leisurely pace along the broad

pavement and I commenced my narration. As well as I could remember, I related the circumstances that had led up to the present disposition of the property and then proceeded to the actual provisions of the will; to all of which my two friends listened with rapt interest, Thorndyke occasionally stopping me to jot down a memorandum in his pocket-book.

"Why, the fellow must have been a stark lunatic!" Jervis exclaimed, when I had finished. "He seems to have laid himself out with the most devilish ingenuity to defeat his own ends."

"That is not an uncommon peculiarity with testators," Thorndyke remarked. "A direct and perfectly intelligible will is rather the exception. But we can hardly judge until we have seen the actual document. I suppose Bellingham hasn't a copy?"

"I don't know," said I, " but I will ask him."

"If he has one, I should like to look through it," said Thorndyke. "The provisions are very peculiar, and, as Jervis says, admirably calculated to defeat the testator's wishes if they have been correctly reported. And, apart from that, they have a remarkable bearing on the circumstances of the disappearance. I daresay you noticed that."

"I noticed that it is very much to Hurst's advantage that the body has not been found."

"Yes, of course. But there are some other points that are very significant. However, it would be premature to discuss the terms of the will until we have seen the actual document or a certified copy."

"If there is a copy extant," I said, "I will try to get hold of it. But Bellingham is terribly afraid of being suspected of a desire to get professional advice gratis."

"That," said Thorndyke, "is natural enough, and not

discreditable. But you must overcome his scruples somehow. I expect you will be able to. You are a plausible young gentleman, as I remember of old, and you seem to have established yourself as quite the friend of the family."

"They are rather interesting people," I explained; "very cultivated and with a strong leaning towards archæology. It seems to be in the blood."

"Yes," said Thorndyke; "a family tendency, probably due to contact and common surroundings rather than heredity. So you like Godfrey Bellingham?"

"Yes. He is a trifle peppery and impulsive, but quite an agreeable, genial old buffer."

"And the daughter," said Jervis, "what is she like?"

"Oh, she is a learned lady; works up bibliographies and references at the Museum."

"Ah!" Jervis exclaimed, with disfavour, "I know the breed. Inky fingers; no chest to speak of; all side and spectacles."

I rose artlessly at the gross and palpable bait.

"You're quite wrong," I exclaimed indignantly, contrasting Jervis's hideous presentment with the comely original. "She is an exceedingly good-looking girl, and her manners all that a lady's should be. A little stiff, perhaps, but then I am only an acquaintance—almost a stranger."

"But," Jervis persisted, "what is she like, in appearance, I mean? Short? Fat? Sandy? Give us intelligible details."

I made a rapid mental inventory, assisted by my recent cogitations.

"She is about five feet seven, slim but rather plump, very erect in carriage and graceful in movements; black hair, loosely parted in the middle and falling very prettily away from the forehead; pale, clear complexion, dark grey eyes, straight eyebrows, straight, well-shaped nose, short mouth, rather full; round chin—what the deuce are you grinning at, Jervis?" For my friend had suddenly unmasked his batteries and now threatened, like the Cheshire cat, to dissolve into a mere abstraction of amusement.

"If there is a copy of that will, Thorndyke," he said, "we shall get it. I think you agree with me, reverend senior?

"I have already said," was the reply, "that I put my trust in Berkeley. And now let us dismiss professional topics. This is our hostelry."

He pushed open an unpretentious glazed door, and we followed him into the restaurant, whereof the atmosphere was pervaded by an appetising meatiness mingled with less agreeable suggestions of the destructive distillation of fat.

It was some two hours later when I wished my friends adieu under the golden-leaved plane trees of King's Bench Walk.

"I won't ask you to come in now," said Thorndyke, "as we have some consultations this afternoon. But come in and see us soon; don't wait for that copy of the will."

"No," said Jervis. "Drop in in the evening when your work is done; unless, of course, there is more attractive society elsewhere. Oh, you needn't turn that colour, my dear child; we have all been young once; there is even a tradition that Thorndyke was young some time back in the pre-dynastic period."

"Don't take any notice of him, Berkeley," said Thorndyke. "The egg-shell is sticking to his head still. He'll know better when he is my age."

"Methuselah!" exclaimed Jervis; "I hope I shan't have

to wait as long as that!"

Thorndyke smiled benevolently at his irrepressible junior, and, shaking my hand cordially, turned into the entry.

From the Temple I wended northward, to the adjacent College of Surgeons, where I spent a couple of profitable hours examining the "pickles" and refreshing my memory on the subjects of pathology and anatomy; marvelling afresh (as every practical anatomist must marvel) at the incredibly perfect technique of the dissections, and inwardly paying tribute to the founder of the collection. At length the warning of the clock, combined with an increasing craving for tea, drove me forth and bore me towards the scene of my not very strenuous labours. My mind was still occupied with the contents of the cases and the great glass jars, so that I found myself at the corner of Fetter Lane without a very clear idea of how I had got there. But at that point I was aroused from my reflections rather abruptly by a raucous voice in my ear.

"'Orrible discovery at Sidcup!"

I turned wrathfully—for a London street-boy's yell, let off at point-blank range, is, in effect, like the smack of an open hand—but the inscription on the staring yellow poster that was held up for my inspection changed my anger to curiosity.

"Horrible discovery in a watercress-bed!"

Now, let prigs deny it if they will, but there is something very attractive in a "horrible discovery." It hints at tragedy, at mystery, at romance. It promises to bring into our grey and commonplace life that element of the dramatic which is the salt that our existence is savoured withal. "In a watercress-bed," too! The rusticity of the background seemed to emphasise the horror of the discovery, whatever it might be.

I bought a copy of the paper, and, tucking it under my arm, hurried on to the surgery, promising myself a mental feast of watercress; but as I opened the door I found myself confronted by a corpulent woman of piebald and pimply aspect who saluted me with a deep groan. It was the lady from the coal shop in Fleur-de-Lys Court.

"Good-evening, Mrs. Jablett," I said briskly; "not come about yourself, I hope."

"Yes, I have," she answered, rising and following me gloomily into the consulting-room; and then, when I had seated her in the patient's chair and myself at the writing table, she continued: "It's my inside, you know, Doctor."

The statement lacked anatomical precision and merely excluded the domain of the skin specialist. I accordingly waited for enlightenment and speculated on the watercress-beds, while Mrs. Jablett regarded me expectantly with a dim and watery eye.

"Ah!" I said at length; "it's your—your inside, is it, Mrs. Jablett?"

"Yus. *And* my 'ead," she added, with a voluminous sigh that filled the apartment with odorous reminiscences of "unsweetened."

"Your head aches, does it?"

"Somethink chronic! " said Mrs. Jablett. "Feels as if it was a-opening and a-shutting, a-opening and a-shutting, and when I sit down I feel as if I should *bust*."

This picturesque description of her sensations—not wholly inconsistent with her figure—gave the clue to Mrs. Jablett's sufferings. Resisting a frivolous impulse to reassure her as to the elasticity of the human integument, I considered her case in exhaustive detail, coasting delicately round the subject of "unsweetened" and finally sent her away, revived in spirits and grasping a bottle of

Mist. Sodæ cum Bismutho from Barnard's big stock-jar. Then I went back to investigate the Horrible Discovery; but before I could open the paper, another patient arrived (*Impetigo contagiosa,* this time, affecting the "wide and archéd-front sublime" of a juvenile Fetter Laner), and then yet another, and so on through the evening, until at last I forgot the watercress-beds altogether. It was only when I had purified myself from the evening consultations with hot water and a nail-brush and was about to sit down to a frugal supper, that I remembered the newspaper and fetched it from the drawer of the consulting-room table, where it had been hastily thrust out of sight. I folded it into a convenient form, and, standing it upright against the water-jug, read the report at my ease as I supped.

There was plenty of it. Evidently the reporter had regarded it as a "scoop," and the editor had backed him up with ample space and hair-raising head-lines:

"HORRIBLE DISCOVERY
IN A WATERCRESS-BED AT
SIDCUP!

"A startling discovery was made yesterday afternoon in the course of clearing out a watercress-bed near the erstwhile rural village of Sidcup in Kent; a discovery that will occasion many a disagreeable qualm to those persons who have been in the habit of regaling themselves with this refreshing esculent. But before proceeding to a description of the circumstances of the actual discovery or of the objects found—which, however, it may be stated at once, are nothing more or less than the fragments of a dismembered human body—it will be interesting to trace the remarkable chain of coincidences by virtue of which the discovery was made.

"The beds in question have been laid out in a small artificial lake fed by a tiny streamlet which forms one of the numerous tributaries of the River Cray. Its depth is greater than usual in the watercress-beds, otherwise the gruesome relics could never have been concealed beneath its surface, and the flow of water through it, though continuous, is slow. The tributary streamlet meanders through a succession of pasture meadows, in one of which the beds themselves are situated, and here throughout most of the year the fleecy victims of the human carnivore carry on the industry of converting grass into mutton. Now it happened some years ago that the sheep frequenting these pastures became affected with the disease known as 'liver-rot'; and here we must make a short digression into the domain of pathology.

"'Liver-rot' is a disease of quite romantic antecedents. Its cause is a small, flat worm—the liver-fluke—which infests the liver and bile-ducts of the affected sheep.

"Now how does the worm get into the sheep's liver? That is where the romance comes in. Let us see.

"The cycle of transformations begins with the deposit of the eggs of the fluke in some shallow stream or ditch running through pasture lands. Now each egg has a sort of lid, which presently opens and lets out a minute, hairy creature who swims away in search of a particular kind of water-snail—the kind called by naturalists *Limnæa truncatula*. If he finds a snail, he bores his way into its flesh and soon begins to grow and wax fat. Then he brings forth a family of tiny worms quite unlike himself, little creatures called *rediæ,* which soon give birth to families of young *rediæ*. So they go on for several generations, but at last there comes a generation of *rediæ* which, instead of giving birth to fresh *rediæ,* produce families of totally different offspring; big-headed, long-tailed creatures like miniature tadpoles, called by the learned *cercariæ*. The *cercariæ* soon wriggle their way out of the body of the snail, and then complications arise: for it is the habit of this particular snail to leave the water occasionally and take a stroll in the fields. Thus the *cercariæ,* escaping from the snail, find themselves on the grass, whereupon they promptly drop their tails and stick themselves to the grass-blades. Then comes the unsuspecting sheep to take his frugal meal, and, cropping the grass, swallows it, *cercariæ* and all. But the latter, when they find themselves in the sheep's stomach, make their way straight to the bile-ducts, up which they travel to the liver. Here, in a few weeks, they grow up into full-blown flukes and begin the important business of producing eggs.

"Such is the pathological romance of the 'liver-rot'; and now what is its connection with this mysterious discovery? It is this. After the outbreak of 'liver-rot' above referred to, the ground landlord, a Mr. John Bellingham, instructed his solicitor to insert a clause in the lease of the beds directing that the latter should be periodically cleared and examined by an expert to make sure that they were free from the noxious water-snails. The last lease expired about two years ago, and since then the beds have been out of cultivation; but, for the safety of the adjacent pastures, it was considered necessary to make the customary periodical inspection, and it was in the course of cleaning the beds for this purpose that the present discovery was made.

"The operation began two days ago. A gang of three men proceeded systematically to grub up the plants and collect the multitudes of water-snails that they might be examined by the expert to see if any obnoxious species were present. They had cleared nearly half of the beds when, yesterday afternoon, one of the men working in the deepest part came upon some bones, the appearance of which excited his suspicion. Thereupon he called his mates, and they carefully picked away the plants piecemeal, a process that soon laid bare an unmistakable human hand lying on the mud amongst the roots. Fortunately they had the wisdom not to disturb the remains, but at once sent off a message to the police. Very soon, an inspector and a sergeant, accompanied by the divisional surgeon, arrived on the scene, and were able to view the remains lying as they had been found. And now another very strange fact came to light; for it was seen that the hand—a left one—lying on the mud was minus its third finger. This is regarded by the police as a very important fact as bearing on the question of identification, seeing that the number of persons having the third finger of the left hand missing must be quite small. After a thorough examination on the spot, the bones were carefully collected and conveyed to the mortuary, where they now lie awaiting further inquiries.

"The divisional surgeon, Dr. Brandon, in an interview with our representative, made the following statements:

"'The bones are those of the left arm of a middle-aged or elderly man about five feet eight inches in height. All the bones of the arm are present, including the scapula, or shoulder-blade, and the clavicle, or collar-bone, but the three bones of the third finger are missing.'

"'Is this a deformity or has the finger been cut off?' our correspondent asked.

"'The finger has been amputated,' was the reply. 'If it had been absent from birth, the corresponding hand bone, or metacarpal, would have been wanting or deformed, whereas it is present and quite normal.'

"'How long have the bones been in the water?' was the next question.

"'More than a year, I should say. They are quite clean; there is not a vestige of the soft structures left.'

"'Have you any theory as to how the arm came to be deposited where it was found?'

"'I should rather not answer that question,' was the guarded response.

"'One more question,' our correspondent urged. 'The ground landlord, Mr. John Bellingham; is not he the gentleman who disappeared so mysteriously some time ago?'

"'So I understand,' Dr. Brandon replied.

"'Can you tell me if Mr. Bellingham had lost the third finger of his left hand?'

"'I cannot say,' said Dr. Brandon; and he added with a smile, 'you had better ask the police.'

"That is how the matter stands at present. But we understand that the police are making active inquiries for any missing man who has lost the third finger of his left hand, and if any of our readers know of such a person, they are earnestly requested to communicate at once, either with us or with the authorities.

"Also we believe that a systematic search is to be made for further remains."

I laid the newspaper down and fell into a train of reflection. It was certainly a most mysterious affair. The thought that had evidently come to the reporter's mind stole naturally into mine. Could these remains be those of John Bellingham? It was obviously possible, though I could not but see that the fact of the bones having been found on his land, while it undoubtedly furnished the suggestion, did not in any way add to its probability. The connection was accidental and in no wise relevant.

Then, too, there was the missing finger. No reference to any such deformity had been made in the original report of the disappearance, though it could hardly have been overlooked. But it was useless to speculate without facts. I should be seeing Thorndyke in the course of the next few days, and, undoubtedly, if the discovery had any bearing upon the disappearance of John Bellingham, I should hear of it. With which reflection I rose from the table, and, adopting the advice contained in the spurious Johnsonian quotation, proceeded to "take a walk in Fleet Street" before settling down for the evening.

CHAPTER VI   Sidelights

The association of coal with potatoes is one upon which I have frequently speculated, without arriving at any more satisfactory explanation than that both products are of the earth, earthy. Of the connection itself Barnard's practice furnished several instances besides Mrs. Jablett's establishment in Fleur-de-Lys Court, one of which was a dark and mysterious cavern a foot below the level of the street, that burrowed under an ancient house on the west side of Fetter Lane—a crinkly, timber house of the three-decker type that leaned back drunkenly from the road as if about to sit down in its own back yard.

Passing this repository of the associated products about ten o'clock in the morning, I perceived in the shadows of the cavern no less a person than Miss Oman. She saw me at the same moment, and beckoned peremptorily with a hand that held a large Spanish onion. I approached with a deferential smile.

"What a magnificent onion, Miss Oman! and how

generous of you to offer it to me——"

"I wasn't offering it to you. But there! Isn't it just like a man——"

"Isn't what just like a man?" I interrupted. "If you mean the onion——"

"I don't!" she snapped, "and I wish you wouldn't talk such a parcel of nonsense. A grown man and a member of a serious profession, too! You ought to know better."

"I suppose I ought," I said reflectively. And she continued:

"I called in at the surgery just now."

"To see me?"

"What else should I come for? Do you suppose that I called to consult the bottle-boy?"

"Certainly not, Miss Oman. So you find the lady doctor no use, after all?"

Miss Oman gnashed her teeth at me (and very fine teeth they were too).

"I called," she said majestically, "on behalf of Miss Bellingham."

My facetiousness evaporated instantly. "I hope Miss Bellingham is not ill," I said with a sudden anxiety that elicited a sardonic smile from Miss Oman.

"No," was the reply, "she is not ill, but she has cut her hand rather badly. It's her right hand too, and she can't afford to lose the use of it, not being a great, hulking, lazy, lolloping man. So you had better go and put some stuff on it."

With this advice, Miss Oman whisked to the right-about and vanished into the depths of the cavern like the witch of Wokey, while I hurried on to the surgery to provide myself with the necessary instruments and materials, and thence proceeded to Nevill's Court.

Miss Oman's juvenile maidservant, who opened the

door to me, stated the existing conditions with epigrammatic conciseness.

"Mr. Bellingham is hout, sir; but Miss Bellingham is hin."

Having thus delivered herself she retreated towards the kitchen and I ascended the stairs, at the head of which I found Miss Bellingham awaiting me with her right hand encased in what looked like a white boxing-glove.

"I'm glad you have come," she said. "Phyllis—Miss Oman, you know—has kindly bound up my hand, but I should like you to see that it is all right."

We went into the sitting-room, where I laid out my paraphernalia on the table while I inquired into the particulars of the accident.

"It is most unfortunate that it should have happened just now," she said, as I wrestled with one of those remarkable feminine knots that, while they seem to defy the utmost efforts of human ingenuity to untie, yet have a singular habit of untying themselves at inopportune moments.

"Why just now in particular?" I asked.

"Because I have some specially important work to do. A very learned lady who is writing an historical book has commissioned me to collect all the literature relating to the Tell el Amarna letters—the cuneiform tablets, you know, of Amenhotep the Fourth."

"Well," I said soothingly, "I expect your hand will soon be well."

"Yes, but that won't do. The work has to be done immediately. I have to send in completed notes not later than this day week, and it will be quite impossible. I am dreadfully disappointed."

By this time I had unwound the voluminous wrappings and exposed the injury—a deep gash in the palm that must have narrowly missed a good-sized artery. Obviously the hand would be useless for fully a week.

"I suppose," she said, "you couldn't patch it up so that I could write with it?"

I shook my head.

"No, Miss Bellingham. I shall have to put it on a splint. We can't run any risks with a deep wound like this."

"Then I shall have to give up the commission, and I don't know how my client will get the work done in the time. You see, I am pretty well up in the literature of Ancient Egypt; in fact, I was to receive special payment on that account. And it would have been such an interesting task, too. However, it can't be helped."

I proceeded methodically with the application of the dressings, and meanwhile reflected. It was evident that she was deeply disappointed. Loss of work meant loss of money, and it needed but a glance at her rusty black dress to see that there was little margin for that. Possibly, too, there was some special need to be met. Her manner seemed almost to imply that there was. And at this point I had a brilliant idea.

"I'm not sure that it can't be helped," said I.

She looked at me inquiringly, and I continued: "I am going to make a proposition, and I shall ask you to consider it with an open mind."

"That sounds rather portentous," said she; "but I promise. What is it?"

"It is this: When I was a student I acquired the useful art of writing shorthand. I am not a lightning reporter, you understand, but I can take matter down from dictation at quite respectable speed."

"Yes."

"Well, I have several hours free every day—usually

the whole afternoon up to six or half-past—and it occurs to me that if you were to go to the Museum in the mornings you could get out your books, look up passages (you could do that without using your right hand), and put in book-marks. Then I could come along in the afternoon and you could read out the selected passages to me, and I could take them down in shorthand. We should get through as much in a couple of hours as you could in a day using long-hand."

"Oh, but how kind of you, Dr. Berkeley!" she exclaimed. "How very kind! Of course, I couldn't think of taking up all your leisure in that way; but I do appreciate your kindness very much."

I was rather chapfallen at this very definite refusal, but persisted feebly:

"I wish you would. It may seem rather a cheek for a comparative stranger like me to make such a proposal to a lady: but if you'd been a man—in these special circumstances—I should have made it all the same, and you would have accepted as a matter of course."

"I doubt that. At any rate, I am not a man. I sometimes wish I were."

"Oh, I am sure you are much better as you are!" I exclaimed, with such earnestness that we both laughed. And at this moment Mr. Bellingham entered the room carrying several large brand-new books in a strap.

"Well, I'm sure!" he exclaimed genially; "here are pretty goings on. Doctor and patient giggling like a pair of schoolgirls! What's the joke?"

He thumped his parcel of books down on the table and listened smilingly while my unconscious witticism was expounded.

"The Doctor's quite right," he said. "You'll do as you are, chick; but the Lord knows what sort of man you would make. You take his advice and let well alone."

Finding him in this genial frame of mind, I ventured to explain my proposition to him and to enlist his support. He considered it with attentive approval, and when I had finished turned to his daughter.

"What is your objection, chick?" he asked.

"It would give Dr. Berkeley such a fearful lot of work," she answered.

"It would give him a fearful lot of pleasure," I said. "It would really."

"Then why not?" said Mr. Bellingham. "We don't mind being under an obligation to the Doctor, do we?"

"Oh, it isn't that!" she exclaimed hastily.

"Then take him at his word. He means it. It is a kind action and he'll like doing it, I'm sure. That's all right, Doctor; she accepts, don't you, chick?"

"Yes, if you say so, I do; and most thankfully."

She accompanied the acceptance with a gracious smile that was in itself a large repayment on account, and when we had made the necessary arrangements, I hurried away in a state of the most perfect satisfaction to finish my morning's work and order an early lunch.

When I called for her a couple of hours later I found her waiting in the garden with the shabby handbag, of which I relieved her, and we set forth together, watched jealously by Miss Oman, who had accompanied her to the gate.

As I walked up the court with this wonderful maid by my side I could hardly believe in my good fortune. By her presence and my own resulting happiness the mean surroundings became glorified and the commonest objects transfigured into things of beauty. What a delightful thoroughfare, for instance, was Fetter Lane, with its quaint charm and mediæval grace! I snuffed the cabbage-laden atmosphere and seemed to breathe the scent of the asphodel. Holborn was even as the Elysian Fields; the omnibus that bore us westward was a chariot of glory; and the people who swarmed verminously on the pavements bore the semblance of the children of light.

Love is a foolish thing judged by workaday standards, and the thoughts and actions of lovers foolish beyond measure. But the workaday standard is the wrong one, after all; for the utilitarian mind does but busy itself with the trivial and transitory interests of life, behind which looms the great and everlasting reality of the love of man and woman. There is more significance in a nightingale's song in the hush of a summer night than in all the wisdom of Solomon (who, by the way, was not without his little experiences of the tender passion).

The janitor in the little glass box by the entrance to the library inspected us and passed us on, with a silent benediction, to the lobby, whence (when I had handed my stick to a bald-headed demigod and received a talismanic disc in exchange) we entered the enormous rotunda of the reading-room.

I have often thought that, if some lethal vapour of highly preservative properties—such as formaldehyde, for instance—could be shed into the atmosphere of this apartment, the entire and complete collection of books and book-worms would be well worth preserving, for the enlightenment of posterity, as a sort of anthropological appendix to the main collection of the Museum. For, surely, nowhere else in the world are so many strange and abnormal human beings gathered together in one place. And a curious question that must have occurred to many observers is: Whence do these singular creatures come, and whither do they go when the very distinct-faced clock (adjusted to literary eyesight) proclaims closing time? The tragic-faced gentleman, for instance, with the corkscrew ringlets that bob up and down like spiral springs as he walks? Or the short, elderly gentleman in the black cassock and bowler hat, who shatters your nerves by turning suddenly and revealing himself as a middle-aged woman? Whither do they go? One never sees them elsewhere. Do they steal away at closing time into the depths of the Museum and hide themselves until morning in sarcophagi or mummy cases? Or do they creep through spaces in the bookshelves and spend the night behind the volumes in a congenial atmosphere of leather and antique paper? Who can say? What I do know is that when Ruth Bellingham entered the reading-room she appeared in comparison with these like a creature of another order; even as the head of Antinous, which formerly stood (it has since been moved) amidst the portrait-busts of the Roman Emperors, seemed like the head of a god set in a portrait gallery of illustrious baboons.

"What have we got to do?" I asked when we had found a vacant seat. "Do you want to look up the catalogue?"

"No, I have the tickets in my bag. The books are waiting in the 'kept books' department."

I placed my hat on the leather-covered shelf, dropped her gloves into it—how delightfully intimate and companionable it seemed! —altered the numbers on the tickets, and then we proceeded together to the "kept books" desk to collect the volumes that contained the material for our day's work.

It was a blissful afternoon. Two and a half hours of happiness unalloyed did I spend at that shiny, leather-clad desk, guiding my nimble pen across the pages of the notebook. It introduced me to a new world—a world in which love and learning, sweet intimacy and crusted archæology, were mingled into the oddest, most whimsical and most delicious confection that the mind of man can conceive. Hitherto, these recondite histories had been far beyond my ken. Of the wonderful heretic, Amenhotep the Fourth, I had barely heard—at the most he had been a mere name; the Hittites a mythical race of undetermined habitat; while cuneiform tablets had presented themselves to my mind merely as an uncouth kind of fossil biscuit suited to the digestion of a prehistoric ostrich.

Now all this was changed. As we sat with our chairs creaking together and she whispered the story of those stirring times into my receptive ear—talking is strictly forbidden in the reading-room—the disjointed fragments arranged themselves into a romance of supreme fascination. Egyptian, Babylonian, Aramæan, Hittite, Memphis, Babylon, Hamath, Megiddo—I swallowed them all thankfully, wrote them down, and asked for more. Only once did I disgrace myself. An elderly clergyman of ascetic and acidulous aspect had passed us with a glance of evident disapproval, clearly setting us down as intruding philanderers; and when I contrasted the parson's probable conception of the whispered communications that were being poured into my ear so tenderly and confidentially with the dry reality, I chuckled aloud. But my fair taskmistress only paused, with her finger on the page, smilingly to rebuke me, and then went on with the dictation. She was certainly a Tartar for work.

It was a proud moment for me when, in response to my interrogative "Yes?" my companion said "That is all," and closed the book. We had extracted the pith and marrow of six considerable volumes in two and a half hours.

"You have been better than your word," she said. "It would have taken me two full days of really hard work to make the notes that you have written down since we commenced. I don't know how to thank you."

"There's no need to. I've enjoyed myself and polished up my shorthand. What is the next thing? We shall want some books for to-morrow, shan't we?"

"Yes. I have made out a list, so if you will come with me to the catalogue desk I will look out the numbers and ask you to write the tickets."

The selection of a fresh batch of authorities occupied us for another quarter of an hour, and then, having handed in the volumes that we had squeezed dry, we took our way out of the reading-room.

"Which way shall we go?" she asked as we passed out of the gate, where stood a massive policeman, like the guardian angel at the gate of Paradise (only, thank Heaven! he bore no flaming sword forbidding re-entry).

"We are going," I replied, "to Museum Street, where is a milkshop in which one can get an excellent cup of tea."

She looked as if she would have demurred, but eventually followed obediently, and we were soon settled side by side at the little marble-topped table, retracing the ground we had covered in the afternoon's work and discussing various points of interest over a joint teapot.

"Have you been doing this sort of work long?" I asked, as she handed me my second cup of tea.

"Professionally," she answered, "only about two years; since we broke up our home, in fact. But long before that I used to come to the Museum with my Uncle John—the one who disappeared, you know, in that dreadfully mysterious way—and help him to look up references. We were good friends, he and I."

"I suppose he was a very learned man?" I suggested.

"Yes, in a certain way; in the way of the better-class collector he was very learned indeed. He knew the contents of every museum in the world, in so far as they were connected with Egyptian antiquities, and had studied them specimen by specimen. Consequently, as Egyptology is largely a museum science, he was a learned Egyptologist. But his real interest was in things rather than events. Of course, he knew a great deal—a very great deal—about Egyptian history, but still he was, before all, a collector."

"And what will happen to his collection if he is really dead?"

"The greater part of it goes to the British Museum by his will, and the remainder he has left to his solicitor, Mr. Jellicoe."

"To Mr. Jellicoe! Why, what will Mr. Jellicoe do with Egyptian antiquities?"

"Oh, he is an Egyptologist too, and quite an enthusiast. He has really a fine collection of scarabs and other small objects such as it is possible to keep in a private house. I have always thought that it was his enthusiasm for everything Egyptian that brought him and my uncle together on terms of such intimacy; though I believe he is an excellent lawyer, and he is certainly a very discreet, cautious man."

"Is he? I shouldn't have thought so, judging by your uncle's will."

"Oh, but that was not Mr. Jellicoe's fault. He assures us that he entreated my uncle to let him draw up a fresh document with more reasonable provisions. But he says Uncle John was immovable; and he really was a rather obstinate man. Mr. Jellicoe repudiates any responsibility in the matter. He washes his hands of the whole affair, and says that it is the will of a lunatic. And so it is. I was glancing through it only a night or two ago, and really I cannot conceive how a sane man could have written such nonsense."

"You have a copy then?" I asked eagerly, remembering Thorndyke's parting instructions.

"Yes. Would you like to see it? I know my father has told you about it, and it is worth reading as a curiosity of perverseness."

"I should very much like to show it to my friend, Dr. Thorndyke," I replied. "He said he would be interested to read it and learn the exact provisions; and it might be well to let him, and hear what he has to say about it."

"I see no objection," she rejoined, "but you know what my father is: his horror, I mean, of what he calls 'cadging for advice gratis.'"

"Oh, but he need have no scruples on that score. Dr. Thorndyke wants to see the will because the case interests him. He is an enthusiast, you know, and he put the request as a personal favour to himself."

"That is very nice and delicate of him, and I will explain the position to my father. If he is willing for Dr. Thorndyke to see the copy I will send or bring it over this evening. Have we finished?"

I regretfully admitted that we had, and, when I had paid the modest reckoning, we sallied forth, turning back with one accord into Great Russell Street, to avoid the noise and bustle of the larger thoroughfares.

"What sort of man was your uncle?" I asked presently, as we walked along the quiet, dignified street. And then I added hastily: "I hope you don't think me inquisitive, but, to my mind, he presents himself as a kind of mysterious abstraction; the unknown quantity of a legal problem."

"My Uncle John," she answered reflectively, "was a

very peculiar man, rather obstinate, very self-willed, what
people call masterful, and decidedly wrong-headed and
unreasonable."

"That is certainly the impression that the terms of his
will convey," I said.

"Yes, and not the will only. There was the absurd
allowance that he made to my father. That was a
ridiculous arrangement, and very unfair too. He ought to
have divided the property up as my grandfather intended.
And yet he was by no means ungenerous, only he would
have his own way, and his own way was very commonly
the wrong way.

"I remember," she continued, after a short pause, "a
very odd instance of his wrong-headedness and
obstinacy. It was a small matter, but very typical of him.
He had in his collection a beautiful little ring of the
eighteenth dynasty. It was said to have belonged to
Queen Ti, the mother of our friend Amenhotep the
Fourth; but I don't think that could have been so, because
the device on it was the Eye of Osiris, and Ti, as you
know, was an Aten-worshipper. However, it was a very
charming ring, and Uncle John, who had a queer sort of
devotion to the mystical Eye of Osiris, commissioned a
very clever goldsmith to make two exact copies of it, one
for himself and one for me. The goldsmith naturally
wanted to take the measurements of our fingers, but this
Uncle John would not hear of; the rings were to be exact
copies, and an exact copy must be the same size as the
original. You can imagine the result; my ring was so
loose that I couldn't keep it on my finger, and Uncle
John's was so tight that though he did manage to get it
on, he was never able to get it off. And it was only the
circumstance that his left hand was decidedly smaller
than his right that made it possible for him to wear it at

all."

"So you never wore your copy?"

"No. I wanted to have it altered to make it fit, but he objected strongly; so I put it away, and have it in a box still."

"He must have been an extraordinarily pig-headed old fellow," I remarked.

"Yes; he was very tenacious. He annoyed my father a good deal, too, by making unnecessary alterations in the house in Queen Square when he fitted up his museum. We have a certain sentiment with regard to that house. Our people have lived in it ever since it was built, when the square was first laid out in the reign of Queen Anne, after whom it was named. It is a dear old house. Would you like to see it? We are quite near it now."

I assented eagerly. If it had been a coal-shed or a fried-fish shop I would still have visited it with pleasure, for the sake of prolonging our walk; but I was also really interested in this old house as a part of the background of the mystery of the vanished John Bellingham.

We crossed into Cosmo Place, with its quaint row of the now rare, cannon-shaped iron posts, and passing through stood for a few moments looking into the peaceful, stately old square. A party of boys disported themselves noisily on the range of stone posts that form a bodyguard round the ancient lamp-surmounted pump, but otherwise the place was wrapped in dignified repose suited to its age and station. And very pleasant it looked on this summer afternoon with the sunlight gilding the foliage of its widespreading plane trees and lighting up the warm-toned brick of the house-fronts. We walked slowly down the shady west side, near the middle of which my companion halted.

"This is the house," she said. "It looks gloomy and

forsaken now; but it must have been a delightful house in the days when my ancestors could look out of the windows through the open end of the square across the fields and meadows to the heights of Hampstead and Highgate."

She stood at the edge of the pavement looking up with a curious wistfulness at the old house; a very pathetic figure I thought, with her handsome face and proud carriage, her threadbare dress and shabby gloves, standing at the threshold of the home that had been her family's for generations, that should now have been hers, and that was shortly to pass away into the hands of strangers.

I, too, looked up at it with a strange interest, impressed by something gloomy and forbidding in its aspect. The windows were shuttered from basement to attic, and no sign of life was visible. Silent, neglected, desolate, it breathed an air of tragedy. It seemed to mourn in sackcloth and ashes for its lost master. The massive door within the splendid carven portico was crusted with grime, and seemed to have passed out of use as completely as the ancient lamp-irons or the rusted extinguishers wherein the footmen were wont to quench their torches when some Bellingham dame was borne up the steps in her gilded chair, in the days of good Queen Anne.

It was in a somewhat sobered frame of mind that we presently turned away and started homeward by way of Great Ormond Street. My companion was deeply thoughtful, relapsing for a while into that sombreness of manner that had so impressed me when I first met her. Nor was I without a certain sympathetic pensiveness; as if, from the great, silent house, the spirit of the vanished man had issued forth to bear us company.

But still it was a delightful walk, and I was sorry when at last we arrived at the entrance to Nevill's Court, and Miss Bellingham halted and held out her hand.

"Good-bye," she said; "and many, many thanks for your invaluable help. Shall I take the bag?"

"If you want it. But I must take out the notebooks."

"Why must you take them?" she asked.

"Why, haven't I got to copy the notes out into long-hand?"

An expression of utter consternation spread over her face; in fact, she was so completely taken aback that she forgot to release my hand.

"Heavens!" she exclaimed. "How idiotic of me! But it is impossible, Dr. Berkeley! It will take you hours!"

"It is perfectly possible, and it is going to be done; otherwise the notes would be useless. Do you want the bag?"

"No, of course not. But I am positively appalled. Hadn't you better give up the idea?"

"And this is the end of our collaboration!" I exclaimed tragically, giving her hand a final squeeze (whereby she became suddenly aware of its position, and withdrew it rather hastily). "Would you throw away a whole afternoon's work? I won't certainly; so, good-bye until to-morrow. I shall turn up in the reading-room as early as I can. You had better take the tickets. Oh, and you won't forget about the copy of the will for Dr. Thorndyke, will you?"

"No; if my father agrees, you shall have it this evening."

She took the tickets from me, and, thanking me yet again, retired into the court.

CHAPTER VII   John Bellingham's Will

The task upon which I had embarked so light-heartedly, when considered in cold blood, did certainly appear, as Miss Bellingham had said, rather appalling. The result of two and a half hours' pretty steady work, at an average speed of nearly a hundred words a minute, would take some time to transcribe into long-hand; and if the notes were to be delivered punctually on the morrow, the sooner I got to work the better.

Recognising this truth, I lost no time, but, within five minutes of my arrival at the surgery, was seated at the writing-table with my copy before me busily converting the sprawling, inexpressive characters into good, legible round-hand.

The occupation was by no means unpleasant, apart from the fact that it was a labour of love; for the sentences, as I picked them up, were fragrant with the reminiscences of the gracious whisper in which they had first come to me. And then the matter itself was full of interest. I was gaining a fresh outlook on life, was crossing the threshold of a new world (which was *her* world); and so the occasional interruptions from the patients, while they gave me intervals of enforced rest, were far from welcome.

The evening wore on without any sign from Nevill's Court, and I began to fear that Mr. Bellingham's scruples had proved insurmountable. Not, I am afraid, that I was so much concerned for the copy of the will as for the possibility of a visit, no matter howsoever brief, from my fair employer; and when, on the stroke of half-past seven, the surgery door flew open with startling abruptness, my fears were allayed and my hopes shattered simultaneously. For it was Miss Oman who stalked in, holding out a blue foolscap envelope with a warlike air as if it were an ultimatum.

"I've brought you this from Mr. Bellingham," she said. "There's a note inside."

"May I read the note, Miss Oman?" I asked.

"Bless the man!" she exclaimed. "What else would you do with it? Isn't that what it's brought for?"

I supposed it was; and, thanking her for her gracious permission, I glanced through the note—a few lines authorising me to show the copy of the will to Dr. Thorndyke. When I looked up from the paper I found her eyes fixed on me with an expression critical and rather disapproving.

"You seem to be making yourself mighty agreeable in a certain quarter," she remarked.

"I make myself universally agreeable. It is my nature to."

"Ha!" she snorted.

"Don't you find me rather agreeable?" I asked.

"Oily," said Miss Oman. And then, with a sour smile at the open notebooks, she remarked:

"You've got some work to do now; quite a change for you."

"A delightful change, Miss Oman. 'For Satan findeth'—but no doubt you are acquainted with the philosophical works of Dr. Watts?"

"If you are referring to 'idle hands,'" she replied, "I'll give you a bit of advice. Don't you keep that hand idle any longer than is really necessary. I have my suspicions about that splint—oh, you know what I mean," and before I had time to reply, she had taken advantage of the entrance of a couple of patients to whisk out of the surgery with the abruptness that had distinguished her arrival.

The evening consultations were considered to be over by half-past eight; at which time Adolphus was wont with exemplary punctuality to close the outer door of the surgery. To-night he was not less prompt than usual; and having performed this, his last daily office, and turned down the surgery gas, he reported the fact and took his departure.

As his retreating footsteps died away and the slamming of the outer door announced his final disappearance, I sat up and stretched myself. The envelope containing the copy of the will lay on the table, and I considered it thoughtfully. It ought to be conveyed to Thorndyke with as little delay as possible, and, as it certainly could not be trusted out of my hands, it ought to be conveyed by me.

I looked at the notebooks. Nearly two hours' work had made a considerable impression on the matter that I had to transcribe, but still, a great deal of the task yet remained to be done. However, I reflected, I could put in a couple of hours or more before going to bed and there would be an hour or two to spare in the morning. Finally I locked the notebooks, open as they were, in the writing-table drawer, and, slipping the envelope into my pocket, set out for the Temple.

The soft chime of the Treasury clock was telling out, in confidential tones, the third quarter as I rapped with my stick on the forbidding "oak" of my friends' chambers. There was no response, nor had I perceived any gleam of light from the windows as I approached, and I was considering the advisability of trying the laboratory on the next floor, when footsteps on the stone stairs and familiar voices gladdened my ear.

"Hallo, Berkeley!" said Thorndyke, "do we find you

waiting like a Peri at the gates of Paradise? Polton is upstairs, you know, tinkering at one of his inventions. If you ever find the nest empty, you had better go up and bang at the laboratory door. He's always there in the evenings."

"I haven't been waiting long," said I, "and I was just thinking of rousing him up when you came."

"That was right," said Thorndyke, turning up the gas. "And what news do you bring? Do I see a blue envelope sticking out of your pocket?"

"You do."

"Is it a copy of the will?" he asked.

I answered "yes," and added that I had full permission to show it to him.

"What did I tell you?" exclaimed Jervis. "Didn't I say that he would get the copy for us if it existed?"

"We admit the excellence of your prognosis," said Thorndyke, "but there is no need to be boastful. Have you read through the document, Berkeley?"

"No, I haven't taken it out of the envelope."

"Then it will be equally new to us all, and we shall see if it tallies with your description."

He placed three easy chairs at a convenient distance from the light, and Jervis, watching him with a smile, remarked:

"Now Thorndyke is going to enjoy himself. To him, a perfectly unintelligible will is a thing of beauty and a joy for ever; especially if associated with some kind of recondite knavery."

"I don't know," said I, "that this will is particularly unintelligible. The mischief seems to be that it is rather too intelligible. However, here it is," and I handed it over to Thorndyke.

"I suppose that we can depend on this copy," said the

latter, as he drew out the document and glanced at it. "Oh, yes," he added, "I see it is copied by Godfrey Bellingham, compared with the original and certified correct. In that case I will get you to read it out slowly, Jervis, and I will make a rough copy for reference. Let us make ourselves comfortable and light our pipes before we begin."

He provided himself with a writing-pad, and, when we had seated ourselves and got our pipes well alight, Jervis opened the document, and with a premonitory "hem!" commenced the reading.

"In the name of God Amen. This is the last will and testament of me John Bellingham of number 141 Queen Square in the parish of St. George Bloomsbury London in the county of Middlesex Gentleman made this twenty-first day of September in the year of our Lord one thousand eight hundred and ninety-two.

"1. I give and bequeath unto Arthur Jellicoe of number 184 New Square Lincoln's Inn London in the county of Middlesex Attorney-at-law the whole of my collection of seals and scarabs and those my cabinets marked A B and D together with the contents thereof and the sum of two thousand pounds sterling free of legacy duty.

"Unto the trustees of the British Museum the residue of my collection of antiquities.

"Unto my cousin George Hurst of The Poplars Eltham in the county of Kent the sum of five thousand pounds free of legacy duty and unto my brother Godfrey Bellingham or if he should die before the occurrence of my death unto his daughter Ruth Bellingham the residue of my estate and effects real and personal subject to the conditions set forth hereinafter namely:

"2. That my body shall be deposited with those of my ancestors in the churchyard appertaining to the church and parish of St. George the Martyr or if that shall not be possible in some other churchyard cemetery burial ground church or chapel or other authorised place for the reception of the bodies of the dead situate within or appertaining to the parishes of St. Andrew above the Bars and St. George the Martyr or St. George Bloomsbury and St. Giles in the Fields. But if the conditions in this clause be not carried out then

"3. I give and devise the said residue of my estate and effects unto my cousin George Hurst aforesaid and I hereby revoke all wills and codicils made by me at any time heretofore and I appoint Arthur Jellicoe aforesaid to be the executor of this my will jointly with the principal beneficiary and residuary legatee that is to say with the aforesaid Godfrey Bellingham if the conditions set forth hereinbefore in clause 2 shall be duly carried out but with the aforesaid George Hurst if the said conditions in the said clause 2 be not carried out.

"JOHN BELLINGHAM.

"Signed by the said testator John Bellingham in the presence of us present at the same time who at his request and in his presence and in the presence of each other have subscribed our names as witnesses.

"Frederick Wilton, 16 Medford Road, London, N., clerk.

"James Barber, 32 Wadbury Crescent, London, S.W., clerk."

"Well," said Jervis, laying down the document as Thorndyke detached the last sheet from his writing-pad, "I have met with a good many idiotic wills, but this one can give them all points. I don't see how it is ever going to be administered. One of the two executors is a mere abstraction—a sort of algebraical problem with no answer."

"I think that difficulty could be overcome," said Thorndyke.

"I don't see how," retorted Jervis. "If the body is deposited in a certain place, A is the executor; if it is somewhere else, B is the executor. But as you cannot produce the body, and no one has the least idea where it is, it is impossible to prove either that it is or that it is not in any specified place."

"You are magnifying the difficulty, Jervis," said Thorndyke. "The body may, of course, be anywhere in the entire world, but the place where it is lying is either inside or outside the general boundary of those two parishes. If it has been deposited within the boundary of those two parishes, the fact must be ascertainable by examining the burial certificates issued since the date when the missing man was last seen alive and by consulting the registers of those specified places of burial. I think that if no record can be found of any such interment within the boundary of those two parishes, that fact will be taken by the Court as proof that no such interment has taken place, and that therefore the body must have been deposited somewhere else. Such a decision would constitute George Hurst the co-executor and residuary legatee."

"That is cheerful for your friends, Berkeley," Jervis remarked, "for we may take it as pretty certain that the body has not been deposited in any of the places named."

"Yes," I agreed gloomily, "I'm afraid there is very little doubt of that. But what an ass the fellow must have been to make such a to-do about his beastly carcass! What the deuce could it have mattered to him where it was dumped, when he had done with it?"

Thorndyke chuckled softly. "Thus the irreverent youth of to-day," said he. "But yours is hardly a fair comment, Berkeley. Our training makes us materialists, and puts us a little out of sympathy with those in whom primitive beliefs and emotions survive. A worthy priest who came to look at our dissecting-room expressed surprise to me that the students, thus constantly in the presence of relics of mortality, should be able to think of anything but the resurrection and the life hereafter. He was a bad psychologist. There is nothing so dead as a dissecting-room subject; and the contemplation of the human body in the process of being quietly taken to pieces—being resolved into its structural units like a worn-out clock or an old engine in the scrapper's yard—is certainly not conducive to a vivid realisation of the doctrine of the resurrection."

"No; but this absurd anxiety to be buried in some particular place has nothing to do with religious belief; it is merely silly sentiment."

"It is sentiment, I admit," said Thorndyke, "but I wouldn't call it silly. The feeling is so widespread in time and space that we must look on it with respect as something inherent in human nature. Think—as doubtless John Bellingham did—of the ancient Egyptians, whose chief aspiration was that of everlasting repose for the dead. See the trouble they took to achieve it. Think of the great Pyramid, or that of Amenemhat the Fourth with its labyrinth of false passages and its sealed and hidden sepulchral chambers. Think of Jacob, borne after death all those hundreds of weary miles in order that he might sleep with his fathers, and then remember Shakespeare and his solemn adjuration to posterity to let him rest undisturbed in his grave. No, Berkeley, it is not a silly sentiment. I am as indifferent as you as to what becomes of my body 'when I have done with it,' to use your irreverent phrase; but I recognise the solicitude that some other men display on the subject as a natural feeling that has to be taken seriously."

"But even so," I said, "if this man had a hankering for a freehold residence in some particular bone-yard, he might have gone about the business in a more reasonable way."

"There I am entirely with you," Thorndyke replied. "It is the absurd way in which this provision is worded that not only creates all the trouble but also makes the whole document so curiously significant in view of the testator's disappearance."

"How significant?" Jervis demanded eagerly.

"Let us consider the provisions of the will point by point," said Thorndyke; "and first note that the testator commanded the services of a very capable lawyer."

"But Mr. Jellicoe disapproved of the will," said I; "in fact, he protested strongly against the form of it."

"We will bear that in mind too," Thorndyke replied. "And now with reference to what we may call the contentious clauses; the first thing that strikes us is their preposterous injustice. Godfrey's inheritance is made conditional on a particular disposal of the testator's body. But this is a matter not necessarily under Godfrey's control. The testator might have been lost at sea, or killed in a fire or explosion, or have died abroad and been buried where his grave could not have been identified.

There are numerous probable contingencies besides the improbable one that has happened that might prevent the body from being recovered.

"But even if the body had been recovered, there is another difficulty. The places of burial in the parishes have all been closed for many years. It would be impossible to reopen any of them without a special faculty, and I doubt whether such a faculty would be granted. Possibly cremation might meet the difficulty, but even that is doubtful; and, in any case, the matter would not be in the control of Godfrey Bellingham. Yet, if the required interment should prove impossible, he is to be deprived of his legacy."

"It is a monstrous and absurd injustice," I exclaimed.

"It is," Thorndyke agreed; "but this is nothing to the absurdity that comes to light when we consider clauses two and three in detail. Observe that the testator presumably wished to be buried in a certain place; also he wished that his brother should benefit under the will. Let us take the first point and see how he has set about securing the accomplishment of what he desired. Now if we read clauses two and three carefully, we shall see that he has rendered it virtually impossible that his wishes can be carried out. He desires to be buried in a certain place and makes Godfrey responsible for his being so buried. But he gives Godfrey no power or authority to carry out the provision, and places insuperable obstacles in his way. For until Godfrey is an executor, he has no power or authority to carry out the provisions; and until the provisions are carried out, he does not become an executor."

"It is a preposterous muddle," exclaimed Jervis.

"Yes, but that is not the worst of it," Thorndyke continued. "The moment John Bellingham dies, his dead body has come into existence; and it is 'deposited,' for the time being, wherever he happens to have died. But unless he should happen to have died in one of the places of burial mentioned—which is in the highest degree unlikely—his body will be, for the time being, 'deposited' in some place other than those specified. In that case clause two is—for the time being—not complied with, and consequently George Hurst becomes, automatically, the co-executor.

"But will George Hurst carry out the provisions of clause two? Probably not. Why should he? The will contains no instructions to that effect. It throws the whole duty on Godfrey. On the other hand, if he should carry out clause two, what happens? He ceases to be an executor and he loses some seventy thousand pounds. We may be pretty certain that he will do nothing of the kind. So that, on considering the two clauses, we see that the wishes of the testator could only be carried out in the unlikely event of his dying in one of the burial-places mentioned, or his body being conveyed immediately after death to a public mortuary in one of the said parishes. In any other event, it is virtually certain that he will be buried in some place other than that which he desired, and that his brother will be left absolutely without provision or recognition."

"John Bellingham could never have intended that," I said.

"Clearly not," agreed Thorndyke; "the provisions of the will furnish internal evidence that he did not. You note that he bequeathed five thousand pounds to George Hurst, in the event of clause two being carried out; but he has made no bequest to his brother in the event of its not being carried out. Obviously, he had not entertained the possibility of this contingency at all. He assumed, as a matter of course, that the conditions of clause two would be fulfilled, and regarded the conditions themselves as a mere formality."

"But," Jervis objected, "Jellicoe must have seen the danger of a miscarriage and pointed it out to his client."

"Exactly," said Thorndyke. "There is the mystery. We understand that he objected strenuously, and that John Bellingham was obdurate. Now it is perfectly understandable that a man should adhere obstinately to the most stupid and perverse disposition of his property; but that a man should persist in retaining a particular form of words after it has been proved to him that the use of such form will almost certainly result in the defeat of his own wishes; that, I say, is a mystery that calls for very careful consideration."

"If Jellicoe had been an interested party," said Jervis, "one would have suspected him of lying low. But the form of clause two doesn't affect him at all."

"No," said Thorndyke; "the person who stands to profit by the muddle is George Hurst. But we understand that he was unacquainted with the terms of the will, and there is certainly nothing to suggest that he is in any way responsible for it."

"The practical question is," said I, "what is going to happen? and what can be done for the Bellinghams?"

"The probability is," Thorndyke replied, "that the next move will be made by Hurst. He is the party immediately interested. He will probably apply to the Court for permission to presume death and administer the will."

"And what will the Court do?"

Thorndyke smiled dryly. "Now you are asking a very pretty conundrum. The decisions of Courts depend on idiosyncrasies of temperament that no one can foresee. But one may say that a Court does not lightly grant permission to presume death. There will be a rigorous inquiry—and a decidedly unpleasant one, I suspect—and the evidence will be reviewed by the judge with a strong predisposition to regard the testator as being still alive. On the other hand, the known facts point very distinctly to the probability that he is dead; and, if the will were less complicated and all the parties interested were unanimous in supporting the application, I don't see why it might not be granted. But it will clearly be to the interest of Godfrey to oppose the application, unless he can show that the conditions of clause two have been complied with—which it is virtually certain he cannot; and he may be able to bring forward reasons for believing John to be still alive. But even if he is unable to do this, inasmuch as it is pretty clear that he was intended to be the chief beneficiary, his opposition is likely to have considerable weight with the Court."

"Oh, is it?" I exclaimed eagerly. "Then that accounts for a very peculiar proceeding on the part of Hurst. I have stupidly forgotten to tell you about it. He has been trying to come to a private agreement with Godfrey Bellingham."

"Indeed!" said Thorndyke. "What sort of agreement?"

"His proposal was this: that Godfrey should support him and Jellicoe in an application to the Court for permission to presume death and to administer the will, and that if it was successful, Hurst should pay him four hundred pounds a year for life: the arrangement to hold good in all eventualities."

"By which he means?"

"That if the body should be discovered at any future time, so that the conditions of clause two could be carried out, Hurst should still retain the property and continue to pay Godfrey the four hundred a year for life."

"Hey, ho!" exclaimed Thorndyke; "that is a queer proposal; a very queer proposal indeed."

"Not to say fishy," added Jervis. "I don't fancy the Court would look with approval on that little arrangement."

"The law does not look with much favour on any little arrangements that aim at getting behind the provisions of a will," Thorndyke replied; "though there would be nothing to complain of in this proposal if it were not for the reference to 'all eventualities.' If a will is hopelessly impracticable, it is not unreasonable or improper for the various beneficiaries to make such private arrangements among themselves as may seem necessary to avoid useless litigation and delay in administering the will. If, for instance, Hurst had proposed to pay four hundred a year to Godfrey so long as the body remained undiscovered on condition that, in the event of its discovery, Godfrey should pay him a like sum for life, there would have been nothing to comment upon. It would have been an ordinary sporting chance. But the reference to 'all eventualities' is an entirely different matter. Of course, it may be mere greediness, but all the same it suggests some very curious reflections."

"Yes, it does," said Jervis. "I wonder if he has any reason to expect that the body will be found? Of course it doesn't follow that he has. He may be merely taking the opportunity offered by the other man's poverty to make sure of the bulk of the property whatever happens. But it is uncommonly sharp practice, to say the least."

"Do I understand that Godfrey declined the proposal?" Thorndyke asked.

"Yes, he did, very emphatically; and I fancy the two gentlemen proceeded to exchange opinions on the circumstances of the disappearance with more frankness than delicacy."

"Ah," said Thorndyke, "that is a pity. If the case comes into Court, there is bound to be a good deal of unpleasant discussion, and still more unpleasant comment in the newspapers. But if the parties themselves begin to express suspicions of one another there is no telling where the matter will end."

"No, by Jove!" said Jervis. "If they begin flinging accusations of murder about, the fat will be in the fire with a vengeance. That way lies the Old Bailey."

"We must try to prevent them from making an unnecessary scandal," said Thorndyke. "It may be that an exposure will be unavoidable, and that must be ascertained in advance. But to return to your question, Berkeley, as to what is to be done. Hurst will probably make some move pretty soon. Do you know if Jellicoe will act with him?"

"No, he won't. He declines to take any steps without Godfrey's assent—at least, that is what he says at present. His attitude is one of correct neutrality."

"That is satisfactory so far," said Thorndyke, "though he may alter his tone when the case comes into Court. From what you said just now I gathered that Jellicoe would prefer to have the will administered and be quit of the whole business; which is natural enough, especially as he benefits under the will to the extent of two thousand pounds and a valuable collection. Consequently, we may fairly assume that, even if he maintains an apparent neutrality, his influence will be exerted in favour of Hurst rather than of Bellingham; from which it follows that Bellingham ought certainly to be properly advised, and, when the case goes into Court, properly represented."

"He can't afford either the one or the other," said I. "He's as poor as an insolvent church mouse and as proud as the devil. He wouldn't accept professional aid that he couldn't pay for."

"H'm," grunted Thorndyke, "that's awkward. But we can't allow the case to go 'by default,' so to speak—to fail for the mere lack of technical assistance. Besides, it is one of the most interesting cases that I have ever met with, and I am not going to see it bungled. He couldn't object to a little general advice in a friendly, informal way—*amicus curiæ,* as old Brodribb is so fond of saying; and there is nothing to prevent us from pushing forward the preliminary inquiries."

"Of what nature would they be?"

"Well, to begin with, we have to satisfy ourselves that the conditions of clause two have not been complied with: that John Bellingham has not been buried within the parish boundaries mentioned. Of course he has not, but we must not take anything for granted. Then we have to satisfy ourselves that he is not still alive and accessible. It is perfectly possible that he is, after all, and it is our business to trace him, if he is still in the land of the living. Jervis and I can carry out these investigations without saying anything to Bellingham; my learned brother will look through the register of burials—not forgetting the cremations—in the metropolitan area, and I will take the other matter in hand."

"You really think that John Bellingham may still be alive?" said I.

"Since his body has not been found, it is obviously a possibility. I think it in the highest degree improbable, but the improbable has to be investigated before it can be excluded."

"It sounds a rather hopeless quest," I remarked. "How do you propose to begin?"

"I think of beginning at the British Museum. The

people there may be able to throw some light on his movements. I know that there are some important excavations in progress at Heliopolis—in fact, the Director of the Egyptian Department is out there at the present moment; and Dr. Norbury, who is taking his place temporarily, is an old friend of Bellingham's. I shall call on him and try to discover if there is anything that might have induced Bellingham suddenly to go abroad to Heliopolis, for instance. Also he may be able to tell me what it was that took the missing man to Paris on that last, rather mysterious journey. That might turn out to be an important clue. And meanwhile, Berkeley, you must endeavour tactfully to reconcile your friend to the idea of letting us give an eye to the case. Make it clear to him that I am doing this entirely for the enlargement of my own knowledge."

"But won't you have to be instructed by a solicitor?" I asked.

"Yes, nominally; but only as a matter of etiquette. We shall do all the actual work. Why do you ask?"

"I was thinking of the solicitor's costs, and I was going to mention that I have a little money of my own——"

"Then keep it, my dear fellow. You'll want it when you go into practice. There will be no difficulty about the solicitor; I shall ask one of my friends to act nominally as a personal favour to me—Marchmont would take the case for us, Jervis, I am sure."

"Yes," said Jervis. "Or old Brodribb, if we put it to him *amicus curiæ.*"

"It is excessively kind of both of you to take this benevolent interest in the case of my friends," I said; "and it is to be hoped that they won't be foolishly proud and stiff-necked about it. It's rather the way with poor gentlefolk."

"I'll tell you what!" exclaimed Jervis. "I have a most brilliant idea. You shall give us a little supper at your rooms and invite the Bellinghams to meet us. Then you and I will attack the old gentleman, and Thorndyke shall exercise his persuasive powers on the lady. These chronic incurable old bachelors, you know, are quite irresistible."

"You observe that my respected junior condemns me to lifelong celibacy," Thorndyke remarked. "But," he added, "his suggestion is quite a good one. Of course, we mustn't put any sort of pressure on Bellingham to employ us—for that is what it amounts to, even if we accept no payment—but a friendly talk over the supper-table would enable us to put the matter delicately and yet convincingly."

"Yes," said I, "I see that, and I like the idea immensely. But it won't be possible for several days, because I've got a job that takes up all my spare time—and that I ought to be at work on now," I added, with a sudden qualm at the way in which I had forgotten the passage of time in the interest of Thorndyke's analysis.

My two friends looked at me inquiringly, and I felt it necessary to explain about the injured hand and the Tell el Amarna tablets; which I accordingly did rather shyly and with a nervous eye upon Jervis. The slow grin, however, for which I was watching, never came; on the contrary, he not only heard me through quite gravely, but when I had finished said with some warmth and using my old hospital pet name:

"I'll say one thing for you, Polly; you're a good chum, and you always were. I hope your Nevill's Court friends appreciate the fact."

"They are far more appreciative than the occasion warrants," I answered. "But to return to this question: how will this day week suit you?"

"It will suit me," Thorndyke answered, with a glance at his junior.

"And me too," said the latter; "so, if it will do for the Bellinghams, we will consider it settled; but if they can't come, you must fix another night."

"Very well," I said, rising and knocking out my pipe, "I will issue the invitation to-morrow. And now I must be off to have another slog at those notes."

As I walked homewards I speculated cheerfully on the prospect of entertaining my friends under my own (or rather Barnard's) roof, if they could be lured out of their eremitical retirement. The idea had, in fact, occurred to me already, but I had been deterred by the peculiarities of Barnard's housekeeper. For Mrs. Gummer was one of those housewives who make up for an archaic simplicity of production by preparations on the most portentous and alarming scale. But this time I would not be deterred. If only the guests could be enticed into my humble lair it would be easy to furnish the raw materials of the feast from outside; and the consideration of ways and means occupied me pleasantly until I found myself once more at my writing-table, confronted by my voluminous notes on the incidents of the North Syrian War.

CHAPTER VIII   A Museum Idyll

Whether it was that practice revived a forgotten skill on my part, or that Miss Bellingham had over-estimated the amount of work to be done, I am unable to say. But whichever may have been the explanation, the fact is that the fourth afternoon saw our task so nearly completed that I was fain to plead that a small remainder might be left over to form an excuse for yet one more visit to the reading-room.

Short, however, as had been the period of our collaboration, it had been long enough to produce a great change in our relations to one another. For there is no friendship so intimate and satisfying as that engendered by community of work, and none—between man and woman, at any rate—so frank and wholesome.

Every day I had arrived to find a pile of books with the places duly marked and the blue-covered quarto notebooks in readiness. Every day we had worked steadily at the allotted task, had then handed in the books and gone forth together to enjoy a most companionable tea in the milk-shop; thereafter to walk home by way of Queen Square, talking over the day's work and discussing the state of the world in the far-off days when Ahkhenaten was king and the Tell el Amarna tablets were a-writing.

It had been a pleasant time, so pleasant, that as I handed in the books for the last time, I sighed to think that it was over; that not only was the task finished, but that the recovery of my fair patient's hand, from which I had that morning removed the splint, had put an end to the need of my help.

"What shall we do?" I asked, as we came out into the central hall. "It is too early for tea. Shall we go and look at some of the galleries?"

"Why not?" she answered. "We might look over some of the things connected with what we have been doing. For instance, there is a relief of Ahkhenaten upstairs in the Third Egyptian Room; we might go and look at it."

I fell in eagerly with the suggestion, placing myself under her experienced guidance, and we started by way of the Roman Gallery, past the long row of extremely commonplace and modern-looking Roman Emperors.

"I don't know," she said, pausing for a moment opposite a bust labelled "Trajan" (but obviously a portrait of Phil May), "how I am ever even to thank you for all that you have done, to say nothing of repayment."

"There is no need to do either," I replied. "I have enjoyed working with you so I have had my reward. But still," I added, "if you want to do me a great kindness, you have it in your power."

"How?"

"In connection with my friend, Dr. Thorndyke. I told you he was an enthusiast. Now he is, for some reason, most keenly interested in everything relating to your uncle, and I happen to know that, if any legal proceedings should take place, he would very much like to keep a friendly eye on the case."

"And what do you want me to do?"

"I want you, if an opportunity should occur for him to give your father advice or help of any kind, to use your influence with your father in favour of, rather than in opposition to, his accepting it—always assuming that you have no real feeling against his doing so."

Miss Bellingham looked at me thoughtfully for a few moments, and then laughed softly.

"So the great kindness that I am to do you is to let you do me a further kindness through your friend!"

"No," I protested; "that is where you are mistaken. It isn't benevolence on Dr. Thorndyke's part; it is professional enthusiasm."

She smiled sceptically.

"You don't believe in it," I said; "but consider other cases. Why does a surgeon get out of bed on a winter's night to do an emergency operation at a hospital? He doesn't get paid for it. Do you think it is altruism?"

"Yes, of course. Isn't it?"

"Certainly not. He does it because it is his job, because it is his business to fight with disease—and win."

"I don't see much difference," she said. "It is work done for love instead of for payment. However, I will do as you ask if the opportunity arises; but I shan't suppose that I am repaying your kindness to me."

"I don't mind so long as you do it," I said, and we walked on for some time in silence.

"Isn't it odd," she said presently, "how our talk always seems to come back to my uncle? Oh, and that reminds me that the things he gave to the Museum are in the same room as the Ahkhenaten relief. Would you like to see them?"

"Of course I should."

"Then we will go and look at them first." She paused, and then, rather shyly and with a rising colour, she continued: "And I think I should like to introduce you to a very dear friend of mine—with your permission, of course."

This last addition she made hastily, seeing, I suppose, that I looked rather glum at the suggestion. Inwardly I consigned her friend to the devil, especially if of the masculine gender; outwardly I expressed my felicity at making the acquaintance of any person whom she should honour with her friendship. Whereat, to my discomfiture, she laughed enigmatically; a very soft laugh, low-pitched and musical, like the cooing of a glorified pigeon.

I strolled on by her side, speculating a little anxiously on the coming introduction. Was I being conducted to the lair of one of the savants attached to the establishment? and would he add a superfluous third to our little party of two, so complete and companionable, *solus cum sola*, in this populated wilderness? Above all, would he turn out to be a young man, and bring my aerial castles tumbling about my ears? The shy look and the blush with which she had suggested the introduction were ominous indications, upon which I mused gloomily as we ascended the stairs and passed through the wide doorway. I glanced apprehensively at my companion, and met a quiet, inscrutable smile; and at that moment she halted opposite a wall-case and faced me.

"This is my friend," she said. "Let me present you to Artemidorus, late of the Fayyum. Oh, don't smile!" she pleaded. "I am quite serious. Have you never heard of pious Catholics who cherish a devotion to some long-departed saint? That is my feeling towards Artemidorus, and if you only knew what comfort he has shed into the heart of a lonely woman; what a quiet, unobtrusive friend he has been to me in my solitary, friendless days, always ready with a kindly greeting on his gentle, thoughtful face, you would like him for that alone. And I want you to like him and to share our silent friendship. Am I very silly, very sentimental?"

A wave of relief swept over me, and the mercury of my emotional thermometer, which had shrunk almost into the bulb, leaped up to summer heat. How charming it was of her and how sweetly intimate, to wish to share this mystical friendship with me! And what a pretty conceit it was, too, and how like this strange, inscrutable maiden, to come here and hold silent converse with this long-departed Greek. And the pathos of it all touched me deeply amidst the joy of this new-born intimacy.

"Are you scornful?" she asked, with a shade of disappointment, as I made no reply.

"No, indeed I am not," I answered earnestly. "I want to make you aware of my sympathy and my appreciation without offending you by seeming to exaggerate, and I don't know how to express it."

"Oh, never mind about the expression, so long as you feel it. I thought you would understand," and she gave me a smile that made me tingle to my finger-tips.

We stood awhile gazing in silence at the mummy—for such, indeed, was her friend Artemidorus. But not an ordinary mummy. Egyptian in form, it was entirely Greek in feeling; and brightly coloured as it was, in accordance with the racial love of colour, the tasteful refinement with which the decoration of the case was treated made those around look garish and barbaric. But the most striking feature was a charming panel portrait which occupied the place of the usual mask. This painting was a revelation to me. Except that it was executed in tempera instead of oil, it differed in no respect from modern work. There was nothing archaic or ancient about it. With its freedom of handling and its correct rendering of light and shade, it might have been painted yesterday; indeed, enclosed in an ordinary gilt frame, it might have passed without remark in an exhibition of modern portraits.

Miss Bellingham observed my admiration and smiled approvingly.

"It is a charming little portrait, isn't it?" she said; "and such a sweet face too; so thoughtful and human, with just a shade of melancholy. But the whole thing is full of charm. I fell in love with it the first time I saw it. And it is so Greek!"

"Yes, it is, in spite of the Egyptian gods and symbols."

"Rather because of them, I think," said she. "There we have the typical Greek attitude, the genial, cultivated eclecticism that appreciated the fitness of even the most alien forms of art. There is Anubis standing beside the bier; there are Isis and Nephthys, and there below Horus and Tahuti. But we can't suppose Artemidorus worshipped or believed in those gods. They are there because they are splendid decoration and perfectly appropriate in character. The real feeling of those who loved the dead man breaks out in the inscription." She pointed to a band below the pectoral, where, in gilt capital letters, was written the two words, "ÁÑÔÅÌÉÄÙÑÅ ÅÔØÕ×É."

"Yes," I said, "it is very dignified and very human."

"And so sincere and full of real emotion," she added. "I find it unspeakably touching. 'O Artemidorus, farewell!' There is the real note of human grief, the sorrow of eternal parting. How much finer it is than the vulgar boastfulness of the Semitic epitaphs, or our own miserable, insincere make-believe of the 'Not lost but gone before' type. He was gone from them for ever; they would look on his face and hear his voice no more; they realised that this was their last farewell. Oh, there is a world of love and sorrow in those two simple words!"

For some time neither of us spoke. The glamour of this touching memorial of a long-buried grief had stolen over me, and I was content to stand silent by my beloved companion and revive, with a certain pensive pleasure, the ghosts of human emotions over which so many centuries had rolled. Presently she turned to me with a frank smile. "You have been weighed in the balance of friendship," she said, "and not found wanting. You have the gift of sympathy, even with a woman's sentimental fancies."

I suspected that a good many men would have developed this precious quality under the circumstances, but I refrained from saying so. There is no use in crying down one's own wares. I was glad enough to have earned her good opinion so easily, and when she at length turned away from the case and passed through into the adjoining room, it was a very complacent young man who bore her company.

"Here is Ahkhenaten—or Khu-en-aten, as the authorities here render the hieroglyphics." She indicated a fragment of a coloured relief labelled: "Portion of a painted stone tablet with a portrait figure of Amenhetep IV.," and we stopped to look at the frail, effeminate figure of the great king, with his large cranium, his queer, pointed chin, and the Aten rays stretching out their weird hands as if caressing him.

"We mustn't stay here if you want to see my uncle's gift, because this room closes at four to-day." With this admonition she moved on to the other end of the room, where she halted before a large floor-case containing a mummy and a large number of other objects. A black label with white lettering set forth the various contents with a brief explanation as follows:

> "Mummy of Sebek-hotep, a scribe of the twenty-second dynasty, together with the objects found in the tomb. These include the four Canopic jars, in which the internal organs were deposited, the Ushabti figures, tomb provisions and various articles that had belonged to the deceased; his favourite chair, his head-rest, his ink-palette, inscribed with his name and the name of the king, Osorkon I., in whose reign he lived, and other smaller articles. Presented by John Bellingham, Esq."

"They have put all the objects together in one case," Miss Bellingham explained, "to show the contents of an ordinary tomb of the better class. You see that the dead man was provided with all his ordinary comforts: provisions, furniture, the ink-palette that he had been accustomed to use in writing on papyri, and a staff of servants to wait on him."

"Where are the servants?" I asked.

"The little Ushabti figures," she answered; "they were the attendants of the dead, you know, his servants in the under-world. It was a quaint idea, wasn't it? But it was all very complete and consistent, and quite reasonable, too, if one once accepts the belief in the persistence of the individual apart from the body."

"Yes," I agreed, "and that is the only fair way to judge a religious system, by taking the main beliefs for granted. But what a business it must have been, bringing all these things from Egypt to London."

"It was worth the trouble, though, for it is a fine and instructive collection. And the work is all very good of its kind. You notice that the Ushabti figures and the heads that form the stoppers of the Canopic jars are quite finely modelled. The mummy itself, too, is rather handsome, though that coat of bitumen on the back doesn't improve it. But Sebek-hotep must have been a fine-looking man."

"The mask on the face is a portrait, I suppose?"

"Yes; in fact, it's rather more. To some extent it is the actual face of the man himself. This mummy is enclosed in what is called a cartonnage, that is a case moulded on the figure. The cartonnage was formed of a number of layers of linen or papyrus united by glue or cement, and when the case had been fitted to a mummy it was moulded to the body, so that the general form of the features and limbs was often apparent. After the cement was dry the case was covered with a thin layer of stucco and the face modelled more completely, and then decorations and inscriptions were painted on. So that, you see, in a cartonnage, the body was sealed up like a nut in its shell, unlike the more ancient forms in which the mummy was merely rolled up and enclosed in a wooden coffin."

At this moment there smote upon our ears a politely protesting voice announcing in sing-song tones that it was closing time; and simultaneously a desire for tea suggested the hospitable milk-shop. With leisurely dignity that ignored the official who shepherded us along the galleries, we made our way to the entrance, still immersed in conversation on matters sepulchral.

It was rather earlier than our usual hour for leaving the Museum, and, moreover, it was our last day—for the present. Wherefore we lingered over our tea to an extent that caused the milk-shop lady to view us with some disfavour, and, when at length we started homeward, we took so many short cuts that six o'clock found us no nearer our destination than Lincoln's Inn Fields; whither we had journeyed by a slightly indirect route that traversed (among other places) Russell Square, Red Lion Square, with the quaint passage of the same name, Bedford Row, Jockey's Fields, Hand Court, and Great Turnstile.

It was in the latter thoroughfare that our attention was attracted by a flaming poster outside a news-vendor's bearing the startling inscription:

> ## "MORE MEMENTOES
> ## OF MURDERED MAN."

Miss Bellingham glanced at the poster and shuddered.

"Horrible, isn't it?" she said. "Have you read about them?"

"I haven't been noticing the papers the last few days," I replied.

"No, of course you haven't. You've been slaving at those wretched notes. We don't very often see the papers, at least we don't take them in, but Miss Oman has kept us supplied during the last day or two. She is a perfect little ghoul; she delights in horrors of every kind, and the more horrible the better."

"But," I asked, "what is it they have found?"

"Oh, they are the remains of some poor creature who seems to have been murdered and cut into pieces. It is dreadful. It made me shudder to read of it, for I couldn't help thinking of poor Uncle John, and, as for my father, he was really quite upset."

"Are these the bones that were found in a watercress-bed at Sidcup?"

"Yes, but they have found several more. The police have been most energetic. They seem to have been making a systematic search, and the result has been that they have discovered several portions of the body, scattered about in very widely separated places—Sidcup, Lee, St. Mary Cray; and yesterday it was reported that an arm had been found in one of the ponds called 'the Cuckoo Pits,' close to our old home."

"What! in Essex?" I exclaimed.

"Yes, in Epping Forest, quite near Woodford. Isn't it dreadful to think of it? They were probably hidden when we were living there. I think it was that that horrified my father so much. When he read it he was so upset that he gathered up the whole bundle of newspapers and tossed them out of the window; and they blew over the wall, and poor Miss Oman had to rush out and pursue them up the court."

"Do you think he suspects that these remains may be those of your uncle?"

"I think so, though he has said nothing to that effect, and, of course, I have not made any suggestion to him. We always preserve the fiction between ourselves of believing that Uncle John is still alive."

"But you don't think he is, do you?"

"No, I'm afraid I don't; and I feel pretty sure that my father doesn't think so either, but he doesn't like to admit it to me."

"Do you happen to remember what bones have been found?"

"No, I don't. I know that an arm was found in the Cuckoo Pits, and I think a thigh-bone was dredged up out of a pond near St. Mary Cray. But Miss Oman will be able to tell you all about it, if you are interested. She will be delighted to meet a kindred spirit," Miss Bellingham added, with a smile.

"I don't know that I claim spiritual kinship with a ghoul," said I; "especially such a very sharp-tempered ghoul."

"Oh, don't disparage her, Dr. Berkeley!" Miss Bellingham pleaded. "She isn't really bad-tempered; only a little prickly on the surface. I oughtn't to have called her a ghoul; she is just the sweetest, most affectionate, most unselfish little angelic human hedgehog that you could find if you travelled the wide world through. Do you know that she has been working her fingers to the bone making an old dress of mine presentable, because she is so anxious that I shall look nice at your little supper party."

"You are sure to do that in any case," I said, "but I withdraw my remark as to her temper unreservedly. And I really didn't mean it, you know; I've always liked the little lady."

"That's right; and now won't you come in and have a few minutes' chat with my father? We are quite early in spite of the short cuts."

I accepted readily, and the more so inasmuch as I

wanted a few words with Miss Oman on the subject of catering and did not want to discuss it before my friends. Accordingly I went in and gossiped with Mr. Bellingham, chiefly about the work we had done at the Museum, until it was time for me to return to the surgery.

Having taken my leave, I walked down the stairs with reflective slowness and as much creaking of my boots as I could manage; with the result, hopefully anticipated, that as I approached the door of Miss Oman's room it opened and the lady's head protruded.

"I'd change my cobbler if I were you," she said.

I thought of the "angelic human hedgehog," and nearly sniggered in her face.

"I am sure you would, Miss Oman, instantly; though, mind you, the poor fellow can't help his looks."

"You are a very flippant young man," she said severely. Whereat I grinned, and she regarded me silently with a baleful glare. Suddenly I remembered my mission and became serious and sober.

"Miss Oman," I said, "I very much want to take your advice on a matter of some importance—to me, at least." (That ought to fetch her, I thought. The "advice fly"— strangely neglected by Izaak Walton—is guaranteed to kill in any weather. And it did fetch her. She rose in a flash and gorged it, cock's feathers, worsted body, and all.)

"What is it about?" she asked eagerly. "But don't stand out there where everybody can hear but me. Come in and sit down."

Now I didn't want to discuss the matter here, and, besides, there was not time. I therefore assumed an air of mystery.

"I can't, Miss Oman. I'm due at the surgery now. But if you should be passing and should have a few minutes to spare, I should be greatly obliged if you would look in. I really don't quite know how to act."

"No, I expect not. Men very seldom do. But you're better than most, for you know when you are in difficulties and have the sense to consult a woman. But what is it about? Perhaps I might be thinking it over."

"Well, you know," I began evasively, "it's a simple matter, but I can't very well—no, by Jove!" I added, looking at my watch, "I must run, or I shall keep the multitude waiting." And with this I bustled away, leaving her literally dancing with curiosity.

CHAPTER IX   The Sphinx of Lincoln's Inn

At the age of twenty-six one cannot claim to have attained to the position of a person of experience. Nevertheless, the knowledge of human nature accumulated in that brief period sufficed to make me feel confident that, at some time during the evening, I should receive a visit from Miss Oman. And circumstances justified my confidence; for the clock yet stood at two minutes to seven when a premonitory tap at the surgery door heralded her arrival.

"I happened to be passing," she explained—and I forbore to smile at the coincidence—"so I thought I might as well drop in and hear what you wanted to ask me about."

She seated herself in the patients' chair, and, laying a bundle of newspapers on the table, glared at me expectantly.

"Thank you, Miss Oman," said I. "It is very good of you to look in on me. I am ashamed to give you all this trouble about such a trifling matter."

She rapped her knuckles impatiently on the table.

"Never mind about the trouble," she exclaimed tartly. "What—is—it—that—you—want—to—*ask*—me about?"

I stated my difficulties in respect of the supper-party, and, as I proceeded, an expression of disgust and disappointment spread over her countenance.

"I don't see why you need have been so mysterious about it," she said glumly.

"I didn't mean to be mysterious; I was only anxious not to make a mess of the affair. It's all very fine to assume a lofty scorn of the pleasures of the table, but there is great virtue in a really good feed, especially when low-living and high-thinking have been the order of the day."

"Coarsely put," said Miss Oman, "but perfectly true."

"Very well. Now, if I leave the management to Mrs. Gummer, she will probably provide a tepid Irish stew with flakes of congealed fat on it, and a plastic suet-pudding or something of that kind, and turn the house upside down in getting it ready. So I thought of having a cold spread and getting the things from outside. But I don't want it to look as if I had beer making enormous preparations."

"They won't think the things came down from heaven," said Miss Oman.

"No, I suppose they won't. But you know what I mean. Now, where do you advise me to go for the raw materials of conviviality?"

Miss Oman reflected. "You had better let me do your shopping and manage the whole business," was her final verdict.

This was precisely what I wanted, and I accepted thankfully, regardless of the feelings of Mrs. Gummer. I handed her two pounds, and, after some protests at my extravagance, she bestowed them in her purse; a process that occupied time, since that receptacle, besides being a sort of miniature Record Office of frayed and time-stained bills, already bulged with a lading of draper's samples, ends of tape, a card of linen buttons, another of hooks and eyes, a lump of beeswax, a rat-eaten stump of lead-pencil, and other trifles that I have forgotten. As she closed the purse at the imminent risk of wrenching off its fastenings she looked at me severely and pursed her lips.

"You're a very plausible young man," she remarked.

"What makes you say that?" I asked.

"Philandering about museums," she continued, "with handsome young ladies on the pretence of work. Work, indeed! Oh, I heard her telling her father about it. She thinks you were perfectly enthralled by the mummies and dried cats and chunks of stone and all the other trash. She doesn't know what humbugs men are."

"Really, Miss Oman—" I began.

"Oh, don't talk to me!" she snapped. "I can see it all. You can't impose upon me. I can see you staring into those glass cases, egging her on to talk, and listening open-mouthed and bulging-eyed and sitting at her feet—now, didn't you?"

"I don't know about sitting at her feet," I said, "though it might easily have come to that with those infernal slippery floors; but I had a very jolly time, and I mean to go again if I can. Miss Bellingham is the cleverest and most accomplished woman I have ever spoken to."

This was a poser for Miss Oman, whose admiration and loyalty, I knew, were only equalled by my own. She would have liked to contradict me, but the thing was impossible. To cover her defeat she snatched up the bundle of newspapers and began to open them out.

"What sort of stuff is 'hibernation'?" she demanded

suddenly.

"Hibernation!" I exclaimed.

"Yes. They found a patch of it on a bone that was discovered in a pond at St. Mary Cray, and a similar patch on one that was found at some other place in Essex. Now, I want to know what 'hibernation' is."

"You must mean 'eburnation,'" I said, after a moment's reflection.

"The newspapers say 'hibernation,' and I suppose they know what they are talking about. If you don't know what it is, don't be ashamed to say so."

"Well, then, I don't."

"In that case you had better read the papers and find out," she said, a little illogically. And then: "Are you fond of murders? I am, awfully."

"What a shocking little ghoul you must be!" I exclaimed.

She stuck out her chin at me. "I'll trouble you," she said, " to be a little more respectful in your language. Do you realise that I am old enough to be your mother?"

"Impossible!" I ejaculated.

"Fact," said Miss Oman.

"Well, anyhow," said I, "age is not the only qualification. And besides, you are too late for the billet. The vacancy's filled."

Miss Oman slapped the papers down on the table and rose abruptly.

"You had better read the papers and see if you can learn a little sense," she said severely as she turned to go. "Oh, and don't forget the finger!" she added eagerly. "That is really thrilling."

"The finger?" I repeated.

"Yes. They found a hand with one missing. The police think it is an important clue. I don't know what they mean; but you read the account and tell me what you think."

With this parting injunction she bustled out through the surgery, and I followed to bid her a ceremonious adieu on the doorstep. I watched her little figure tripping with quick, bird-like steps down Fetter Lane, and was about to turn back into the surgery when my attention was attracted by the evolutions of an elderly gentleman on the opposite side of the street. He was a somewhat peculiar-looking man, tall, gaunt, and bony, and the way in which he carried his head suggested to the medical mind a pronounced degree of near sight and a pair of "deep" spectacle glasses. Suddenly he espied me and crossed the road with his chin thrust forward and a pair of keen blue eyes directed at me through the centres of his spectacles.

"I wonder if you can and will help me," said he, with a courteous salute. "I wish to call on an acquaintance, and I have forgotten his address. It is in some court, but the name of that court has escaped me for the moment. My friend's name is Bellingham. I suppose you don't chance to know it? Doctors know a great many people, as a rule."

"Do you mean Mr. Godfrey Bellingham?"

"Ah! Then you do know him. I have not consulted the oracle in vain. He is a patient of yours, no doubt?"

"A patient and a personal friend. His address is Forty-nine Nevill's Court."

"Thank you, thank you. Oh, and as you are a friend, perhaps you can inform me as to the customs of the household. I am not expected, and I do not wish to make an untimely visit. What are Mr. Bellingham's habits as to his evening meal? Would this be a convenient time to call?"

"I generally make my evening visits a little later than this—say about half-past eight; they have finished their meal by then."

"Ah! Half-past eight? Then I suppose I had better take a walk until that time. I don't want to disturb them."

"Would you care to come in and smoke a cigar until it is time to make your call? If you would, I could walk over with you and show you the house."

"That is very kind of you," said my new acquaintance, with an inquisitive glance at me through his spectacles. "I think I should like to sit down. It's a dull affair, mooning about the streets, and there isn't time to go back to my chambers—in Lincoln's Inn."

"I wonder," said I, as I ushered him into the room lately vacated by Miss Oman, "if you happen to be Mr. Jellicoe?"

He turned his spectacles full on me with a keen, suspicious glance. "What makes you think I am Mr. Jellicoe?" he asked.

"Oh, only that you live in Lincoln's Inn."

"Ha! I see. I live in Lincoln's Inn; Mr. Jellicoe lives in Lincoln's Inn; therefore I am Mr. Jellicoe. Ha! ha! Bad logic, but a correct conclusion. Yes, I am Mr. Jellicoe. What do you know about me?"

"Mighty little, excepting that you were the late John Bellingham's man of business."

"The '*late* John Bellingham,' hey? How do you know he is the late John Bellingham?"

"As a matter of fact, I don't; only I rather understood that that was your own belief."

"You understood! Now from whom did you 'understand' that? From Godfrey Bellingham? H'm! And how did he know what I believe? I never told him. It is a very unsafe thing, my dear sir, to expound another man's beliefs."

"Then you think that John Bellingham is alive?"

"Do I? Who said so? I did not, you know."

"But he must be either dead or alive."

"There," said Mr. Jellicoe, "I am entirely with you. You have stated an undeniable truth."

"It is not a very illuminating one, however," I replied, laughing.

"Undeniable truths often are not," he retorted. "They are apt to be extremely general. In fact, I would affirm that the certainty of the truth of a given proposition is directly proportional to its generality."

"I suppose that is so," said I.

"Undoubtedly. Take an instance from your own profession. Given a million normal human beings under twenty, and you can say with certainty that a majority of them will die before reaching a certain age, that they will die in certain circumstances and of certain diseases. Then take a single unit from that million, and what can you predict concerning him? Nothing. He may die to-morrow; he may live to be a couple of hundred. He may die of a cold in the head, or a cut finger, or from falling off the cross of St. Paul's. In a particular case you can predict nothing."

"That is perfectly true," said I. And then realising that I had been led away from the topic of John Bellingham, I ventured to return to it.

"That was a very mysterious affair—the disappearance of John Bellingham, I mean."

"Why mysterious?" asked Mr. Jellicoe. "Men disappear from time to time, and when they reappear, the explanations that they give (when they give any) seem more or less adequate."

"But the circumstances were surely rather mysterious."

"What circumstances?" asked Mr. Jellicoe.

"I mean the way in which he vanished from Mr. Hurst's house."

"In what way did he vanish from it?"

"Well, of course, I don't know."

"Precisely. Neither do I. Therefore I can't say whether that way was a mysterious one or not."

"It is not even certain that he did leave it," I remarked, rather recklessly.

"Exactly," said Mr. Jellicoe. "And if he did not, he is there still. And if he is there still, he has not disappeared—in the sense understood. And if he has not disappeared, there is no mystery."

I laughed heartily, but Mr. Jellicoe preserved a wooden solemnity and continued to examine me through his spectacles (which I, in my turn, inspected and estimated at about minus five dioptres). There was something highly diverting about this grim lawyer, with his dry contentiousness and almost farcical caution. His ostentatious reserve encouraged me to ply him with fresh questions, the more indiscreet the better.

"I suppose," said I, "that, under these circumstances, you would hardly favour Mr. Hurst's proposal to apply for permission to presume death?"

"Under what circumstances?" he inquired.

"I was referring to the doubt you have expressed as to whether John Bellingham is, after all, really dead."

"My dear sir," said he, "I fail to see your point. If it were certain that the man was alive, it would be impossible to presume that he was dead; and if it were certain that he was dead, presumption of death would still be impossible. You do not presume a certainty. The uncertainty is of the essence of the transaction."

"But," I persisted, "if you really believe that he may be

alive, I should hardly have thought that you would take the responsibility of presuming his death and dispersing his property."

"I don't," said Mr. Jellicoe. "I take no responsibility. I act in accordance with the decision of the Court and have no choice in the matter."

"But the Court may decide that he is dead and he may nevertheless be alive."

"Not at all. If the Court decides that he is presumably dead, then he is presumably dead. As a mere irrelevant, physical circumstance he may, it is true, be alive. But legally speaking, and for testamentary purposes, he is dead. You fail to perceive the distinction, no doubt?"

"I am afraid I do," I admitted.

"Yes; the members of your profession usually do. That is what makes them such bad witnesses in a court of law. The scientific outlook is radically different from the legal. The man of science relies on his own knowledge and observation and judgment, and disregards testimony. A man comes to you and tells you he is blind in one eye. Do you accept his statement? Not in the least. You proceed to test his eyesight with some infernal apparatus of coloured glasses, and you find that he can see perfectly well with both eyes. Then you decide that he is not blind in one eye; that is to say, you reject his testimony in favour of facts of your own ascertaining."

"But surely that is the rational method of coming to a conclusion?"

"In science, no doubt. Not in law. A court of law must decide according to the evidence which is before it; and that evidence is of the nature of sworn testimony. If a witness is prepared to swear that black is white and no evidence to the contrary is offered, the evidence before the Court is that black is white, and the Court must decide accordingly. The judge and the jury may think otherwise—they may even have private knowledge to the contrary—but they have to decide according to the evidence."

"Do you mean to say that a judge would be justified in giving a decision which he knew to be contrary to the facts? Or that he might sentence a man whom he knew to be innocent?"

"Certainly. It has been done. There is a case of a judge who sentenced a man to death and allowed the execution to take place, notwithstanding that he—the judge—had actually seen the murder committed by another man. But that was carrying correctness of procedure to the verge of pedantry."

"It was, with a vengeance," I agreed. "But to return to the case of John Bellingham. Supposing that after the Court has decided that he is dead he should return alive? What then?"

"Ah! It would then be his turn to make an application, and the Court, having fresh evidence laid before it, would probably decide that he was alive."

"And meantime his property would have been dispersed?"

"Probably. But you will observe that the presumption of death would have arisen out of his own proceedings. If a man acts in such a way as to create a belief that he is dead, he must put up with the consequences."

"Yes, that is reasonable enough," said I. And then, after a pause, I asked: "Is there any immediate likelihood of proceedings of the kind being commenced?"

"I understood from what you said just now that Mr. Hurst was contemplating some action of the kind. No doubt you had your information from a reliable quarter." This answer Mr. Jellicoe delivered without moving a muscle, regarding me with the fixity of a spectacled figurehead.

I smiled feebly. The operation of pumping Mr. Jellicoe was rather like the sport of boxing with a porcupine, being chiefly remarkable as a demonstration of the power of passive resistance. I determined, however, to make one more effort, rather, I think, for the pleasure of witnessing his defensive manœuvres than with the expectation of getting anything out of him. I accordingly "opened out" on the subject of the "remains."

"Have you been following these remarkable discoveries of human bones that have been appearing in the papers?" I asked.

He looked at me stonily for some moments, and then replied:

"Human bones are rather more within your province than mine, but, now that you mention it, I think I recall having read of some such discoveries. They were disconnected bones, I believe."

"Yes; evidently parts of a dismembered body."

"So I should suppose. No, I have not followed the accounts. As we get on in life our interests tend to settle into grooves, and my groove is chiefly connected with conveyancing. These discoveries would be of more interest to a criminal lawyer."

"I thought you might, perhaps, have connected them with the disappearance of your client?"

"Why should I? What could be the nature of the connection?"

"Well," I said, "these are the bones of a man——"

"Yes; and my client was a man with bones. That is a connection, certainly, though not a very specific or distinctive one. But perhaps you had something more particular in your mind?"

"I had," I replied. "The fact that some of the bones were actually found on land belonging to your client seemed to me rather significant."

"Did it, indeed?" said Mr. Jellicoe. He reflected for a few moments, gazing steadily at me the while, and then continued: "In that I am unable to follow you. It would have seemed to me that the finding of human remains upon a certain piece of land might conceivably throw a *prima facie* suspicion upon the owner or occupant of the land as being the person who deposited them. But the case that you suggest is the one case in which this would be impossible. A man cannot deposit his own dismembered remains."

"No, of course not. I was not suggesting that he deposited them himself, but merely that the fact of their being deposited on his land, in a way, connected these remains with him."

"Again," said Mr. Jellicoe, "I fail to follow you, unless you are suggesting that it is customary for murderers who mutilate bodies to be punctilious in depositing the dismembered remains upon land belonging to their victims. In which case I am sceptical as to your facts. I am not aware of the existence of any such custom. Moreover, it appears that only a portion of the body was deposited on Mr. Bellingham's land, the remaining portions having been scattered broadcast over a wide area. How does that agree with your suggestion?"

"It doesn't, of course," I admitted. "But there is another fact that I think you will admit to be more significant. The first remains that were discovered were found at Sidcup. Now, Sidcup is close to Eltham; and Eltham is the place where Mr. Bellingham was last seen alive."

"And what is the significance of this? Why do you

connect the remains with one locality rather than the various other localities in which other portions of the body were found?"

"Well," I replied, rather gravelled by this very pertinent question, " the appearances seem to suggest that the person who deposited these remains started from the neighbourhood of Eltham, where the missing man was last seen."

Mr. Jellicoe shook his head. "You appear," said he, "to be confusing the order of deposition with the order of discovery. What evidence is there that the remains found at Sidcup were deposited before those found elsewhere?"

"I don't know that there is any," I admitted.

"Then," said he, "I don't see how you support your suggestion that the person started from the neighbourhood of Eltham."

On consideration, I had to admit that I had nothing to offer in support of my theory; and, having thus shot my last arrow in this very unequal contest, I thought it time to change the subject.

"I called in at the British Museum the other day," said I, "and had a look at Mr. Bellingham's last gift to the nation. The things are very well shown in that central case."

"Yes. I was very pleased with the position they have given to the exhibit, and so would my poor old friend have been. I wished, as I looked at the case, that he could have seen it. But perhaps he may, after all."

"I am sure I hope he will," said I, with more sincerity, perhaps, than the lawyer gave me credit for. For the return of John Bellingham would most effectually have cut the Gordian knot of my friend Godfrey's difficulties. "You are a good deal interested in Egyptology yourself, aren't you?" I added.

"Greatly interested," replied Mr. Jellicoe, with more animation than I had thought possible in his wooden face. "It is a fascinating subject, the study of this venerable civilisation, extending back to the childhood of the human race, preserved for ever for our instruction in its own unchanging monuments like a fly in a block of amber. Everything connected with Egypt is full of an impressive solemnity. A feeling of permanence, of stability, defying time and change, pervades it. The place, the people, and the monuments alike breathe of eternity."

I was mightily surprised at this rhetorical outburst on the part of this dry, taciturn lawyer. But I liked him the better for the touch of enthusiasm that made him human, and determined to keep him astride of his hobby.

"Yet," said I, "the people must have changed in the course of centuries."

"Yes, that is so. The people who fought against Cambyses were not the race who marched into Egypt five thousand years before—the dynastic people whose portraits we see on the early monuments. In those fifty centuries the blood of Hyksos and Syrians and Ethiopians and Hittites, and who can say how many more races, must have mingled with that of the old Egyptians. But still the national life went on without a break; the old culture leavened the new peoples, and the immigrant strangers ended by becoming Egyptians. It is a wonderful phenomenon. Looking back on it from our own time, it seems more like a geological period than the life history of a single nation. Are you at all interested in the subject?"

"Yes, decidedly, though I am completely ignorant of it. The fact is that my interest is of quite recent growth. It is only of late that I have been sensible of the glamour of things Egyptian."

"Since you made Miss Bellingham's acquaintance, perhaps?" suggested Mr. Jellicoe, himself as unchanging in aspect as an Egyptian effigy.

I suppose I must have reddened—I certainly resented the remark—for he continued in the same even tone: "I made the suggestion because I know that she takes an intelligent interest in the subject and is, in fact, quite well informed on it."

"Yes; she seems to know a great deal about the antiquities of Egypt, and I may as well admit that your surmise was correct. It was she who showed me her uncle's collection."

"So I had supposed," said Mr. Jellicoe. "And a very instructive collection it is, in a popular sense; very suitable for exhibition in a public museum, though there is nothing in it of unusual interest to the expert. The tomb furniture is excellent of its kind, and the cartonnage case of the mummy is well made and rather finely decorated."

"Yes, I thought it quite handsome. But can you explain to me why, after taking all that trouble to decorate it, they should have disfigured it with those great smears of bitumen?"

"Ah!" said Mr. Jellicoe, "that is quite an interesting question. It is not unusual to find mummy cases smeared with bitumen; there is a mummy of a priestess in the next gallery which is completely coated with bitumen except the gilded face. Now, this bitumen was put on for a purpose—for the purpose of obliterating the inscriptions and thus concealing the identity of the deceased from the robbers and desecrators of tombs. And there is the oddity of this mummy of Sebek-hotep. Evidently there was an intention of obliterating the inscriptions. The whole of the back is covered thickly with bitumen, and so are the feet. Then the workers seem to have changed their minds and left the inscriptions and decoration untouched. Why they intended to cover it, and why, having commenced, they left it partially covered only, is a mystery. The mummy was found in its original tomb and quite undisturbed, so far as tomb-robbers are concerned. Poor Bellingham was greatly puzzled as to what the explanation could be."

"Speaking of bitumen," said I, "reminds me of a question that has occurred to me. You know that this substance has been used a good deal by modern painters and that it has a very dangerous peculiarity; I mean its tendency to liquefy, without any obvious reason, long after it has dried."

"Yes, I know. Isn't there some story about a picture of Reynolds' in which bitumen had been used? A portrait of a lady, I think. The bitumen softened, and one of the lady's eyes slipped down on to her cheek; and they had to hang the portrait upside down and keep it warm until the eye slipped back again into its place. But what was your question?"

"I was wondering whether the bitumen used by the Egyptian artists has ever been known to soften after this great lapse of time."

"Yes, I think it has. I have heard of instances in which the bitumen coatings have softened under certain circumstances and become quite 'tacky.' But, bless my soul! here am I gossiping with you and wasting your time, and it is nearly a quarter to nine!"

My guest rose hastily, and I, with many apologies for having detained him, proceeded to fulfil my promise to guide him to his destination. As we sallied forth together the glamour of Egypt faded by degrees, and when he shook my hand stiffly at the gate of the Bellinghams' house, all his vivacity and enthusiasm had vanished, leaving the taciturn lawyer, dry, uncommunicative, and not a little suspicious.

CHAPTER X   The New Alliance

The "Great Lexicographer"—tutelary deity of my adopted habitat—has handed down to shuddering posterity a definition of the act of eating which might have been framed by a dyspeptic ghoul. "Eat: to devour with the mouth." It is a shocking view to take of so genial a function: cynical, indelicate, and finally unforgivable by reason of its very accuracy. For, after all, that is what eating amounts to, if one must needs express it with such crude brutality. But if "the ingestion of alimentary substances"—to ring a modern change upon the older formula—is in itself a process material even unto carnality, it is undeniable that it forms a highly agreeable accompaniment to more psychic manifestations.

And so, as the lamplight, reinforced by accessory candles, falls on the little table in the first-floor room looking on Fetter Lane—only now the curtains are drawn—the conversation is not the less friendly and bright for a running accompaniment executed with knives and forks, for clink of goblet, and jovial gurgle of wine-flask. On the contrary, to one of us, at least—to wit, Godfrey Bellingham—the occasion is one of uncommon festivity, and his boyish enjoyment of the simple feast makes pathetic suggestions of hard times, faced uncomplainingly, but keenly felt nevertheless.

The talk flitted from topic to topic, mainly concerning itself with matters artistic, and never for one moment approaching the critical subject of John Bellingham's will. From the stepped pyramid of Sakkara with its encaustic tiles to mediæval church floors; from

Elizabethan woodwork to Mycenæan pottery, and thence to the industrial arts of the Stone Age and the civilisation of the Aztecs. I began to suspect that my two legal friends were so carried away by the interest of the conversation that they had forgotten the secret purpose of the meeting; for the dessert had been placed on the table (by Mrs. Gummer with the manner of a bereaved dependant dispensing funeral bakemeats), and still no reference had been made to the "case." But it seemed that Thorndyke was but playing a waiting game; was only allowing the intimacy to ripen while he watched for the opportunity. And that opportunity came, even as Mrs. Gummer vanished spectrally with a tray of plates and glasses.

"So you had a visitor last night, Doctor," said Mr. Bellingham. "I mean my friend Jellicoe. He told us he had seen you, and mighty curious he was about you. I have never known Jellicoe to be so inquisitive before. What did you think of him?"

"A quaint old cock. I found him highly amusing. We entertained one another for quite a long time with cross-questions and crooked answers; I affecting eager curiosity, he replying with a defensive attitude of universal ignorance. It was a most diverting encounter."

"He needn't have been so close," Miss Bellingham remarked, "seeing that all the world will be regaled with our affairs before long."

"They are proposing to take the case into Court, then?" said Thorndyke.

"Yes," said Mr Bellingham. "Jellicoe came to tell me that my cousin, Hurst, has instructed his solicitors to make the application and to invite me to join him. Actually he came to deliver an ultimatum from Hurst— but I mustn't disturb the harmony of this festive gathering with litigious discords."

"Now, why mustn't you?" asked Thorndyke. "Why is a subject in which we are all keenly interested to be taboo? You don't mind telling us about it, do you?"

"No, of course not. But what do you think of a man who button-holes a doctor at a dinner-party to retail a list of ailments?"

"It depends on what his ailments are," replied Thorndyke. "If he is a chronic dyspeptic and wishes to expound the virtues of Dr. Snaffler's Purple Pills for Pimply People, he is merely a bore. But if he chances to suffer from some rare and choice disease, such as Trypanosomiasis or Acromegaly, the doctor will be delighted to listen."

"Then are we to understand," Miss Bellingham asked, "that we are rare and choice products, in a legal sense?"

"Undoubtedly," replied Thorndyke. "The case of John Bellingham is, in many respects, unique. It will be followed with the deepest interest by the profession at large, and especially by medical jurists."

"How gratifying that should be to us!" said Miss Bellingham. "We may even attain undying fame in text-books and treatises; and yet we are not so very much puffed up with our importance."

"No," said her father; "we could do without the fame quite well, and so, I think, could Hurst. Did Berkeley tell you of the proposal that he made?"

"Yes," said Thorndyke; "and I gather from what you say that he has repeated it."

"Yes. He sent Jellicoe to give me another chance, and I was tempted to take it; but my daughter was strongly against any compromise, and probably she is right. At any rate, she is more concerned than I am."

"What view did Mr. Jellicoe take?" Thorndyke asked.

"Oh, he was very cautious and reserved, but he didn't disguise his feeling that I should be wise to take a certainty in lieu of a very problematical fortune. He would certainly like me to agree, for he naturally wishes to get the affair settled and pocket his legacy."

"And have you definitely refused?"

"Yes; quite definitely. So Hurst will apply for permission to presume death and prove the will, and Jellicoe will support him; he says he has no choice."

"And you?"

"I suppose I shall oppose the application, though I don't quite know on what grounds."

"Before you take definite steps," said Thorndyke, "you ought to give the matter very careful consideration. I take it that you have very little doubt that your brother is dead. And if he is dead, any benefit that you may receive under the will must be conditional on the previous presumption or proof of death. But perhaps you have taken advice?"

"No, I have not. As our friend the Doctor has probably told you, my means—or rather, the lack of them—do not admit of my getting professional advice. Hence my delicacy about discussing the case with you."

"Then do you propose to conduct your case in person?"

"Yes; if it is necessary for me to appear in Court, as I suppose it will be, if I oppose the application."

Thorndyke reflected for a few moments and then said gravely:

"You had much better not appear in person to conduct your case, Mr. Bellingham, for several reasons. To begin with, Mr. Hurst is sure to be represented by a capable counsel, and you will find yourself quite unable to meet the sudden exigencies of a contest in Court. You will be out-manoeuvred. Then there is the judge to be considered."

"But surely one can rely on the judge dealing fairly with a man who is unable to afford a solicitor and counsel?"

"Undoubtedly, as a rule, a judge will give an unrepresented litigant every assistance and consideration. English judges in general are high-minded men with a deep sense of their great responsibilities. But you cannot afford to take any chances. You must consider the exceptions. A judge has been a counsel, and he may carry to the bench some of the professional prejudices of the bar. Indeed, if you consider the absurd licence permitted to counsel in their treatment of witnesses, and the hostile attitude adopted by some judges towards medical and other scientific men who have to give their evidence, you will see that the judicial mind is not always quite as judicial as one would wish, especially when the privileges and immunities of the profession are concerned. Now, your appearance in person to conduct your case must, unavoidably, cause some inconvenience to the Court. Your ignorance of procedure and legal details must occasion some delay; and if the judge should happen to be an irritable man he might resent the inconvenience and delay. I don't say that would affect his decision—I don't think it would—but I am sure it would be wise to avoid giving offence to the judge. And, above all, it is most desirable to be able to detect and reply to any manoeuvres on the part of the opposing counsel, which you certainly would not be able to do."

"This is excellent advice, Dr. Thorndyke," said Bellingham, with a grim smile; "but I'm afraid I shall have to take my chance."

"Not necessarily," said Thorndyke. "I am going to make a little proposal, which I will ask you to consider without prejudice as a mutual accommodation. You see, your case is one of exceptional interest—it will become a text-book case, as Miss Bellingham prophesied; and, since it lies within my speciality, it will be necessary for me to follow it in the closest detail. Now, it would be much more satisfactory to me to study it from within than from without, to say nothing of the credit which would accrue to me if I should be able to conduct it to a successful issue. I am therefore going to ask you to put your case in my hands and let me see what can be done with it. I know this is an unusual course for a professional man to take, but I think it is not improper under the circumstances."

Mr. Bellingham pondered in silence for a few moments, and then, after a glance at his daughter, began rather hesitatingly: "It's very generous of you, Dr. Thorndyke——"

"Pardon me," interrupted Thorndyke, "it is not. My motives, as I have explained, are purely egoistic."

Mr. Bellingham laughed uneasily and again glanced at his daughter, who, however, pursued her occupation of peeling a pear with calm deliberation and without lifting her eyes. Getting no help from her, he asked: "Do you think that there is any possibility whatever of a successful issue?"

"Yes, a remote possibility—very remote, I fear, as things look at present; but if I thought the case absolutely hopeless I should advise you to stand aside and let events take their course."

"Supposing the case should come to a favourable termination, would you allow me to settle your fees in the ordinary way?"

"If the choice lay with me," replied Thorndyke, "I should say 'yes' with pleasure. But it does not. The attitude of the profession is very definitely unfavourable to 'speculative' practice. You may remember the well-known firm of Dodson and Fogg, who gained thereby much profit, but little credit. But why discuss contingencies of this kind? If I bring your case to a successful issue I shall have done very well for myself. We shall have benefited one another mutually. Come now, Miss Bellingham, I appeal to you. We have eaten salt together, to say nothing of pigeon pie and other cates. Won't you back me up, and at the same time do a kindness to Dr. Berkeley?"

"Why, is Dr. Berkeley interested in our decision?"

"Certainly he is, as you will appreciate when I tell you that he actually tried to bribe me secretly out of his own pocket."

"Did you?" she asked, looking at me with an expression that rather alarmed me.

"Well, not exactly," I replied, mighty hot and uncomfortable, and wishing Thorndyke at the devil with his confidences. "I merely mentioned that the—the—solicitor's costs, you know, and that sort of thing—but you needn't jump on me, Miss Bellingham; Dr. Thorndyke did all that was necessary in that way."

She continued to look at me thoughtfully as I stammered out my excuses, and then said: "I wasn't going to. I was only thinking that poverty has its compensations. You are all so very good to us; and, for my part, I should accept Dr. Thorndyke's generous offer most gratefully, and thank him for making it so easy for us."

"Very well, my dear," said Mr. Bellingham; "we will enjoy the sweets of poverty, as you say—we have sampled the other kind of thing pretty freely—and do ourselves the pleasure of accepting a great kindness, most delicately offered."

"Thank you," said Thorndyke. "You have justified my faith in you, Miss Bellingham, and in the power of Dr. Berkeley's salt. I understand that you place your affairs in my hands?"

"Entirely and thankfully," replied Mr. Bellingham. "Whatever you think best to be done we agree to beforehand."

"Then," said I, "let us drink success to the cause. Port, if you please, Miss Bellingham; the vintage is not recorded, but it is quite wholesome, and a suitable medium for the sodium chloride of friendship." I filled her glass, and when the bottle had made its circuit, we stood up and solemnly pledged the new alliance.

"There is just one thing I would say before we dismiss the subject for the present," said Thorndyke. "It is a good thing to keep one's own counsel. When you get formal notice from Mr. Hurst's solicitors that proceedings are being commenced, you may refer them to Mr. Marchmont of Gray's Inn, who will nominally act for you. He will actually have nothing to do, but we must preserve the fiction that I am instructed by a solicitor. Meanwhile, and until the case goes into Court, I think it very necessary that neither Mr. Jellicoe nor anyone else should know that I am connected with it. We must keep the other side in the dark, if we can."

"We will be as secret as the grave," said Mr. Bellingham; "and, as a matter of fact, it will be quite easy, since it happens, by a curious coincidence, that I am already acquainted with Mr. Marchmont. He acted for Stephen Blackmore, you remember, in that case that you unravelled so wonderfully. I knew the Blackmores."

"Did you?" said Thorndyke. "What a small world it is. And what a remarkable affair that was! The intricacies and cross-issues made it quite absorbingly interesting; and it is noteworthy for me in another respect, for it was one of the first cases in which I was associated with Dr. Jervis."

"Yes, and a mighty useful associate I was," remarked Jervis, "though I did pick up one or two facts by accident. And, by the way, the Blackmore case had certain points in common with your case, Mr. Bellingham. There was a disappearance and a disputed will, and the man who vanished was a scholar and an antiquarian."

"Cases in our speciality are apt to have certain general resemblances," Thorndyke said; and as he spoke he directed a keen glance at his junior, the significance of which I partly understood when he abruptly changed the subject.

"The newspaper reports of your brother's disappearance, Mr. Bellingham, were remarkably full of detail. There were even plans of your house and that of Mr. Hurst. Do you know who supplied the information?"

"No, I don't," replied Mr. Bellingham. "I know that I didn't. Some newspaper men came to me for information, but I sent them packing. So, I understand, did Hurst; and as for Jellicoe, you might as well cross-examine an oyster."

"Well," said Thorndyke, "the pressmen have queer methods of getting 'copy'; but still, some one must have given them that description of your brother and those plans. It would be interesting to know who it was. However, we don't know; and now let us dismiss these legal topics, with suitable apologies for having introduced them."

"And perhaps," said I, "we may as well adjourn to what we will call the drawing-room—it is really Barnard's den—and leave the housekeeper to wrestle with the debris."

We migrated to the cheerfully shabby little apartment, and, when Mrs. Gummer had served coffee, with gloomy resignation (as who should say: "If you will drink this sort of stuff I suppose you must, but don't blame me for the consequences"), I settled Mr. Bellingham in Barnard's favourite lop-sided easy chair—the depressed seat of which suggested its customary use by an elephant of sedentary habits—and opened the diminutive piano.

"I wonder if Miss Bellingham would give us a little music?" I said.

"I wonder if she could?" was the smiling response. "Do you know," she continued, "I have not touched a piano for nearly two years? It will be quite an interesting experiment—to me; but, if it fails, you will be the sufferers. So you must choose."

"My verdict," said Mr. Bellingham, "is *fiat experimentum*, though I won't complete the quotation, as that would seem to disparage Dr. Barnard's piano. But before you begin, Ruth, there is one rather disagreeable matter that I want to dispose of, so that I may not disturb the harmony with it later."

He paused and we all looked at him expectantly.

"I suppose, Dr. Thorndyke," he said, "you read the newspapers?"

"I don't," replied Dr. Thorndyke. "But I ascertain, for purely business purposes, what they contain."

"Then," said Mr. Bellingham, "you have probably met with some accounts of the finding of certain human remains, apparently portions of a mutilated body."

"Yes, I have seen those reports and filed them for future reference."

"Exactly. Well, now, it can hardly be necessary for me to tell you that those remains—the mutilated remains of some poor murdered creature, as there can be no doubt they are—have seemed to have a very dreadful significance for me. You will understand what I mean and I want to ask you if—if they have made a similar suggestion to you?"

Thorndyke paused before replying, with his eyes bent thoughtfully on the floor, and we all looked at him anxiously.

"It is very natural," he said at length, "that you should associate these remains with the mystery of your brother's disappearance. I should like to say that you are wrong in doing so, but if I did I should be uncandid. There are certain facts that do, undoubtedly, seem to suggest a connection, and, up to the present, there are no definite facts of a contrary significance."

Mr. Bellingham sighed deeply and shifted uncomfortably in his chair.

"It is a horrible affair!" he said huskily; "horrible! Would you mind, Dr. Thorndyke, telling us just how the matter stands in your opinion—what the probabilities are, for and against?"

Again Thorndyke reflected awhile, and it seemed to me that he was not very willing to discuss the subject. However, the question had been asked pointedly, and eventually he answered:

"At the present stage of the investigation it is not very easy to state the balance of probabilities. The matter is still quite speculative. The bones which have been found hitherto (for we are dealing with a skeleton, not with a body) have been exclusively those which are useless for personal identification; which is, in itself, a rather curious and striking fact. The general character and dimensions of the bones seem to suggest a middle-aged man of about your brother's height, and the date of deposition appears to be in agreement with the date of his disappearance."

"Is it known, then, when they were deposited?" asked Mr. Bellingham.

"In the case of those found at Sidcup it seems possible to deduce an approximate date. The watercress-bed was cleaned out about two years ago, so they could not have been lying there longer than that; and their condition suggests that they could not have been there much less than two years, as there is apparently no vestige of the soft structures left. Of course, I am speaking from the newspaper reports only; I have no direct knowledge of the matter."

"Have they found any considerable part of the body yet? I haven't been reading the papers myself. My little friend, Miss Oman, brought a great bundle of 'em for me to read, but I couldn't stand it; I pitched the whole boiling of 'em out of the window."

I thought I detected a slight twinkle in Thorndyke's eye, but he answered quite gravely:

"I think I can give you the particulars from memory, though I won't guarantee the dates. The original discovery was made, apparently quite accidentally, at Sidcup on the fifteenth of July. It consisted of a complete left arm, minus the third finger and including the bones of the shoulder—the shoulder-blade and collar-bone. This discovery seems to have set the local population, especially the juvenile part of it, searching all the ponds and streams of the neighbourhood——"

"Cannibals!" interjected Mr. Bellingham.

"With the result that there was dredged up out of a pond near St. Mary Cray, in Kent, a right thigh-bone. There is a slight clue to identity in respect of this bone, since the head of it has a small patch of 'eburnation'— that is a sort of porcelain-like polish that occurs on the parts of bones that form a joint when the natural covering of cartilage is destroyed by disease. It is produced by the unprotected surface of the bone grinding against the similarly unprotected surface of another."

"And how," Mr. Bellingham asked, "would that help the identification?"

"It would indicate," Thorndyke replied, "that the deceased had probably suffered from rheumatoid arthritis—what is commonly known as rheumatic gout—and he would probably have limped slightly and complained of some pain in the right hip."

"I'm afraid that doesn't help us very much," said Mr. Bellingham; "for you see, John had a pretty pronounced limp from another cause, an old injury to his left ankle; and as to complaining of pain—well, he was a hardy old fellow and not much given to making complaints of any kind. But don't let me interrupt you."

"The next discovery," continued Thorndyke, "was made near Lee, by the police this time. They seem to have developed sudden activity in the matter, and in searching the neighbourhood of West Kent they dragged out of a pond near Lee the bones of a right foot. Now, if it had been the left instead of the right we might have a clue, as I understand your brother had fractured his left ankle, and there might have been some traces of the injury on the foot itself."

"Yes," said Mr. Bellingham. "I suppose there might. The injury was described as a Pott's fracture."

"Exactly. Well, now, after this discovery at Lee it seems that the police set on foot a systematic search of all the ponds and small pieces of water around London, and, on the twenty-third, they found in the Cuckoo Pits in Epping Forest, not far from Woodford, the bones of a right arm (including those of the shoulder, as before), which seem to be part of the same body."

"Yes," said Mr. Bellingham, "I heard of that. Quite close to my old house. Horrible! horrible! It gave me the shudders to think of it—to think that poor old John may have been waylaid and murdered when he was actually coming to see me. He may even have got into the grounds by the back gate, if it was left unfastened, and been followed in there and murdered. You remember that a scarab from his watch-chain was found there? But is it clear that this arm was the fellow of the arm that was found at Sidcup?"

"It seems to agree in character and dimensions," said Thorndyke, "and the agreement is strongly supported by a discovery made two days later."

"What is that?" Mr. Bellingham demanded.

"It is the lower half of a trunk which the police dragged out of a rather deep pond on the skirts of the forest at Loughton—Staple's Pond, it is called. The bones found were the pelvis—that is, the two hipbones—and six vertebra, or joints of the backbone. Having discovered these, the police dammed the stream and pumped the pond dry, but no other bones were found; which is rather odd, as there should have been a pair of ribs belonging to the upper vertebra—the twelfth dorsal vertebra. It suggests some curious questions as to the method of dismemberment; but I mustn't go into unpleasant details. The point is that the cavity of the right hip-joint showed a patch of eburnation corresponding to that on the head of the right thigh-bone that was found at St. Mary Cray. So there can be very little doubt that these bones are all part of the same body."

"I see," grunted Mr. Bellingham; and he added, after a moment's thought: "Now, the question is, Are these bones the remains of my brother John? What do you say,

Dr. Thorndyke?"

"I say that the question cannot be answered on the facts at present known to us. It can only be said that they may be, and that some of the circumstances suggest that they are. But we can only wait for further discoveries. At any moment the police may light upon some portion of the skeleton which will settle the question definitely one way or the other."

"I suppose," said Mr. Bellingham, "I can't be of any service to you in the matter of identification?"

"Indeed you can," said Thorndyke, "and I was going to ask you to assist me. What I want you to do is this: Write down a full description of your brother, including every detail known to you, together with an account of every illness or injury from which you know him to have suffered; also the names and, if possible, the addresses of any doctors, surgeons, or dentists who may have attended him at any time. The dentists are particularly important, as their information would be invaluable if the skull belonging to these bones should be discovered."

Mr. Bellingham shuddered.

"It's a shocking idea," he said, "but, of course you are right. You must have the facts if you are to form an opinion. I will write out what you want and send it to you without delay. And now, for God's sake, let us throw off this nightmare, for a little while, at least! What is there, Ruth, among Dr. Barnard's music that you can manage?"

Barnard's collection in general inclined to the severely classical, but we disinterred from the heap a few lighter works of an old-fashioned kind, including a volume of Mendelssohn's *Lieder ohne Worte*, and with one of these Miss Bellingham made trial of her skill, playing it with excellent taste and quite adequate execution. That, at least, was her father's verdict; for, as to me, I found it the perfection of happiness merely to sit and look at her—a state of mind that would have been in no wise disturbed even by "Silvery Waves" or "The Maiden's Prayer."

Thus with simple, homely music, and conversation always cheerful and sometimes brilliant, slipped away one of the pleasantest evenings of my life, and slipped away all too soon. St. Dunstan's clock was the fly in the ointment, for it boomed out intrusively the hour of eleven just as my guests were beginning thoroughly to appreciate one another, and thereby carried the sun (with a minor paternal satellite) out of the firmament of my heaven. For I had, in my professional capacity, given strict injunctions that Mr Bellingham should on no account sit up late; and now, in my social capacity, I had smilingly to hear "the doctor's orders" quoted. It was a scurvy return for all my care.

When Mr. and Miss Bellingham departed, Thorndyke and Jervis would have gone too; but noting my bereaved condition, and being withal compassionate and tender of heart, they were persuaded to stay awhile and bear me company in a consolatory pipe.

CHAPTER XI   The Evidence Reviewed

"So the game has opened," observed Thorndyke, as he struck a match. "The play has begun with a cautious lead off by the other side. Very cautious and not very confident."

"Why do you say 'not very confident'?" I asked.

"Well, it is evident that Hurst—and, I fancy, Jellicoe too—is anxious to buy off Bellingham's opposition, and at a pretty long price, under the circumstances. And when we consider how very little Bellingham has to offer against the presumption of his brother's death, it looks as if Hurst hadn't much to say on his side."

"No," said Jervis, "he can't hold many trumps or he wouldn't be willing to pay four hundred a year for his opponent's chance; and that is just as well, for it seems to me that our own hand is a pretty poor one."

"We must look through our hand and see what we do hold," said Thorndyke. "Our trump card at present—a rather small one, I'm afraid—is the obvious intention of the testator that the bulk of the property should go to his brother."

"I suppose you will begin your inquiries now?" I said.

"We began them some time ago—the day after you brought us the will, in fact. Jervis has been through the registers and has ascertained that no interment under the name of John Bellingham has taken place since the disappearance; which was just what we expected. He has also discovered that some other person has been making similar inquiries; which, again, is what we expected."

"And your own investigations?"

"Have given negative results for the most part. I found Dr. Norbury, at the British Museum, very friendly and helpful; so friendly, in fact, that I am thinking whether I may not be able to enlist his help in certain private researches of my own, with reference to the change effected by time in the physical properties of certain substances."

"Oh; you haven't told me about that," said Jervis.

"No; I haven't really commenced to plan my experiments yet, and they will probably lead to nothing when I do. It occurred to me that, possibly, in the course of time, certain molecular changes might take place in substances such as wood, bone, pottery, stucco, and other common materials, and that these changes might alter their power of conducting or transmitting molecular vibrations. Now, if this should turn out to be the case, it would be a fact of considerable importance, medico-legally and otherwise; for it would be possible to determine approximately the age of any object of known composition by testing its reactions to electricity, heat, light, and other molecular vibrations. I thought of seeking Dr. Norbury's assistance because he can furnish me with materials for experiment of such great age that the reactions, if any, should be extremely easy to demonstrate. But to return to our case. I learned from him that John Bellingham had certain friends in Paris—collectors and museum officials—whom he was in the habit of visiting for the purpose of study and exchange of specimens. I have made inquiries of all these, and none of them had seen him during his last visit. In fact, I have not yet discovered anyone who had seen Bellingham in Paris on this occasion. So his visit there remains a mystery for the present."

"It doesn't seem to be of much importance, since he undoubtedly came back," I remarked; but to this Thorndyke demurred.

"It is impossible to estimate the importance of the unknown," said he.

"Well, how does the matter stand," asked Jervis, "on the evidence that we have? John Bellingham disappeared on a certain date. Is there anything to show what was the manner of his disappearance?"

"The facts in our possession," said Thorndyke, "which are mainly those set forth in the newspaper report, suggest several alternative possibilities; and in view of the coming inquiry—for they will, no doubt, have to be gone into in Court, to some extent—it may be worth while to consider them There are five conceivable hypotheses"—here Thorndyke checked them on his fingers as he proceeded—"First, he may still be alive. Second, he may have died and been buried without identification. Third, he may have been murdered by some unknown person. Fourth, he may have been murdered by Hurst and his body concealed. Fifth, he may have been murdered by his brother. Let us examine these possibilities seriatim.

"First, he may still be alive. If he is, he must either have disappeared voluntarily, have lost his memory suddenly and not been identified, or have been imprisoned—on a false charge or otherwise. Let us take the first case—that of voluntary disappearance. Obviously, its improbability is extreme."

"Jellicoe doesn't think so," said I. " He thinks it quite on the cards that John Bellingham is alive. He says that it is not a very unusual thing for a man to disappear for a time."

"Then why is he applying for a presumption of death?"

"Just what I asked him. He says that it is the correct thing to do; that the entire responsibility rests on the Court."

"That is all nonsense," said Thorndyke. "Jellicoe is the trustee for his absent client, and, if he thinks that client is alive, it is his duty to keep the estate intact; and he knows that perfectly well. We may take it that Jellicoe is of the same opinion as I am, that John Bellingham is dead."

"Still," I urged, "men do disappear from time to time, and turn up again after years of absence."

"Yes, but for a definite reason. Either they are irresponsible vagabonds who take this way of shuffling off their responsibilities, or they are men who have been caught in a net of distasteful circumstances. For instance, a civil servant or a solicitor or a tradesman finds himself bound for life to a locality and an occupation of intolerable monotony. Perhaps he has an ill-tempered wife, who after the amiable fashion of a certain type of woman, thinking that her husband is pinned down without a chance of escape, gives a free rein to her temper. The man puts up with it for years, but at last it becomes unbearable. Then he suddenly disappears; and small blame to him. But this was not Bellingham's case. He was a wealthy bachelor with an engrossing interest in life, free to go whither he would and to do whatsoever he wished. Why should he disappear? The thing is incredible.

"As to his having lost his memory and remained unidentified, that, also, is incredible in the case of a man who had visiting-cards and letters in his pocket, whose linen was marked, and who was being inquired for everywhere by the police. As to his being in prison, we may dismiss that possibility, inasmuch as a prisoner, both before and after conviction, would have full opportunity of communicating with his friends.

"The second possibility, that he may have died suddenly and been buried without identification, is highly improbable; but, as it is conceivable that the body might have been robbed and the means of identification thus lost, it remains as a possibility that has to be considered, remote as it is.

"The third hypothesis, that he may have been murdered by some unknown person, is, under the circumstances, not wildly improbable; but, as the police were on the lookout and a detailed description of the missing man's person was published in the papers, it would involve the complete concealment of the body. But this would exclude the most probable form of crime—the casual robbery with violence. It is therefore possible, but highly improbable.

"The fourth hypothesis is that Bellingham was murdered by Hurst. Now the one fact which militates against this view is that Hurst apparently had no motive for committing the murder. We are assured by Jellicoe that no one but himself knew the contents of the will, and if this is so—but mind, we have no evidence that it is so—Hurst would have no reason to suppose that he had anything material to gain by his cousin's death. Otherwise the hypothesis presents no inherent improbabilities. The man was last seen alive at Hurst's house. He was seen to enter it and he was never seen to leave it—we are still taking the facts as stated in the newspapers, remember—and it now appears that he stands to benefit enormously by that man's death."

"But," I objected, "you are forgetting that, directly the man was missed, Hurst and the servants together searched the entire house."

"Yes. What did they search for?"

"Why, for Mr. Bellingham, of course."

"Exactly; for Mr. Bellingham. That is, for a living man. Now how do you search a house for a living man? You look in all the rooms. When you look in a room if he is there, you see him; if you do not see him, you assume that he is not there. You don't look under the sofa or behind the piano, you don't pull out large drawers or open cupboards. You just look into the rooms. That is what these people seem to have done. And they did not see Mr. Bellingham. Mr. Bellingham's corpse might have been stowed away out of sight in any one of the rooms that they looked into."

"That is a grim thought," said Jervis; "but it is perfectly true. There is no evidence that the man was not lying dead in the house at the very time of the search."

"But even so," said I, "there was the body to be disposed of somehow. Now how could he possibly have got rid of the body without being observed?"

"Ah!" said Thorndyke, "now we are touching on a point of crucial importance. If anyone should ever write a treatise on the art of murder—not an exhibition of literary fireworks like De Quincey's, but a genuine working treatise—he might leave all other technical details to take care of themselves if he could describe some really practicable plan for disposing of the body. That is, and always has been, the great stumbling block to the murderer: to get rid of the body. The human body," he continued, thoughtfully regarding his pipe, just as, in the days of my pupilage, he was wont to regard the blackboard chalk, "is a very remarkable object. It presents a combination of properties that makes it singularly difficult to conceal permanently. It is bulky and of an awkward shape, it is heavy, it is completely incombustible, it is chemically unstable, and its decomposition yields great volumes of highly odorous gases, and it nevertheless contains identifiable structures of the highest degree of permanence. It is extremely difficult to preserve unchanged, and it is still more difficult completely to destroy. The essential permanence of the human body is well shown in the classical case of Eugene Aram; but a still more striking instance is that of Sekenen-Ra the Third, one of the last kings of the seventeenth Egyptian dynasty. Here, after a lapse of four thousand years, it has been possible to determine not only the cause of death and the manner of its occurrence, but the way in which the king fell, the nature of the weapon with which the fatal wound was inflicted, and even the position of the assailant. And the permanence of the body under other conditions is admirably shown in the case of

Dr. Parkman, of Boston, U.S.A., in which identification was actually effected by means of remains collected from the ashes of a furnace."

"Then we may take it," said Jervis, "that the world has not yet seen the last of John Bellingham."

"I think we may regard that as almost a certainty," replied Thorndyke. "The only question—and a very important one—is as to when the reappearance may take place. It may be to-morrow or it may be centuries hence, when all the issues involved have been forgotten."

"Assuming," said I, "for the sake of argument, that Hurst did murder him and that the body was concealed in the study at the time the search was made. How could it have been disposed of? If you had been in Hurst's place, how would you have gone to work?"

Thorndyke smiled at the bluntness of my question.

"You are asking me for an incriminating statement," said he, "delivered in the presence of a witness too. But, as a matter of fact, there is no use in speculating *a priori*; we should have to reconstruct a purely imaginary situation, the circumstances of which are unknown to us, and we should almost certainly reconstruct it wrong. What we may fairly assume is that no reasonable person, no matter how immoral, would find himself in the position that you suggest. Murder is usually a crime of impulse, and the murderer a person of feeble self-control. Such persons are most unlikely to make elaborate and ingenious arrangements for the disposal of the bodies of their victims. Even the cold-blooded perpetrators of the most carefully planned murders appear, as I have said, to break down at this point. The almost insuperable difficulty of getting rid of the human body is not appreciated until the murderer suddenly finds himself face to face with it.

"In the case you are suggesting, the choice would seem to lie between burial on the premises or dismemberment and dispersal of the fragments; and either method would be pretty certain to lead to discovery."

"As illustrated by the remains of which you were speaking to Mr. Bellingham," Jervis remarked.

"Exactly," Thorndyke answered, "though we could hardly imagine a reasonably intelligent criminal adopting a watercress-bed as a hiding-place."

"No. That was certainly an error of judgment. By the way, I thought it best to say nothing while you were talking to Bellingham, but I noticed that, in discussing the possibility of those being the bones of his brother, you made no comment on the absence of the third finger of the left hand. I am sure you didn't overlook it, but isn't it a point of some importance?"

"As to identification? Under the present circumstances, I think not. If there were a man missing who had lost that finger it would, of course, be an important fact. But I have not heard of any such man. Or, again, if there were any evidence that the finger had been removed before death, it would be highly important. But there is no such evidence. It may have been cut off after death, and that is where the real significance of its absence lies."

"I don't quite see what you mean," said Jervis.

"I mean that, if there is no report of any missing man who had lost that particular finger, the probability is that the finger was removed after death. And then arises the interesting question of motive. Why should it have been removed? It could hardly have become detached accidentally. What do you suggest?"

"Well," said Jervis, "it might have been a peculiar finger; a finger, for instance, with some characteristic deformity such as an ankylosed joint, which would be easy to identify."

"Yes; but that explanation introduces the same difficulty. No person with a deformed or ankylosed finger has been reported as missing."

Jervis puckered up his brows, and looked at me.

"I'm hanged if I see any other explanation," he said. "Do you, Berkeley?"

I shook my head.

"Don't forget which finger it is that is missing," said Thorndyke. "The third finger of the left hand."

"Oh, I see!" said Jervis. "The ring-finger. You mean that it may have been removed for the sake of a ring that wouldn't come off."

"Yes. It would not be the first instance of the kind. Fingers have been severed from dead hands—and even from living ones—for the sake of rings that were too tight to be drawn off. And the fact that it is the left hand supports the suggestion; for a ring that was inconveniently tight would be worn by preference on the left hand, as that is usually slightly smaller than the right. What is the matter, Berkeley?"

A sudden light had burst upon me, and I suppose my countenance betrayed the fact.

"I am a confounded fool!" I exclaimed.

"Oh, don't say that," said Jervis. "Give your friends a chance."

"I ought to have seen this long ago and told you about it. John Bellingham did wear a ring, and it was so tight that, when once he had got it on, could never get it off again."

"Do you happen to know on which hand he wore it?" Thorndyke asked.

"Yes. It was on the left hand; because Miss Bellingham, who told me about it, said that he would never have been able to get the ring on at all but for the fact that his left hand was slightly smaller than his right."

"There it is, then," said Thorndyke. "With this new fact in our possession, the absence of the finger furnishes the starting-point of some very curious speculations."

"As for instance?" said Jervis.

"Ah, under the circumstances, I must leave you to pursue those speculations independently. I am now acting for Mr. Bellingham."

Jervis grinned and was silent for a while, refilling his pipe thoughtfully; but when he had got it alight he resumed.

"To return to the question of the disappearance; you don't consider it highly improbable that Bellingham might have been murdered by Hurst?"

"Oh, don't imagine I am making an accusation. I am considering the various probabilities merely in the abstract. The same reasoning applies to the Bellinghams. As to whether any of them did commit the murder, that is a question of personal character. I certainly do not suspect the Bellinghams after having seen them, and with regard to Hurst, I know nothing, or at least very little, to his disadvantage."

"Do you know anything?" asked Jervis.

"Well," Thorndyke said, with some hesitation, "it seems a thought unkind to rake up the little details of a man's past, and yet it has to be done. I have, of course, made the usual routine inquiries concerning the parties to this affair, and this is what they have brought to light:

"Hurst, as you know, is a stockbroker—a man of good position and reputation; but, about ten years ago, he seems to have committed an indiscretion, to put it mildly, which nearly got him into rather serious difficulties. He appears to have speculated rather heavily and considerably beyond his means, for, when a sudden spasm of the markets upset his calculations, it turned out that he had been employing his clients' capital and securities. For a time it looked as if there was going to be serious trouble; then, quite unexpectedly, he managed to raise the necessary amount in some way and settle all claims. Whence he got the money has never been discovered to this day, which is a curious circumstance, seeing that the deficiency was rather over five thousand pounds; but the important fact is that he did get it and that he paid up all that he owed. So that he was only a potential defaulter, so to speak; and discreditable as the affair undoubtedly was, it does not seem to have any direct bearing on this present case."

"No," Jervis agreed, "though it makes one consider his position with more attention than one would otherwise."

"Undoubtedly," said Thorndyke. "A reckless gambler is a man whose conduct cannot be relied on. He is subject to vicissitudes of fortune which may force him into other kinds of wrongdoing. Many an embezzlement has been preceded by an unlucky plunge on the turf."

"Assuming the responsibility for this disappearance to lie between Hurst and—and the Bellinghams," said I, with an uncomfortable gulp as I mentioned the names of my friends, "to which side does the balance of probability incline?"

"To the side of Hurst, I should say, without doubt," replied Thorndyke. "The case stands thus—on the facts presented to us: Hurst appears to have had no motive for killing the deceased (as we will call him); but the man was seen to enter the house, was never seen to leave it, and was never again seen alive. Bellingham, on the other hand, had a motive, as he had believed himself to be the principal beneficiary under the will. But the deceased was not seen at his house, and there is no evidence that he went to the house or to the neighbourhood, excepting the scarab that was found there. But the evidence of the scarab is vitiated by the fact that Hurst was present when it was picked up, and that it was found on a spot over which Hurst had passed only a few minutes previously. Until Hurst is cleared, it seems to me that the presence of the scarab proves nothing against the Bellinghams."

"Then your opinions on the case," said I, "are based entirely on the facts that have been made public."

"Yes, mainly. I do not necessarily accept those facts just as they are presented, and I may have certain views of my own on the case. But if I have, I do not feel in a position to discuss them. For the present, discussion has to be limited to the facts and inferences offered by the parties concerned."

"There!" exclaimed Jervis, rising to knock his pipe out, "that is where Thorndyke has you. He lets you think you're in the thick of the 'know' until one fine morning you wake up and discover that you have only been a gaping outsider; and then you are mightily astonished— and so are the other side, too, for that matter. But we must really be off now, mustn't we, reverend senior?"

"I suppose we must," replied Thorndyke; and, as he drew on his gloves, he asked: "Have you heard from Barnard lately?"

"Oh, yes," I answered. "I wrote to him at Smyrna to say that the practice was flourishing and that I was quite happy and contented, and that he might stay away as long as he liked. He writes by return that he will prolong his holiday if an opportunity offers, but will let me know later."

"Gad," said Jervis, "it was a stroke of luck for Barnard that Bellingham happened to have such a magnificent daughter—there! don't mind me, old man. You go in and win—she's worth it, isn't she, Thorndyke?"

"Miss Bellingham is a very charming young lady," replied Thorndyke. "I am most favourably impressed by both the father and the daughter, and I only trust that we may be able to be of some service to them." With this sedate little speech Thorndyke shook my hand, and I watched my two friends go on their way until their fading shapes were swallowed up in the darkness of Fetter Lane.

CHAPTER XII   A Voyage of Discovery

It was two or three mornings after my little supper party that, as I stood in the consulting-room brushing my hat preparatory to starting on my morning round, Adolphus appeared at the door to announce two gentlemen waiting in the surgery. I told him to bring them in, and a moment later Thorndyke entered, accompanied by Jervis. I noted that they looked uncommonly large in that little apartment, especially Thorndyke, but I had no time to consider this phenomenon, for the latter, when he had shaken my hand, proceeded at once to explain the object of their visit.

"We have come to ask a favour, Berkeley," he said; "to ask you to do us a very great service in the interests of your friends the Bellinghams."

"You know I shall be delighted," I said warmly. "What is it?"

"I will explain. You know—or perhaps you don't—that the police have collected all the bones that have been discovered and deposited them in the mortuary at Woodford, where they are to be viewed by the coroner's jury. Now, it has become imperative that I should have more definite and reliable information than I can get from the newspapers. The natural thing for me would be to go down and examine them myself, but there are circumstances that make it very desirable that my connection with the case should not leak out. Consequently, I can't go myself, and, for the same reason, I can't send Jervis. On the other hand, as it is now stated pretty openly that the police consider the bones to be almost certainly those of John Bellingham, it would seem perfectly natural that you, as Godfrey Bellingham's doctor, should go down to view them on his behalf."

"I should like to," I said. "I would give anything to go; but how is it to be managed? It would mean a whole day off and leaving the practice to look after itself."

"I think it could be managed," said Thorndyke; "and the matter is really important for two reasons. One is that the inquest opens to-morrow, and some one certainly ought to be there to watch the proceedings on Godfrey's behalf; and the other is that our client has received notice from Hurst's solicitors that the application will be heard in the Probate Court in a few days."

"Isn't that rather sudden?" I asked.

"It certainly suggests that there has been a good deal more activity than we were given to understand. But you see the importance of the affair. The inquest will be a sort of dress rehearsal for the Probate Court, and it is quite essential that we should have a chance of estimating the management."

"Yes, I see that. But how are we to manage about the practice?"

"We shall find you a substitute."

"Through a medical agent?"

"Yes," said Jervis, "Turcival will find us a man; in fact, he has done it. I saw him this morning; he has a man who is waiting up in town to negotiate for the purchase of a practice and who would do the job for a couple of guineas. Quite a reliable man. Only say the word, and I will run off to Adam Street and engage him definitely."

"Very well. You engage the locum tenens, and I will be prepared to start for Woodford as soon as he turns up."

"Excellent!" said Thorndyke. "That is a great weight off my mind. And if you could manage to drop in this evening and smoke a pipe with us we could talk over the plan of campaign and let you know what items of information we are particularly in want of."

I promised to turn up at King's Bench Walk as soon after half-past eight as possible, and my two friends then took their departure, leaving me to set out in high spirits on my scanty round of visits.

It is surprising what different aspects things present from different points of view; how relative are our estimates of the conditions and circumstances of life. To the urban workman—the journeyman baker, or tailor, for instance, labouring year in year out in a single building—a holiday ramble on Hampstead Heath is a veritable voyage of discovery; whereas to the sailor the shifting panorama of the whole wide world is but the commonplace of the day's work.

So I reflected as I took my place in the train at Liverpool Street on the following day. There had been a time when a trip by rail to the borders of Epping Forest would have been far from a thrilling experience; now, after vegetating in the little world of Fetter Lane, it was quite an adventure.

The enforced inactivity of a railway journey is favourable to thought, and I had much to think about. The last few weeks had witnessed momentous changes in my outlook. New interests had arisen, new friendships had grown up, and, above all, there had stolen into my life that supreme influence that, for good or for evil, according to my fortune, was to colour and pervade it even to its close. Those few days of companionable labour in the reading-room, with the homely hospitalities of the milk-shop and the pleasant walks homeward through the friendly London streets, had called into existence a new world—a world in which the gracious personality of Ruth Bellingham was the one dominating reality. And thus, as I leaned back in the corner of the railway carriage with an unlighted pipe in my hand, the events of the immediate past, together with those more problematical ones of the impending future, occupied me rather to the exclusion of the business of the moment, which was to review the remains collected in the Woodford mortuary, until, as the train approached Stratford, the odours of the soap and bone-manure factories poured in at the open window and (by a natural association of ideas) brought me back to the object of my quest.

As to the exact purpose of this expedition, I was not very clear; but I knew that I was acting as Thorndyke's proxy and thrilled with pride at the thought. But what particular light my investigations were to throw upon the intricate Bellingham case I had no very definite idea. With a view to fixing the procedure in my mind, I took Thorndyke's written instructions from my pocket and read them over carefully. They were very full and explicit, making ample allowance for my lack of experience in medico-legal matters:

"1. Do not appear to make minute investigations or in any way excite remark.

"2. Ascertain if all the bones belonging to each region are present, and if not, which are missing.

"3. Measure the extreme length of the principal bones and compare those of opposite sides.

"4. Examine the bones with reference to age, sex, and muscular development of the deceased.

"5. Note the presence or absence of signs of constitutional disease, local disease of bone or adjacent structures, old or recent injuries, and any other departures from the normal or usual.

"6. Observe the presence or absence of adipocere and its position, if present.

"7. Note any remains of tendons, ligaments, or other soft structures.

"8. Examine the Sidcup hand with reference to the question as to whether the finger was separated before or after death.

"9. Estimate the probable period of submersion and note any changes (as e.g. mineral or organic staining) due to the character of the water or mud.

"10. Ascertain the circumstances (immediate and remote) that led to the discovery of the bones and the names of the persons concerned in those circumstances.

"11. Commit all information to writing as soon as possible, and make plans and diagrams on the spot, if circumstances permit.

"12. Preserve an impassive exterior; listen attentively but without eagerness; ask as few questions as possible; pursue any inquiry that your observations on the spot may suggest."

These were my instructions, and, considering that I was going merely to inspect a few dry bones, they appeared rather formidable; in fact, the more I read them over the greater became my misgivings as to my qualifications for the task.

As I approached the mortuary it became evident that some, at least, of Thorndyke's admonitions were by no means unnecessary. The place was in charge of a police sergeant, who watched my approach suspiciously; and some half-dozen men, obviously newspaper reporters, hovered about the entrance like a pack of jackals. I presented the coroner's order which Mr. Marchmont had obtained, and which the sergeant read with his back against the wall, to prevent the newspaper men from looking over his shoulder.

My credentials being found satisfactory, the door was unlocked and I entered, accompanied by three enterprising reporters, whom, however, the sergeant summarily ejected and locked out, returning to usher me into the presence and to observe my proceedings with intelligent but highly embarrassing interest.

The bones were laid out on a large table and covered with a sheet, which the sergeant slowly turned back, watching my face intently as he did so to note the impression that the spectacle made upon me. I imagine that he must have been somewhat disappointed by my impassive demeanour, for the remains suggested to me nothing more than a rather shabby set of "student's osteology." The whole collection had been set out by the police surgeon (as the sergeant informed me) in their proper anatomical order; notwithstanding which I counted them over carefully to make sure that none were missing, checking them by the list with which Thorndyke had furnished me.

"I see you have found the left thigh-bone," I remarked, observing that this did not appear in the list.

"Yes," said the sergeant; "that turned up yesterday evening in a big pond called Baldwin's Pond in the

Sandpit plain, near Little Monk Wood."

"Is that near here?" I asked.

"In the forest up Loughton way," was the reply.

I made a note of the fact (on which the sergeant looked as if he was sorry he had mentioned it), and then turned my attention to a general consideration of the bones before examining them in detail. Their appearance would have been improved and examination facilitated by a thorough scrubbing, for they were just as they had been taken from their respective resting-places, and it was difficult to decide whether their reddish-yellow colour was an actual stain or due to a deposit on the surface. In any case, as it affected them all alike, I thought it an interesting feature and made a note of it. They bore numerous traces of their sojourn in the various ponds from which they had been recovered, but these gave me little help in determining the length of time during which they had been submerged. They were, of course, encrusted with mud, and little wisps of pond-weed stuck to them in places; but these facts furnished only the vaguest measure of time.

Some of the traces were, indeed, more informing. To several of the bones, for instance, there adhered the dried egg-clusters of the common pond-snail, and in one of the hollows of the right shoulder-blade (the "infra-spinous fossa") was a group of the mud-built tubes of the red river-worm. These remains gave proof of a considerable period of submersion, and since they could not have been deposited on the bones until all the flesh had disappeared they furnished evidence that some time—a month or two, at any rate—had elapsed since this had happened. Incidentally, too, their distribution showed the position in which the bones had lain, and though this appeared to be of no importance in the existing circumstances, I made careful notes of the situation of each adherent body, illustrating their position by rough sketches.

The sergeant watched my proceedings with an indulgent smile.

"You're making a regular inventory, sir," he remarked, "as if you were going to put 'em up for auction. I shouldn't think those snails' eggs would be much help in identification. And all that has been done already," he added as I produced my measuring-tape.

"No doubt," I replied; "but my business is to make independent observations, to check the others, if necessary." And I proceeded to measure each of the principal bones separately and to compare those of the opposite sides. The agreement in dimensions and general characteristics of the pairs of bones left little doubt that all were parts of one skeleton, a conclusion that was confirmed by the eburnated patch on the head of the right thigh-bone and the corresponding patch in the socket of the right hip-bone. When I had finished my measurements I went over the entire series of bones in detail, examining each with the closest attention for any of those signs which Thorndyke had indicated, and eliciting nothing but a monotonously reiterated negative. They were distressingly and disappointingly normal.

"Well, sir, what do you make of 'em?" the sergeant asked cheerfully as I shut up my notebook and straightened my back. "Whose bones are they? Are they Mr. Bellingham's, think ye?"

"I should be very sorry to say whose bones they are," I replied. "One bone is very much like another, you know."

"I suppose it is," he agreed; "but I thought that, with all that measuring and all those notes, you might have arrived at something definite." Evidently he was disappointed in me; and I was somewhat disappointed in myself when I contrasted Thorndyke's elaborate instructions with the meagre result of my investigations. For what did my discoveries amount to? And how much was the inquiry advanced by the few entries in my notebook?

The bones were apparently those of a man of fair though not remarkable muscular development; over thirty years of age, but how much older I was unable to say. His height I judged roughly to be five feet eight inches, but my measurements would furnish data for more exact estimate by Thorndyke. Beyond this the bones were quite uncharacteristic. There were no signs of disease either local or general, no indications of injuries either old or recent, no departures of any kind from the normal or usual; and the dismemberment had been effected with such care that there was not a single scratch on any of the separated surfaces. Of adipocere (the peculiar waxy or soapy substance that is commonly found in bodies that have slowly decayed in damp situations) there was not a trace; and the only remnant of the soft structures was a faint indication, like a spot of dried glue, of the tendon on the tip of the right elbow.

The sergeant was in the act of replacing the sheet, with the air of a showman who has just given an exhibition, when there came a sharp rapping on the mortuary door. The officer finished spreading the sheet with official precision, and, having ushered me out into the lobby, turned the key and admitted three persons, holding the door open after they had entered for me to go out. But the appearance of the newcomers inclined me to linger. One of them was a local constable, evidently in official charge; a second was a labouring man, very wet and muddy, who carried a small sack; while in the third I thought I scented a professional brother.

The sergeant continued to hold the door open.

"Nothing more I can do for you, sir?" he asked genially.

"Is that the divisional surgeon?" I inquired.

"Yes. I am the divisional surgeon," the new-comer answered. "Did you want anything of me?"

"This," said the sergeant, "is a medical gentleman who has got permission from the coroner to inspect the remains. He is acting for the family of the deceased—I mean, for the family of Mr. Bellingham," he added in answer to an inquiring glance from the surgeon.

"I see," said the latter. "Well, they have found the rest of the trunk, including, I understand, the ribs that were missing from the other part. Isn't that so, Davis?"

"Yes, sir," replied the constable. "Inspector Badger says all the ribs is here, and all the bones of the neck as well."

"The inspector seems to be an anatomist," I remarked.

The sergeant grinned. "He is a very knowing gentleman, is Mr. Badger. He came down here this morning quite early and spent a long time looking over the bones and checking them by some notes in his pocket-book. I fancy he's got something on, but he was precious close about it."

Here the sergeant shut up rather suddenly—perhaps contrasting his own conduct with that of his superior.

"Let us have these new bones out on the table," said the police surgeon. "Take the sheet off, and don't shoot them out as if they were coals. Hand them out carefully."

The labourer fished out the wet and muddy bones one by one from the sack, and as he laid them on the table the surgeon arranged them in their proper relative positions.

"This has been a neatly executed job," he remarked; "none of your clumsy hacking with a chopper or a saw.

The bones have been cleanly separated at the joints. The fellow who did this must have had some anatomical knowledge, unless he was a butcher, which by the way, is not impossible. He has used his knife uncommonly skilfully, and you notice that each arm was taken off with the scapula attached, just as a butcher takes off a shoulder of mutton. Are there any more bones in that bag?"

"No, sir," replied the labourer, wiping his hands with an air of finality on the posterior aspect of his trousers; "that's the lot."

The surgeon looked thoughtfully at the bones as he gave a final touch to their arrangement, and remarked:

"The inspector is right. All the bones of the neck are there. Very odd. Don't you think so?"

"You mean——"

"I mean that this very eccentric murderer seems to have given himself such an extraordinary amount of trouble for no reason that one can see. There are these neck vertebrae, for instance. He must have carefully separated the skull from the atlas instead of just cutting through the neck. Then there is the way he divided the trunk; the twelfth ribs have just come in with this lot, but the twelfth dorsal vertebra to which they belong was attached to the lower half. Imagine the trouble he must have taken to do that, and without cutting or hacking the bones about, either. It is extraordinary. This is rather interesting, by the way. Handle it carefully."

He picked up the breast-bone daintily—for it was covered with wet mud—and handed it to me with the remark:

"That is the most definite piece of evidence we have."

"You mean," I said, "that the union of the two parts into a single mass fixes this as the skeleton of an elderly man?"

"Yes, that is the obvious suggestion, which is confirmed by the deposit of bone in the rib-cartilages. You can tell the inspector, Davis, that I have checked this lot of bones and that they are all here."

"Would you mind writing it down, sir?" said the constable. "Inspector Badger said I was to have everything in writing."

The surgeon took out his pocket-book, and, while he was selecting a suitable piece of paper, he asked: "Did you form any opinion as to the height of the deceased?"

"Yes, I thought he would be about five feet eight" (here I caught the sergeant's eyes, fixed on me with a knowing leer).

"I made it five eight and a half," said the police surgeon; "but we shall know better when we have seen the lower leg-bones. Where was this lot found, Davis?"

"In the pond just off the road in Lord's Bushes, sir, and the inspector has gone off now to——"

"Never mind where he's gone," interrupted the sergeant. "You just answer questions and attend to your business."

The sergeant's reproof conveyed a hint to me on which I was not slow to act. Friendly as my professional colleague was, it was clear that the police were disposed to treat me as an interloper who was to be kept out of the "know" as far as possible. Accordingly I thanked my colleague and the sergeant for their courtesy, and, bidding them adieu until we should meet at the inquest, took my departure and walked away quickly until I found an inconspicuous position from which I could keep the door of the mortuary in view. A few moments later I saw Constable Davis emerge and stride away up the road.

I watched his rapidly diminishing figure until he had gone as far as I considered desirable, and then I set forth in his wake. The road led straight away from the village, and in less than half a mile entered the outskirts of the forest. Here I quickened my pace to close up somewhat, and it was well that I did so, for suddenly he diverged from the road into a green lane, where for a while I lost sight of him. Still hurrying forward, I again caught sight of him just as he turned off into a narrow path that entered a beech wood with a thickish undergrowth of holly, along which I followed him for several minutes, gradually decreasing the distance between us, until suddenly there fell on my ear a rhythmical sound like the clank of a pump. Soon after I caught the sound of men's voices, and then the constable struck off the path into the wood.

I now advanced more cautiously, endeavouring to locate the search party by the sound of the pump, and when I had done this I made a little detour so that I might approach from the opposite direction to that from which the constable had appeared.

Still guided by the noise of the pump, I at length came out into a small opening among the trees and halted to survey the scene. The centre of the opening was occupied by a small pond, not more than a dozen yards across, by the side of which stood a builder's handcart. The little two-wheeled vehicle had evidently been used to convey the appliances which were deposited on the ground near it, and which consisted of a large tub—now filled with water—a shovel, a rake, a sieve, and a portable pump, the latter being fitted with a long delivery hose. There were three men besides the constable, one of whom was working the handle of the pump, while another was glancing at a paper that the constable had just delivered to him. He looked up sharply as I appeared, and viewed me with unconcealed disfavour.

"Hallo, sir!" said he. "You can't come here."

Now, seeing that I was actually here, this was clearly a mistake, and I ventured to point out the fallacy.

"Well, I can't allow you to stay here. Our business is of a private nature."

"I know exactly what your business is, Inspector Badger."

"Oh, do you?" said he, surveying me with a foxy smile. "And I expect I know what yours is, too. But we can't have any of you newspaper gentry spying on us just at present, so you just be off."

I thought it best to undeceive him at once, and accordingly, having explained who I was, I showed him the coroner's permit, which he read with manifest annoyance.

"This is all very well, sir," said he as he handed me back the paper, "but it doesn't authorise you to come spying on the proceedings of the police. Any remains that we discover will be deposited in the mortuary, where you can inspect them to your heart's content; but you can't stay here and watch us."

I had no defined object in keeping a watch on the inspector's proceedings; but the sergeant's indiscreet hint had aroused my curiosity, which was further excited by Mr. Badger's evident desire to get rid of me. Moreover, while we had been talking, the pump had stopped (the muddy floor of the pond being now pretty fully exposed), and the inspector's assistant was handling the shovel impatiently.

"Now I put it to you, Inspector," said I persuasively, "is it politic of you to allow it to be said that you refused an authorised representative of the family facilities for verifying any statements that you may make hereafter?"

"What do you mean?" he asked.

"I mean that if you should happen to find some bone which could be identified as part of the body of Mr. Bellingham, that fact would be of more importance to his family than to anyone else. You know that there is a very valuable estate and a rather difficult will."

"I didn't know it, and I don't see the bearing of it now" (neither did I for that matter); "but if you make such a point of being present at the search, I can't very well refuse. Only you mustn't get in our way, that's all."

On hearing this conclusion, his assistant, who looked like a plain-clothes officer, took up his shovel and stepped into the mud that formed the bottom of the pond, stooping as he went and peering among the masses of weed that had been left stranded by the withdrawal of the water. The inspector watched him anxiously, cautioning him from time to time to "look out where he was treading"; the labourer left the pump and craned forward from the margin of the mud, and the constable and I looked on from our respective points of vantage. For some time the search was fruitless. Once the searcher stooped and picked up what turned out to be a fragment of. decayed wood; then the remains of a long-deceased jay were discovered, examined, and rejected. Suddenly the man bent down by the side of a small pool that had been left in one of the deeper hollows, stared intently into the mud, and stood up.

"There's something here that looks like a bone, sir," he sang out.

"Don't grub about then," said the inspector. "Drive your shovel right into the mud where you saw it and bring it to the sieve."

The man followed out these instructions, and as he came shorewards with a great pile of the slimy mud on his shovel we all converged on the sieve, which the inspector took up and held over the tub, directing the constable and labourer to "lend a hand," meaning thereby that they were to crowd round the tub and exclude me as completely as possible. This, in fact, they did very effectively with his assistance, for, when the shovelful of mud had been deposited on the sieve, the four men leaned over it and so nearly hid it from view that it was only by craning over, first on one side and then on the other, that I was able to catch an occasional glimpse of it, and to observe it gradually melting away as the sieve, immersed in the water, was shaken to and fro.

Presently the inspector raised the sieve from the water and stooped over it more closely to examine its contents. Apparently the examination yielded no very conclusive results, for it was accompanied by a series of rather dubious grunts.

At length the officer stood up, and, turning to me with a genial but foxy smile, held out the sieve for my inspection.

"Like to see what we have found, Doctor?" said he.

I thanked him and stood over the sieve. It contained the sort of litter of twigs, skeleton leaves, weed, pond-snails, dead shells, and fresh-water mussels that one would expect to strain out from the mud of an ancient pond; but in addition to these there were three small bones which at first glance gave me quite a start until I saw what they were.

The inspector looked at me inquiringly. "H'm?" said he.

"Yes," I replied. "Very interesting."

"Those will be human bones, I fancy; h'm?"

"I should say so, undoubtedly," I answered.

"Now," said the inspector, "could you say, off-hand, which finger those bones belong to?"

I smothered a grin (for I had been expecting this question), and answered:

"I can say off-hand that they don't belong to any finger. They are the bones of the left great toe."

The inspector's jaw dropped.

"The deuce they are!" he muttered. "H'm. I thought they looked a bit stout."

"I expect," said I, "that if you go through the mud close to where this came from you'll find the rest of the foot."

The plain-clothes man proceeded at once to act on my suggestion, taking the sieve with him to save time. And sure enough, after filling it twice with the mud from the bottom of the pool, the entire skeleton of the foot was brought to light.

"Now you're happy, I suppose," said the inspector, when I had checked the bones and found them all present.

"I should be more happy," I replied, "if I knew what you were searching for in this pond. You weren't looking for the foot, were you?"

"I was looking for anything that I might find," he answered. "I shall go on searching until we have the whole body. I shall go through all the streams and ponds around here, excepting Connaught Water. That I shall leave to the last, as it will be a case of dredging from a boat and isn't so likely as the smaller ponds. Perhaps the head will be there; it's deeper than any of the others."

It now occurred to me that as I had learned all that I was likely to learn, which was little enough, I might as well leave the inspector to pursue his researches unembarrassed by my presence. Accordingly I thanked him for his assistance and departed by the way I had come.

But as I retraced my steps along the shady path I

speculated profoundly on the officer's proceedings. My examination of the mutilated hand had yielded the conclusion that the finger had been removed after death or shortly before, but more probably after. Some one else had evidently arrived at the same conclusion, and had communicated his opinion to Inspector Badger; for it was clear that that gentleman was in full cry after the missing finger. But why was he searching for it here when the hand had been found at Sidcup? And what did he expect to learn from it when he found it? There is nothing particularly characteristic about a finger, or, at least, the bones of one; and the object of the present researches was to determine the identity of the person of whom these bones were the remains. There was something mysterious about the affair, something suggesting that Inspector Badger was in possession of private information of some kind. But what information could he have? And whence could he have obtained it? These were questions to which I could find no answer, and I was still fruitlessly revolving them when I arrived at the modest inn where the inquest was to be held, and where I proposed to fortify myself with a correspondingly modest lunch as a preparation for my attendance at the inquiry.

CHAPTER XIII   The Crowner's Quest

The proceedings of that fine old institution, the coroner's court, are apt to have their dignity impaired by the somewhat unjudicial surroundings amidst which they are conducted. The present inquiry was to be held in a long room attached to the inn, ordinarily devoted, as its various appurtenances testified, to gatherings of a more convivial character.

Hither I betook myself after a protracted lunch and a meditative pipe, and, being the first to arrive—the jury having already been sworn and conducted to the mortuary to view the remains—whiled away the time by considering the habits of the customary occupants of the room by the light of the objects contained in it. A wooden target with one or two darts sticking in it hung on the end wall and invited the Robin Hoods of the village to try their skill; a system of incised marks on the oaken table made sinister suggestions of shove-halfpenny; and a large open box filled with white wigs, gaudily coloured robes and wooden spears, swords and regalia, crudely coated with gilded paper, obviously appertained to the puerile ceremonials of the Order of Druids.

I had exhausted the interest of these relics and had transferred my attention to the picture gallery when the other spectators and the witnesses began to arrive. Hastily I seated myself in the only comfortable chair besides the one placed at the head of the table, presumably for the coroner; and I had hardly done so when the latter entered accompanied by the jury. Immediately after them came the sergeant, Inspector Badger, one or two plain-clothes men, and finally the divisional surgeon.

The coroner took his seat at the head of the table and opened his book, and the jury seated themselves on a couple of benches on one side of the long table.

I looked with some interest at the twelve "good men and true." They were a representative group of British tradesmen, quiet, attentive, and rather solemn; but my attention was particularly attracted by a small man with a very large head and a shock of upstanding hair whom I had diagnosed, after a glance at his intelligent but truculent countenance and the shiny knees of his trousers, as the village cobbler. He sat between the broad-shouldered foreman, who looked like a blacksmith, and a dogged, red-faced man whose general aspect of prosperous greasiness suggested the calling of a butcher.

"The inquiry, gentlemen," the coroner commenced, "upon which we are now entering concerns itself with two questions. The first is that of identity: who was this person whose body we have just viewed? The second is: How, when, and by what means did he come by his death? We will take the identity first and begin with the circumstances under which the body was discovered."

Here the cobbler stood up and raised an excessively dirty hand.

"I rise, Mr. Chairman," said he, "to a point of order." The other jurymen looked at him curiously and some of them, I regret to say, grinned. "You have referred, sir," he continued, "to the body which we have just viewed. I wish to point out that we have not viewed a body; we have viewed a collection of bones."

"We will refer to them as the remains, if you prefer it," said the coroner.

"I do prefer it," was the reply, and the objector sat down.

"Very well," rejoined the coroner, and he proceeded to call the witnesses, of whom the first was a labourer who had discovered the bones in the watercress-bed.

"Do you happen to know how long it was since the watercress-beds had been cleaned out previously?" the coroner asked, when the witness had told the story of the discovery.

"They was cleaned out by Mr. Tapper's orders just before he gave them up. That will be a little better than two years ago. In May it were. I helped to clean 'em. I worked on this very same place and there wasn't no bones there then."

The coroner glanced at the jury. "Any questions, gentlemen?" he asked.

The cobbler directed an intimidating scowl at the witness and demanded:

"Were you searching for bones when you came on these remains?"

"Me?" exclaimed the witness. "What should I be searching for bones for?"

"Don't prevaricate," said the cobbler sternly; "answer the question: Yes or no."

"No, of course I wasn't."

The juryman shook his enormous head dubiously as though implying that he would let it pass this time but it mustn't happen again; and the examination of the witnesses continued, without eliciting anything that was new to me or giving rise to any incident, until the sergeant had described the finding of the right arm in the Cuckoo Pits.

"Was this an accidental discovery?" the coroner asked.

"No. We had instructions from Scotland Yard to search any likely ponds in this neighbourhood."

The coroner discreetly forbore to press this matter any further, but my friend the cobbler was evidently on the qui vive, and I anticipated a brisk cross-examination for Mr. Badger when his turn came. The inspector was apparently of the same opinion, for I saw him cast a glance of the deepest malevolence at the too inquiring disciple of St. Crispin. In fact, his turn came next, and the cobbler's hair stood up with unholy joy.

The finding of the lower half of the trunk in Staple's Pond at Loughton was the inspector's own achievement, but he was not boastful about it. The discovery, he remarked, followed naturally on the previous one in the Cuckoo Pits.

"Had you any private information that led you to search this particular neighbourhood?" the cobbler asked.

"We had no private information whatever," replied Badger.

"Now I put it to you," pursued the juryman, shaking a forensic, and very dirty, forefinger at the inspector; "here are certain remains found at Sidcup; here are certain other remains found at St. Mary Cray, and certain others at Lee. All those places are in Kent. Now isn't it very remarkable that you should come straight down to Epping Forest, which is in Essex, and search for those bones and find 'em?"

"We were making a systematic search of all likely places," replied Badger.

"Exactly," said the cobbler, with a ferocious grin, "that's just my point. I say, isn't it very funny that, after finding the remains in Kent some twenty miles from here, with the River Thames between, you should come here to look for the bones and go straight to Staple's Pond, where they happen to be—and find 'em?"

"It would have been more funny," Badger replied sourly, "if we'd gone straight to a place where they happened *not* to be—and found them."

A gratified snigger arose from the other eleven good men and true, and the cobbler grinned savagely; but before he could think of a suitable rejoinder the coroner interposed.

"The question is not very material," he said, "and we mustn't embarrass the police by unnecessary inquiries."

"It's my belief," said the cobbler, "that he knew they were there all the time."

"The witness has stated that he had no private information," said the coroner; and he proceeded to take the rest of the inspector's evidence, watched closely by the critical juror.

The account of the finding of the remains having been given in full, the police surgeon was called and sworn; the jurymen straightened their backs with an air of expectancy, and I turned over a page of my notebook.

"You have examined the bones at present lying in the mortuary and forming the subject of this inquiry?" the coroner asked.

"I have."

"Will you kindly tell us what you have observed?"

"I find that the bones are human bones, and are, in my opinion, all parts of the same person. They form a skeleton which is complete with the exception of the skull, the third finger of the left hand, the knee-caps, and the leg-bones—I mean the bones between the knees and the ankles."

"Is there anything to account for the absence of the missing finger?"

"No. There is no deformity and no sign of its having been amputated during life. In my opinion it was removed after death."

"Can you give us any description of the deceased?"

"I should say that these are the bones of an elderly man, probably over sixty years of age, about five feet eight and a half inches in height, of rather stout build, fairly muscular, and well preserved. There are no signs of disease excepting some old-standing rheumatic gout of the right hip-joint."

"Can you form any opinion as to the cause of death?"

"No. There are no marks of violence or signs of injury. But it will be impossible to form any opinion as to the cause of death until we have seen the skull."

"Did you note anything else of importance?"

"Yes. I was struck by the appearance of anatomical

knowledge and skill on the part of the person who dismembered the body. The knowledge of anatomy is proved by the fact that the corpse has been divided into definite anatomical regions. For instance, the bones of the neck are complete and include the top joint of the backbone known as the atlas; whereas a person without anatomical knowledge would probably take off the head by cutting through the neck. Then the arms have been separated with the scapula (or shoulder-blade) and clavicle (or collar-bone) attached, just as an arm would be removed for dissection.

"The skill is shown by the neat way in which the dismemberment has been carried out. The parts have not been rudely hacked asunder, but have been separated at the joints so skilfully that I have not discovered a single scratch or mark of the knife on any of the bones."

"Can you suggest any class of person who would be likely to possess the knowledge and skill to which you refer?"

"It would, of course, be possessed by a surgeon or medical student, and possibly by a butcher."

"You think that the person who dismembered this body may have been a surgeon or a medical student?"

"Yes; or a butcher. Some one accustomed to the dismemberment of bodies and skilful with the knife."

Here the cobbler suddenly rose to his feet.

"I rise, Mr. Chairman," said he, "to protest against the statement that has just been made."

"What statement?" demanded the coroner.

"Against the aspersion," continued the cobbler, with an oratorical flourish, "that has been cast upon a honourable calling."

"I don't understand you," said the coroner.

"Dr. Summers has insinuated that this murder was

committed by a butcher. Now a member of that honourable calling is sitting on this jury——"

"You let me alone," growled the butcher.

"I will not let you alone," persisted the cobbler. "I desire——"

"Oh, shut up, Pope!" This was from the foreman, who, at the same moment, reached out an enormous hairy hand with which he grabbed the cobbler's coat-tails and brought him into a sitting posture with a thump that shook the room.

But Mr. Pope, though seated, was not silenced. "I desire," he said, "to have my protest put on record."

"I can't do that," said the coroner, "and I can't allow you to interrupt the witnesses."

"I am acting," said Mr. Pope, "in the interests of my friend here and the members of a honourable——"

But here the butcher turned on him savagely, and, in a hoarse stage-whisper, exclaimed:

"Look here, Pope; you've got too much of what the cat licks——"

"Gentlemen! gentlemen!" the coroner protested sternly; "I cannot permit this unseemly conduct. You are forgetting the solemnity of the occasion and your own responsible positions. I must insist on more decent and decorous behaviour."

There was profound silence, in the midst of which the butcher concluded in the same hoarse whisper:

"—licks 'er paws with."

The coroner cast a withering glance at him, and, turning to the witness, resumed the examination.

"Can you tell us, Doctor, how long a time has elapsed since the death of the deceased?"

"I should say not less than eighteen months, but probably more. How much more it is impossible from inspection alone to say. The bones are perfectly clean—that is, clean of all soft structures—and will remain substantially in their present condition for many years."

"The evidence of the man who found the remains in the watercress-bed suggests that they could not have been there for more than two years. Do the appearances in your opinion agree with that view?"

"Yes; perfectly."

"There is one more point, Doctor; a very important one. Do you find anything in any of the bones, or all of them together, which would enable you to identify them as the bones of any particular individual?"

"No," replied Dr. Summers; "I found no peculiarity that could furnish the means of personal identification."

"The description of a missing individual has been given to us," said the coroner; "a man, fifty-nine years of age, five feet eight inches in height, healthy, well preserved, rather broad in build, and having an old Pott's fracture of the left ankle. Do the remains that you have examined agree with that description?"

"Yes, so far as agreement is possible. There is no disagreement."

"The remains might be those of that individual?"

"They might; but there is no positive evidence that they are. The description would apply to a large proportion of elderly men, except as to the fracture."

"You found no signs of such a fracture?"

"No. Pott's fracture affects the bone called the fibula. That is one of the bones that has not yet been found, so there is no evidence on that point. The left foot was quite normal, but then it would be in any case, unless the fracture had resulted in great deformity."

"You estimated the height of the deceased as half an inch greater than that of the missing person. Does that constitute a disagreement?"

"No; my estimate is only approximate. As the arms are complete and the legs are not, I have based my calculations on the width across the two arms. But measurement of the thigh-bones gives the same result. The length of the thigh-bones is one foot seven inches and five-eighths."

"So the deceased might have been taller than five feet eight?"

"That is so; from five feet eight to five feet nine."

"Thank you. I think that is all we want to ask you, Doctor; unless the jury wish to put any questions."

He glanced uneasily at that august body, and instantly the irrepressible Pope rose to the occasion.

"About that finger that is missing," said the cobbler. "You say that it was cut off after death?"

"That is my opinion."

"Now can you tell us why it was cut off?"

"No, I cannot."

"Oh, come now, Dr. Summers, you must have formed some opinion on the subject."

Here the coroner interposed. "The Doctor is only concerned with the evidence arising out of the actual examination of the remains. Any personal opinions or conjectures that he may have formed are not evidence, and he must not be asked about them."

"But, sir," objected Pope, "we want to know why that finger was cut off. It couldn't have been took off for no reason. May I ask, sir, if the person who is missing had anything peculiar about that finger?"

"Nothing is stated to that effect in the written description," replied the coroner.

"Perhaps," suggested Pope, "Inspector Badger can tell us."

"I think," said the coroner, "we had better not ask the police too many questions. They will tell us anything that they wish to be made public."

"Oh, very well," snapped the cobbler. "If it's a matter of hushing it up I've got no more to say; only I don't see how we are to arrive at a verdict if we don't have the facts put before us."

All the witnesses having now been examined, the coroner proceeded to sum up and address the jury.

"You have heard the evidence, gentlemen, of the various witnesses, and you will have perceived that it does not enable us to answer either of the questions that form the subject of this inquiry. We now know that the deceased was an elderly man, about sixty years of age, and about five feet eight to nine in height; and that his death took place from eighteen months to two years ago. That is all we know. From the treatment to which the body has been subjected we may form conjectures as to the circumstances of his death. But we have no actual knowledge. We do not know who the deceased was or how he came by his death. Consequently, it will be necessary to adjourn this inquiry until fresh facts are available, and as soon as that is the case, you will receive due notice that your attendance is required."

The silence of the Court gave place to the confused noise of moving chairs and a general outbreak of eager talk, amidst which I rose and made my way out into the street. At the door I encountered Dr. Summers, whose dog-cart was waiting close by.

"Are you going back to town now?" he asked.

"Yes," I answered; "as soon as I can catch a train."

"If you jump into my cart I'll run you down in time for the five-one. You'll miss it if you walk."

I accepted his offer thankfully, and a minute later was

spinning briskly down the road to the station.

"Queer little devil, that man Pope," Dr. Summers remarked. "Quite a character; a socialist, labourite, agitator, general crank; anything for a row."

"Yes," I answered; "that was what his appearance suggested. It must be trying for the coroner to get a truculent rascal like that on a jury."

Summers laughed. "I don't know. He supplies the comic relief. And then, you know, those fellows have their uses. Some of his questions were pretty pertinent."

"So Badger seemed to think."

"Yes, by Jove," chuckled Summers. "Badger didn't like him a bit; and I suspect the worthy inspector was sailing pretty close to the wind in his answers."

"You think he really has some private information?"

"Depends upon what you mean by 'information.' The police are not a speculative body. They wouldn't be taking all this trouble unless they had a pretty straight tip from somebody. How are Mr. and Miss Bellingham? I used to know them when they lived here."

I was considering a discreet answer to this question when we swept into the station yard. At the same moment the train drew up at the platform, and, with a hurried hand-shake and hastily spoken thanks, I sprang from the dog-cart and darted into the station.

During the rather slow journey homewards I read over my notes and endeavoured to extract from the facts they set forth some significance other than that which lay on the surface, but without much success. Then I fell to speculating on what Thorndyke would think of the evidence at the inquest and whether he would be satisfied with the information that I had collected. These speculations lasted me, with occasional digressions, until I arrived at the Temple and ran up the stairs rather eagerly to my friends' chambers.

But here a disappointment awaited me. The nest was empty with the exception of Polton, who appeared at the laboratory door in his white apron, with a pair of flat-nosed pliers in his hand.

"The Doctor had to go down to Bristol to consult over an urgent case," he explained, "and Dr. Jervis has gone with him. They'll be away a day or two, I expect, but the Doctor left this note for you."

He took a letter from the shelf, where it had been stood conspicuously on edge, and handed it to me. It was a short note from Thorndyke apologising for his sudden departure and asking me to give Polton my notes with any comments that I had to make.

"You will be interested to learn," he added, "that the application will be heard in the Probate Court the day after to-morrow. I shall not be present, of course, nor will Jervis, so I should like you to attend and keep your eyes open for anything that may happen during the hearing and that may not appear in the notes that Marchmont's clerk will be instructed to take. I have retained Dr. Payne to stand by and help you with the practice, so that you can attend the Court with a clear conscience."

This was highly flattering and quite atoned for the small disappointment; with deep gratification at the trust that Thorndyke had reposed in me, I pocketed the letter, handed my notes to Polton, wished him "Good-evening," and betook myself to Fetter Lane.

CHAPTER XIV   Which Carries the Reader into the Probate Court

The Probate Court wore an air of studious repose when I entered with Miss Bellingham and her father. Apparently the great and inquisitive public had not become aware of the proceedings that were about to take place, or had not realised their connection with the sensational "Mutilation Case"; but barristers and Pressmen, better informed, had gathered in some strength, and the hum of their conversation filled the air like the droning of the voluntary that ushers in a cathedral service.

As we entered, a pleasant-faced, elderly gentleman rose and came forward to meet us, shaking Mr. Bellingham's hand cordially and saluting Miss Bellingham with a courtly bow.

"This is Mr. Marchmont, Doctor," said the former, introducing me; and the solicitor, having thanked me for the trouble I had taken in attending at the inquest, led us to a bench, at the farther end of which was seated a gentleman whom I recognised as Mr. Hurst.

Mr. Bellingham recognised him at the same moment and glared at him wrathfully.

"I see that scoundrel is here!" he exclaimed in a distinctly audible voice, "pretending that he doesn't see me, because he is ashamed to look me in the face, but——"

"Hush! Hush! my dear sir," exclaimed the horrified solicitor; "we mustn't talk like that, especially in this place. Let me beg you—let me entreat you to control your feelings, to make no indiscreet remarks; in fact, to make no remarks at all," he added, with the evident conviction that any remarks that Mr. Bellingham might make would be certain to be indiscreet.

"Forgive me, Marchmont," Mr. Bellingham replied contritely. "I will control myself: I will really be quite discreet. I won't even look at him again—because, if I do, I shall probably go over and pull his nose."

This form of discretion did not appear to be quite to Mr. Marchmont's liking, for he took the precaution of insisting that Miss Bellingham and I should sit on the farther side of his client, and thus effectually separate him from his enemy.

"Who's the long-nosed fellow talking to Jellicoe?" Mr. Bellingham asked.

"That is Mr. Loram, K.C., Mr. Hurst's counsel; and the convivial-looking gentleman next to him is our counsel, Mr. Heath, a most able man and"—here Mr. Marchmont whispered behind his hand—"fully instructed by Dr. Thorndyke."

At this juncture the judge entered and took his seat; the usher proceeded with great rapidity to swear in the jury, and the Court gradually settled down into that state of academic quiet which it maintained throughout the proceedings, excepting when the noisy swing-doors were set oscillating by some bustling clerk or reporter.

The judge was a somewhat singular-looking old gentleman, very short as to his face and very long as to his mouth; which peculiarities, together with a pair of large and bulging eyes (which he usually kept closed), suggested a certain resemblance to a frog. And he had a curious frog-like trick of flattening his eyelids—as if in the act of swallowing a large beetle—which was the only outward and visible sign of emotion that he ever displayed.

As soon as the swearing-in of the jury was completed Mr. Loram rose to introduce the case; whereupon his lordship leaned back in his chair and closed his eyes, as if bracing himself for a painful operation.

"The present proceedings," Mr. Loram explained, "are occasioned by the unaccountable disappearance of Mr. John Bellingham, of 141, Queen Square, Bloomsbury, which occurred about two years ago, or, to be more precise, on the twenty-third of November, nineteen hundred and two. Since that date nothing has been heard of Mr. Bellingham, and, as there are certain substantial reasons for believing him to be dead, the principal beneficiary under his will, Mr. George Hurst, is now applying to the Court for permission to presume the death of the testator and prove the will. As the time which has elapsed since the testator was last seen alive is only two years, the application is based upon the circumstances of the disappearance, which were, in many respects, very singular, the most remarkable feature of that disappearance being, perhaps, its suddenness and completeness."

Here the judge remarked in a still, small voice that, "It would, perhaps, have been even more remarkable if the testator had disappeared gradually and incompletely."

"No doubt, my lord," agreed Mr. Loram; "but the point is that the testator, whose habits had always been regular and orderly, disappeared on the date mentioned without having made any of the usual provisions for the conduct of his affairs, and has not since then been seen or heard of."

With this preamble Mr. Loram proceeded to give a narrative of the events connected with the disappearance of John Bellingham, which was substantially identical with that which I had read in the newspapers; and having laid the actual facts before the jury, he went on to discuss their probable import.

"Now, what conclusion," he asked, "will this strange, this most mysterious train of events suggest to an intelligent person who shall consider it impartially? Here is a man who steps forth from the house of his cousin or his brother, as the case may be, and forthwith, in the twinkling of an eye, vanishes from human ken. What is the explanation? Did he steal forth and, without notice or hint of his intention, take train to some seaport, thence to embark for some distant land, leaving his affairs to take care of themselves and his friends to speculate vainly as to his whereabouts? Is he now hiding abroad, or even at home, indifferent alike to the safety of his own considerable property and the peace of mind of his friends? Or is it that death has come upon him unawares by sickness, by accident, or, more probably, by the hand of some unknown criminal? Let us consider the probabilities.

"Can he have disappeared by his own deliberate act? Why not? it may be asked. Men undoubtedly do disappear from time to time, to be discovered by chance or to reappear voluntarily after intervals of years and find their names almost forgotten and their places filled by new-comers. Yes; but there is always some reason for a disappearance of this kind, even though it be a bad one. Family discords that make life a weariness; pecuniary difficulties that make life a succession of anxieties; distaste for particular circumstances and surroundings from which there seems no escape; inherent restlessness and vagabond tendencies, and so on.

"Do any of these explanations apply to the present case? No, they do not. Family discords—at least those capable of producing chronic misery—appertain exclusively to a married state. But the testator was a bachelor with no encumbrances whatever. Pecuniary anxieties can be equally excluded. The testator was in easy, in fact, in affluent circumstances. His mode of life was apparently agreeable and full of interest and activity, and he had full liberty of change if he wished. He had been accustomed to travel, and could do so again without absconding. He had reached an age when radical changes do not seem desirable. He was a man of fixed and regular habits, and his regularity was of his own choice and not due to compulsion or necessity. When last seen by his friends, as I shall prove, he was proceeding to a definite destination with the expressed intention of returning for purposes of his own appointing. He did return and then vanished, leaving those purposes unachieved.

"If we conclude that he has voluntarily disappeared and is at present in hiding, we adopt an opinion that is entirely at variance with all these weighty facts. If, on the other hand, we conclude that he has died suddenly, or has been killed by an accident or otherwise, we are adopting a view that involves no inherent improbabilities and that is entirely congruous with the known facts; facts that will be proved by the testimony of the witnesses whom I shall call. The supposition that the testator is dead is not only more probable than that he is alive; I submit it is the only reasonable explanation of the circumstances of his disappearance.

"But this is not all. The presumption of death which arises so inevitably out of the mysterious and abrupt manner in which the testator disappeared has recently received most conclusive and dreadful confirmation. On the fifteenth of July last there were discovered at Sidcup the remains of a human arm—a left arm, gentlemen, from the hand of which the third, or ring, finger was missing. The doctor who has examined that arm will tell you that the finger was cut off either after death or immediately before; and his evidence will prove conclusively that that arm must have been deposited in the place where it was found just about the time when the testator disappeared. Since that first discovery, other portions of the same mutilated body have come to light; and it is a strange and significant fact that they have all been found in the immediate neighbourhood of Eltham or Woodford. You will remember, gentlemen, that it was either at Eltham or Woodford that the testator was last seen alive.

"And now observe the completeness of the coincidence. These human remains, as you will be told presently by the experienced and learned medical gentleman who has examined them most exhaustively, are those of a man of about sixty years of age, about five feet eight inches in height, fairly muscular and well preserved, apparently healthy, and rather stoutly built. Another witness will tell you that the missing man was about sixty years of age, about five feet eight inches in height, fairly muscular and well preserved, apparently healthy, and rather stoutly built. And—another most significant and striking fact—the testator was accustomed to wear upon the third finger of his left hand—the very finger that is missing from the remains that were found— a most peculiar ring, which fitted so tightly that he was unable to get it off after once putting it on; a ring, gentleman, of so peculiar a pattern that had it been found on the body must have instantly established the identity of the remains. In a word, gentlemen, the remains which have been found are those of a man exactly like the testator; they differ from him in no respect whatever; they display a mutilation which suggests an attempt to conceal an identifying peculiarity which he undoubtedly presented; and they were deposited in their various hiding-places about the time of the testator's disappearance. Accordingly, when you have heard these facts proved by the sworn testimony of competent witnesses, together with the facts relating to the disappearance, I shall ask you for a verdict in accordance with that evidence."

Mr. Loram sat down, and, adjusting a pair of pince-nez, rapidly glanced over his brief while the usher was administering the oath to the first witness.

This was Mr. Jellicoe, who stepped into the box and directed a stony gaze at the (apparently) unconscious judge. The usual preliminaries having been gone through, Mr. Loram proceeded to examine him.

"You were the testator's solicitor and confidential agent, I believe?"

"I was—and am."

"How long have you known him?"

"Twenty-seven years."

"Judging from your experience of him, should you say that he was a person likely to disappear voluntarily, and suddenly to cease to communicate with his friends?"

"No."

"Kindly give your reasons for that opinion."

"Such conduct on the part of the testator would be entirely opposed to his habits and character as they are known to me. He was exceedingly regular and business-like in his dealings with me. When travelling abroad he always kept me informed as to his whereabouts, or, if he was likely to be beyond reach of communications, he always advised me beforehand. One of my duties was to collect a pension which he drew from the Foreign Office, and on no occasion, previous to his disappearance, has he ever failed to furnish me punctually with the necessary documents."

"Had he, so far as you know, any reasons for wishing to disappear?"

"No."

"When and where did you last see him alive?"

"At six o'clock in the evening, on the fourteenth of October, nineteen hundred and two, at 141, Queen Square, Bloomsbury."

"Kindly tell us what happened on that occasion."

"The testator had called for me at my office at a quarter past three, and asked me to come with him to his house to meet Dr. Norbury. I accompanied him to 141, Queen Square, and shortly after we arrived Dr. Norbury came to look at some antiquities that the testator proposed to give to the British Museum. The gift consisted of a mummy with four Canopic jars and other tomb-furniture which the testator stipulated should be exhibited together in a single case and in the state in which they were then presented. Of these objects, the mummy only was ready for inspection. The tomb-furniture had not yet arrived in England, but was expected within a week. Dr. Norbury accepted the gift on behalf of the Museum, but could not take possession of the objects until he had communicated with the Director and obtained his formal authority. The testator accordingly gave me certain instructions concerning the delivery of the gift, as he was leaving England that evening."

"Are those instructions relevant to the subject of this inquiry?"

"I think they are. The testator was going to Paris, and perhaps from thence to Vienna. He instructed me to receive and unpack the tomb-furniture on its arrival, and to store it, with the mummy, in a particular room, where it was to remain for three weeks. If he returned within that time he was to hand it over in person to the Museum authorities; if he had not returned within that time, he desired me to notify the Museum authorities that they were at liberty to take possession of and remove the collection at their convenience. From these instructions I gathered that the testator was uncertain as to the length of his absence from England and the extent of his journey."

"Did he state precisely where he was going?"

"No. He said he was going to Paris and perhaps to Vienna, but he gave no particulars and I asked for none."

"Do you, in fact, know where he went?"

"No. He left the house at six o'clock wearing a long, heavy overcoat and carrying a suit-case and an umbrella. I wished him 'Good-bye' at the door and watched him walk away as if going towards Southampton Row. I have no idea where he went, and I never saw him again."

"Had he no other luggage than the suit-case?"

"I do not know, but I believe not. He was accustomed to travel with the bare necessaries, and to buy anything further that he wanted *en route*."

"Did he say nothing to the servants as to the probable date of his return?"

"There were no servants excepting the caretaker. The house was not used for residential purposes. The testator slept and took his meals at his club, though he kept his clothes at the house."

"Did you receive any communication from him after he left?"

"No. I never heard from him again in any way. I waited for three weeks as he had instructed me, and then notified the Museum authorities that the collection was ready for removal. Five days later Dr. Norbury came and took formal possession of it, and it was transferred to the Museum forthwith."

"When did you next hear of the testator?"

"On the twenty-third of November following at a quarter-past seven in the evening. Mr. George Hurst came to my rooms, which are over my office, and informed me that the testator had called at his house during his absence and had been shown into the study to wait for him. That on his—Mr. Hurst's—arrival it was found that the testator had disappeared without acquainting the servants of his intended departure, and without being seen by anyone to leave the house. Mr. Hurst thought this so remarkable that he had hastened up to town to inform me. I also thought it a remarkable circumstance, especially as I had received no communication from the testator, and we both decided that it was advisable to inform the testator's brother, Godfrey, of what had happened.

"Accordingly Mr. Hurst and I proceeded as quickly as possible to Liverpool Street and took the first train available to Woodford, where Mr. Godfrey Bellingham then resided. We arrived at his house at five minutes to nine, and were informed by the servant that he was not at home, but that his daughter was in the library, which was a detached building situated in the grounds. The servant lighted a lantern and conducted us through the grounds to the library, where we found Mr. Godfrey Bellingham and Miss Bellingham. Mr. Godfrey had only just come in and had entered by the back gate, which had a bell that rang in the library. Mr. Hurst informed Mr. Godfrey of what had occurred, and then we left the library to walk up to the house. A few paces from the library I noticed by the light of the lantern, which Mr. Godfrey was carrying, a small object lying on the lawn. I pointed it out to him and he picked it up, and then we all recognised it as a scarab that the testator was accustomed to wear on his watch-chain. It was fitted with a gold wire passed through the suspension hole and a gold ring. Both the wire and the ring were in position, but the ring was broken. We went to the house and questioned the servants as to visitors; but none of them had seen the testator, and they all agreed that no visitor whatsoever had come to the house during the afternoon or evening. Mr. Godfrey and Miss Bellingham both declared that they had neither seen nor heard anything of the testator, and were both unaware that he had returned to England. As the circumstances were somewhat disquieting, I communicated, on the following morning, with the police and requested them to make inquiries; which they did, with the result that a suit-case, bearing the initials 'J. B.', was found to be lying unclaimed in the cloak-room at Charing Cross Station. I was able to identify the suit-case as that which I had seen the testator carry away from Queen Square. I was also able to identify some of the contents. I interviewed the cloak-room attendant, who informed me that the suit-case had been deposited on the twenty-third about 4.15 p.m. He had no recollection of the person who deposited it. It remained unclaimed in the possession of the railway company for three months, and was then surrendered to me."

"Were there any marks or labels on it showing the route by which it had travelled?"

"There were no labels on it and no marks other than the initials 'J. B.'"

"Do you happen to know the testator's age?"

"Yes. He was fifty-nine on the eleventh of October, nineteen hundred and two."

"Can you tell us what his height was?"

"Yes. He was exactly five feet eight inches."

"What sort of health had he?"

"So far as I know his health was good. I am not aware that he suffered from any disease. I am only judging by his appearance, which was that of a healthy man."

"Should you describe him as well preserved or otherwise?"

"I should describe him as a well preserved man for his age."

"How should you describe his figure?"

"I should describe him as rather broad and stout in build, and fairly muscular, though not exceptionally so."

Mr. Loram made a rapid note of these answers and then said:

"You have told us, Mr. Jellicoe, that you have known the testator intimately for twenty-seven years. Now, did you ever notice whether he was accustomed to wear any rings upon his fingers?"

"He wore upon the third finger of his left hand a copy of an antique ring which bore the device of the Eye of Osiris. That was the only ring he ever wore as far as I know."

"Did he wear it constantly?"

"Yes, necessarily; because it was too small for him, and having once squeezed it on he was never able to get it off again."

This was the sum of Mr. Jellicoe's evidence, and at its conclusion the witness glanced inquiringly at Mr. Bellingham's counsel. But Mr. Heath remained seated, attentively considering the notes that he had just made, and, finding that there was to be no cross-examination, Mr. Jellicoe stepped down from the box. I leaned back on my bench, and, turning my head, observed Miss Bellingham deep in thought.

"What do you think of it?" I asked.

"It seems very complete and conclusive," she replied.

And then, with a sigh, she murmured: "Poor old Uncle John! How horrid it sounds to talk of him in this cold-blooded, business-like way as 'the testator,' as if he were nothing but a sort of algebraical sign."

"There isn't much room for sentiment, I suppose, in the proceedings of the Probate Court," I replied. To which she assented, and then asked: "Who is this lady?"

"This lady" was a fashionably dressed young woman who had just bounced into the witness-box and was now being sworn. The preliminaries being finished, she answered Miss Bellingham's question and Mr. Loram's by stating that her name was Augustina Gwendoline Dobbs, and that she was housemaid to Mr. George Hurst, of "The Poplars," Eltham.

"Mr. Hurst lives alone, I believe?" said Mr. Loram.

"I don't know what you mean by that," Miss Dobbs began; but the barrister explained:

"I mean that I believe he is unmarried?"

"Well, and what about it?" the witness demanded tartly.

"I am asking you a question."

"I know that," said the witness viciously; "and I say that you've no business to make any such insinuations to a respectable young lady when there's a cook-housekeeper and a kitchenmaid living in the house, and him old enough to be my father——"

Here his lordship flattened his eyelids with startling effect, and Mr. Loram interrupted: "I make no insinuations. I merely ask, Is your employer, Mr. Hurst, an unmarried man, or is he not?"

"I never asked him," said the witness sulkily.

"Please answer my question—yes or no."

"How can I answer your question? He may be married or he may not. How do I know? I'm not a private detective."

Mr. Loram directed a stupefied gaze at the witness, and in the ensuing silence a plaintive voice came from the bench:

"Is that point material?"

"Certainly, my lord," replied Mr. Loram.

"Then, as I see that you are calling Mr. Hurst, perhaps you had better put the question to him. He will probably know."

Mr. Loram bowed, and as the judge subsided into his normal state of coma he turned to the triumphant witness.

"Do you remember anything remarkable occurring on the twenty-third of November the year before last?"

"Yes. Mr. John Bellingham called at our house."

"How did you know he was Mr. John Bellingham?"

"I didn't; but he said he was, and I supposed he knew."

"At what time did he arrive?"

"At twenty minutes past five in the evening."

"What happened then?"

"I told him that Mr. Hurst had not come home yet, and he said he would wait for him in the study and write some letters; so I showed him into the study and shut the door."

"What happened next?"

"Nothing. Then Mr. Hurst came home at his usual time—a quarter to six—and let himself in with his key. He went straight into the study where I supposed Mr. Bellingham still was, so I took no notice, but laid the table for two. At six o'clock Mr. Hurst came into the dining-room—he has tea in the City and dines at six—and when he saw the table laid for two he asked the reason. I said I thought Mr. Bellingham was staying to dinner.

"'Mr. Bellingham!' says he, 'I didn't know he was

here. Why didn't you tell me?' he says. 'I thought he was with you, sir,' I said. 'I showed him into the study,' I said. 'Well, he wasn't there when I came in,' he said, 'and he isn't there now,' he said. 'Perhaps he has gone to wait in the drawing-room,' he said. So we went and looked in the drawing-room, but he wasn't there. Then Mr. Hurst said he thought Mr. Bellingham must have got tired of waiting and gone away; but I told him I was quite sure he hadn't, because I had been watching all the time. Then he asked me if Mr. Bellingham was alone or whether his daughter was with him, and I said that it wasn't that Mr. Bellingham at all, but Mr. John Bellingham, and then he was more surprised than ever. I said we had better search the house to make sure whether he was there or not, and Mr. Hurst said he would come with me; so we went all over the house and looked in all the rooms, but there was not a sign of Mr. Bellingham in any of them. Then Mr. Hurst got very nervous and upset, and when he had just snatched a little dinner he ran off to catch the six-thirty-one train up to town."

"You say that Mr. Bellingham could not have left the house because you were watching all the time. Where were you while you were watching?"

"I was in the kitchen. I could see the front gate from the kitchen window."

"You say that you laid the table for two. Where did you lay it?"

"In the dining-room, of course."

"Could you see the front gate from the dining-room?"

"No, but I could see the study door. The study is opposite the dining-room."

"Do you have to come upstairs to get from the kitchen to the dining-room?"

"Yes, of course you do!"

"Then, might not Mr. Bellingham have left the house while you were coming up the stairs?"

"No, he couldn't have done."

"Why not?"

"Because it would have been impossible."

"But why would it have been impossible?"

"Because he couldn't have done it."

"I suggest that Mr. Bellingham left the house quietly while you were on the stairs?"

"No, he didn't."

"How do you know he did not?"

"I am quite sure he didn't."

"But how can you be certain?"

"Because I should have seen him if he had."

"But I mean when you were on the stairs."

"He was in the study when I was on the stairs."

"How do you know he was in the study?"

"Because I showed him in there and he hadn't come out."

Mr. Loram paused and took a deep breath, and his lordship flattened his eyelids.

"Is there a side gate to the premises?" the barrister resumed wearily.

"Yes. It opens into a narrow lane at the side of the house."

"And there is a French window in the study, is there not?"

"Yes. It opens on to the small grass plot opposite the side gate."

"Were the window and the gate locked or would it have been possible for Mr. Bellingham to let himself out into the lane?"

"The window and the gate both have catches on the inside. He could have got out that way, but, of course, he didn't."

"Why not?"

"Well, no gentleman would go creeping out the back way like a thief."

"Did you look to see if the French window was shut and fastened after you missed Mr. Bellingham?"

"I looked at it when we shut the house up for the night. It was then shut and fastened on the inside."

"And the side gate?"

"That gate was shut and latched. You have to slam the gate to make the latch fasten, so no one could have gone out of the gate without being heard."

Here the examination-in-chief ended, and Mr. Loram sat down with an audible sigh of relief. Miss Dobbs was about to step down from the witness-box when Mr. Heath rose to cross-examine.

"Did you see Mr. Bellingham in a good light?" he asked.

"Pretty good. It was dark outside, but the hall-lamp was alight."

"Kindly look at this"—here a small object was passed across to the witness. "It is a trinket that Mr. Bellingham is stated to have carried suspended from his watch-guard. Can you remember if he was wearing it in that manner when he came to the house?"

"No, he was not."

"You are sure of that?"

"Quite sure."

"Thank you. And now I want to ask you about the search that you have mentioned. You say that you went all over the house. Did you go into the study?"

"No—at least, not until Mr. Hurst had gone to London."

"When you did go in, was the window fastened?"

"Yes."

"Could it have been fastened from the outside?"

"No; there is no handle outside."

"What furniture is there in the study?"

"There is a writing-table, a revolving-chair, two easy chairs, two large book-cases, and a wardrobe that Mr. Hurst keeps his overcoats and hats in."

"Does the wardrobe lock?"

"Yes."

"Was it locked when you went in?"

"I'm sure I don't know. I don't go about trying the cupboards and drawers."

"What furniture is there in the drawing-room?"

"A cabinet, six or seven chairs, a Chesterfield sofa, a piano, a silver-table, and one or two occasional tables."

"Is the piano a grand or upright?"

"It is an upright grand."

"In what position is it placed?"

"It stands across a corner near the window."

"Is there sufficient room behind it for a man to conceal himself?"

Miss Dobbs was amused and did not dissemble. "Oh, yes," she sniggered, "there's plenty of room for a man to hide behind it."

"When you searched the drawing-room, did you look behind the piano?"

"No, I didn't," Miss Dobbs replied scornfully.

"Did you look under the sofa?"

"Certainly not!"

"What did you do then?"

"We opened the door and looked into the room. We were not looking for a cat or a monkey, we were looking for a middle-aged gentleman."

"And am I to take it that your search over the rest of

the house was conducted in a similar manner?"

"Certainly. We looked into the rooms, but we did not search under the beds or in the cupboards."

"Are all the rooms in the house in use as living or sleeping rooms?"

"No; there is one room on the second floor that is used as a store and lumber-room, and one on the first floor that Mr. Hurst uses to store trunks and things that he is not using."

"Did you look in those rooms when you searched the house?"

"No."

"Have you looked in them since?"

"I have been in the lumber-room since, but not in the other. It is always kept locked."

At this point an ominous flattening became apparent in his lordship's eyelids, but these symptoms passed when Mr. Heath sat down and indicated that he had no further questions to ask.

Miss Dobbs once more prepared to step down from the witness box, when Mr. Loram shot up like a jack-in-the-box.

"You have made certain statements," said he, "concerning the scarab which Mr. Bellingham was accustomed to wear suspended from his watch-guard. You say that he was not wearing it when he came to Mr. Hurst's house on the twenty-third of November, nineteen hundred and two. Are you quite sure of that?"

"Quite sure."

"I must ask you to be very careful in your statement on this point. The question is a highly important one. Do you swear that the scarab was not hanging from his watch-guard?"

"Yes, I do."

"Did you notice the watch-guard particularly?"

"No; not particularly."

"Then what makes you sure that the scarab was not attached to it?"

"It couldn't have been."

"Why could it not?"

"Because if it had been there I should have seen it."

"What kind of watch-guard was Mr. Bellingham wearing?"

"Oh, an ordinary sort of watch-guard."

"I mean was it a chain or a ribbon or a strap?"

"A chain, I think—or perhaps a ribbon—or it might have been a strap."

His lordship flattened his eyelids, but made no further sign and Mr. Loram continued:

"Did you or did you not notice what kind of watch-guard Mr. Bellingham was wearing?"

"I did not. Why should I? It was no business of mine."

"But yet you are quite sure about the scarab?"

"Yes, quite sure."

"You noticed that, then?"

"No, I didn't. How could I when it wasn't there?"

Mr. Loram paused and looked helplessly at the witness; a suppressed titter arose from the body of the Court, and a faint voice from the bench inquired:

"Are you *quite* incapable of giving a straightforward answer?"

Miss Dobbs's only reply was to burst into tears; whereupon Mr. Loram abruptly sat down and abandoned his re-examination.

The witness-box vacated by Miss Dobbs was occupied successively by Dr. Norbury, Mr. Hurst and the cloak-room attendant, none of whom contributed any new facts, but merely corroborated the statements made by Mr.

Jellicoe and the housemaid. Then came the labourer who discovered the bones at Sidcup, and who repeated the evidence that he had given at the inquest, showing that the remains could not have been lying in the watercress-bed more than two years. Finally Dr. Summers was called, and, after he had given a brief description of the bones that he had examined, was asked by Mr. Loram:

"You have heard the description that Mr. Jellicoe has given of the testator?"

"I have."

"Does that description apply to the person whose remains you examined?"

"In a general way it does."

"I must ask you for a direct answer—yes or no. Does it apply?"

"Yes. But I ought to say that my estimate of the height of the deceased is only approximate."

"Quite so. Judging from your examination of those remains and from Mr. Jellicoe's description, might those remains be the remains of the testator, John Bellingham?"

"Yes, they might."

On receiving this admission Mr. Loram sat down, and Mr. Heath immediately rose to cross-examine.

"When you examined these remains, Dr. Summers, did you discover any personal peculiarities which would enable you to identify them as the remains of any one individual rather than any other individual of similar size, age, and proportions?"

"No. I found nothing that would identify the remains as those of any particular individual."

As Mr. Heath asked no further questions, the witness received his dismissal, and Mr. Loram informed the Court that that was his case. The judge bowed somnolently, and then Mr. Heath rose to address the

Court on behalf of the respondent. It was not a long speech, nor was it enriched by any displays of florid rhetoric; it concerned itself exclusively with a rebutment of the arguments of the counsel for the petitioner.

Having briefly pointed out that the period of absence was too short to give rise of itself to the presumption of death, Mr. Heath continued:

"The claim therefore rests upon evidence of a positive character. My learned friend asserts that the testator is presumably dead, and it is for him to prove what he has affirmed. Now, has he done this? I submit that he has not. He has argued with great force and ingenuity that the testator, being a bachelor, a solitary man without wife or child, dependant or master, public or private office or duty, or any bond, responsibility, or any other condition limiting his freedom of action, had no reason or inducement for absconding. This is my learned friend's argument, and he has conducted it with so much skill and ingenuity that he has not only succeeded in proving his case; he has proved a great deal too much. For if it is true, as my learned friend so justly argues, that a man thus unfettered by obligations of any kind has no reason for disappearing, is it not even more true that he has no reason for *not* disappearing? My friend has urged that the testator was at liberty to go where he pleased, when he pleased, and how he pleased; and that therefore there was no need for him to abscond. I reply, if he was at liberty to go away, whither, when, and how he pleased, why do we express surprise that he has made use of his liberty? My learned friend points out that the testator notified to nobody his intention of going away and has acquainted no one with his whereabouts; but, I ask, whom should he have notified? He was responsible to nobody; there was no one dependent upon him; his presence or absence was the concern of nobody but himself. If circumstances suddenly arising made it desirable that he should go abroad, why should he not go? I say there was no reason whatever.

"My learned friend has said that the testator went away leaving his affairs to take care of themselves. Now, gentlemen, I ask you if this can fairly be said of a man whose affairs are, as they have been for many years, in the hands of a highly capable, completely trustworthy agent who is better acquainted with them than the testator himself? Clearly it cannot.

"To conclude this part of the argument: I submit that the circumstances of the so-called disappearance of the testator present nothing out of the ordinary. The testator is a man of ample means, without any responsibilities to fetter his movements, and has been in the constant habit of travelling, often into remote and distant regions. The mere fact that he has been absent somewhat longer than usual affords no ground whatever for the drastic proceeding of presumption of death and taking possession of his property.

"With reference to the human remains which have been mentioned in connection with the case I need say but little. The attempt to connect them with the testator has failed completely. You yourselves have heard Dr. Summers state on oath that they cannot be identified as the remains of any particular person. That would seem to dispose of them effectually. I must remark upon a very singular point that has been raised by the learned counsel for the petitioner, which is this:

"My learned friend points out that these remains were discovered near Eltham and near Woodford and that the testator was last seen alive at one of these two places. This he considers for some reason to be a highly significant fact. But I cannot agree with him. If the testator had been last seen alive at Woodford, and the remains had been found at Woodford, or if he had disappeared from Eltham, and the remains had been found at Eltham, that would have had some significance. But he can only have been last seen at one of the places, whereas the remains have been found at both places. Here again my learned friend seems to have proved too much.

"But I need not occupy your time further. I repeat that, in order to justify us in presuming the death of the testator, clear and positive evidence would be necessary. That no such evidence has been brought forward. Accordingly, seeing that the testator may return at any time and is entitled to find his property intact, I shall ask you for a verdict that will secure to him this measure of ordinary justice."

At the conclusion of Mr. Heath's speech the judge, as if awakening from a refreshing nap, opened his eyes; and uncommonly shrewd, intelligent eyes they were when the expressive eyelids were duly tucked up out of the way. He commenced by reading over a part of the will and certain notes—which he appeared to have made in some miraculous fashion with his eyes shut—and then proceeded to review the evidence and the counsels' arguments for the instruction of the jury.

"Before considering the evidence which you have heard, gentlemen," he said, "it will be well for me to say a few words to you on the general aspects of the case which is occupying our attention.

"If a person goes abroad or disappears from his home and his ordinary places of resort and is absent for a long period of time, the presumption of death arises at the expiration of seven years from the date on which he was last heard of. That is to say, that the total disappearance of an individual for seven years constitutes presumptive evidence that the said individual is dead; and the presumption can be set aside only by the production of evidence that he was alive at some time within that period of seven years. But if, on the other hand, it is sought to presume the death of a person who has been absent for a shorter period than seven years, it is necessary to produce such evidence as shall make it highly probable that the said person is dead. Of course, presumption implies supposition as opposed to actual demonstration; but, nevertheless, the evidence in such a case must be of a kind that tends to create a very strong belief that death has occurred; and I need hardly say that the shorter the period of absence, the more convincing must be the evidence.

"In the present case, the testator, John Bellingham, has been absent somewhat under two years. This is a relatively short period, and in itself gives rise to no presumption of death. Nevertheless, death has been presumed in a case where the period of absence was even shorter and the insurance recovered; but here the evidence supporting the belief in the occurrence of death was exceedingly weighty.

"The testator in this case was a shipmaster, and his disappearance was accompanied by the disappearance of the ship and the entire ship's company in the course of a voyage from London to Marseilles. The loss of the ship and her crew was the only reasonable explanation of the disappearance, and, short of actual demonstration, the facts offered convincing evidence of the death of all persons on board. I mention this case as an illustration. You are not dealing with speculative probabilities. You are contemplating a very momentous proceeding, and you must be very sure of your ground. Consider what it is that you are asked to do.

"The petitioner asks permission to presume the death of the testator in order that the testator's property may be distributed among the beneficiaries under the will. The granting of such permission involves us in the gravest responsibility. An ill-considered decision might be productive of a serious injustice to the testator, an injustice that could never be remedied. Hence it is incumbent upon you to weigh the evidence with the greatest care, to come to no decision without the profoundest consideration of all the facts.

"The evidence that you have heard divides itself into two parts—that relating to the circumstances of the testator's disappearance, and that relating to certain human remains. In connection with the latter I can only express my surprise and regret that the application was not postponed until the completion of the coroner's inquest, and leave you to consider the evidence. You will bear in mind that Dr. Summers has stated explicitly that the remains cannot be identified as those of any particular individual, but that the testator and the unknown deceased had so many points of resemblance that they might possibly be one and the same person.

"With reference to the circumstances of the disappearance, you have heard the evidence of Mr. Jellicoe to the effect that the testator has on no previous occasion gone abroad without informing him as to his proposed destination. But in considering what weight you are to give to this statement you will bear in mind that when the testator set out for Paris after his interview with Dr. Norbury he left Mr. Jellicoe without any information as to his specific destination, his address in Paris, or the precise date when he should return, and that Mr. Jellicoe was unable to tell us where the testator went or what was his business. Mr. Jellicoe was, in fact, for a time without any means of tracing the testator or ascertaining his whereabouts.

"The evidence of the housemaid, Dobbs, and of Mr. Hurst is rather confusing. It appears that the testator came to the house, and when looked for later was not to be found. A search of the premises showed that he was not in the house, whence it seems to follow that he must have left it; but since no one was informed of his intention to leave, and he had expressed the intention of staying to see Mr. Hurst, his conduct in thus going away surreptitiously must appear somewhat eccentric. The point that you have to consider, therefore, is whether a person who is capable of thus departing in a surreptitious and eccentric manner from a house, without giving notice to the servants, is capable also of departing in a surreptitious and eccentric manner from his usual places of resort without giving notice to his friends or thereafter informing them of his whereabouts.

"The questions, then, gentlemen, that you have to ask yourselves before deciding on your verdict are two: first, Are the circumstances of the testator's disappearance and his continued absence incongruous with his habits and personal peculiarities as they are known to you? and second, Are there any facts which indicate in a positive manner that the testator is dead? Ask yourselves these questions, gentlemen, and the answers to them, furnished by the evidence that you have heard, will guide you to your decision."

Having delivered himself of the above instructions, the judge applied himself to the perusal of the will with professional gusto, in which occupation he was presently disturbed by the announcement of the foreman of the jury that a verdict had been agreed upon.

The judge sat up and glanced at the jury-box, and when the foreman proceeded to state that "We find no sufficient reason for presuming the testator, John Bellingham, to be dead," he nodded approvingly. Evidently that was his opinion, too, as he was careful to explain when he conveyed to Mr. Loram the refusal of the Court to grant the permission applied for.

The decision was a great relief to me, and also, I think, to Miss Bellingham; but most of all to her father who, with instinctive good manners, since he could not suppress a smile of triumph, rose and hastily stumped out of the Court, so that the discomfited Hurst should not see him. His daughter and I followed, and as we left the Court she remarked, with a smile:

"So our pauperism is not, after all, made absolute. There is still a chance for us in the Chapter of Accidents—and perhaps even for poor old Uncle John."

CHAPTER XV   **Circumstantial Evidence**

The morning after the hearing saw me setting forth on my round in more than usually good spirits. The round itself was but a short one, for my list contained only a couple of "chronics," and this, perhaps, contributed to my cheerful outlook on life. But there were other reasons. The decision of the Court had come as an unexpected reprieve and the ruin of my friends' prospects was at least postponed. Then, I had learned that Thorndyke was back from Bristol and wished me to look in on him; and, finally, Miss Bellingham had agreed to spend this very afternoon with me, browsing round the galleries at the British Museum.

I had disposed of my two patients by a quarter to eleven, and three minutes later was striding down Mitre Court, all agog to hear what Thorndyke had to say with reference to my notes on the inquest. The "oak" was open when I arrived at his chambers, and a modest flourish on the little brass knocker of the inner door was answered by my quondam teacher himself.

"How good of you, Berkeley," he said, shaking hands genially, "to look me up so early. I am alone, just looking through the report of the evidence in yesterday's proceedings."

He placed an easy chair for me, and, gathering up a bundle of typewritten papers, laid them aside on the table.

"Were you surprised at the decision?" I asked.

"No," he answered. "Two years is a short period of absence; but still, it might easily have gone the other way. I am greatly relieved. The respite gives us time to carry out our investigations without undue hurry."

"Did you find my notes of any use?" I asked.

"Heath did. Polton handed them to him, and they were invaluable to him for his cross-examination. I haven't seen them yet; in fact, I have only just got them back from him. Let us go through them together now."

He opened a drawer, and taking from it my notebook, seated himself, and began to read through my notes with grave attention, while I stood and looked shyly over his shoulder. On the page that contained my sketches of the Sidcup arm, showing the distribution of the snails' eggs on the bones, he lingered with a faint smile that made me turn hot and red.

"Those sketches look rather footy," I said; "but I had to put something in my notebook."

"You did not attach any importance, then, to the facts that they illustrated?"

"No. The egg-patches were there, so I noted the fact. That's all."

"I congratulate you, Berkeley. There is not one man in twenty who would have had the sense to make a careful note of what he considers an unimportant or irrelevant fact; and the investigator who notes only those things that appear significant is perfectly useless. He gives himself no material for reconsideration. But you don't mean that these egg-patches and worm-tubes appeared to you to have no significance at all?"

"Oh, of course, they show the position in which the bones were lying."

"Exactly. The arm was lying, fully extended, with the dorsal side uppermost. But we also learn from these egg-patches that the hand had been separated from the arm before it was thrown into the pond; and there is something very remarkable in that."

I leaned over his shoulder and gazed at my sketches, amazed at the rapidity with which he had reconstructed the limb from my rough drawings of the individual bones.

"I don't quite see how you arrived at it, though," I said.

"Well, look at your drawings. The egg-patches are on the dorsal surface of the scapula, the humerus, and the bones of the fore-arm. But here you have shown six of the bones of the hand: two metacarpals, the os magnum, and three phalanges; and they all have egg-patches on the *palmar* surface. Therefore the hand was lying palm upwards."

"But the hand may have been pronated."

"If you mean pronated in relation to the arm, that is impossible, for the position of the egg-patches shows clearly that the bones of the arm were lying in the position of supination. Thus the dorsal surface of the arm and the palmar surface of the hand respectively were uppermost, which is an anatomical impossibility so long as the hand is attached to the arm."

"But might not the hand have become detached after lying in the pond some time?"

"No. It could not have been detached until the ligaments had decayed, and if it had been separated after the decay of the soft parts, the bones would have been thrown into disorder. But the egg-patches are all on the palmar surface, showing that the bones were still in their normal relative positions. No, Berkeley, that hand was thrown into the pond separately from the arm."

"But why should it have been?" I asked.

"Ah, there is a very pretty little problem for you to consider. And, meantime, let me tell you that your expedition has been a brilliant success. You are an excellent observer. Your only fault is that when you have noted certain facts you don't seem fully to appreciate their significance—which is merely a matter of inexperience. As to the facts that you have collected, several of them are of prime importance."

"I am glad you are satisfied," said I, "though I don't see that I have discovered much excepting those snails' eggs; and they don't seem to have advanced matters very much."

"A definite fact, Berkeley, is a definite asset. Perhaps we may presently find a little space in our Chinese puzzle which this fact of the detached hand will just drop into. But, tell me, did you find nothing unexpected or suggestive about those bones—as to their number and condition, for instance?"

"Well, I thought it a little queer that the scapula and clavicle should be there. I should have expected him to cut the arm off at the shoulder-joint."

"Yes," said Thorndyke; "so should I; and so it has been done in every case of dismemberment that I am acquainted with. To an ordinary person, the arm seems to join on to the trunk at the shoulder-joint, and that is where he would naturally sever it. What explanation do you suggest of this unusual mode of severing the arm?"

"Do you think the fellow could have been a butcher?" I asked, remembering Dr. Summers' remark. "This is the way a shoulder of mutton is taken off."

"No," replied Thorndyke. "A butcher includes the scapula in a shoulder of mutton for a specific purpose, namely, to take off a given quantity of meat. And also, as a sheep has no clavicle, it is the easiest way to detach the limb. But I imagine a butcher would find himself in difficulties if he attempted to take off a man's arm in that way. The clavicle would be a new and perplexing feature. Then, too, a butcher does not deal very delicately with his subject; if he has to divide a joint, he just cuts through it and does not trouble himself to avoid marking the bones. But you note here that there is not a single scratch or score on any one of the bones, not even where the finger was removed. Now, if you have ever prepared bones for a museum, as I have, you will remember the extreme care that is necessary in disarticulating joints to avoid disfiguring the articular ends of the bones with cuts and scratches."

"Then you think that the person who dismembered this body must have had some anatomical knowledge and skill?"

"That is what has been suggested. The suggestion is not mine."

"Then I infer that you don't agree?"

Thorndyke smiled. "I am sorry to be so cryptic, Berkeley, but you understand that I can't make statements. Still, I am trying to lead you to make certain inferences from the facts that are in your possession."

"If I make the right inference, will you tell me?" I asked.

"It won't be necessary," he answered, with the same quiet smile. "When you have fitted the puzzle together you don't need to be told you have done it."

It was most infernally tantalising. I pondered on the problem with a scowl of such intense cogitation that Thorndyke laughed outright.

"It seems to me," I said, at length, "that the identity of the remains is the primary question and that it is a question of fact. It doesn't seem any use to speculate about it."

"Exactly. Either these bones are the remains of John Bellingham or they are not. There will be no doubt on the subject when all the bones are assembled—if ever they are. And the settlement of that question will probably throw light on the further question: Who deposited them in the places in which they were found? But to return to your observations: did you gather nothing from the other bones? From the complete state of the neck vertebra, for instance?"

"Well, it did strike me as rather odd that the fellow should have gone to the trouble of separating the atlas from the skull. He must have been pretty handy with the scalpel to have done it as cleanly as he seems to have done; but I don't see why he should have gone about the business in the most inconvenient way."

"You notice the uniformity of method. He has separated the head from the spine, instead of cutting through the spine lower down, as most persons would have done; he removed the arms with the entire shoulder-girdle, instead of simply cutting them off at the shoulder-joints. Even in the thighs the same peculiarity appears; for in neither case was the knee-cap found with the thigh-bone, although it seems to have been searched for. Now the obvious way to divide the leg is to cut through the patella ligament, leaving the knee-cap attached to the thigh. But in this case, the knee-cap appears to have been left attached to the shank. Can you explain why this person should have adopted this unusual and rather inconvenient method? Can you suggest a motive for this procedure, or can you think of any circumstances which might lead a person to adopt this method by preference?"

"It seems as if he wished, for some reason, to divide the body into definite anatomical regions."

Thorndyke chuckled. "You are not offering that suggestion as an explanation, are you? Because it would require more explaining than the original problem. And it is not even true. Anatomically speaking, the knee-cap appertains to the thigh rather than to the shank. It is a sesamoid bone belonging to the thigh muscles; yet in this case it has been left attached, apparently, to the shank. No, Berkeley, that cat won't jump. Our unknown operator was not preparing a skeleton as a museum specimen; he was dividing a body up into convenient sized portions for the purpose of conveying them to various ponds. Now what circumstances might have led him to divide it in this peculiar manner?"

"I am afraid I have no suggestion to offer. Have you?"

Thorndyke suddenly lapsed into ambiguity. "I think," he said, "it is possible to conceive such circumstances, and so, probably, will you if you think it over."

"Did you gather anything of importance from the evidence at the inquest?" I asked.

"It is difficult to say," he replied. "The whole of my conclusions in this case are based on what is virtually circumstantial evidence. I have not one single fact of which I can say that it admits only of a single interpretation. Still, it must be remembered that even the most inconclusive facts, if sufficiently multiplied, yield a highly conclusive total. And my little pile of evidence is growing, particle by particle; but we mustn't sit here gossiping at this hour of the day; I have to consult with Marchmont and you say that you have an early afternoon engagement. We can walk together as far as Fleet Street."

A minute or two later we went our respective ways, Thorndyke towards Lombard Street and I to Fetter Lane, not unmindful of those coming events that were casting so agreeable a shadow before them.

There was only one message awaiting me, and when Adolphus had delivered it (amidst mephitic fumes that rose from the basement, premonitory of fried plaice), I pocketed my stethoscope and betook myself to Gunpowder Alley, the aristocratic abode of my patient; joyfully threading the now familiar passages of Gough Square and Wine Office Court, and meditating pleasantly on the curious literary flavour that pervades these little-known regions. For the shade of the author of *Rasselas* still seems to haunt the scenes of his Titanic labours and his ponderous but homely and temperate rejoicings. Every court and alley whispers of books and of the making of books; formes of type, trundled noisily on trolleys by ink-smeared boys, salute the wayfarer at odd corners; piles of strawboard, rolls or bales of paper, drums of printing-ink or roller composition stand on the pavement outside dark entries; basement windows give glimpses into Hadean caverns tenanted by legions of printer's devils; and the very air is charged with the hum of press and with odours of glue and paste and oil. The entire neighbourhood is given up to the printer and binder; and even my patient turned out to be a guillotine-knife grinder—a ferocious and revolutionary calling strangely at variance with his harmless appearance and meek bearing.

I was in good time at my tryst, despite the hindrances of fried plaice and invalid guillotinists; but early as I was, Miss Bellingham was already waiting in the garden—she had been filling a bowl with flowers—ready to sally forth.

"It is quite like old times," she said, as we turned into Fetter Lane, "to be going to the Museum together. It brings back the Tell el Amarna tablets and all your kindness and unselfish labour. I suppose we shall walk there to-day?"

"Certainly," I replied; "I am not going to share your society with the common mortals who ride in omnibuses. That would be sheer, sinful waste. Besides, it is more companionable to walk."

"Yes, it is; and the bustle of the streets makes one more appreciative of the quiet of the Museum. What are we going to look at when we get there?"

"You must decide that," I replied. "You know the collection much better than I do."

"Well, now," she mused, "I wonder what you would like to see; or, in other words, what I should like you to see. The old English pottery is rather fascinating, especially the Fulham ware. I rather think I shall take you to see that."

She reflected a while, and then, just as we reached the gate of Staple Inn, she stopped and looked thoughtfully down the Gray's Inn Road.

"You have taken a great interest in our 'case,' as Dr. Thorndyke calls it. Would you like to see the churchyard where Uncle John wished to be buried? It is a little out of our way, but we are not in a hurry, are we?"

I, certainly, was not. Any deviation that might prolong our walk was welcome, and, as to the place—why, all places were alike to me if only she were by my side. Besides, the churchyard was really of some interest, since it was undoubtedly the "exciting cause" of the obnoxious paragraph two of the will. I accordingly expressed a desire to make its acquaintance, and we crossed to the entrance to Gray's Inn Road.

"Do you ever try," she asked, as we turned down the dingy thoroughfare, "to picture familiar places as they looked a couple of hundred years ago?"

"Yes," I answered, "and very difficult I find it. One has to manufacture the materials for reconstruction, and then the present aspect of the place will keep obtruding itself. But some places are easier to reconstitute than others."

"That is what I find," said she. "Now Holborn, for example, is quite easy to reconstruct, though I daresay the imaginary form isn't a bit like the original. But there are fragments left, like Staple Inn and the front of Gray's Inn; and then one has seen prints of the old Middle Row and some of the taverns, so that one has some material with which to help out one's imagination. But this road we are walking in always baffles me. It looks so old and yet is, for the most part, so new that I find it impossible to make a satisfactory picture of its appearance, say, when Sir Roger de Coverley might have strolled in Gray's Inn Walks, or farther back, when Francis Bacon had chambers in the Inn."

"I imagine," said I, "that part of the difficulty is in the mixed character of the neighbourhood. Here, on the one side, is old Gray's Inn, not much changed since Bacon's time—his chambers are still to be seen, I think, over the gateway; and there, on the Clerkenwell side, is a dense and rather squalid neighbourhood which has grown up over a region partly rural and wholly fugitive in character. Places like Bagnigge Wells and Hockley in the Hole would not have had many buildings that were likely to survive; and in the absence of surviving specimens the imagination hasn't much to work from."

"I daresay you are right," said she. "Certainly, the purlieus of old Clerkenwell present a very confused picture to me; whereas, in the case of an old street like, say, Great Ormond Street, one has only to sweep away the modern buildings and replace them with glorious old houses like the few that remain, dig up the roadway and pavements and lay down cobble-stones, plant a few wooden posts, hang up one or two oil-lamps, and the transformation is complete. And a very delightful transformation it is."

"Very delightful; which, by the way, is a melancholy thought. For we ought to be doing better work than our forefathers; whereas what we actually do is to pull down the old buildings, clap the doorways, porticoes, panelling, and mantels in our museums, and then run up something inexpensive and useful and deadly uninteresting in their place."

My companion looked at me and laughed softly. "For a naturally cheerful, and even gay young man," said she, "you are most amazingly pessimistic. The mantle of Jeremiah—if he ever wore one—seems to have fallen on you, but without in the least impairing your good spirits excepting in regard to matters architectural."

"I have much to be thankful for," said I. "Am I not taken to the Museum by a fair lady? And does she not stay me with mummy cases and comfort me with crockery?"

"Pottery," she corrected; and then as we met a party of grave-looking women emerging from a side-street, she said: "I suppose those are lady medical students."

"Yes, on their way to the Royal Free Hospital. Note the gravity of their demeanour and contrast it with the levity of the male student."

"I was doing so," she answered, "and wondering why professional women are usually so much more serious than men."

"Perhaps," I suggested, "it is a matter of selection. A peculiar type of woman is attracted to the professions, whereas every man has to earn his living as a matter of course."

"Yes, I daresay that is the explanation. This is our turning."

We passed into Heathcote Street, at the end of which was an open gate giving entrance to one of those disused and metamorphosed burial-grounds that are to be met with in the older districts of London; in which the dispossessed dead are jostled into corners to make room for the living. Many of the headstones were still standing, and others, displaced to make room for asphalted walks and seats, were ranged around by the walls exhibiting inscriptions made meaningless by their removal. It was a pleasant enough place on this summer afternoon, contrasted with the dingy streets whence we had come, though its grass was faded and yellow and the twitter of the birds in the trees mingled with the hideous Board-school drawl of the children who played around the seats and the few remaining tombs.

"So this is the last resting-place of the illustrious house of Bellingham," said I.

"Yes; and we are not the only distinguished people who repose in this place. The daughter of no less a person than Richard Cromwell is buried here; the tomb is still standing—but perhaps you have been here before, and know it."

"I don't think I have ever been here before; and yet there is something about the place that seems familiar." I looked around, cudgelling my brains for the key to the dimly reminiscent sensations that the place evoked; until, suddenly, I caught sight of a group of buildings away to the west, enclosed within a wall heightened by a wooden trellis.

"Yes, of course!" I exclaimed. "I remember the place now. I have never been in this part before, but in that enclosure beyond, which opens at the end of Henrietta Street, there used to be and may be still, for all I know, a school of anatomy, at which I attended in my first year; in fact, I did my first dissection there."

"There was a certain gruesome appropriateness in the position of the school," remarked Miss Bellingham. "It would have been really convenient in the days of the resurrection men. Your material would have been delivered at your very door. Was it a large school?"

"The attendance varied according to the time of the year. Sometimes I worked there quite alone. I used to let myself in with a key and hoist my subject out of a sort of sepulchral tank by means of a chain tackle. It was a ghoulish business. You have no idea how awful the body used to look to my unaccustomed eyes, as it rose slowly out of the tank. It was like the resurrection scenes that you see on some old tombstones, where the deceased is shown rising out of his coffin while the skeleton, Death, falls vanquished with his dart shattered and his crown toppling off.

"I remember, too, that the demonstrator used to wear a blue apron, which created a sort of impression of a cannibal butcher's shop. But I am afraid I am shocking you."

"No you are not. Every profession has its unpresentable aspects, which ought not to be seen by outsiders. Think of the sculptor's studio and of the sculptor himself when he is modelling a large figure or group in the clay. He might be a bricklayer or a road-sweeper if you judge by his appearance. This is the tomb I was telling you about."

We halted before the plain coffer of stone, weathered and wasted by age, but yet kept in decent repair by some pious hands, and read the inscription, setting forth with modest pride, that here reposed Anna, sixth daughter of Richard Cromwell, "The Protector." It was a simple monument and commonplace enough, with the crude severity of the ascetic age to which it belonged. But still, it carried the mind back to those stirring times when the leafy shades of Gray's Inn Lane must have resounded with the clank of weapons and the tramp of armed men; when this bald recreation-ground was a rustic churchyard, standing amidst green fields and hedgerows, and countrymen leading their pack-horses into London through the Lane would stop to look in over the wooden gate.

Miss Bellingham looked at me critically as I stood thus reflecting, and presently remarked: "I think you and I have a good many mental habits in common."

I looked up inquiringly, and she continued: "I notice that an old tombstone seems to set you meditating. So it does me. When I look at an ancient monument, and especially an old headstone, I find myself almost unconsciously retracing the years to the date that is written on the stone. Why do you think that is? Why should a monument be so stimulating to the imagination?

And why should a common headstone be more so than any other?"

"I suppose it is," I answered reflectively, "that a churchyard monument is a peculiarly personal thing and appertains in a peculiar way to a particular time. And the circumstance that it has stood untouched by the passing years while everything around has changed, helps the imagination to span the interval. And the common headstone, the memorial of some dead and gone farmer or labourer who lived and died in the village hard by, is still more intimate and suggestive. The rustic, childish sculpture of the village mason and the artless doggerel of the village schoolmaster, bring back the time and place and the conditions of life more vividly than the more scholarly inscriptions and the more artistic enrichments of monuments of greater pretensions. But where are your own family tombstones?"

"They are over in that farther corner. There is an intelligent, but inopportune, person apparently copying the epitaphs. I wish he would go away. I want to show them to you."

I now noticed, for the first time, an individual engaged, notebook in hand, in making a careful survey of a group of old headstones. Evidently he was making a copy of the inscriptions, for not only was he poring attentively over the writing on the face of the stone, but now and again he helped out his vision by running his fingers over the worn lettering.

"That is my grandfather's tombstone that he is copying now," said Miss Bellingham; and even as she spoke, the man turned and directed a searching glance at us with a pair of keen, spectacled eyes.

Simultaneously we uttered an exclamation of surprise; for the investigator was Mr. Jellicoe.

CHAPTER XVI   "O Artemidorus, Farewell!"

Whether or not Mr. Jellicoe was surprised to see us, it is impossible to say. His countenance (which served the ordinary purposes of a face, inasmuch as it contained the principal organs of special sense, with inlets to the alimentary and respiratory tracts) was, as an apparatus for the expression of the emotions, a total failure. To a thought-reader it would have been about as helpful as the face carved upon the handle of an umbrella; a comparison suggested, perhaps, by a certain resemblance to such an object. He advanced, holding his open notebook and pencil, and, having saluted us with a stiff bow and an old-fashioned flourish of his hat, shook hands rheumatically and waited for us to speak.

"This is an unexpected pleasure, Mr. Jellicoe," said Miss Bellingham.

"It is very good of you to say so," he replied.

"And quite a coincidence—that we should all happen to come here on the same day."

"A coincidence, certainly," he admitted; "and if we had all happened not to come—which must have occurred frequently—that also would have been a coincidence."

"I suppose it would," said she, "but I hope we are not interrupting you."

"Thank you, no. I had just finished when I had the pleasure of perceiving you."

"You were making some notes in reference to the case, I imagine," said I. It was an impertinent question, put with malice aforethought for the mere pleasure of hearing him evade it.

226

"The case?" he repeated. "You are referring, perhaps, to Stevens versus the Parish Council?"

"I think Dr. Berkeley was referring to the case of my uncle's will," Miss Bellingham said quite gravely, though with a suspicious dimpling about the corners of her mouth.

"Indeed," said Mr. Jellicoe. "There is a case, is there; a suit?"

"I mean the proceedings instituted by Mr. Hurst."

"Oh, but that was merely an application to the Court, and is, moreover, finished and done with. At least, so I understand. I speak, of course, subject to correction; I am not acting for Mr. Hurst, you will be pleased to remember. As a matter of fact," he continued, after a brief pause, "I was just refreshing my memory as to the wording of the inscriptions on these stones, especially that of your grandfather, Francis Bellingham. It has occurred to me that if it should appear by the finding of the coroner's jury that your uncle is deceased, it would be proper and decorous that some memorial should be placed here. But, as the burial ground is closed, there might be some difficulty about erecting a new monument, whereas there would probably be none in adding an inscription to one already existing. Hence these investigations. For if the inscriptions on your grandfather's stone had set forth that 'here rests the body of Francis Bellingham,' it would have been manifestly improper to add 'also that of John Bellingham, son of the above.' Fortunately the inscription was more discreetly drafted, merely recording the fact that this monument is 'sacred to the memory of the said Francis,' and not committing itself as to the whereabouts of the remains. But perhaps I am interrupting you."

"No, not at all," replied Miss Bellingham (which was

grossly untrue; he was interrupting *me* most intolerably); "we were going to the British Museum and just looked in here on our way."

"Ha," said Mr. Jellicoe, "now I happen to be going to the Museum too, to see Dr. Norbury. I suppose that is another coincidence?"

"Certainly it is," Miss Bellingham replied; and then she asked: "Shall we walk together?" and the old curmudgeon actually said "yes"—confound him!

We returned to the Gray's Inn Road, where, as there was now room for us to walk abreast, I proceeded to indemnify myself for the lawyer's unwelcome company by leading the conversation back to the subject of the missing man.

"Was there anything, Mr. Jellicoe, in Mr. John Bellingham's state of health that would make it probable that he might die suddenly?"

The lawyer looked at me suspiciously for a few moments and then remarked:

"You seem to be greatly interested in John Bellingham and his affairs."

"I am. My friends are deeply concerned in them, and the case itself is of more than common interest from a professional point of view."

"And what is the bearing of this particular question?"

"Surely it is obvious," said I. "If a missing man is known to have suffered from some affection, such as heart disease, aneurism, or arterial degeneration, likely to produce sudden death, that fact will surely be highly material to the question as to whether he is probably dead or alive."

"No doubt you are right," said Mr. Jellicoe. "I have little knowledge of medical affairs, but doubtless you are right. As to the question itself, I am Mr. Bellingham's lawyer, not his doctor. His health is a matter that lies outside my jurisdiction. But you heard my evidence in Court, to the effect that the testator appeared, to my untutored observation, to be a healthy man. I can say no more now."

"If the question is of any importance," said Miss Bellingham, "I wonder they did not call his doctor and settle it definitely. My own impression is that he was—or is—rather a strong and sound man. He certainly recovered very quickly and completely after his accident."

"What accident was that?" I asked.

"Oh, hasn't my father told you? It occurred while he was staying with us. He slipped from a kerb and broke one of the bones of the left ankle—somebody's fracture—"

"Pott's?"

"Yes; that was the name—Pott's fracture; and he broke both his knee-caps as well. Sir Morgan Bennet had to perform an operation, or he would have been a cripple for life. As it was, he was about again in a few weeks, apparently none the worse excepting for a slight weakness of the left ankle."

"Could he walk upstairs?" I asked.

"Oh, yes; and play golf and ride a bicycle."

"You are sure he broke both knee-caps?"

"Quite sure. I remember that it was mentioned as an uncommon injury, and that Sir Morgan seemed quite pleased with him for doing it."

"That sounds rather libellous; but I expect he was pleased with the result of the operation. He might well be."

Here there was a brief lull in the conversation, and, even as I was trying to think of a poser for Mr. Jellicoe, that gentleman took the opportunity to change the subject.

"Are you going to the Egyptian rooms?" he asked.

"No," replied Miss Bellingham; "we are going to look at the pottery."

"Ancient or modern?"

"That old Fulham ware is what chiefly interests us at present; that of the seventeenth century. I don't know whether you call that ancient or modern."

"Neither do I," said Mr. Jellicoe. "Antiquity and modernity are terms that have no fixed connotation. They are purely relative and their application in a particular instance has to be determined by a sort of sliding-scale. To a furniture collector, a Tudor chair or a Jacobean chest is ancient; to an architect, their period is modern, whereas an eleventh-century church is ancient; but to an Egyptologist, accustomed to remains of a vast antiquity, both are products of modern periods separated by an insignificant interval. And, I suppose," he added reflectively, "that to a geologist, the traces of the very earliest dawn of human history appertain only to the recent period. Conceptions of time, like all other conceptions, are relative."

"You would appear to be a disciple of Herbert Spencer," I remarked.

"I am a disciple of Arthur Jellicoe, sir," he retorted. And I believed him.

By the time we had reached the Museum he had become almost genial, and if less amusing in this frame he was so much more instructive and entertaining that I refrained from baiting him, and permitted him to discuss his favourite topic unhindered, especially since my companion listened with lively interest. Nor, when we entered the great hall, did he relinquish possession of us,

and we followed submissively, as he led the way past the
winged bulls of Nineveh and the great seated statues,
until we found ourselves, almost without the exercise of
our volition, in the upper room amidst the glaring
mummy cases that had witnessed the birth of my
friendship with Ruth Bellingham.

"Before I leave you," said Mr. Jellicoe, "I should like
to show you that mummy that we were discussing the
other evening; the one, you remember, that my friend,
John Bellingham, presented to the Museum a little time
before his disappearance. The point that I mentioned is
only a trivial one, but it may become of interest hereafter
if any plausible explanation should be forthcoming." He
led us along the room until we arrived at the case
containing John Bellingham's gift, where he halted and
gazed in at the mummy with the affectionate
reflectiveness of the connoisseur.

"The bitumen coating was what we were discussing,
Miss Bellingham," said he. "You have seen it, of course."

"Yes," she answered. "It is a dreadful disfigurement,
isn't it?"

"Æsthetically it is to be deplored, but it adds a certain
speculative interest to the specimen. You notice that the
black coating leaves the principal decoration and the
whole of the inscription untouched, which is precisely the
part that one would expect to find covered up; whereas
the feet and the back, which probably bore no writing, are
quite thickly crusted. If you stoop down, you can see that
the bitumen was daubed freely into the lacings of the
back, where it served no purpose, so that even the strings
are embedded." He stooped as he spoke, and peered up
inquisitively at the back of the mummy, where it was
visible between the supports.

"Has Dr. Norbury any explanation to offer?" asked

Miss Bellingham.

"None whatever," replied Mr. Jellicoe. "He finds it as great a mystery as I do. But he thinks that we may get some suggestion from the Director when he comes back. He is a very great authority, as you know, and a practical excavator of great experience too. But I mustn't stay here talking of these things, and keeping you from your pottery. Perhaps I have stayed too long already. If I have I ask your pardon, and I will now wish you a very good afternoon." With a sudden return to his customary wooden impassivity, he shook hands with us, bowed stiffly, and took himself off towards the curator's office.

"What a strange man that is," said Miss Bellingham, as Mr. Jellicoe disappeared through the doorway at the end of the room, "or perhaps I should say, a strange being, for I can hardly think of him as a man. I have never met any other human creature at all like him."

"He is certainly a queer old fogey," I agreed.

"Yes, but there is something more than that. He is so emotionless, so remote and aloof from all mundane concerns. He moves among ordinary men and women, but as a mere presence, an unmoved spectator of their actions, quite dispassionate and impersonal."

"Yes; he is astonishingly self-contained; in fact, he seems, as you say, to go to and fro among men, enveloped in a sort of infernal atmosphere of his own, like Marley's ghost. But he is lively and human enough as soon as the subject of Egyptian antiquities is broached."

"Lively, but not human. He is always, to me, quite unhuman. Even when he is most interested, and even enthusiastic, he is a mere personification of knowledge. Nature ought to have furnished him with an ibis's head like Tahuti; then he would have looked his part."

"He would have made a rare sensation in Lincoln's Inn if he had," said I; and we both laughed heartily at the imaginary picture of Tahuti Jellicoe, slender-beaked and top-hatted, going about his business in Lincoln's Inn and the Law Courts.

Insensibly, as we talked, we had drawn near to the mummy of Artemidorus, and now my companion halted before the case with her thoughtful grey eyes bent dreamily on the face that looked out at us. I watched her with reverent admiration. How charming she looked as she stood with her sweet, grave face turned so earnestly to the object of her mystical affection! How dainty and full of womanly dignity and grace! And then, suddenly, it was borne in upon me that a great change had come over her since the day of our first meeting. She had grown younger, more girlish, and more gentle. At first she had seemed much older than I; a sad-faced woman, weary, solemn, enigmatic, almost gloomy, with a bitter, ironic humour and a bearing distant and cold. Now she was only maidenly and sweet; tinged, it is true, with a certain seriousness, but frank and gracious and wholly lovable.

Could the change be due to our friendship? As I asked myself the question, my heart leaped with a new hope. I yearned to tell her all that she was to me—all that I hoped we might be to one another in the years to come.

At length I ventured to break in upon her reverie.

"What are you thinking about so earnestly, fair lady?"

She turned quickly with a bright smile and sparkling eyes that looked frankly into mine. "I was wondering," said she, "if he was jealous of my new friend. But what a baby I am to talk such nonsense!"

She laughed softly and happily with just an adorable hint of shyness.

"Why should he be jealous?" I asked.

"Well, you see, before—we were friends, he had me all to himself. I have never had a man friend before— except my father—and no really intimate friend at all. And I was very lonely in those days, after our troubles had befallen. I am naturally solitary, but still, I am only a girl; I am not a philosopher. So when I felt very lonely, I used to come here and look at Artemidorus and make believe that he knew all the sadness of my life and sympathised with me. It was very silly, I know, but yet, somehow, it was a real comfort to me."

"It was not silly of you at all. He must have been a good man, a gentle, sweet-faced man who had won the love of those who knew him, as this beautiful memorial tells; and it was wise and good of you to sweeten the bitterness of your life with the fragrance of this human love that blossoms in the dust after the lapse of centuries. No, you were not silly, and Artemidorus is not jealous of your new friend."

"Are you sure?" She still smiled as she asked the question, but her glance was soft—almost tender—and there was a note of whimsical anxiety in her voice.

"Quite sure. I give you my confident assurance."

She laughed gaily. "Then," said she, "I am satisfied, for I am sure you know. But here is a mighty telepathist who can read the thoughts even of a mummy. A most formidable companion. But tell me how you know."

"I know because it is he who gave you to me to be my friend. Don't you remember?"

"Yes, I remember," she answered softly. "It was when you were so sympathetic with my foolish whim that I felt we were really friends."

"And I, when you confided your pretty fancy to me, thanked you for the gift of your friendship, and treasured it, and do still treasure it, above everything on earth."

She looked at me quickly with a sort of nervousness in her manner, and cast down her eyes. Then, after a few moments' almost embarrassed silence, as if to bring back our talk to a less emotional plane, she said:

"Do you notice the curious way in which this memorial divides itself up into two parts?"

"How do you mean?" I asked, a little disconcerted by the sudden descent.

"I mean that there is a part of it that is purely decorative and a part that is expressive or emotional. You notice that the general design and scheme of decoration, although really Greek in feeling, follows rigidly the Egyptian conventions. But the portrait is entirely in the Greek manner, and when they came to that pathetic farewell, it had to be spoken in their own tongue, written in their own familiar characters."

"Yes. I have noticed that and admired the taste with which they have kept the inscription so inconspicuous as not to clash with the decoration. An obtrusive inscription in Greek characters would have spoiled the consistency of the whole scheme."

"Yes, it would." She assented absently as if she were thinking of something else, and once more gazed thoughtfully at the mummy. I watched her with deep content: noted the lovely contour of her cheek, the soft masses of hair that strayed away so gracefully from her brow, and thought her the most wonderful creature that had ever trod the earth. Suddenly she looked at me reflectively.

"I wonder," she said, "what made me tell you about Artemidorus. It was a rather silly, childish sort of make-believe, and I wouldn't have told anyone else for the world; not even my father. How did I know that you would sympathise and understand?"

She asked the question in all simplicity, with her serious grey eyes looking inquiringly into mine. And the answer came to me in a flash, with the beating of my own heart.

"I will tell you how you knew, Ruth," I whispered passionately. "It was because I loved you more than anyone else in the world has ever loved you, and you felt my love in your heart and called it sympathy."

I stopped short, for she had blushed scarlet and then turned deathly pale. And now she looked at me wildly, almost with terror.

"Have I shocked you, Ruth dearest?" I exclaimed penitently, "have I spoken too soon? If I have, forgive me. But I had to tell you. I have been eating my heart out for love of you for I don't know how long. I think I have loved you from the first day we met. Perhaps I shouldn't have spoken yet, but, Ruth dear, if you only knew what a sweet girl you are, you wouldn't blame me."

"I don't blame you," she said, almost in a whisper; "I blame myself. I have been a bad friend to you, who have been so loyal and loving to me. I ought not to have let this happen. For it can't be, Paul; I can't say what you want me to say. We can never be anything more to one another than friends."

A cold hand seemed to grasp my heart—a horrible fear that I had lost all that I cared for—all that made life desirable.

"Why can't we?" I asked. "Do you mean that—that the gods have been gracious to some other man?"

"No, no," she answered hastily—almost indignantly, "of course I don't mean that."

"Then it is only that you don't love me yet. Of course you don't. Why should you? But you will, dear, some day. And I will wait patiently until that day comes and not trouble you with entreaties. I will wait for you as Jacob waited for Rachel; and as the long years seemed to him but as a few days because of the love he bore her, so it shall be with me, if only you will not send me away quite without hope."

She was looking down, white-faced, with a hardening of the lips as if she were in bodily pain. "You don't understand," she whispered. "It can't be—it can never be. There is something that makes it impossible, now and always. I can't tell you more than that."

"But, Ruth dearest," I pleaded despairingly, "may it not become possible some day? Can it not be made possible? I can wait, but I can't give you up. Is there no chance whatever that this obstacle may be removed?"

"Very little, I fear. Hardly any. No, Paul; it is hopeless, and I can't bear to talk about it. Let me go now. Let us say good-bye here and see one another no more for a while. Perhaps we may be friends again some day—when you have forgiven me."

"Forgiven you, dearest!" I exclaimed. "There is nothing to forgive. And we are friends, Ruth. Whatever happens, you are the dearest friend I have on earth, or can ever have."

"Thank you, Paul," she said faintly. "You are very good to me. But let me go, please. I must be alone."

She held out a trembling hand, and, as I took it, I was shocked to see how terribly agitated and ill she looked.

"May I not come with you, dear?" I pleaded.

"No, no!" she exclaimed breathlessly; "I must go away by myself. I want to be alone. Good-bye."

"Before I let you go, Ruth—if you must go—I must have a most solemn promise from you."

Her sad grey eyes met mine and her lips quivered with an unspoken question.

"You must promise me," I went on, "that if ever this barrier that parts us should be removed, you will let me know instantly. Remember that I love you always, and that I am waiting for you always on this side of the grave."

She caught her breath in a quick little sob, and pressed my hand.

"Yes," she whispered: "I promise. Good-bye."

She pressed my hand again and was gone; and, as I gazed at the empty doorway through which she had passed, I caught a glimpse of her reflection in a glass on the landing, where she had paused for a moment to wipe her eyes. I felt it, in a manner, indelicate to have seen her, and turned away my head quickly; and yet I was conscious of a certain selfish satisfaction in the sweet sympathy that her grief bespoke.

But now that she was gone a horrible sense of desolation descended on me. Only now, by the consciousness of irreparable loss, did I begin to realise the meaning of this passion of love that had stolen unawares into my life. How it had glorified the present and spread a glamour of delight over the dimly considered future: how all pleasures and desires, hopes and ambitions, had converged upon it as a focus; how it had stood out as the one great reality behind which the other circumstances of life were as a background, shimmering, half seen, immaterial and unreal. And now it was gone—lost, as it seemed, beyond hope; and that which was left to me was but the empty frame from which the picture had vanished.

I have no idea how long I stood rooted to the spot where she had left me, wrapped in a dull consciousness of pain, immersed in a half-numb reverie. Recent events flitted dream-like through my mind; our happy labours in the reading-room; our first visit to the Museum; and this present day that had opened so brightly and with such joyous promise. One by one these phantoms of a vanished happiness came and went. Occasional visitors sauntered into the room—but the galleries were mostly empty that day—gazed inquisitively at my motionless figure and went their way. And still the dull intolerable ache in my breast went on, the only vivid consciousness that was left to me.

Presently I raised my eyes and met those of the portrait. The sweet, pensive face of the old Greek settler looked out at me wistfully as though he would offer comfort; as though he would tell me that he, too, had known sorrow when he lived his life in the sunny Fayyum. And a subtle consolation, like the faint scent of old rose leaves, seemed to exhale from that friendly face that had looked on the birth of my happiness and had seen it wither and fade. I turned away, at last, with a silent farewell; and, when I looked back, he seemed to speed me on my way with gentle valediction.

CHAPTER XVII   The Accusing Finger

Of my wanderings after I left the Museum on that black and dismal *dies iræ* I have but a dim recollection. But I must have travelled a quite considerable distance, since it wanted an hour or two to the time for returning to the surgery, and I spent the interval walking swiftly through streets and squares, unmindful of the happenings around, intent only on my present misfortune, and driven by a natural impulse to seek relief in bodily exertion. For mental distress sets up, as it were, a sort of induced current of physical unrest; a beneficent arrangement, by which a dangerous excess of emotional excitement may be transformed into motor energy, and so safely got rid of. The motor apparatus acts as a safety-valve to the psychical; and, if the engine races for a while, with the onset of bodily fatigue the emotional pressure-gauge returns to a normal reading.

And so it was with me. At first I was conscious of nothing but a sense of utter bereavement, of the shipwreck of all my hopes. But, by degrees, as I threaded my way among the moving crowds, I came to a better and more worthy frame of mind. After all, I had lost nothing that I had ever had. Ruth was still all that she had ever been to me—perhaps even more; and if that had been a rich endowment yesterday, why not to-day also? And how unfair it would be to her if I should mope and grieve over a disappointment that was no fault of hers and for which there was no remedy! Thus I reasoned with myself, and to such purpose that, by the time I reached Fetter Lane, my dejection had come to quite manageable proportions and I had formed the resolution to get back to the *status quo ante bellum* as soon as possible.

About eight o'clock, as I was sitting alone in the consulting-room, gloomily persuading myself that I was now quite resigned to the inevitable, Adolphus brought me a registered packet, at the handwriting on which my heart gave such a bound that I had much ado to sign the receipt. As soon as Adolphus had retired (with undissembled contempt of the shaky signature) I tore open the packet, and as I drew out a letter a tiny box dropped on the table.

The letter was all too short, and I devoured it over and over again with the eagerness of a condemned man reading a reprieve:

"MY DEAR PAUL,—Forgive me for leaving you so abruptly this afternoon, and leaving you so unhappy, too. I am more sane and reasonable now, and so send you greeting and beg you not to grieve for that which can never be. It is quite impossible, dear friend, and I entreat you, as you care for me, never to speak of it again; never again to make me feel that I can give you so little when you have given so much. And do not try to see me for a little while. I shall miss your visits, and so will my father, who is very fond of you; but it is better that we should not meet, until we can take up our old relations—if that can ever be.

"I am sending you a little keepsake in case we should drift apart on the eddies of life. It is the ring that I told you about—the one that my uncle gave me. Perhaps you may be able to wear it as you have a small hand, but in any case keep it in remembrance of our friendship. The device on it is the Eye of Osiris, a mystic symbol for which I have a sentimentally superstitious affection, as also had my poor uncle, who actually bore it tattooed in scarlet on his breast. It signifies that the great judge of the dead looks down on men to see that justice is done and that truth prevails. So I commend you to the good Osiris; may his eye be upon you, ever watchful over your welfare in the absence of

"Your affectionate friend,

"RUTH."

It was a sweet letter, I thought, even if it carried little comfort; quiet and reticent like its writer, but with an undertone of affection. I laid it down at length, and, taking the ring from its box, examined it fondly. Though but a copy, it had all the quaintness and feeling of the antique original, and, above all, it was fragrant with the spirit of the giver. Dainty and delicate, wrought of silver and gold, with an inlay of copper, I would not have exchanged it for the Koh-i-noor; and when I had slipped it on my finger its tiny eye of blue enamel looked up at me so friendly and companionable that I felt the glamour of the old-world superstition stealing over me too.

Not a single patient came in this evening, which was well for me (and also for the patient), as I was able forthwith to write in reply a long letter; but this I shall spare the long-suffering reader excepting its concluding paragraph:

"And now, dearest, I have said my say: once for all I have said it, and I will not open my mouth on the subject again (I am not actually opening it now) 'until the times do alter.' And if the times do never alter—if it shall come to pass, in due course, that we two shall sit side by side, white-haired, and crinkly-nosed, and lean our poor old chins upon our sticks and mumble and gibber amicably over the things that might have been if the good Osiris had come up to the scratch—I will still be content, because your friendship, Ruth, is better than another woman's love. So you see, I have taken my gruel and come up to time smiling—if you will pardon the pugilistic metaphor—and I promise you loyally to do your bidding and never again to distress you.

"Your faithful and loving friend,

"PAUL."

This letter I addressed and stamped, and then, with a wry grimace which I palmed off on myself (but not on Adolphus) as a cheerful smile, I went out and dropped it into the post-box; after which I further deluded myself by murmuring *Nunc dimittis* and assuring myself that the incident was now absolutely closed.

But despite this comfortable assurance I was, in the days that followed, an exceedingly miserable young man. It is all very well to write down troubles of this kind as trivial and sentimental. They are nothing of the kind. When a man of essentially serious nature has found the one woman of all the world who fulfils his highest ideals of womanhood, who is, in fact, a woman in ten thousand, to whom he has given all that he has to give of love and worship, the sudden wreck of all his hopes is no small calamity. And so I found it. Resign myself as I would to the bitter reality, the ghost of the might-have-been haunted me night and day, so that I spent my leisure wandering abstractedly about the streets, always trying to banish thought and never for an instant succeeding. A great unrest was upon me; and when I received a letter from Dick Barnard announcing his arrival at Madeira, homeward bound, I breathed a sigh of relief. I had no plans for the future, but I longed to be rid of the, now irksome, routine of the practice—to be free to come and go when and how I pleased.

One evening, as I sat consuming with little appetite my solitary supper, there fell on me a sudden sense of loneliness. The desire that I had hitherto felt to be alone with my own miserable reflections gave place to a yearning for human companionship. That, indeed, which I craved for most was forbidden, and I must abide by my lady's wishes; but there were my friends in the Temple. It was more than a week since I had seen them; in fact, we had not met since the morning of that unhappiest day of my life. They would be wondering what had become of me. I rose from the table, and having filled my pouch from a tin of tobacco, set forth for King's Bench Walk.

As I approached the entry of No. 5A in the gathering darkness I met Thorndyke himself emerging encumbered with two deck-chairs, a reading-lantern, and a book.

"Why, Berkeley!" he exclaimed, "is it indeed thou? We have been wondering what had become of you."

"It is a long time since I looked you up," I admitted.

He scrutinised me attentively by the light of the entry lamp, and then remarked: "Fetter Lane doesn't seem to be agreeing with you very well, my son. You are looking quite thin and peaky."

"Well, I've nearly done with it. Barnard will be back in about ten days. His ship is putting in at Madeira to coal and take in some cargo, and then he is coming home. Where are you going with those chairs?"

"I am going to sit down at the end of the Walk by the railings. It is cooler there than indoors. If you will wait a moment I will go and fetch another chair for Jervis, though he won't be back for a little while." He ran up the stairs, and presently returned with a third chair, and we carried our impedimenta down to the quiet corner of the Walk.

"So your term of servitude is coming to an end," said he, when we had placed the chairs and hung the lantern on the railings. "Any other news?"

"No. Have you any?"

"I am afraid I have not. All my inquiries have yielded negative results. There is, of course, a considerable body of evidence, and it all seems to point one way. But I am unwilling to make a decisive move without something more definite. I am really waiting for confirmation or otherwise of my ideas on the subject; for some new item of evidence."

"I didn't know there was any evidence."

"Didn't you?" said Thorndyke. "But you know as much as I know. You have all the essential facts; but apparently you haven't collated them and extracted their meaning. If you had, you would have found them curiously significant."

"I suppose I mustn't ask what their significance is?"

"No, I think not. When I am conducting a case I mention my surmises to nobody—not even to Jervis. Then I can say confidently that there has been no leakage. Don't think I distrust you. Remember that my thoughts are my client's property, and that the essence of strategy is to keep the enemy in the dark."

"Yes, I see that. Of course I ought not to have asked."

"You ought not to need to ask," Thorndyke replied, with a smile; "you should put the facts together and reason from them yourself."

While we had been talking I had noticed Thorndyke glance at me inquisitively from time to time. Now after an interval of silence, he asked suddenly:

"Is anything amiss, Berkeley? Are you worrying about your friends' affairs?"

"No, not particularly; though their prospects don't look very rosy."

"Perhaps they are not quite so bad as they look," said he. "But I am afraid something is troubling you. All your gay spirits seem to have evaporated." He paused for a few moments, and then added: "I don't want to intrude on your private affairs, but if I can help you by advice or otherwise, remember that we are old friends and that you are my academic offspring."

Instinctively, with a man's natural reticence, I began to

mumble a half-articulate disclaimer; and then I stopped. After all, why should I not confide in him? He was a good man and a wise man, full of human sympathy, as I knew, though so cryptic and secretive in his professional capacity. And I wanted a friend badly just now.

"I'm afraid," I began shyly, "it is not a matter that admits of much help, and it's hardly the sort of thing that I ought to worry you by talking about—"

"If it is enough to make you unhappy, my dear fellow, it is enough to merit serious consideration by your friend; so if you don't mind telling me—"

"Of course I don't, sir!" I exclaimed.

"Then fire away; and don't call me 'sir.' We are brother practitioners now."

Thus encouraged, I poured out the story of my little romance; bashfully at first and with halting phrases, but later, with more freedom and confidence. He listened with grave attention, and once or twice put a question when my narrative became a little disconnected. When I had finished he laid his hand softly on my arm.

"You have had rough luck, Berkeley. I don't wonder that you are miserable. I am more sorry than I can tell you."

"Thank you," I said. "It's exceedingly good of you to listen so patiently, but it's a shame for me to pester you with my sentimental troubles."

"Now, Berkeley, you don't think that, and I hope you don't think that I do. We should be bad biologists and worse physicians if we should underestimate the importance of that which is nature's chiefest care. The one salient biological truth is the paramount importance of sex; and we are deaf and blind if we do not hear and see it in everything that lives when we look abroad upon the world; when we listen to the spring song of the birds, or when we consider the lilies of the field. And as is man to the lower organisms, so is human love to their merely reflex manifestations of sex. I will maintain, and you will agree with me, I know, that the love of a serious and honourable man for a woman who is worthy of him is the most momentous of all human affairs. It is the foundation of social life, and its failure is a serious calamity, not only to those whose lives may be thereby spoilt, but to society at large."

"It's a serious enough matter for the parties concerned," I agreed; "but that is no reason why they should bore their friends."

"But they don't. Friends should help one another and think it a privilege."

"Oh, I shouldn't mind coming to you for help, knowing you as I do. But no one can help a poor devil in a case like this—and certainly not a medical jurist."

"Oh, come, Berkeley!" he protested, "don't rate us too low. The humblest of creatures has its uses—'even the little pismire,' you know, as Isaak Walton tells us. Why, I have got substantial help from a stamp-collector. And then reflect upon the motor-scorcher and the earthworm and the blow-fly. All these lowly creatures play their parts in the scheme of nature; and shall we cast out the medical jurist as nothing worth?"

I laughed dejectedly at my teacher's genial irony.

"What I meant," said I, "was that there is nothing to be done but wait—perhaps for ever. I don't know why she isn't able to marry me, and I mustn't ask her. She can't be married already."

"Certainly not. She told you explicitly that there was no man in the case."

"Exactly. And I can think of no other valid reason, excepting that she doesn't care enough for me. That would be a perfectly sound reason, but then it would only be a temporary one, not the insuperable obstacle that she assumes to exist, especially as we really got on excellently together. I hope it isn't some confounded perverse feminine scruple. I don't see how it could be; but women are most frightfully tortuous and wrong-headed at times."

"I don't see," said Thorndyke, "why we should cast about for perversely abnormal motives when there is a perfectly reasonable explanation staring us in the face."

"Is there?" I exclaimed. "I see none."

"You are, not unnaturally, overlooking some of the circumstances that affect Miss Bellingham; but I don't suppose she has failed to grasp their meaning. Do you realise what her position really is? I mean with regard to her uncle's disappearance?"

"I don't think I quite understand you."

"Well, there is no use in blinking the facts," said Thorndyke. "The position is this: if John Bellingham ever went to his brother's house at Woodford, it is nearly certain that he went there after his visit to Hurst. Mind, I say '*if* he went'; I don't say that I believe he did. But it is stated that he appears to have gone there: and if he did go, he was never seen alive afterwards. Now, he did not go in at the front door. No one saw him enter the house. But there was a back gate, which John Bellingham knew, and which had a bell which rang in the library. And you will remember that, when Hurst and Jellicoe called, Mr. Bellingham had only just come in. Previous to that time Miss Bellingham had been alone in the library; that is to say, she was alone in the library at the very time when John Bellingham is said to have made his visit. That is the position, Berkeley. Nothing pointed has been said up to the present. But, sooner or later, if John Bellingham is not found, dead or alive, the question will be opened. Then it is certain that Hurst, in self-defence, will make the most of any facts that may transfer suspicion from him to some one else. And that some one else will be Miss Bellingham."

I sat for some moments literally paralysed with horror. Then my dismay gave place to indignation. "But, damn it!" I exclaimed, starting up, "I beg your pardon—but could anyone have the infernal audacity to insinuate that that gentle, refined lady murdered her uncle?"

"That is what will be hinted, if not plainly asserted; and she knows it. And that being so, is it difficult to understand why she should refuse to allow you to be publicly associated with her? To run the risk of dragging your honourable name into the sordid transactions of the police-court or the Old Bailey? To invest it, perhaps, with a dreadful notoriety?"

"Oh, don't! for God's sake! It is too horrible! Not that I would care for myself. I would be proud to share her martyrdom of ignominy, if it had to be; but it is the sacrilege, the blasphemy of even thinking of her in such terms, that enrages me."

"Yes," said Thorndyke; "I understand and sympathise with you. Indeed, I share your righteous indignation at this dastardly affair. So you mustn't think me brutal for putting the case so plainly."

"I don't. You have only shown me the danger that I was fool enough not to see. But you seem to imply that this hideous position has been brought about deliberately."

"Certainly I do! This is no chance affair. Either the appearances indicate the real events—which I am sure they do not—or they have been created of a set purpose to lead to false conclusions. But the circumstances convince me that there has been a deliberate plot; and I am waiting—in no spirit of Christian patience, I can tell you—to lay my hand on the wretch who has done this."

"What are you waiting for?" I asked.

"I am waiting for the inevitable," he replied; "for the false move that the most artful criminal invariably makes. At present he is lying low; but presently he will make a move, and then I shall have him."

"But he may go on lying low. What will you do then?"

"Yes, that is the danger. We may have to deal with the perfect villain who knows when to leave well alone. I have never met him, but he may exist, nevertheless."

"And then we should have to stand by and see our friends go under."

"Perhaps," said Thorndyke; and we both subsided into gloomy and silent reflection.

The place was peaceful and quiet, as only a backwater of London can be. Occasional hoots from faraway tugs and steamers told of the busy life down below in the crowded pool. A faint hum of traffic was borne in from the streets outside the precincts, and the shrill voices of newspaper boys came in unceasing chorus from the direction of Carmelite Street. They were too far away to be physically disturbing, but the excited yells, toned down as they were by distance, nevertheless stirred the very marrow in my bones, so dreadfully suggestive were they of those possibilities of the future at which Thorndyke had hinted. They seemed like the sinister shadows of coming misfortunes.

Perhaps they called up the same association of ideas in Thorndyke's mind, for he remarked presently: "The newsvendor is abroad to-night like a bird of ill-omen. Something unusual has happened; some public or private calamity, most likely, and these yelling ghouls are out to feast on the remains. The newspaper men have a good deal in common with the carrion-birds that hover over a battle-field."

Again we subsided into silence and reflection. Then, after an interval, I asked:

"Would it be possible for me to help in any way in this investigation of yours?"

"That is exactly what I have been asking myself," replied Thorndyke. "It would be right and proper that you should, and I think you might."

"How?" I asked eagerly.

"I can't say off-hand; but Jervis will be going away for his holiday almost at once—in fact, he will go off actual duty to-night. There is very little doing; the long vacation is close upon us, and I can do without him. But if you would care to come down here and take his place, you would be very useful to me; and if there should be anything to be done in the Bellinghams' case, I am sure you would make up in enthusiasm for any deficiency in experience."

"I couldn't really take Jervis's place," said I, "but if you would let me help you in any way it would be a great kindness. I would rather clean your boots than be out of it altogether."

"Very well. Let us leave it that you come here as soon as Barnard has done with you. You can have Jervis's room, which he doesn't often use nowadays, and you will be more happy here than elsewhere, I know. I may as well give you my latch-key now. I have a duplicate upstairs, and you understand that my chambers are yours too from this moment."

He handed me the latch-key and I thanked him warmly from my heart; for I felt sure that the suggestion was made, not for any use that I should be to him, but for my own peace of mind. I had hardly finished speaking when a quick step on the paved walk caught my ear.

"Here is Jervis," said Thorndyke. "We will let him know that there is a locum-tenens ready to step into his shoes when he wants to be off." He flashed the lantern across the path, and a few moments later his junior stepped up briskly with a bundle of newspapers tucked under his arm.

It struck me that Jervis looked at me a little queerly when he recognised me in the dim light; also he was a trifle constrained in his manner, as if my presence were an embarrassment. He listened to Thorndyke's announcement of our newly made arrangement without much enthusiasm and with none of his customary facetious comments. And again I noticed a quick glance at me, half curious, half uneasy, and wholly puzzling to me.

"That's all right," he said when Thorndyke had explained the situation. "I daresay you'll find Berkeley as useful as me, and, in any case, he'll be better here than staying on with Barnard." He spoke with unwonted gravity, and there was in his tone a solicitude for me that attracted my notice and that of Thorndyke as well, for the latter looked at him curiously, though he made no comment. After a short silence, however, he asked: "And what news does my learned brother bring? There is a mighty shouting among the outer barbarians, and I see a bundle of newspapers under my learned friend's arm. Has anything in particular happened?"

Jervis looked more uncomfortable than ever. "Well— yes," he replied hesitatingly, "something has happened— there. It's no use beating about the bush; Berkeley may as well learn it from me as from those yelling devils outside." He took a couple of papers from his bundle and silently handed one to me and the other to Thorndyke.

Jervis's ominous manner, naturally enough, alarmed me not a little. I opened the paper with a nameless dread. But whatever my vague fears, they fell far short of the occasion; and when I saw those yells from without crystallised into scare head-lines and flaming capitals I turned for a moment sick and dizzy with fear.

The paragraph was only a short one, and I read it through in less than a minute:

"THE MISSING FINGER
"DRAMATIC DISCOVERY AT WOODFORD

"The mystery that has surrounded the remains of a mutilated human body, portions of which have been found in various places in Kent and Essex, has received a partial and very sinister solution. The police have, all along, suspected that those remains were those of a Mr. John Bellingham who disappeared under circumstances of some suspicion about two years ago. There is now no doubt upon the subject, for the finger which was missing from the hand that was found at Sidcup has been discovered at the bottom of a disused well *together with a ring*, which has been identified as one habitually worn by Mr. John Bellingham.

"The house in the garden of which the well is situated was the property of the murdered man, and was occupied at the time of the disappearance by his brother, Mr. Godfrey Bellingham. But the latter left it very soon after, and it has been empty ever since. Just lately it has been put in repair, and it was in this way that the well came to be emptied and cleaned out. It seems that Detective-Inspector Badger, who was searching the neighbourhood for further remains, heard of the emptying of the well and went down in the bucket to examine the bottom, where he found the three bones and the ring.

"Thus the identity of the body is established beyond all doubt, and the question that remains is, Who killed John Bellingham? It may be remembered that a trinket, apparently broken from his watch-chain, was found in the grounds of this house on the day that he disappeared, and that he was never again seen alive. What may be the import of these facts time will show."

That was all; but it was enough. I dropped the paper to the ground and glanced round furtively at Jervis, who sat gazing gloomily at the toes of his boots. It was horrible! It was incredible! The blow was so crushing that it left my faculties numb, and for a while I seemed unable even to think intelligibly.

I was aroused by Thorndyke's voice—calm, business-like, composed:

"Time will show, indeed! But meanwhile we must go warily. And don't be unduly alarmed, Berkeley. Go home, take a good dose of bromide with a little stimulant, and turn in. I am afraid this has been rather a shock to you."

I rose from my chair like one in a dream and held out my hand to Thorndyke; and even in the dim light and in my dazed condition I noticed that his face bore a look that I had never seen before; the look of a granite mask of Fate—grim, stern, inexorable.

My two friends walked with me as far as the gateway at the top of Inner Temple Lane, and as we reached the entry a stranger, coming quickly up the Lane, overtook and passed us. In the glare of the lamp outside the porter's lodge he looked at us quickly over his shoulder; and, though he passed on without halt or greeting, I recognised him with a certain dull surprise which I did not understand then and do not understand now. It was Mr. Jellicoe.

I shook hands once more with my friends and strode out into Fleet Street, but as soon as I was outside the gate I made direct for Nevill's Court. What was in my mind I do not know; only that some instinct of protection led me there, where my lady lay unconscious of the hideous menace that hung over her. At the entrance to the Court a tall, powerful man was lounging against the wall, and he seemed to look at me curiously as I passed; but I hardly noticed him and strode forward into the narrow passage. By the shabby gateway of the house I halted and looked up at such of the windows as I could see over the wall. They were all dark. All the inmates, then, were in bed. Vaguely comforted by this, I walked on to the New Street end of the Court and looked out. Here, too, a man—a tall, thick-set man—was loitering; and as he looked inquisitively into my face I turned and re-entered the Court, slowly retracing my steps. As I again reached the gate of the house I stopped to look once more at the windows, and turning I found the man whom I had last noticed close behind me. Then, in a flash of dreadful comprehension, I understood. These two were plain-clothes policemen.

For a moment a blind fury possessed me. An insane impulse urged me to give battle to this intruder; to avenge upon this person the insult of his presence. Fortunately the impulse was but momentary, and I recovered myself without making any demonstration. But the appearance of those two policemen brought the peril into the immediate present, imparted to it a horrible actuality. A chilly sweat of terror stood on my forehead, and my ears were ringing when I walked with faltering steps out into

Fetter Lane.

CHAPTER XVIII　　　John Bellingham

The next few days were a very nightmare of horror and gloom. Of course, I repudiated my acceptance of the decree of banishment that Ruth had passed upon me. I was her friend, at least, and in time of peril my place was at her side. Tacitly—though thankfully enough, poor girl! —she had recognised the fact and made me once more free of the house.

For there was no disguising the situation. Newspaper boys yelled the news up and down Fleet Street from morning to night; soul-shaking posters grinned on gaping crowds; and the newspapers fairly wallowed in the "Shocking details."

It is true that no direct accusations were made; but the original reports of the disappearance were reprinted with such comments as made me gnash my teeth with fury.

The wretchedness of those days will live in my memory until my dying day. Never can I forget the dread that weighed me down, the horrible suspense, the fear that clutched at my heart as I furtively scanned the posters in the streets. Even the wretched detectives who prowled about the entrances to Nevill's Court became grateful to my eyes, for, embodying as they did the hideous menace that hung over my dear lady, their presence at least told me that the blow had not yet fallen. Indeed, we came, after a time, to exchange glances of mutual recognition, and I thought that they seemed to be sorry for her and for me, and had no great liking for their task. Of course, I spent most of my leisure at the old house, though my heart ached more there than elsewhere;

and I tried, with but poor success, I fear, to maintain a cheerful, confident manner, cracking my little jokes as of old, and even essaying to skirmish with Miss Oman. But this last experiment was a dead failure; and, when she had suddenly broken down in a stream of brilliant repartee to weep hysterically on my breast, I abandoned the attempt and did not repeat it.

A dreadful gloom had settled down upon the old house. Poor Miss Oman crept silently but restlessly up and down the ancient stairs with dim eyes and a tremulous chin, or moped in her room with a parliamentary petition (demanding, if I remember rightly, the appointment of a female judge to deal with divorce and matrimonial causes) which lay on her table languidly awaiting signatures that never came. Mr. Bellingham, whose mental condition at first alternated between furious anger and absolute panic, was fast sinking into a state of nervous prostration that I viewed with no little alarm. In fact, the only really self-possessed person in the entire household was Ruth herself, and even she could not conceal the ravages of sorrow and suspense and overshadowing peril. Her manner was almost unchanged; or rather, I should say, she had gone back to that which I had first known—quiet, reserved, taciturn, with a certain bitter humour showing through her unvarying amiability. When she and I were alone, indeed, her reserve melted away and she was all sweetness and gentleness. But it wrung my heart to look at her, to see how, day by day, she grew ever more thin and haggard; to watch the growing pallor of her cheek; to look into her solemn grey eyes, so sad and tragic and yet so brave and defiant of fate.

It was a terrible time; and through it all the dreadful questions haunted me continually: When will the blow fall? What is it that the police are waiting for? And when they do strike, what will Thorndyke have to say?

So things went on for four dreadful days. But on the fourth day, just as the evening consultations were beginning and the surgery was filled with waiting patients, Polton appeared with a note, which he insisted, to the indignation of Adolphus, on delivering into my own hands. It was from Thorndyke, and was to the following effect:

"I learn from Dr. Norbury that he has recently heard from Herr Lederbogen, of Berlin—a learned authority on Oriental antiquities—who makes some reference to an English Egyptologist whom he met in Vienna about a year ago. He cannot recall the Englishman's name, but there are certain expressions in the letter which make Dr. Norbury suspect that he is referring to John Bellingham.

"I want you to bring Mr. and Miss Bellingham to my chambers this evening at 8.30, to meet Dr. Norbury and talk over his letter; and in view of the importance of the matter, I look to you not to fail me."

A wave of hope and relief swept over me. It was still possible that this Gordian knot might be cut; that the deliverance might come before it was too late. I wrote a hasty note to Thorndyke and another to Ruth, making the appointment; and, having given them both to the trusty Polton, returned somewhat feverishly to my professional duties. To my profound relief, the influx of patients ceased, and the practice sank into its accustomed torpor; whereby I was able without base and mendacious subterfuge to escape in good time to my tryst.

It was near upon eight o'clock when I passed through

the archway into Nevill's Court. The warm afternoon light had died away, for the summer was running out apace. The last red glow of the setting sun had faded from the ancient roofs and chimney stacks, and down in the narrow court the shades of evening had begun to gather in nooks and corners. I was due at eight, and, as it still wanted some minutes to the hour, I sauntered slowly down the Court, looking reflectively on the familiar scene and the well-known friendly faces.

The day's work was drawing to a close. The little shops were putting up their shutters; lights were beginning to twinkle in parlour windows; a solemn hymn arose in the old Moravian chapel, and its echoes stole out through the dark entry that opens into the court under the archway.

Here was Mr. Finneymore (a man of versatile gifts, with a leaning towards paint and varnish) sitting, white-aproned and shirt-sleeved, on a chair in his garden, smoking his pipe with a complacent eye on his dahlias. There, at an open window, a young man, with a brush in his hand and another behind his ear, stood up and stretched himself, while an older lady deftly rolled up a large map. The barber was turning out the gas in his little saloon; the greengrocer was emerging with a cigarette in his mouth and an aster in his button-hole, and a group of children were escorting the lamp-lighter on his rounds.

All these good, homely folk were Nevill's Courtiers of the genuine breed; born in the court, as had been their fathers before them for generations. And of such to a great extent was the population of the place. Miss Oman herself claimed aboriginal descent and so did the sweet-faced Moravian lady next door—a connection of the famous La Trobes of the old Conventicle, whose history went back to the Gordon Riots; and as to the gentleman who lived in the ancient timber-and-plaster house at the bottom of the court, it was reported that his ancestors had dwelt in that very house since the days of James the First.

On these facts I reflected as I sauntered down the court; on the strange phenomenon of an old-world hamlet with its ancient population lingering in the very heart of the noisy city; an island of peace set in an ocean of unrest, an oasis in a desert of change and ferment.

My meditations brought me to the shabby gate in the high wall, and, as I raised the latch and pushed it open, I saw Ruth standing at the door of the house talking to Miss Oman. She was evidently waiting for me, for she wore her sombre black coat and hat and a black veil, and when she saw me she came out, closing the door after her, and holding out her hand.

"You are punctual," said she. "St. Dunstan's clock is striking now."

"Yes," I answered. "But where is your father?"

"He has gone to bed, poor old dear. He didn't feel well enough to come, and I did not urge him. He is really very ill. This dreadful suspense will kill him if it goes on much longer."

"Let us hope it won't," I said, but with little conviction, I fear, in my tone.

It was harrowing to see her torn by anxiety for her father, and I yearned to comfort her. But what was there to say? Mr. Bellingham was breaking up visibly under the stress of the terrible menace that hung over his daughter, and no words of mine could make the fact less manifest.

We walked silently up the court. The lady at the window greeted us with a smiling salutation, Mr. Finneymore removed his pipe and raised his cap, receiving a gracious bow from Ruth in return, and then we passed through the covered way into Fetter Lane, where my companion paused and looked about her.

"What are you looking for?" I asked.

"The detective," she answered quietly. "It would be a pity if the poor man should miss me after waiting so long. However, I don't see him." And she turned away towards Fleet Street. It was an unpleasant surprise to me that her sharp eyes had detected the secret spy upon her movements; and the dry, sardonic tone of her remark pained me too, recalling, as it did, the frigid self-possession that had so repelled me in the early days of our acquaintance. And yet I could not but admire the cool unconcern with which she faced her horrible peril.

"Tell me a little more about this conference," she said, as we walked down Fetter Lane. "Your note was rather more concise than lucid; but I suppose you wrote it in a hurry."

"Yes, I did. And I can't give you any details now. All I know is that Dr. Norbury has had a letter from a friend of his in Berlin, an Egyptologist, as I understand, named Lederbogen, who refers to an English acquaintance of his and Norbury's whom he saw in Vienna about a year ago. He cannot remember the Englishman's name, but from some of the circumstances Norbury seems to think that he is referring to your Uncle John. Of course, if this should turn out to be really the case, it would set everything straight; so Thorndyke was anxious that you and your father should meet Norbury and talk it over."

"I see," said Ruth. Her tone was thoughtful but by no means enthusiastic.

"You don't seem to attach much importance to the matter," I remarked.

"No. It doesn't seem to fit the circumstances. What is the use of suggesting that poor Uncle John is alive—and behaving like an imbecile, which he certainly was not—

when his dead body has actually been found?"

"But," I suggested lamely, "there may be some mistake. It may not be his body after all."

"And the ring?" she asked, with a bitter smile.

"That may be just a coincidence. It was a copy of a well-known form of antique ring. Other people may have had copies made as well as your uncle. Besides," I added with more conviction, "we haven't seen the ring. It may not be his at all."

She shook her head. "My dear Paul," she said quietly, "it is useless to delude ourselves. Every known fact points to the certainty that it is his body. John Bellingham is dead; there can be no doubt of that. And to every one except his unknown murderer, and one or two of my own loyal friends, it must seem that his death lies at my door. I realised from the beginning that the suspicion lay between George Hurst and me; and the finding of the ring fixes it definitely on me. I am only surprised that the police have made no move yet."

The quiet conviction of her tone left me for a while speechless with horror and despair. Then I recalled Thorndyke's calm, even confident, attitude, and I hastened to remind her of it.

"There is one of your friends," I said, "who is still undismayed. Thorndyke seems to anticipate no difficulties."

"And yet," she replied, "he is ready to consider a forlorn hope like this. However, we shall see."

I could think of nothing more to say, and it was in gloomy silence that we pursued our way down Inner Temple Lane and through the dark entries and tunnel-like passages that brought us out, at length, by the Treasury.

"I don't see any light in Thorndyke's chambers," I said, as we crossed King's Bench Walk; and I pointed out the row of windows all dark and blank.

"No; and yet the shutters are not closed. He must be out."

"He can't be after making an appointment with you and your father. It is most mysterious. Thorndyke is so very punctilious about his engagements."

The mystery was solved, when we reached the landing, by a slip of paper fixed by a tack on the iron-bound "oak."

"A note for P. B. is on the table," was the laconic message: on reading which I inserted my key, swung the heavy door outward, and opened the lighter inner door. The note was lying on the table and I brought it out to the landing to read by the light of the staircase lamp.

> "Apologise to our friends," it ran, "for the slight change of programme. Norbury is anxious that I should get my experiments over before the Director returns, so as to save discussion. He has asked me to begin to-night and says he will see Mr. and Miss Bellingham here, at the Museum. Please bring them along at once. I think some matters of importance may transpire at the interview.—J. E. T."

"I hope you don't mind," I said apologetically, when I had read the note to Ruth.

"Of course I don't," she replied. "I am rather pleased. We have so many associations with the dear old Museum, haven't we?" She looked at me for a moment with a strange and touching wistfulness and then turned to descend the stone stairs.

At the Temple gate I hailed a hansom, and we were soon speeding westward and north to the soft tinkle of the horse's bell.

"What are these experiments that Dr. Thorndyke refers to?" she asked presently.

"I can only answer you vaguely," I replied. "Their object, I believe, is to ascertain whether the penetrability of organic substances by the X-rays becomes altered by age; whether, for instance, an ancient block of wood is more or less transparent to the rays than a new block of the same size."

"And of what use would the knowledge be, if it were obtained?"

"I can't say. Experiments are made to obtain knowledge without regard to its utility. The use appears when the knowledge has been acquired. But in this case, if it should be possible to determine the age of any organic substance by its reaction to X-rays, the discovery might be found of some value in legal practice—as in demonstrating a new seal on an old document, for instance. But I don't know whether Thorndyke has anything definite in view; I only know that the preparations have been on a most portentous scale."

"How do you mean?"

"In regard to size. When I went into the workshop yesterday morning, I found Polton erecting a kind of portable gallows about nine feet high, and he had just finished varnishing a pair of enormous wooden trays each over six feet long. It looked as if he and Thorndyke were contemplating a few private executions with subsequent post-mortems on the victims."

"What a horrible suggestion!"

"So Polton said, with his quaint, crinkly smile. But he was mighty close about the use of the apparatus all the same. I wonder if we shall see anything of the experiments, when we get there. This is Museum Street, isn't it?"

"Yes." As she spoke, she lifted the flap of one of the little windows in the back of the cab and peered out. Then, closing it with a quiet, ironic smile, she said:

"It is all right; he hasn't missed us. It will be quite a nice little change for him."

The cab swung round into Great Russell Street, and, glancing out as it turned, I saw another hansom following; but before I had time to inspect its solitary passenger, we drew up at the Museum gates.

The gate porter, who seemed to expect us, ushered us up the drive to the great portico and into the Central Hall, where he handed us over to another official.

"Dr. Norbury is in one of the rooms adjoining the Fourth Egyptian Room," the latter stated in answer to our inquiries; and, providing himself with a wire-guarded lantern, he prepared to escort us thither.

Up the great staircase, now wrapped in mysterious gloom, we passed in silence with bitter-sweet memories of that day of days when we had first trodden its steps together; through the Central Saloon, the Mediæval Room and the Asiatic Saloon, and so into the long range of the Ethnographical Galleries.

It was a weird journey. The swaying lantern shot its beams abroad into the darkness of the great, dim galleries, casting instantaneous flashes on the objects in the cases, so that they leaped into being and vanished in the twinkling of an eye. Hideous idols with round, staring eyes started forth from the darkness, glared at us for an instant and were gone. Grotesque masks, suddenly revealed by the shimmering light, took on the semblance of demon faces that seemed to mow and gibber at us as we passed. As for the life-sized models—realistic enough by daylight—their aspect was positively alarming; for the moving light and shadow endowed them with life and movement, so that they seemed to watch us furtively, to lie in wait and to hold themselves in readiness to steal out and follow us. The illusion evidently affected Ruth as well as me, for she drew nearer to me and whispered:

"These figures are quite startling. Did you see that Polynesian? I really felt as if he were going to spring out on us."

"They are rather uncanny," I admitted, "but the danger is over now. We are passing out of their sphere of influence."

We came out on a landing as I spoke and then turned sharply to the left along the North Gallery, from the centre of which we entered the Fourth Egyptian Room.

Almost immediately, a door in the opposite wall opened; a peculiar, high-pitched humming sound became audible, and Jervis came out on tiptoe with his hand raised.

"Tread as lightly as you can," he said. "We are just making an exposure."

The attendant turned back with his lantern, and we followed Jervis into the room from whence he had come. It was a large room, and little lighter than the galleries, for the single glow-lamp that burned at the end where we entered left the rest of the apartment in almost complete obscurity. We seated ourselves at once on the chairs that had been placed for us, and, when the mutual salutations had been exchanged, I looked about me. There were three people in the room besides Jervis; Thorndyke, who sat with his watch in his hand, a grey-headed gentleman whom I took to be Dr. Norbury, and a smaller person at the dim farther end—undistinguishable, but probably Polton. At our end of the room were the two large trays that I had seen in the workshop, now mounted on trestles and each fitted with a rubber drain-tube leading down to a bucket. At the farther end of the room the sinister shape of the gallows reared itself aloft in the gloom; only now I could see that it was not a gallows at all. For affixed to the top cross-bar was a large, bottomless glass basin, inside which was a glass bulb that glowed with a strange green light; and in the heart of the bulb a bright spot of red.

It was all clear enough so far. The peculiar sound that filled the air was the hum of the interrupter; the bulb was, of course, a Crookes' tube, and the red spot inside it, the glowing red-hot disc of the anti-cathode. Clearly an X-ray photograph was being made; but of what? I strained my eyes, peering into the gloom at the foot of the gallows, but though I could make out an elongated object lying on the floor directly under the bulb, I could not resolve the dimly seen shape into anything recognisable. Presently, however, Dr. Norbury supplied the clue.

"I am rather surprised," said he, "that you chose so composite an object as a mummy to begin on. I should have thought that a simpler object, such as a coffin or a wooden figure, would have been more instructive."

"In some ways it would," replied Thorndyke, "but the variety of materials that the mummy gives us has its advantages. I hope your father is not ill, Miss Bellingham."

"He is not at all well," said Ruth, "and we agreed that it was better for me to come alone. I knew Herr Lederbogen quite well. He stayed with us for a time when he was in England."

"I trust," said Dr. Norbury, "that I have not troubled you for nothing. Herr Lederbogen speaks of 'our erratic English friend with the long name that I can never remember,' and it seemed to me that he might be referring to your uncle."

"I should hardly have called my uncle erratic," said Ruth.

"No, no. Certainly not," Dr. Norbury agreed hastily. "However, you shall see the letter presently and judge for yourself. We mustn't introduce irrelevant topics while the experiment is in progress, must we, Doctor?"

"You had better wait until we have finished," said Thorndyke, "because I am going to turn out the light. Switch off the current, Polton."

The green light vanished from the bulb, the hum of the interrupter swept down an octave or two and died away. Then Thorndyke and Dr. Norbury rose from their chairs and went towards the mummy, which they lifted tenderly while Polton drew from beneath it what presently turned out to be a huge black paper envelope. The single glow-lamp was switched off, leaving the room in total darkness until there burst out suddenly a bright orange-red light immediately above one of the trays.

We all gathered round to watch, as Polton—the high priest of these mysteries—drew from the black envelope a colossal sheet of bromide paper, laid it carefully in the tray and proceeded to wet it with a large brush which he had dipped in a pail of water.

"I thought you always used plates for this kind of work," said Dr. Norbury.

"We do, by preference; but a six-foot plate would be impossible, so I had a special paper made to the size."

There is something singularly fascinating in the appearance of a developing photograph; in the gradual, mysterious emergence of the picture from the blank, white surface of plate or paper. But a skiagraph, or X-ray photograph, has a fascination all its own. Unlike the ordinary photograph, which yields a picture of things already seen, it gives a presentment of objects hitherto invisible; and hence, when Polton poured the developer on the already wet paper, we all craned over the tray with the keenest curiosity.

The developer was evidently a very slow one. For fully half a minute no change could be seen in the uniform surface. Then, gradually, almost insensibly, the marginal portion began to darken, leaving the outline of the mummy in pale relief. The change, once started, proceeded apace. Darker and darker grew the margin of the paper until from slaty grey it had turned to black; and still the shape of the mummy, now in strong relief, remained an elongated patch of bald white. But not for long. Presently the white shape began to be tinged with grey, and, as the colour deepened, there grew out of it a paler form that seemed to steal out of the enshrouding grey like an apparition, spectral, awesome, mysterious. The skeleton was coming into view.

"It is rather uncanny," said Dr. Norbury. "I feel as if I were assisting at some unholy rite. Just look at it now!"

The grey shadow of the cartonnage, the wrappings and the flesh was fading away into the background, and the white skeleton stood out in sharp contrast. And it certainly was rather a weird spectacle.

"You'll lose the bones if you develop much farther," said Dr. Norbury.

"I must let the bones darken," Thorndyke replied, "in case there are any metallic objects. I have three more papers in the envelope."

The white shape of the skeleton now began to grey over and, as Dr. Norbury had said, its distinctness became less and yet less. Thorndyke leaned over the tray with his eyes fixed on a point in the middle of the breast and we all watched him in silence. Suddenly he rose. "Now, Polton," he said sharply; "get the hypo on as quickly as you can."

Polton, who had been waiting with his hand on the stop-cock of the drain-tube, rapidly ran off the developer into the bucket and flooded the paper with the fixing solution.

"Now we can look at it at our leisure," said Thorndyke. After waiting a few seconds, he switched on one of the glow-lamps, and as the flood of light fell on the photograph, he added: "you see we haven't quite lost the skeleton."

"No." Dr. Norbury put on a pair of spectacles and bent down over the tray; and at this moment I felt Ruth's hand touch my arm, lightly, at first, and then with a strong nervous grasp; and I could feel that her hand was trembling. I looked round at her anxiously and saw that she had turned deathly pale.

"Would you rather go out into the gallery?" I asked; for the room with its tightly shut windows was close and hot.

"No," she replied quietly, " I will stay here. I am quite well." But still she kept hold of my arm.

Thorndyke glanced at her keenly and then looked away as Dr. Norbury turned to ask him a question.

"Why is it, think you, that some of the teeth show so much whiter than others?"

"I think the whiteness of the shadows is due to the presence of metal," Thorndyke replied.

"Do you mean that the teeth have metal fillings?" asked Dr. Norbury.

"Yes."

"Really! This is very interesting. The use of gold stoppings—and artificial teeth, too—by the ancient Egyptians is well known, but we have no examples in this Museum. This mummy ought to be unrolled. Do you think all those teeth are filled with the same metal? They are not equally white."

"No," replied Thorndyke. "Those teeth that are perfectly white are undoubtedly filled with gold, but that greyish one is probably filled with tin."

"Very interesting," said Dr. Norbury. "*Very* interesting! And what do you make of that faint mark across the chest, near the top of the sternum?"

It was Ruth who answered his question.

"It is the Eye of Osiris!" she exclaimed in a hushed voice.

"Dear me!" exclaimed Dr. Norbury, "so it is. You are quite right. It is the Utchat—the Eye of Horus—or Osiris, if you prefer to call it so. That, I presume, will be a gilded device on some of the wrappings."

"No; I should say it is a tattoo mark. It is too indefinite for a gilded device. And I should say further that the tattooing is done in vermilion, as carbon tattooing would cast no visible shadow."

"I think you must be mistaken about that," said Dr. Norbury, "but we shall see, if the Director allows us to unroll the mummy. By the way, those little objects in front of the knees are metallic, I suppose?"

"Yes, they are metallic. But they are not in front of the knees; they are in the knees. They are pieces of silver wire which have been used to repair fractured knee-caps."

"Are you sure of that?" exclaimed Dr. Norbury, peering at the little white marks with ecstasy; "because if you are, and if these objects are what you say they are, the mummy of Sebek-hotep is an absolutely unique specimen."

"I am quite certain of it," said Thorndyke.

"Then," said Dr. Norbury, "we have made a discovery,

thanks to your inquiring spirit. Poor John Bellingham! He little knew what a treasure he was giving us! How I wish he could have known! How I wish he could have been here with us to-night!"

He paused once more to gaze in rapture at the photograph. And then Thorndyke, in his quiet, impassive way, said:

"John Bellingham is here, Dr. Norbury. This is John Bellingham."

Dr. Norbury started back and stared at Thorndyke in speechless amazement.

"You don't mean," he exclaimed, after a long pause, "that this mummy is the body of John Bellingham!"

"I do indeed. There is no doubt of it."

"But it is impossible! The mummy was here in the gallery a full three weeks before he disappeared."

"Not so," said Thorndyke. "John Bellingham was last seen alive by you and Mr. Jellicoe on the fourteenth of October, more than three weeks before the mummy left Queen Square. After that date he was never seen alive or dead by any person who knew him and could identify him."

Dr. Norbury reflected awhile in silence. Then, in a faint voice, he asked:

"How do you suggest that John Bellingham's body came to be inside that cartonnage?"

"I think Mr. Jellicoe is the most likely person to be able to answer that question," Thorndyke replied dryly.

There was another interval of silence, and then Dr. Norbury asked suddenly:

"But what do you suppose has become of Sebek-hotep? The real Sebek-hotep, I mean?"

"I take it," said Thorndyke, "that the remains of Sebek-hotep, or at least a portion of them, are at present lying in the Woodford mortuary awaiting an adjourned inquest."

As Thorndyke made this statement a flash of belated intelligence, mingled with self-contempt, fell on me. Now that the explanation was given, how obvious it was! And yet I, a competent anatomist and physiologist and actually a pupil of Thorndyke's, had mistaken those ancient bones for the remains of a recent body!

Dr. Norbury considered the last statement for some time in evident perplexity. "It is all consistent enough, I must admit," said he, at length, "and yet—are you quite sure there is no mistake? It seems so incredible."

"There is no mistake, I assure you," Thorndyke answered. "To convince you, I will give you the facts in detail. First, as to the teeth. I have seen John Bellingham's dentist and obtained particulars from his case-book. There were in all five teeth that had been filled. The right upper wisdom-tooth, the molar next to it, and the second lower molar on the left side, all had extensive gold fillings. You can see them all quite plainly in the skiagraph. The left lower lateral incisor had a very small gold filling, which you can see as a nearly circular white dot. In addition to these, a filling of tin amalgam had been inserted while the deceased was abroad, in the second left upper bicuspid, the rather grey spot that we have already noticed. These would, by themselves, furnish ample means of identification. But, in addition, there is the tattooed device of the Eye of Osiris—"

"Horus," murmured Dr. Norbury.

"Horus, then—in the exact locality in which it was borne by the deceased, and tattooed, apparently, with the same pigment. There are, further, the suture wires in the knee-caps; Sir Morgan Bennet, having looked up the notes of the operation, informs me that he introduced three suture wires into the left patella and two into the right; which is what the skiagraph shows. Lastly, the deceased had an old Pott's fracture on the left side. It is not very apparent now, but I saw it quite distinctly just now when the shadows of the bones were whiter. I think that you may take it that the identification is beyond all doubt or question."

"Yes," agreed Dr. Norbury, with gloomy resignation, "it sounds, as you say, quite conclusive. Well, well, it is a most horrible affair. Poor old John Bellingham! It looks uncommonly as if he had met with foul play. Don't you think so?"

"I do," replied Thorndyke. "There was a mark on the right side of the skull that looked rather like a fracture. It was not very clear, being at the side, but we must develop a negative to show it."

Dr. Norbury drew his breath in sharply through his teeth. "This is a gruesome business, Doctor," said he. "A terrible business. Awkward for our people, too. By the way, what is our position in the matter? What steps ought we to take?"

"You should give notice to the coroner—I will manage the police—and you should communicate with one of the executors of the will."

"Mr. Jellicoe?"

"No, not Mr. Jellicoe, under the peculiar circumstances. You had better write to Mr. Godfrey Bellingham."

"But I rather understood that Mr. Hurst was the co-executor," said Dr. Norbury.

"He is, surely, as matters stand," said Jervis.

"Not at all," replied Thorndyke. "He *was* as matters *stood*; but he is not now. You are forgetting the conditions of clause two. That clause sets forth the conditions under which Godfrey Bellingham shall inherit the bulk of the estate and become the co-executor; and those conditions are: 'that the body of the testator shall be deposited in some authorised place for the reception of the bodies of the dead, situate within the boundaries of, or appertaining to some place of worship within, the parish of St. George, Bloomsbury, and St. Giles in the Fields, or St. Andrew above the Bars and St. George the Martyr.' Now Egyptian mummies are bodies of the dead, and this Museum is an authorised place for their reception; and this building is situate within the boundaries of the parish of St. George, Bloomsbury. Therefore the provisions of clause two have been duly carried out and therefore Godfrey Bellingham is the principal beneficiary under the will, and the co-executor, in accordance with the wishes of the testator. Is that quite clear?"

"Perfectly," said Dr. Norbury; "and a most astonishing coincidence—but, my dear young lady, had you not better sit down? You are looking very ill."

He glanced anxiously at Ruth, who was pale to the lips and was now leaning heavily on my arm.

"I think, Berkeley," said Thorndyke, "you had better take Miss Bellingham out into the gallery, where there is more air. This has been a tremendous climax to all the trials she has borne so bravely. Go out with Berkeley," he added gently, laying his hand on her shoulder, "and sit down while we develop the other negatives. You mustn't break down now, you know, when the storm has passed and the sun is beginning to shine." He held the door open and as we passed out his face softened into a smile of infinite kindness. "You won't mind my locking you out," said he; "this is a photographic dark-room at present."

The key grated in the lock and we turned away into the dim gallery. It was not quite dark, for a beam of moonlight filtered in here and there through the blinds that covered the sky-lights. We walked on slowly, her arm linked in mine, and for a while neither of us spoke. The great rooms were very silent and peaceful and solemn. The hush, the stillness, the mystery of the half-seen forms in the cases around, were all in harmony with the deeply-felt sense of a great deliverance that filled our hearts.

We had passed through into the next room before either of us broke the silence. Insensibly our hands had crept together, and, as they met and clasped with mutual pressure, Ruth exclaimed: "How dreadful and tragic it is! Poor, poor Uncle John! It seems as if he had come back from the world of shadows to tell us of this awful thing. But, O God! what a relief it is!"

She caught her breath in one or two quick sobs and pressed my hand passionately.

"It is over, dearest," I said. "It is gone for ever. Nothing remains but the memory of your sorrow and your noble courage and patience."

"I can't realise it yet," she murmured. "It has been like a frightful, interminable dream."

"Let us put it away," said I, "and think only of the happy life that is opening."

She made no reply, and only a quick catch in her breath, now and again, told of the long agony that she had endured with such heroic calm.

We walked on slowly, scarcely disturbing the silence with our soft footfalls, through the wide doorway into the second room. The vague shapes of mummy-cases standing erect in the wall-cases, loomed out dim and gigantic, silent watchers keeping their vigil with the memories of untold centuries locked in their shadowy breasts. They were an awesome company. Reverend survivors from a vanished world, they looked out from the gloom of their abiding-place, but with no shade of menace or of malice in their silent presence; rather with a solemn benison on the fleeting creatures of to-day.

Half-way along the room a ghostly figure, somewhat aloof from its companions, showed a dim, pallid blotch where its face would have been. With one accord we halted before it.

"Do you know who this is, Ruth?" I asked.

"Of course I do," she answered. "It is Artemidorus."

We stood, hand in hand, facing the mummy, letting our memories fill in the vague silhouette with its well-remembered details. Presently I drew her nearer to me and whispered:

"Ruth! do you remember when we last stood here?"

"As if I could ever forget!" she answered passionately. "Oh, Paul! The sorrow of it! The misery! How it wrung my heart to tell you! Were you *very* unhappy when I left you?"

"Unhappy! I never knew, until then, what real, heart-breaking sorrow was. It seemed as if the light had gone out of my life for ever. But there was just one little spot of brightness left."

"What was that?"

"You made me a promise, dear—a solemn promise; and I felt—at least I hoped—that the day would come, if I only waited patiently, when you would be able to redeem it."

She crept closer to me and yet closer, until her head nestled on my shoulder and her soft cheek lay against mine.

"Dear heart," I whispered, "is it now? Is the time fulfilled?"

"Yes, dearest," she murmured softly. "It is now—and

for ever."

Reverently I folded her in my arms; gathered her to the heart that worshipped her utterly. Henceforth no sorrows could hurt us, no misfortunes vex; for we should walk hand in hand on our earthly pilgrimage and find the way all too short.

Time, whose sands run out with such unequal swiftness for the just and the unjust, the happy and the wretched, lagged, no doubt, with the toilers in the room that we had left. But for us its golden grains trickled out apace, and left the glass empty before we had begun to mark their passage. The turning of a key and the opening of a door aroused us from our dream of perfect happiness. Ruth raised her head to listen, and our lips met for one brief moment. Then, with a silent greeting to the friend who had looked on our grief and witnessed our final happiness, we turned and retraced our steps quickly, filling the great empty rooms with chattering echoes.

"We won't go back into the dark-room—which isn't dark now," said Ruth.

"Why not?" I asked.

"Because—when I came out I was very pale; and I'm—well, I don't think I am very pale now. Besides, poor Uncle John is in there—and—I should be ashamed to look at him with my selfish heart overflowing with happiness."

"You needn't be," said I. "It is the day of our lives and we have a right to be happy. But you shan't go in, if you don't wish to," and I accordingly steered her adroitly past the beam of light that streamed from the open door.

"We have developed four negatives," said Thorndyke, as he emerged with the others, "and I am leaving them in the custody of Dr. Norbury, who will sign each when they are dry, as they may have to be put in evidence.

What are you going to do?"

I looked at Ruth to see what she wished.

"If you won't think me ungrateful," said she, "I should rather be alone with my father to-night. He is very weak and—"

"Yes, I understand," I said hastily. And I did. Mr. Bellingham was a man of strong emotions and would probably be somewhat overcome by the sudden change of fortune and the news of his brother's tragic death.

"In that case," said Thorndyke, "I will bespeak your services. Will you go on and wait for me at my chambers, when you have seen Miss Bellingham home?"

I agreed to this, and we set forth under the guidance of Dr. Norbury (who carried an electric lamp) to return by the way we had come; two of us, at least, in a vastly different frame of mind. The party broke up at the entrance gates, and as Thorndyke wished my companion "Good-night," she held his hand and looked up in his face with swimming eyes.

"I haven't thanked you, Dr. Thorndyke," she said, "and I don't feel that I ever can. What you have done for me and my father is beyond all thanks. You have saved his life and you have rescued me from the most horrible ignominy. Good-bye! and God bless you!"

The hansom that bowled along eastward—at most unnecessary speed—bore two of the happiest human beings within the wide boundaries of the town. I looked at my companion as the lights of the street shone into the cab, and was astonished at the transformation. The pallor of her cheek had given place to a rosy pink; the hardness, the tension, the haggard self-repression that had aged her face, were all gone, and the girlish sweetness that had so bewitched me in the early days of our love had stolen back. Even the dimple was there when the sweeping lashes lifted and her eyes met mine in a smile of infinite tenderness.

Little was said on that brief journey. It was happiness enough to sit, hand clasped in hand, and know that our time of trial was past; that no cross of Fate could ever part us now.

The astonished cabman set us down, according to instructions, at the entrance to Nevill's Court, and watched us with open mouth as we vanished into the narrow passage. The court had settled down for the night, and no one marked our return; no curious eye looked down on us from the dark house-front as we said "Good-bye" just inside the gate.

"You will come and see us to-morrow, dear, won't you?" she asked.

"Do you think it possible that I could stay away, then?"

"I hope not, but come as early as you can. My father will be positively frantic to see you; because I shall have told him, you know. And, remember, that it is you who have brought us this great deliverance. Good-night, Paul."

"Good-night, sweetheart."

She put up her face frankly to be kissed and then ran up to the ancient door; whence she waved me a last good-bye. The shabby gate in the wall closed behind me and hid her from my sight; but the light of her love went with me and turned the dull street into a path of glory.

CHAPTER XIX   A Strange Symposium

It came upon me with something of a shock of surprise to find the scrap of paper still tacked to the oak of

Thorndyke's chambers. So much had happened since I had last looked on it that it seemed to belong to another epoch of my life. I removed it thoughtfully and picked out the tack before entering, and then, closing the inner door, but leaving the oak open, I lit the gas and fell to pacing the room.

What a wonderful episode it had been! How the whole aspect of the world had been changed in a moment by Thorndyke's revelation! At another time, curiosity would have led me to endeavour to trace back the train of reasoning by which the subtle brain of my teacher had attained this astonishing conclusion. But now my own happiness held exclusive possession of my thoughts. The image of Ruth filled the field of my mental vision. I saw her again as I had seen her in the cab with her sweet, pensive face and downcast eyes; I felt again the touch of her soft cheek and the parting kiss by the gate, so frank and simple, so intimate and final.

I must have waited quite a long time, though the golden minutes sped unreckoned, for when my two colleagues arrived they tendered needless apologies.

"And I suppose," said Thorndyke, "you have been wondering what I wanted you for."

I had not, as a matter of fact, given the matter a moment's consideration.

"We are going to call on Mr. Jellicoe," Thorndyke explained. "There is something behind this affair, and until I have ascertained what it is, the case is not complete from my point of view."

"Wouldn't it have done as well to-morrow?" I asked.

"It might; and then it might not. There is an old saying as to catching a weasel asleep. Mr. Jellicoe is a somewhat wide-awake person, and I think it best to introduce him to Inspector Badger at the earliest possible moment."

"The meeting of a weasel and a badger suggests a sporting interview," remarked Jervis. "But you don't expect Jellicoe to give himself away, do you?"

"He can hardly do that, seeing that there is nothing to give away. But I think he may make a statement. There were some exceptional circumstances, I feel sure."

"How long have you known that the body was in the Museum?" I asked.

"About thirty or forty seconds longer than you have, I should say."

"Do you mean," I exclaimed, "that you did not know until the negative was developed?"

"My dear fellow," he replied, "do you suppose that, if I had had certain knowledge where the body was, I should have allowed that noble girl to go on dragging out a lingering agony of suspense that I could have cut short in a moment? Or that I should have made these humbugging pretences of scientific experiments if a more dignified course had been open to me?"

"As to the experiments," said Jervis, "Norbury could hardly have refused if you had taken him into your confidence."

"Indeed he could, and probably would. My 'confidence' would have involved a charge of murder against a highly respectable gentleman who was well known to him. He would probably have referred me to the police, and then what could I have done? I had plenty of suspicions, but not a single solid fact."

Our discussion was here interrupted by hurried footsteps on the stairs and a thundering rat-tat on our knocker.

As Jervis opened the door, Inspector Badger burst into the room in a highly excited state.

"What is all this, Dr. Thorndyke?" he asked. "I see

you've sworn an information against Mr. Jellicoe, and I have a warrant to arrest him; but before anything else is done I think it right to tell you that we have more evidence than is generally known pointing to quite a different quarter."

"Derived from Mr. Jellicoe's information," said Thorndyke. "But the fact is that I have just examined and identified the body at the British Museum where it was deposited by Mr. Jellicoe. I don't say that he murdered John Bellingham—though that is what appearances suggest—but I do say that he will have to account for his secret disposal of the body."

Inspector Badger was thunderstruck. Also he was visibly annoyed. The salt which Mr. Jellicoe had so adroitly sprinkled on the constabulary tail appeared to develop irritating properties, for when Thorndyke had given him a brief outline of the facts he stuck his hands in his pockets and exclaimed gloomily:

"Well, I'm hanged! And to think of all the time and trouble I've spent on those damned bones! I suppose they were just a plant?"

"Don't let us disparage them," said Thorndyke. "They have played a useful part. They represent the inevitable mistake that every criminal makes sooner or later. The murderer will always do a little too much. If he would only lie low and let well alone, the detective might whistle for a clue. But it is time we were starting."

"Are we all going?" asked the inspector, looking at me in particular with no very gracious recognition.

"We will all come with you," said Thorndyke; "but you will, naturally, make the arrest in the way that seems best to you."

"It's a regular procession," grumbled the inspector; but he made no more definite objection, and we started forth on our quest.

The distance from the Temple to Lincoln's Inn is not great. In five minutes we were at the gateway in Chancery Lane, and a couple of minutes later saw us gathered round the threshold of the stately old house in New Square.

"Seems to be a light in the first-floor front," said Badger. "You'd better move away before I ring the bell."

But the precaution was unnecessary. As the inspector advanced to the bell-pull a head was thrust out of the open window immediately above the street door.

"Who are you?" inquired the owner of the head in a voice which I recognised as that of Mr. Jellicoe.

"I am Inspector Badger of the Criminal Investigation Department. I wish to see Mr. Arthur Jellicoe."

"Then look at me. I am Mr. Arthur Jellicoe."

"I hold a warrant for your arrest, Mr. Jellicoe. You are charged with the murder of Mr. John Bellingham, whose body has been discovered in the British Museum."

"By whom?"

"By Dr. Thorndyke."

"Indeed," said Mr. Jellicoe. "Is he here?"

"Yes."

"Ha! and you wish to arrest me, I presume?"

"Yes. That is what I am here for."

"Well, I will agree to surrender myself subject to certain conditions."

"I can't make any conditions, Mr. Jellicoe."

"No, I will make them, and you will accept them. Otherwise you will not arrest me."

"It's no use for you to talk like that," said Badger. "If you don't let me in I shall have to break in. And I may as well tell you," he added mendaciously, "that the house is surrounded."

"You may accept my assurance," Mr. Jellicoe replied calmly, "that you will not arrest me if you do not accept my conditions."

"Well, what are your conditions?" demanded Badger.

"I desire to make a statement," said Mr. Jellicoe.

"You can do that, but I must caution you that anything you say may be used in evidence against you."

"Naturally. But I wish to make the statement in the presence of Dr. Thorndyke, and I desire to hear a statement from him of the method of investigation by which he discovered the whereabouts of the body. That is to say, if he is willing."

"If you mean that we should mutually enlighten one another, I am very willing indeed," said Thorndyke.

"Very well. Then my conditions, Inspector, are that I shall hear Dr. Thorndyke's statement and that I shall be permitted to make a statement myself, and that until those statements are completed, with any necessary interrogation and discussion, I shall remain at liberty and shall suffer no molestation or interference of any kind. And I agree that, on the conclusion of the said proceedings, I will submit without resistance to any course that you may adopt."

"I can't agree to that," said Badger.

"Can't you?" said Mr. Jellicoe coldly; and after a pause he added: "Don't be hasty. I have given you warning."

There was something in Mr. Jellicoe's passionless tone that disturbed the inspector exceedingly, for he turned to Thorndyke and said in a low tone:

"I wonder what his game is? He can't get away, you know."

"There are several possibilities," said Thorndyke.

"M'yes," said Badger, stroking his chin perplexedly.

"After all, is there any objection? His statement might save trouble, and you'd be on the safe side. It would take you some time to break in."

"Well," said Mr. Jellicoe, with his hand on the window, "do you agree—yes or no?"

"All right," said Badger sulkily. "I agree."

"You promise not to molest me in any way until I have quite finished?"

"I promise."

Mr. Jellicoe's head disappeared and the window closed. After a short pause we heard the jar of massive bolts and the clank of a chain, and, as the heavy door swung open, Mr. Jellicoe stood revealed, calm and impassive, with an old-fashioned office candlestick in his hand.

"Who are the others?" he inquired, peering out sharply through his spectacles.

"Oh, they are nothing to do with me," replied Badger.

"They are Dr. Berkeley and Dr. Jervis," said Thorndyke.

"Ha!" said Mr. Jellicoe; "very kind and attentive of them to call. Pray, come in, gentlemen. I am sure you will be interested to hear our little discussion."

He held the door open with a certain stiff courtesy, and we all entered the hall led by Inspector Badger. He closed the door softly and preceded us up the stairs and into the apartment from the window of which he had dictated the terms of surrender. It was a fine old room, spacious, lofty, and dignified, with panelled walls and a carved mantelpiece, the central escutcheon of which bore the initials "J. W. P." with the date "1671." A large writing-table stood at the farther end, and behind it an iron safe.

"I have been expecting this visit," Mr. Jellicoe remarked tranquilly as he placed four chairs opposite the table.

"Since when?" asked Thorndyke.

"Since last Monday evening, when I had the pleasure of seeing you conversing with my friend Dr. Berkeley at the Inner Temple gate, and then inferred that you were retained in the case. That was a circumstance that had not been fully provided for. May I offer you gentlemen a glass of sherry?"

As he spoke he placed on the table a decanter and a tray of glasses, and looked at us interrogatively with his hand on the stopper.

"Well, I don't mind if I do, Mr. Jellicoe," said Badger, on whom the lawyer's glance had finally settled. Mr. Jellicoe filled a glass and handed it to him with a stiff bow; then, with the decanter still in his hand, he said persuasively: "Dr. Thorndyke, pray allow me to fill you a glass?"

"No, thank you," said Thorndyke, in a tone so decided that the inspector looked round at him quickly. And as Badger caught his eye, the glass which he was about to raise to his lips became suddenly arrested and was slowly returned to the table untasted.

"I don't want to hurry you, Mr. Jellicoe," said the inspector, "but it's rather late, and I should like to get this business settled. What is it that you wish to do?"

"I desire," replied Mr. Jellicoe, "to make a detailed statement of the events that have happened, and I wish to hear from Dr. Thorndyke precisely how he arrived at his very remarkable conclusion. When this has been done I shall be entirely at your service; and I suggest that it would be more interesting if Dr. Thorndyke would give us his statement before I furnish you with the actual facts."

"I am entirely of your opinion," said Thorndyke.

"Then in that case," said Mr. Jellicoe, "I suggest that you disregard me, and address your remarks to your friends as if I were not present."

Thorndyke acquiesced with a bow, and Mr. Jellicoe, having seated himself in his elbow-chair behind the table, poured himself out a glass of water, selected a cigarette from a neat silver case, lighted it deliberately, and leaned back to listen at his ease.

"My first acquaintance with this case," Thorndyke began without preamble, "was made through the medium of the daily papers about two years ago; and I may say that, although I had no interest in it beyond the purely academic interest of a specialist in a case that lies in his particular speciality, I considered it with deep attention. The newspaper reports contained no particulars of the relations of the parties that could furnish any hints as to motives on the part of any of them, but merely a bare statement of the events. And this was a distinct advantage, inasmuch as it left one to consider the facts of the case without regard to motive—to balance the *prima facie* probabilities with an open mind. And it may surprise you to learn that those *prima facie* probabilities pointed from the very first to that solution which has been put to the test of experiment this evening. Hence it will be well for me to begin by giving the conclusions that I reached by reasoning from the facts set forth in the newspapers before any of the further facts came to my knowledge.

"From the facts as stated in the newspaper reports it is obvious that there were four possible explanations of the disappearance.

"1. The man might be alive and in hiding. This was highly improbable, for the reasons that were stated by

Mr. Loram at the late hearing of the application, and for a further reason that I shall mention presently.

"2. He might have died by accident or disease, and his body failed to be identified. This was even more improbable, seeing that he carried on his person abundant means of identification, including visiting cards.

"3. He might have been murdered by some stranger for the sake of his portable property. This was highly improbable for the same reason: his body could hardly have failed to be identified.

"These three explanations are what we may call the outside explanations. They touched none of the parties mentioned; they were all obviously improbable on general grounds; and to all of them there was one conclusive answer—the scarab which was found in Godfrey Bellingham's garden. Hence I put them aside and gave my attention to the fourth explanation. This was that the missing man had been made away with by one of the parties mentioned in the report. But, since the reports mentioned three parties, it was evident that there was a choice of three hypotheses, namely:

"(*a*) That John Bellingham had been made away with by Hurst; or (*b*) by the Bellinghams; or (*c*) by Mr. Jellicoe.

"Now, I have constantly impressed on my pupils that the indispensable question that must be asked at the outset of such an inquiry as this is, 'When was the missing person last undoubtedly seen or known to be alive?' That is the question that I asked myself after reading the newspaper report; and the answer was, that he was last certainly seen alive on the fourteenth of October, nineteen hundred and two, at 141, Queen Square, Bloomsbury. Of the fact that he was alive at that time and place there could be no doubt whatever; for he was seen at the same moment by two persons, both of whom were intimately acquainted with him, and one of whom, Dr. Norbury, was apparently a disinterested witness. After that date he was never seen, alive or dead, by any person who knew him and was able to identify him. It was stated that he had been seen on the twenty-third of November following by the housemaid of Mr. Hurst; but as this person was unacquainted with him, it was uncertain whether the person whom she saw was or was not John Bellingham.

"Hence the disappearance dated, not from the twenty-third of November, as every one seems to have assumed, but from the fourteenth of October; and the question was not, 'What became of John Bellingham after he entered Mr. Hurst's house?' but, 'What became of him after his interview in Queen Square?'

"But as soon as I had decided that that interview must form the real starting point of the inquiry, a most striking set of circumstances came into view. It became obvious that if Mr. Jellicoe had had any reason for wishing to make away with John Bellingham, he had such an opportunity as seldom falls to the lot of an intending murderer.

"Just consider the conditions. John Bellingham was known to be setting out alone upon a journey beyond the sea. His exact destination was not stated. He was to be absent for an undetermined period, but at least three weeks. His disappearance would occasion no comment; his absence would lead to no inquiries, at least for several weeks, during which the murderer would have leisure quietly to dispose of the body and conceal all traces of the crime. The conditions were, from a murderer's point of view, ideal.

"But that was not all. During that very period of John

Bellingham's absence Mr. Jellicoe was engaged to deliver to the British Museum what was admittedly a dead human body; and that body was to be enclosed in a sealed case. Could any more perfect or secure method of disposing of a body be devised by the most ingenious murderer? The plan would have had only one weak point: the mummy would be known to have left Queen Square *after* the disappearance of John Bellingham, and suspicion might in the end have arisen. To this point I shall return presently; meanwhile we will consider the second hypothesis—that the missing man was made away with by Mr. Hurst.

"Now, there seemed to be no doubt that some person, purporting to be John Bellingham, did actually visit Mr. Hurst's house; and he must either have left the house or remained in it. If he left, he did so surreptitiously; if he remained, there could be no reasonable doubt that he had been murdered and that his body had been concealed. Let us consider the probabilities in each case.

"Assuming—as every one seems to have done—that the visitor was really John Bellingham, we are dealing with a responsible, middle-aged gentleman, and the idea that such a person would enter a house, announce his intention of staying, and then steal away unobserved is very difficult to accept. Moreover, he would appear to have come down to Eltham by rail immediately on landing in England, leaving his luggage in the cloak-room at Charing Cross. This pointed to a definiteness of purpose quite inconsistent with his casual disappearance from the house.

"On the other hand, the idea that he might have been murdered by Hurst was not inconceivable. The thing was physically possible. If Bellingham had really been in the study when Hurst came home, the murder could have been committed—by appropriate means—and the body temporarily concealed in the cupboard or elsewhere. But, although possible, it was not at all probable. There was no real opportunity. The risk and the subsequent difficulties would be very great; there was not a particle of positive evidence that a murder had occurred; and the conduct of Hurst in immediately leaving the house in possession of the servants is quite inconsistent with the supposition that there was a body concealed in it. So that, while it is almost impossible to believe that John Bellingham left the house of his own accord, it is equally difficult to believe that he did not leave it.

"But there is a third possibility, which, strange to say, no one seems to have suggested. Supposing that the visitor was not John Bellingham at all, but some one who was personating him? That would dispose of the difficulties completely. The strange disappearance ceases to be strange, for a personator would necessarily make off before Mr. Hurst should arrive and discover the imposture. But if we accept this supposition, we raise two further questions: 'Who was the personator?' and 'What was the object of the personation?'

"Now, the personator was clearly not Hurst himself, for he would have been recognised by his housemaid; he was therefore either Godfrey Bellingham or Mr. Jellicoe or some other person; and as no other person was mentioned in the newspaper reports I confined my speculations to these two.

"And, first, as to Godfrey Bellingham. It did not appear whether he was or was not known to the housemaid, so I assumed—wrongly, as it turns out—that he was not. Then he might have been the personator. But why should he have personated his brother? He could not have already committed the murder. There had not been time enough. He would have had to leave Woodford before John Bellingham had set out from Charing Cross. And even if he had committed the murder, he would have no object in raising this commotion. His cue would have been to remain quiet and know nothing. The probabilities were all against the personator being Godfrey Bellingham.

"Then could it be Mr. Jellicoe? The answer to this question is contained in the answer to the further question: What could have been the object of the personation?

"What motive could this unknown person have had in appearing, announcing himself as John Bellingham, and forthwith vanishing? There could only have been one motive; that, namely, of fixing the date of John Bellingham's disappearance—of furnishing a definite moment at which he was last seen alive.

"But who was likely to have had such a motive? Let us see.

"I said just now that if Mr. Jellicoe had murdered John Bellingham and disposed of the body in the mummy-case, he would have been absolutely safe for the time being. But there would be a weak spot in his armour. For a month or more the disappearance of his client would occasion no remark. But presently, when he failed to return, inquiries would be set on foot; and then it would appear that no one had seen him since he left Queen Square. Then it would be noted that the last person with whom he was seen was Mr. Jellicoe. It might, further, be remembered that the mummy had been delivered to the Museum some time *after* the missing man was last seen alive. And so suspicion might arise and be followed by disastrous investigations. But supposing it should be made to appear that John Bellingham had been seen alive more than a month after his interview with Mr. Jellicoe and some weeks after the mummy had been deposited in the Museum? Then Mr. Jellicoe would cease to be in any way connected with the disappearance and henceforth would be absolutely safe.

"Hence, after carefully considering this part of the newspaper report, I came to the conclusion that the mysterious occurrence at Mr. Hurst's house had only one reasonable explanation, namely, that the visitor was not John Bellingham, but some one personating him; and that that some one was Mr. Jellicoe.

"It remains to consider the case of Godfrey Bellingham and his daughter, though I cannot understand how any sane person can have seriously suspected either" (here Inspector Badger smiled a sour smile). "The evidence against them was negligible, for there was nothing to connect them with the affair save the finding of the scarab on their premises; and that event, which might have been highly suspicious under other circumstances, was robbed of any significance by the fact that the scarab was found on a spot which had been passed a few minutes previously by the other suspected party, Hurst. The finding of the scarab did, however, establish two important conclusions; namely, that John Bellingham had probably met with foul play, and that, of the four persons present when it was found, one at least had had possession of the body. As to which of the four was the one, the circumstances furnished only a hint, which was this: if the scarab had been purposely dropped, the most likely person to find it was the one who dropped it. And the person who discovered it was Mr. Jellicoe.

"Following up this hint, if we ask ourselves what motive Mr. Jellicoe could have had for dropping it— assuming him to be the murderer—the answer is obvious.

It would not be his policy to fix the crime on any particular person, but rather to set up a complication of conflicting evidence which would occupy the attention of investigators and divert it from himself.

"Of course, if Hurst had been the murderer, he would have had a sufficient motive for dropping the scarab, so that the case against Mr. Jellicoe was not conclusive; but the fact that it was he who found it was highly significant.

"This completes the analysis of the evidence contained in the original newspaper report describing the circumstances of the disappearance. The conclusions that followed from it were, as you will have seen:

"1. That the missing man was almost certainly dead, as proved by the finding of the scarab after his disappearance.

"2. That he had probably been murdered by one or more of four persons, as proved by the finding of the scarab on the premises occupied by two of them and accessible to the others.

"3. That, of those four persons, one—Mr. Jellicoe—was the last person who was known to have been in the company of the missing man; had had an exceptional opportunity for committing the murder; and was known to have delivered a dead body to the Museum subsequently to the disappearance.

"4. That the supposition that Mr. Jellicoe had committed the murder rendered all the other circumstances of the disappearance clearly intelligible, whereas on any other supposition they were quite inexplicable.

"The evidence of the newspaper report, therefore, clearly pointed to the probability that John Bellingham had been murdered by Mr. Jellicoe and his body concealed in the mummy-case.

"I do not wish to give you the impression that I, then and there, believed that Mr. Jellicoe was the murderer. I did not. There was no reason to suppose that the report contained all the essential facts, and I merely considered it speculatively as a study in probabilities. But I did decide that that was the only probable conclusion from the facts that were given.

"Nearly two years had passed before I heard anything more of the case. Then it was brought to my notice by my friend, Dr. Berkeley, and I became acquainted with certain new facts, which I will consider in the order in which they became known to me.

"The first new light on the case came from the will. As soon as I had read the document I felt convinced that there was something wrong. The testator's evident intention was that his brother should inherit the property, whereas the construction of the will was such as almost certainly to defeat that intention. The devolution of the property depended on the burial clause—clause two; but the burial arrangements would ordinarily be decided by the executor, who happened to be Mr. Jellicoe. Thus the will left the disposition of the property under the control of Mr. Jellicoe, though his action could have been contested.

"Now, this will, although drawn up by John Bellingham, was executed in Mr. Jellicoe's office as is proved by the fact that it was witnessed by two of his clerks. He was the testator's lawyer, and it was his duty to insist on the will being properly drawn. Evidently he did nothing of the kind, and this fact strongly suggested some kind of collusion on his part with Hurst, who stood to benefit by the miscarriage of the will. And this was the odd feature in the case; for whereas the party responsible for the defective provisions was Mr. Jellicoe, the party who benefited was Hurst.

"But the most startling peculiarity of the will was the way in which it fitted the circumstances of the disappearance. It looked as if clause two had been drawn up with those very circumstances in view. Since, however, the will was ten years old, this was impossible. But if clause two could not have been devised to fit the disappearance, could the disappearance have been devised to fit clause two? That was by no means impossible: under the circumstances it looked rather probable. And if it had been so contrived, who was the agent in that contrivance? Hurst stood to benefit, but there was no evidence that he even knew the contents of the will. There only remained Mr. Jellicoe, who had certainly connived at the misdrawing of the will for some purpose of his own—some dishonest purpose.

"The evidence of the will, then, pointed to Mr. Jellicoe as the agent in the disappearance, and, after reading it, I definitely suspected him of the crime.

"Suspicion, however, is one thing and proof is another; I had not nearly enough evidence to justify me in laying an information, and I could not approach the Museum officials without making a definite accusation. The great difficulty of the case was that I could discover no motive. I could not see any way in which Mr. Jellicoe would benefit by the disappearance. His own legacy was secure, whenever and however the testator died. The murder and concealment apparently benefited Hurst alone; and, in the absence of any plausible motive, the facts required to be much more conclusive than they were."

"Did you form absolutely no opinion as to motive?" asked Mr. Jellicoe.

He put the question in a quiet, passionless tone, as if he

were discussing some *cause célèbre* in which he had nothing more than a professional interest. Indeed, the calm, impersonal interest that he displayed in Thorndyke's analysis, his unmoved attention, punctuated by little nods of approval at each telling point in the argument, were the most surprising features of this astounding interview.

"I did form an opinion," replied Thorndyke, "but it was merely speculative, and I was never able to confirm it. I discovered that about ten years ago Mr. Hurst had been in difficulties and that he had suddenly raised a considerable sum of money, no one knew how or on what security. I observed that this event coincided with the execution of the will, and I surmised that there might be some connection between them. But that was only a surmise; and as the proverb has it, 'He discovers who proves.' I could prove nothing, so that I never discovered Mr. Jellicoe's motive, and I don't know it now."

"Don't you really?" said Mr. Jellicoe, in something approaching a tone of animation. He laid down the end of his cigarette, and, as he selected another from the silver case, he continued: "I think that is the most interesting feature of your really remarkable analysis. It does you great credit. The absence of motive would have appeared to most persons a fatal objection to the theory of, what I may call, the prosecution. Permit me to congratulate you on the consistency and tenacity with which you have pursued the actual, visible facts."

He bowed stiffly to Thorndyke (who returned his bow with equal stiffness), lighted a fresh cigarette, and once more leaned back in his chair with the calm, attentive manner of a man who is listening to a lecture or a musical performance.

"The evidence, then, being insufficient to act upon,"

Thorndyke resumed, "there was nothing for it but to wait for some new facts. Now, the study of a large series of carefully conducted murders brings into view an almost invariable phenomenon. The cautious murderer, in his anxiety to make himself secure, does too much; and it is this excess of precaution that leads to detection. It happens constantly; indeed, I may say that it always happens—in those murders that are detected; of those that are not we say nothing—and I had strong hopes that it would happen in this case. And it did.

"At the very moment when my client's case seemed almost hopeless, some human remains were discovered at Sidcup. I read the account of the discovery in the evening paper, and, scanty as the report was, it recorded enough facts to convince me that the inevitable mistake had been made."

"Did it, indeed?" said Mr. Jellicoe. "A mere, inexpert, hearsay report! I should have supposed it to be quite valueless from a scientific point of view."

"So it was," said Thorndyke. "But it gave the date of the discovery and the locality, and it also mentioned what bones had been found. Which were all vital facts. Take the question of time. These remains, after lying *perdu* for two years, suddenly come to light just as the parties— who have also been lying *perdu*—have begun to take action in respect of the will; in fact, within a week or two of the hearing of the application. It was certainly a remarkable coincidence. And when the circumstances that occasioned the discovery were considered, the coincidence became more remarkable still. For these remains were found on land actually belonging to John Bellingham, and their discovery resulted from certain operations (the clearing of the watercress-beds) carried out on behalf of the absent landlord. But by whose orders were those works undertaken? Clearly by the orders of the landlord's agent. But the landlord's agent was known to be Mr. Jellicoe. Therefore these remains were brought to light at this peculiarly opportune moment by the action of Mr. Jellicoe. The coincidence, I say again, was very remarkable.

"But what instantly arrested my attention on reading the newspaper report was the unusual manner in which the arm had been separated; for, besides the bones of the arm proper, there were those of what anatomists call the 'shoulder-girdle'—the shoulder-blade and collar-bone. This was very remarkable. It seemed to suggest a knowledge of anatomy, and yet no murderer, even if he possessed such knowledge, would make such a display of it on such an occasion. It seemed to me that there must be some other explanation. Accordingly, when other remains had come to light and all had been collected at Woodford I asked my friend Berkeley to go down there and inspect them. He did so, and this is what he found:

"Both arms had been detached in the same peculiar manner; both were complete, and all the bones were from the same body. The bones were quite clean—of soft structures, I mean. There were no cuts, scratches or marks on them. There was not a trace of adipocere—the peculiar waxy soap that forms in bodies that decay in water or in a damp situation. The right hand had been detached at the time the arm was thrown into the pond, and the left ring finger had been separated and had vanished. This latter fact had attracted my attention from the first, but I will leave its consideration for the moment and return to it later."

"How did you discover that the hand had been detached?" Mr. Jellicoe asked.

"By the submersion marks," replied Thorndyke. "It

was lying on the bottom of the pond in a position which would have been impossible if it had been attached to the arm."

"You interest me exceedingly," said Mr. Jellicoe. "It appears that a medico-legal expert finds 'books in the running brooks, sermons in bones, and evidence in everything.' But don't let me interrupt you."

"Dr. Berkeley's observations," Thorndyke resumed, "together with the medical evidence at the inquest, led me to certain conclusions.

"Let me state the facts which were disclosed.

"The remains which had been assembled formed a complete human skeleton with the exception of the skull, one finger, and the legs from the knee to the ankle, including both knee-caps. This was a very impressive fact; for the bones that were missing included all those which could have been identified as belonging or not belonging to John Bellingham; and the bones that were present were the unidentifiable remainder.

"It had a suspicious appearance of selection.

"But the parts that were present were also curiously suggestive. In all cases the mode of dismemberment was peculiar; for an ordinary person would have divided the knee-joint leaving the knee-cap attached to the thigh, whereas it had evidently been left attached to the shin-bone; and the head would most probably have been removed by cutting through the neck instead of being neatly detached from the spine. And all these bones were entirely free from marks or scratches such as would naturally occur in an ordinary dismemberment, and all were quite free from adipocere. And now as to the conclusions which I drew from these facts. First, there was the peculiar grouping of the bones. What was the meaning of that? Well, the idea of a punctilious anatomist was obviously absurd, and I put it aside. But was there any other explanation? Yes, there was. The bones had appeared in the natural groups that are held together by ligaments; and they had separated at points where they were attached principally by muscles. The knee-cap, for instance, which really belongs to the thigh, is attached to it by muscle, but to the shin-bone by a stout ligament. And so with the bones of the arm; they are connected to one another by ligaments; but to the trunk only by muscle, excepting at one end of the collar-bone.

"But this was a very significant fact. Ligament decays much more slowly than muscle, so that in a body of which the muscles had largely decayed the bones might still be held together by ligament. The peculiar grouping therefore suggested that the body had been partly reduced to a skeleton before it was dismembered; that it had then been merely pulled apart and not divided with a knife.

"This suggestion was remarkably confirmed by the total absence of knife-cuts or scratches.

"Then there was the fact that all the bones were quite free from adipocere. Now, if an arm or a thigh should be deposited in water and left undisturbed to decay, it is certain that large masses of adipocere would be formed. Probably more than half of the flesh would be converted into this substance. The absence of adipocere therefore proved that the bulk of the flesh had disappeared or been removed from the bones before they were deposited in the pond. That, in fact, it was not a body, but a skeleton, that had been deposited.

"But what kind of skeleton? If it was the recent skeleton of a murdered man, then the bones had been carefully stripped of flesh so as to leave the ligaments intact. But this was highly improbable; for there could be no object in preserving the ligaments. And the absence of scratches was against this view.

"Then they did not appear to be graveyard bones. The collection was too complete. It is very rare to find a graveyard skeleton of which many of the small bones are not missing. And such bones are usually more or less weathered and friable.

"They did not appear to be bones such as may be bought at an osteological dealer's, for these usually have perforations to admit the macerating fluid to the marrow cavities. Dealers' bones, too, are very seldom all from the same body; and the small bones of the hand are drilled with holes to enable them to be strung on catgut.

"They were not dissecting-room bones, as there was no trace of red lead in the openings for the nutrient arteries.

"What the appearances did suggest was that these were parts of a body which had decayed in a very dry atmosphere (in which no adipocere would be formed), and which had been pulled or broken apart. Also that the ligaments which held the body—or rather skeleton— together were brittle and friable as suggested by the detached hand, which had probably broken off accidentally. But the only kind of body that completely answered this description is an Egyptian mummy. A mummy, it is true, has been more or less preserved; but on exposure to the air of such a climate as ours it perishes rapidly, the ligaments being the last of the soft parts to disappear.

"The hypothesis that these bones were parts of a mummy naturally suggested Mr. Jellicoe. If he had murdered John Bellingham and concealed his body in the mummy-case, he would have a spare mummy on his hands, and that mummy would have been exposed to the air and to somewhat rough handling.

"A very interesting circumstance connected with these

remains was that the ring finger was missing. Now, fingers have on sundry occasions been detached from dead hands for the sake of the rings on them. But in such cases the object has been to secure a valuable ring uninjured. If this hand was the hand of John Bellingham, there was no such object. The purpose was to prevent identification; and that purpose would have been more easily, and much more completely, achieved by sacrificing the ring, by filing through it or breaking it off the finger. The appearances, therefore, did not quite agree with the apparent purpose.

"Then, could there be any other purpose with which they agreed better? Yes, there could.

"If it had happened that John Bellingham was known to have worn a ring on that finger, and especially if that ring fitted tightly, the removal of the finger would serve a very useful purpose. It would create an impression that the finger had been removed on account of a ring, to prevent identification; which impression would, in turn, produce a suspicion that the hand was that of John Bellingham. And yet it would not be evidence that could be used to establish identity. Now, if Mr. Jellicoe were the murderer and had the body hidden elsewhere, vague suspicion would be precisely what he would desire, and positive evidence what he would wish to avoid.

"It transpired later that John Bellingham did wear a ring on that finger and that the ring fitted very tightly. Whence it followed that the absence of the finger was an additional point tending to implicate Mr. Jellicoe.

"And now let us briefly review this mass of evidence. You will see that it consists of a multitude of items, each either trivial or speculative. Up to the time of the actual discovery I had not a single crucial fact, nor any clue as to motive. But, slight as the individual points of evidence were, they pointed with impressive unanimity to one person—Mr. Jellicoe. Thus:

"The person who had the opportunity to commit murder and dispose of the body was Mr. Jellicoe.

"The deceased was last certainly seen alive with Mr. Jellicoe.

"An unidentified human body was delivered to the Museum by Mr. Jellicoe.

"The only person who could have a motive for personating the deceased was Mr. Jellicoe.

"The only known person who could possibly have done so was Mr. Jellicoe.

"One of the two persons who could have had a motive for dropping the scarab was Mr. Jellicoe. The person who found that scarab was Mr. Jellicoe, although owing to his defective eyesight and his spectacles, he was the most unlikely person of those present to find it.

"The person who was responsible for the execution of the defective will was Mr. Jellicoe.

"Then as to the remains. They were apparently not those of John Bellingham, but parts of a particular kind of body. But the only person who was known to have had such a body in his possession was Mr. Jellicoe.

"The only person who could have had any motive for substituting those remains for the remains of the deceased was Mr. Jellicoe.

"Finally, the person who caused the discovery of those remains at that singularly opportune moment was Mr. Jellicoe.

"This was the sum of the evidence that was in my possession up to the time of the hearing and, indeed, for some time after, and it was not enough to act upon. But when the case had been heard in Court, it was evident either that the proceedings would be abandoned—which was unlikely—or that there would be new developments.

"I watched the progress of events with profound interest. An attempt had been made (by Mr. Jellicoe or some other person) to get the will administered without producing the body of John Bellingham; and that attempt had failed. The coroner's jury had refused to identify the remains; the Probate Court had refused to presume the death of the testator. As affairs stood the will could not be administered.

"What would be the next move?

"It was virtually certain that it would consist in the production of something which would identify the unrecognised remains as those of the testator.

"But what would that something be?

"The answer to that question would contain the answer to another question: Was my solution of the mystery the true solution?

"If I was wrong, it was possible that some of the undoubtedly genuine bones of John Bellingham might presently be discovered; for instance, the skull, the knee-cap, or the left fibula, by any of which the remains could be positively identified.

"If I was right, only one thing could possibly happen. Mr. Jellicoe would have to play the trump card that he had been holding back in case the Court should refuse the application; a card that he was evidently reluctant to play.

"He would have to produce the bones of the mummy's finger, together with John Bellingham's ring. No other course was possible.

"But not only would the bones and the ring have to be found together. They would have to be found in a place which was accessible to Mr. Jellicoe, and so far under his control that he could determine the exact time when the discovery should be made.

"I waited patiently for the answer to my question. Was I right or was I wrong?

"And in due course, the answer came.

"The bones and the ring were discovered in the well in the grounds of Godfrey Bellingham's late house. That house was the property of John Bellingham. Mr. Jellicoe was John Bellingham's agent. Hence it was practically certain that the date on which the well was emptied was settled by Mr. Jellicoe.

"The oracle had spoken.

"The discovery proved conclusively that the bones were not those of John Bellingham (for if they had been the ring would have been unnecessary for identification). But if the bones were not John Bellingham's, the ring was; from which followed the important corollary that whoever had deposited those bones in the well had had possession of the body of John Bellingham. And there could be no doubt that that person was Mr. Jellicoe.

"On receiving this final confirmation of my conclusions, I applied forthwith to Dr. Norbury for permission to examine the mummy of Sebek-hotep, with the result that you are already acquainted with."

As Thorndyke concluded, Mr. Jellicoe regarded him thoughtfully for a moment and then said: "You have given us a most complete and lucid exposition of your method of investigation, sir. I have enjoyed it exceedingly, and should have profited by it hereafter— under other circumstances. Are you sure you won't allow me to fill your glass?" He touched the stopper of the decanter, and Inspector Badger ostentatiously consulted his watch.

"Time is running on, I fear," said Mr. Jellicoe.

"It is, indeed," Badger assented emphatically.

"Well, I need not detain you long," said the lawyer.

"My statement is a narration of events. But I desire to make it, and you, no doubt, will be interested to hear it."

He opened the silver case and selected a fresh cigarette, which, however, he did not light. Inspector Badger produced a funereal notebook, which he laid open on his knee; and the rest of us settled ourselves in our chairs with no little curiosity to hear Mr. Jellicoe's statement.

CHAPTER XX   The End of the Case

A profound silence had fallen on the room and its occupants. Mr. Jellicoe sat with his eyes fixed on the table as if deep in thought, the unlighted cigarette in one hand, the other grasping the tumbler of water. Presently Inspector Badger coughed impatiently and he looked up. "I beg your pardon, gentlemen," he said. "I am keeping you waiting."

He took a sip from the tumbler, opened a match-box and took out a match, but apparently altering his mind, laid it down and commenced:

"The unfortunate affair which has brought you here to-night, had its origin ten years ago. At that time my friend Hurst became suddenly involved in financial difficulties—am I speaking too fast for you, Mr. Badger?"

"No, not at all," replied Badger. "I am taking it down in shorthand."

"Thank you," said Mr. Jellicoe. "He became involved in serious difficulties and came to me for assistance. He wished to borrow five thousand pounds to enable him to meet his engagements. I had a certain amount of money at my disposal, but I did not consider Hurst's security satisfactory; accordingly I felt compelled to refuse. But on the very next day, John Bellingham called on me with a draft of his will which he wished me to look over before it was executed.

"It was an absurd will, and I nearly told him so; but then an idea occurred to me in connection with Hurst. It was obvious to me, as soon as I glanced through the will, that if the burial clause was left as the testator had drafted it, Hurst had a very good chance of inheriting the property; and, as I was named as the executor, I should be able to give full effect to that clause. Accordingly, I asked for a few days to consider the will, and then I called upon Hurst and made a proposal to him; which was this: That I should advance him five thousand pounds without security; that I should ask for no repayment, but that he should assign to me any interest that he might have or acquire in the estate of John Bellingham up to ten thousand pounds, or two-thirds of any sum that he might inherit if over that amount. He asked if John had yet made any will, and I replied, quite correctly, that he had not. He inquired if I knew what testamentary arrangements John intended to make, and again I answered, quite correctly, that I believed John proposed to devise the bulk of his property to his brother, Godfrey.

"Thereupon, Hurst accepted my proposal; I made him the advance and he executed the assignment. After a few days' delay, I passed the will as satisfactory. The actual document was written from the draft by the testator himself; and, a fortnight after Hurst had executed the assignment, John signed the will in my office. By the provisions of that will I stood an excellent chance of becoming virtually the principal beneficiary, unless Godfrey should contest Hurst's claim and the Court should override the conditions of clause two.

"You will now understand the motives which governed my subsequent actions. You will also see, Dr. Thorndyke, how very near to the truth your reasoning carried you; and you will understand, as I wish you to do, that Mr. Hurst was no party to any of those proceedings which I am about to describe.

"Coming now to the interview in Queen Square in October, nineteen hundred and two, you are aware of the general circumstances from my evidence in Court, which was literally correct up to a certain point. The interview took place in a room on the third floor, in which were stored the cases which John had brought with him from Egypt. The mummy was unpacked, as were some other objects that he was not offering to the Museum, but several cases were still unopened. At the conclusion of the interview I accompanied Dr. Norbury down to the street door, and we stood on the doorstep conversing for perhaps a quarter of an hour. Then Dr. Norbury went away and I returned upstairs.

"Now the house in Queen Square is virtually a museum. The upper part is separated from the lower by a massive door which opens from the hall and gives access to the staircase, and which is fitted with a Chubb night-latch. There are two latch-keys, of which John used to keep one and I the other. You will find them both in the safe behind me. The caretaker had no key and no access to the upper part of the house unless admitted by one of us.

"At the time when I came in, after Dr. Norbury had left, the caretaker was in the cellar, where I could hear him breaking coke for the hot-water furnace. I had left John on the third floor opening some of the packing-cases by the light of a lamp with a tool somewhat like a plasterer's hammer; that is, a hammer with a small axe-blade at the reverse of the head. As I stood talking to Dr. Norbury, I could hear him knocking out the nails and wrenching up the lids; and, when I entered the doorway leading to the stairs, I could still hear him. Just as I closed the staircase door behind me, I heard a rumbling noise from above; then all was still.

"I went up the stairs to the second floor, where, as the staircase was all in darkness, I stopped to light the gas. As I turned to ascend the next flight, I saw a hand projecting over the edge of the half-way landing. I ran up the stairs, and there, on the landing, I saw John lying huddled up in a heap at the foot of the top flight. There was a wound at the side of his forehead from which a little blood was trickling. The case-opener lay on the floor close by him and there was blood on the axe-blade. When I looked up the stairs I saw a rag of torn matting over the top stair.

"It was quite easy to see what had happened. He had walked quickly out on the landing with the case-opener in his hand. His foot had caught in the torn matting and he had pitched head foremost down the stairs still holding the case-opener. He had fallen so that his head had come down on the upturned edge of the axe-blade; he had then rolled over and the case-opener had dropped from his hand.

"I lit a wax match and stooped down to look at him. His head was in a very peculiar position, which made me suspect that his neck was broken. There was extremely little bleeding from the wound; he was perfectly motionless; I could detect no sign of breathing; and I felt no doubt that he was dead.

"It was an exceedingly regrettable affair, and it placed me, as I perceived at once, in an extremely awkward position. My first impulse was to send the caretaker for a doctor and a policeman; but a moment's reflection convinced me that there were serious objections to this course.

"There was nothing to show that I had not, myself, knocked him down with the case-opener. Of course, there was nothing to show that I had; but we were alone in the house with the exception of the caretaker, who was down in the basement out of earshot.

"There would be an inquest. At the inquest inquiries would be made as to the will which was known to exist. But as soon as the will was produced, Hurst would become suspicious. He would probably make a statement to the coroner and I should be charged with the murder. Or, even if I were not charged, Hurst would suspect me and would probably repudiate the assignment; and, under the circumstances, it would be practically impossible for me to enforce it. He would refuse to pay and I could not take my claim into Court.

"I sat down on the stairs just above poor John's body and considered the matter in detail. At the worst, I stood a fair chance of hanging; at the best, I stood to lose close upon fifty thousand pounds. These were not pleasant alternatives.

"Supposing, on the other hand, I concealed the body and gave out that John had gone to Paris. There was, of course, the risk of discovery, in which case I should certainly be convicted of the murder. But if no discovery occurred, I was not only safe from suspicion, but I secured the fifty thousand pounds. In either case there was considerable risk, but in one there was the certainty of loss, whereas in the other there was a material advantage to justify the risk. The question was whether it would be possible to conceal the body. If it were, then the contingent profit was worth the slight additional risk. But a human body is a very difficult thing to dispose of, especially to a person of so little scientific culture as myself.

"It is curious that I considered this question for a quite considerable time before the obvious solution presented itself. I turned over at least a dozen methods of disposing of the body and rejected them all as impracticable. Then, suddenly, I remembered the mummy upstairs.

"At first it occurred to me only as a fantastic possibility that I could conceal the body in the mummy-case. But as I turned over the idea I began to see that it was really practicable; and not only practicable but easy; and not only easy but eminently safe. If once the mummy-case was in the Museum, I was rid of it for ever.

"The circumstances were, as you, sir, have justly observed, singularly favourable. There would be no hue and cry, no hurry, no anxiety; but ample time for all the necessary preparations. Then the mummy-case itself was curiously suitable. Its length was ample, as I knew from having measured it. It was a cartonnage of rather flexible material, and had an opening behind, secured with a lacing so that it could be opened without injury. Nothing need be cut but the lacing, which could be replaced. A little damage might be done in extracting the mummy and in introducing the deceased; but such cracks as might occur would be of no importance. For here again Fortune favoured me. The whole of the back of the mummy-case was coated with bitumen, and it would be easy when once the deceased was safely inside to apply a fresh coat, which would cover up not only the cracks but also the new lacing.

"After careful consideration, I decided to adopt the plan. I went downstairs and sent the caretaker on an

errand to the Law Courts. Then I returned and carried the
deceased up to one of the third-floor rooms, where I
removed his clothes and laid him out on a long packing-
case in the position in which he would lie in the mummy-
case. I folded his clothes neatly and packed them, with
the exception of his boots, in a suit-case that he had been
taking to Paris, and which contained nothing but his
night-clothes, toilet articles, and a change of linen. By the
time I had done this and thoroughly washed the oilcloth
on the stairs and landing, the caretaker had returned. I
informed him that Mr. Bellingham had started for Paris
and then I went home. The upper part of the house was,
of course, secured by the Chubb lock, but I had also—*ex
abundantiâ cautelæ*—locked the door of the room in
which I had deposited the deceased.

"I had, of course, some knowledge of the methods of
embalming, but principally of those employed by the
ancients. Hence, on the following day, I went to the
British Museum library and consulted the most recent
works on the subject; and exceedingly interesting they
were, as showing the remarkable improvements that
modern knowledge has effected in this ancient art. I need
not trouble you with details that are familiar to you. The
process that I selected as the simplest for a beginner was
that of formalin injection, and I went straight from the
Museum to purchase the necessary materials. I did not,
however, buy an embalming syringe: the book stated that
an ordinary anatomical injecting syringe would answer
the same purpose, and I thought it a more discreet
purchase.

"I fear that I bungled the injection terribly, although I
had carefully studied the plates in a treatise on
anatomy—Gray's, I think. However, if my methods were
clumsy, they were quite effectual. I carried out the

process on the evening of the third day; and, when I locked up the house that night, I had the satisfaction of knowing that poor John's remains were secure from corruption and decay.

"But this was not enough. The great weight of a fresh body as compared with that of a mummy would be immediately noticed by those who had the handling of the mummy-case. Moreover, the damp from the body would quickly ruin the cartonnage and would cause a steamy film on the inside of the glass case in which it would be exhibited. And this would probably lead to an examination. Clearly, then, it was necessary that the remains of the deceased should be thoroughly dried before they were enclosed in the cartonnage.

"Here my unfortunate deficiency in scientific knowledge was a great drawback. I had no idea how this result would be achieved, and, in the end, was compelled to consult a taxidermist, to whom I represented that I wished to collect some small animals and reptiles and rapidly dry them for convenience of transport. By this person I was advised to immerse the dead animals in a jar of methylated spirit for a week and then expose them in a current of warm, dry air.

, "But the plan of immersing the remains of the deceased in a jar of methylated spirit was obviously impracticable. However, I bethought me that we had in our collection a porphyry sarcophagus, the cavity of which had been shaped to receive a small mummy in its case. I tried the deceased in the sarcophagus and found that he just fitted the cavity loosely. I obtained a few gallons of methylated spirit, which I poured into the cavity, just covering the body, and then I put on the lid and luted it down air-tight with putty. I trust I do not weary you with these particulars?"

"I'll ask you to cut it as short as you can, Mr Jellicoe," said Badger. "It has been a long yarn and time is running on."

"For my part," said Thorndyke, "I find these details deeply interesting and instructive. They fill in the outline that I had drawn by inference."

"Precisely," said Mr Jellicoe; "then I will proceed.

"I left the deceased soaking in the spirit for a fortnight and then took him out, wiped him dry, and laid him on four cane-bottomed chairs just over the hot-water pipes, and I let a free current of air pass through the room. The result interested me exceedingly. By the end of the third day the hands and feet had become quite dry and shrivelled and horny—so that the ring actually dropped off the shrunken finger—the nose looked like a fold of parchment; and the skin of the body was so dry and smooth that you could have engrossed a lease on it. For the first day or two I turned the deceased at intervals so that he should dry evenly, and then I proceeded to get the case ready. I divided the lacing and extracted the mummy with great care—with great care as to the case, I mean; for the mummy suffered some injury in the extraction. It was very badly embalmed, and so brittle that it broke in several places while I was getting it out; and when I unrolled it the head separated and both the arms came off.

"On the sixth day after the removal from the sarcophagus, I took the bandages that I had removed from Sebek-hotep and very carefully wrapped the deceased in them, sprinkling powdered myrrh and gum benzoin freely on the body and between the folds of the wrappings to disguise the faint odour of the spirit and the formalin that still lingered about the body. When the wrappings had been applied, the deceased really had a most workmanlike appearance; he would have looked quite well in a glass case even without the cartonnage, and I felt almost regretful at having to put him out of sight for ever.

"It was a difficult business getting him into the case without assistance, and I cracked the cartonnage badly in several places before he was safely enclosed. But I got him in at last, and then, when I had closed up the case with a new lacing, I applied a fresh layer of bitumen which effectually covered up the cracks and the new cord. A dusty cloth dabbed over the bitumen when it was dry disguised its newness, and the cartonnage with its tenant was ready for delivery. I notified Dr. Norbury of the fact, and five days later he came and removed it to the Museum.

"Now that the main difficulty was disposed of, I began to consider the further difficulty to which you, sir, have alluded with such admirable perspicuity. It was necessary that John Bellingham should make one more appearance in public before sinking into final oblivion.

"Accordingly, I devised the visit to Hurst's house, which was calculated to serve two purposes. It created a satisfactory date for the disappearance, eliminating me from any connection with it, and by throwing some suspicion on Hurst it would make him more amenable— less likely to dispute my claim when he learned the provisions of the will.

"The affair was quite simple. I knew that Hurst had changed his servants since I was last at his house, and I knew his habits. On that day I took the suit-case to Charing Cross and deposited it in the cloak-room, called at Hurst's office to make sure that he was there, and went from thence direct to Cannon Street and caught the train to Eltham. On arriving at the house I took the precaution to remove my spectacles—the only distinctive feature of my exterior—and was duly shown into the study at my request. As soon as the housemaid had left the room I quietly let myself out by the French window, which I closed behind me but could not fasten, went out at the side gate and closed that also behind me, holding the bolt of the latch back with my pocket-knife so that I need not slam the gate to shut it.

"The other events of that day, including the dropping of the scarab, I need not describe, as they are known to you. But I may fitly make a few remarks on the unfortunate tactical error into which I fell in respect of the bones. That error arose, as you have doubtless perceived, from the lawyer's incurable habit of underestimating the scientific expert. I had no idea mere bones were capable of furnishing so much information to a man of science.

"The way in which the affair came about was this: the damaged mummy of Sebek-hotep, perishing gradually by exposure to the air, was not only an eyesore to me; it was a definite danger. It was the only remaining link between me and the disappearance. I resolved to be rid of it and cast about for some means of destroying it. And then, in an evil moment, the idea of utilising it occurred to me.

"There was an undoubted danger that the Court might refuse to presume death after so short an interval; and if the permission should be postponed, the will might never be administered during my lifetime. Hence, if these bones of Sebek-hotep could be made to simulate the remains of the deceased testator, a definite good would be achieved. But I knew that the entire skeleton could never be mistaken for his. The deceased had broken his knee-caps and damaged his ankle, injuries which I assumed would leave some permanent trace. But if a judicious selection of the bones were deposited in a suitable place, together with some object clearly identifiable as appertaining to the deceased, it seemed to me that the difficulty would be met. I need not trouble you with details. The course which I adopted is known to you with the attendant circumstances, even to the accidental detachment of the right hand—which broke off as I was packing the arm in my handbag. Erroneous as that course was, it would have been successful but for the unforeseen contingency of your being retained in the case.

"Thus, for nearly two years, I remained in complete security. From time to time I dropped in at the Museum to see if the deceased was keeping in good condition; and on those occasions I used to reflect with satisfaction on the gratifying circumstance—accidental though it was—that his wishes, as expressed (very imperfectly) in clause two, had been fully complied with, and that without prejudice to my interests.

"The awakening came on that evening when I saw you at the Temple gate talking with Dr. Berkeley. I suspected immediately that something had gone amiss and that it was too late to take any useful action. Since then, I have waited here in hourly expectation of this visit. And now the time has come. You have made the winning move and it remains only for me to pay my debts like an honest gambler."

He paused and quietly lit his cigarette. Inspector Badger yawned and put away his notebook.

"Have you done, Mr. Jellicoe?" the inspector asked. "I want to carry out my contract to the letter, you know, though it's getting devilish late."

Mr. Jellicoe took his cigarette from his mouth and drank a glass of water.

"I forgot to ask," he said, "whether you unrolled the mummy—if I may apply the term to the imperfectly treated remains of my deceased client."

"I did not open the mummy-case," replied Thorndyke.

"You did not!" exclaimed Mr. Jellicoe. "Then how did you verify your suspicions?"

"I took an X-ray photograph."

"Ah! Indeed!" Mr. Jellicoe pondered for some moments. "Astonishing!" he murmured; "and most ingenious. The resources of science at the present day are truly wonderful."

"Is there anything more that you want to say?" asked Badger; "because if you don't, time's up."

"Anything more?" Mr. Jellicoe repeated slowly; "anything more? No—I—think—think—the time—is—up. Yes—the—the—time——"

He broke off and sat with a strange look fixed on Thorndyke.

His face had suddenly undergone a curious change. It looked shrunken and cadaverous and his lips had assumed a peculiar cherry-red colour.

"Is anything the matter, Mr. Jellicoe?" Badger asked uneasily. "Are you not feeling well, sir?"

Mr. Jellicoe did not appear to have heard the question, for he returned no answer but sat motionless, leaning back in his chair, with his hands spread out on the table and his strangely intent gaze bent on Thorndyke.

Suddenly his head dropped on his breast and his body seemed to collapse; and, as with one accord we sprang to our feet, he slid forward off his chair and disappeared under the table.

"Good Lord! The man's fainted!" exclaimed Badger.

In a moment he was down on his hands and knees, trembling with excitement, groping under the table. He dragged the unconscious lawyer out into the light and knelt over him, staring into his face.

"What's the matter with him, Doctor?" he asked, looking up at Thorndyke. "Is it apoplexy? Or is it a heart attack, think you?"

Thorndyke shook his head, though he stooped and put his fingers on the unconscious man's wrist.

"Prussic acid or potassium cyanide is what the appearances suggest," he replied.

"But can't you do anything?" demanded the inspector.

Thorndyke dropped the arm, which fell limply to the floor.

"You can't do much for a dead man," he said.

"Dead! Then he has slipped through our fingers after all!"

"He has anticipated the sentence. That is all." Thorndyke spoke in an even, impassive tone which struck me as rather strange, considering the suddenness of the tragedy, as did also the complete absence of surprise in his manner. He seemed to treat the occurrence as a perfectly natural one.

Not so Inspector Badger; who rose to his feet and stood with his hands thrust into his pockets scowling sullenly down at the dead lawyer.

"I was an infernal fool to agree to his blasted conditions," he growled savagely.

"Nonsense," said Thorndyke. "If you had broken in you would have found a dead man. As it was you found a live man and obtained an important statement. You acted quite properly."

"How do you suppose he managed it?" asked Badger.

Thorndyke held out his hand.

"Let us look at his cigarette case," said he.

Badger extracted the little silver case from the dead man's pocket and opened it. There were five cigarettes in it, two of which were plain, while the other three were gold-tipped. Thorndyke took out one of each kind and gently pinched their ends. The gold-tipped one he returned; the plain one he tore through, about a quarter of an inch from the end; when two little white tabloids dropped out on to the table. Badger eagerly picked one up and was about to smell it when Thorndyke grasped his wrist. "Be careful," said he; and when he had cautiously sniffed at the tabloid—held at a safe distance from his nose—he added: "Yes, potassium cyanide. I thought so when his lips turned that queer colour. It was in that last cigarette; you can see that he has bitten the end off."

For some time we stood silently looking down at the still form stretched on the floor. Presently Badger looked up.

"As you pass the porter's lodge on your way out," said he, "you might just drop in and tell him to send a constable to me."

"Very well," said Thorndyke. "And by the way, Badger, you had better tip that sherry back into the decanter and put it under lock and key, or else pour it out of the window."

"Gad, yes!" exclaimed the inspector. "I'm glad you mentioned it. We might have had an inquest on a constable as well as a lawyer. Good-night, gentlemen, if you are off."

We went out and left him with his prisoner—passive enough, indeed, according to his ambiguously worded promise. As we passed through the gateway Thorndyke gave the inspector's message, curtly and without comment, to the gaping porter, and then we issued forth into Chancery Lane.

We were all silent and very grave, and I thought that Thorndyke seemed somewhat moved. Perhaps Mr. Jellicoe's last intent look—which I suspect he knew to be the look of a dying man—lingered in his memory as it did in mine. Half-way down Chancery Lane he spoke for the first time; and then it was only to ejaculate, "Poor devil!"

Jervis took him up. "He was a consummate villain, Thorndyke."

"Hardly that," was the reply. "I should rather say that he was non-moral. He acted without malice and without scruple or remorse. His conduct exhibited a passionless expediency which was dreadful because utterly unhuman. But he was a strong man—a courageous, self-contained man, and I had been better pleased if it could have been ordained that some other hand than mine should let the axe fall."

Thorndyke's compunction may appear strange and inconsistent, but yet his feeling was also my own. Great as was the misery and suffering that this inscrutable man had brought into the lives of those I loved, I forgave him; and in his downfall forgot the callous relentlessness with which he had pursued his evil purpose. For it was he who had brought Ruth into my life; who had opened for me the Paradise of Love into which I had just entered. And so my thoughts turned away from the still shape that lay on the floor of the stately old room in Lincoln's Inn, away to the sunny vista of the future, where I should walk hand in hand with Ruth until my time, too, should come; until I, too, like the grim lawyer, should hear the solemn evening bell bidding me put out into the darkness of the silent sea.

THE END